BEYOND
the
SURFACE

by

SARAH KRIZEK

©2024 by Sarah Krizek

Published by hope*books
2217 Matthews Township Pkwy
Suite D302
Matthews, NC 28105
www.hopebooks.com

hope*books is a division of hope*media

Printed in the United States of America

First paperback edition.

Paperback ISBN: 979-8-89185-070-5
Hardcover ISBN: 979-8-89185-071-2
Ebook ISBN: 979-8-89185-152-8
Library of Congress Number: 20244931118

hope*books
hopebooks.com

Praise for
Beyond the Surface

"Sarah Krizek's wonderful historical fiction debut Beyond The Surface brings to light the courage, compassion and sacrifice of so many members of the Greatest Generation during WWII. This is a meticulously researched story told from the perspective of army nurse Anna and infantrymen Paul, two main characters so well drawn and relatable that you root for them from the start. This novel also brings to light the lesser known, heartbreaking tragedy of the sinking of the SS Leopoldville, a transport ship carrying members of the 66th Infantry Division, that was hit and sunk by a German U-Boat on Christmas Eve 1944."

Jane Healey
Best selling author of The Beantown Girls,
The Secret Stealers, The Saturday Evening Girls Club,
and Goodnight From Paris

For N –
Together wing to wing and oar to oar.

For C and J –
Higher than heaven and deeper
than the ocean.

For the Black Panther Division –
May your sacrifices always be remembered
and your stories always be told.

CONTENTS

Chapter 1

ANNA
MAY 1944
NEW JERSEY

The crunch of gravel beneath her bare feet was a welcome sensation as she wound through the sprawling garden. She had it memorized now. Camelia trees lined the edges, the bright pink and white blooms reminding her of Alice in Wonderland. Her mother had grafted them together, waiting patiently for the flowers to display their dizzying show of alternating color. Her mother was talented, there was no denying that. Evidence of her hand permeated the entirety of the garden.

She meandered further down the path until it circled around a little white gazebo. To the left, the gravel walk continued, winding through neat rows of vegetables, planted with care. To the right, the enticing aroma of budding fruit trees and blueberry bushes graced the breeze, and little white flowers opened up to the sun with the promise of strawberries to come.

Anna stopped just before the path split and climbed the gazebo steps. She sat on the bench that wrapped around the edges and breathed deeply. She tipped her head back, the delicious scent of tea olive trees filling her nose. She closed her eyes. It was her favorite spot.

The crunch of footsteps warned her of someone approaching. She didn't need to open her eyes to know who it was. Her mother could hardly stand to see her daughter enjoying a moment of quiet in the garden. Since Anna was a little girl, she'd played second fiddle to her mother's precious garden. Hours upon hours, she'd sit in the gazebo, playing games and making up stories with her little rag dolls. She'd wander up and down the rows of plants and flowers, bobbing in and out - a game of hide and seek just for her - waiting for her mother to look up from her digging and weeding and planting. Oh, how her imagination had run wild, barefoot and sweaty, anything just to be near her mother.

She sighed. *How silly,* she thought. *I'm in competition with a garden.* But to that little girl she'd once been, it was a competition, vying for her mother's attention and always falling short.

"I see things haven't changed much." Her mother's voice broke through her thoughts, and she opened one eye.

"Still running about barefoot all over the place." Her mother stood before her, hands on her hips, looking for a fight. She was always ready to argue, lately, though it hadn't been Anna's intention. It was the unfortunate byproduct of doing something her mother hadn't expected - or approved.

"I enjoy feeling the Earth under my feet," Anna said. "I would have thought you, of all people, could understand that." She opened both eyes to look at her mother. Her cream linen pants matched the button-down blouse, perfectly tailored and not a wrinkle in sight. She had tied a blue and yellow kerchief around her neck and carried her straw hat in one hand, gardening gloves in the other.

"What are you talking about, Anna? I've never been so careless as to walk barefoot outdoors." She wrinkled her nose in disgust.

That's half the problem, thought Anna. This is how it had always been. Anna was careless, her head in the clouds, a silly little girl. Her mother had never been able to look past their differences to see her for anything else.

"Why, Mother, you are always digging in the dirt. It's the same thing, really. You like getting your hands dirty, and I," she wiggled her toes, "like getting my feet dirty."

Her mother rolled her eyes. "It is not the same, Anna," she huffed.

"Yes, mother, I know. It's dreadfully disappointing to have raised a daughter with a brown thumb. Though I thought you'd at least be able to appreciate my ability to keep people alive." She didn't know why, when she saw the fire in her mother's eyes, she decided to engage. She had poked the hornet's nest and couldn't outrun it, now.

"And what exactly do you think you'll be able to do with that precious degree you just had to have?"

Anna smiled. "I can do anything with a nursing degree, mother. People always need help." *You included,* she thought.

"Ha!" Her mother's laughter teemed with anger, and Anna wondered what it was that had made her this way. What happened that she'd become this angry?

"What could a sickly thing like you do to take care of someone else? You couldn't take care of a damn cat if you tried."

Having had enough of this conversation, Anna stood, though she knew she'd provoked it herself. It would go nowhere good, but she'd never learn. She tried to edge her way around her mother, but she blocked the steps.

"Answer me, Anna," her mother taunted.

Anna sighed, suddenly drained. "I'd rather not, mother," she answered truthfully.

This seemed to satisfy her as though Anna's refusal was an admission of defeat, and a smile spread across her face. Anna ignored her and tried again to walk down the steps. She reached the bottom step when she was yanked backward by her arm, her mother's grasp holding her in place.

"You have an appointment with Dr. White tomorrow at noon," she said.

"Excuse me?"

"I've arranged for you to see the doctor. Did I not make that clear?"

Anna wrenched free from her mother's grip. "You really do think I'm sickly, don't you?" She looked at her mother, then, really seeing her. *She's aged,* Anna thought. She softened, wondering if she'd not given her mother a fair chance. Tensions were high for everyone, and maybe she was really just worried about her daughter.

"Mother, just because I had one seizure when I was two doesn't mean you need to treat me like an invalid." She reached out to touch her mother's arm, but the older woman tensed under the contact. Anna pulled back again. *Maybe invalid was too strong of a word*, Anna thought. But the sentiment was the same. She couldn't understand how her mother came to the conclusion that she'd be sick all her life. Sure, it was one scary experience, but she'd recovered - she'd just finished nursing school, for goodness sake.

She watched her mother grimace. She did not like to talk about 'the episode' and looked away, pulling on her gloves and hat.

"It's not a checkup, Anna. It's a job interview." She stalked away, taking the path into the orchard.

Anna chased after her mother, bits of gravel sticking to her feet, stinging with every step.

"Why would you ask Dr. White for a job interview?" She blocked her mother from going any further.

"He needs the help, Anna. You've seen how busy he's gotten. With all that training of yours, you should be able to help the poor old doctor."

"Mother, with all that training I can do much more than be a secretary," Anna seethed.

Her mother rolled her eyes. "Don't be so dramatic, dear. And don't embarrass me. Do be on time tomorrow." She elbowed her way past, but Anna stalked after her.

"How dare you, Mother. How dare you." She was too angry to think of anything else to say.

"How dare I what, Anna? Make sure my daughter has a good job? Make sure she'll be well taken care of?" She feigned innocence and Anna saw red.

"Don't pretend like you care about me," Anna shouted. "You only care about yourself, this damn garden, and what everyone else thinks!" She backed away, on the verge of tears that she did not want her mother to have the satisfaction of seeing. She closed her eyes, willing the tears away and taking in a shaky breath when she felt the sting of her mother's hand across her face. Her eyes flew open and she blinked in shock. She could have laughed at the incredulousness of it all. She raised her hand to her cheek, stunned that her mother was angry enough to slap her, and burst into laughter. Giant peals of laughter bubbled up out of her. She bent over, her hands on her knees, to catch her breath. She looked up at her mother, her hands balled into fists, lips pursed.

"Get out," her mother said. Anna straightened and swiped at her eyes.

"Mother, please," she tried.

"Out," her mother said again. "Get out of my garden. Get out of this house. If this is such a joke to you, if *I* am such a joke to you, I'd prefer you not be here at all." She turned her back on Anna and disappeared between the apple trees.

Anna stood for a moment, digesting her mother's words. They had always had their differences. They'd let their tempers get the best of them on more than one occasion, but never before had she laid a hand on her or told her to leave. It was exactly what she'd planned on doing. Anna spun around, looking at all of her favorite parts of the garden before turning to leave. She breathed in the familiar sweet scent of the tea olive and bent to smell her favorite coral rose before walking out of the garden she both loved and hated.

Chapter 2

*M*om,

Would you please stop worrying? I'm fine. Everyone here is fine. I'm in a classroom all day long. It's SCHOOL. I'm not on the front lines. I'm not even in boot camp. Don't worry about me. My precious lil face is just perfect. Just the way it was when I left. Anyway, it's all pretty boring here, and I don't have much news to report. Just wanted to tell you to put your worries away!

Love ya,

Paul

He folded his letter neatly and placed it in the envelope just as his buddy Harry strode into the classroom. He nodded in Paul's direction. "Letters to Mommy again?" he laughed.

Paul just smiled, "Gotta make sure she's not worryin' too much, ya know."

He leaned back in his chair and yawned. Somehow, he had made it to class early, despite tossing and turning all night in the barracks. Not sleeping and not staying asleep were the special bonuses of army life. He looked around the classroom, the four gray walls with posters haphazardly placed to remind them of "who vs. whom" and various other grammar mistakes to avoid. Paul wondered if his impeccable grammar would be of great service to him when he was fighting the Germans. He shook his head at the thought. He hoped he'd never have to find out.

Harry took his seat on the other side of the classroom. Paul looked over to his left, beyond Harry, and out the large windows. The fine mist coming down had turned the sky a bleak gray, and Paul let out a low chuckle as he realized the outside matched the inside. He couldn't escape the gray cover no matter where he went.

He tucked his letter away to send home later today. He wondered how long he'd have before he'd have different news to report. Not that he wanted to have any news to report - he hated the idea of lying to his folks. But for weeks, the sense of impending dread had permeated both the classroom and the barracks. He told his mother everything was fine - what else could he say? That things were looking so low he had a hard time believing he'd stay safe in the Army Specialized Training Program? It had taken everyone here a hell of a lot of determination and intelligence to land a spot. This was the place you wanted to be and rarely got into. He usually tried not to take it for granted. Now, though, he had to wonder, was there really much use for a bunch of brains sitting in a classroom when the world was erupting into chaos just across the Atlantic? Paul didn't want to go to the front lines, but he couldn't help feeling guilty sitting here waiting for another English lesson to bore him to sleep. He wiped his hand down his face, wishing he could wipe away the nerves that swirled in his stomach.

As he looked around the room, his buddies seemed just as thrilled as he was to be up so early for what was bound to be another riveting hour led by none other than Professor Dillard. Or, as Paul had coined him, Professor Dull-ard. His poor attempt at a joke had stuck, largely because it was so terrible, and now he and his buddies had to check themselves before addressing the poor old English teacher. He'd be glad when this semester was over, and he didn't have to worry about accidentally calling his professor the awful nickname.

Paul leaned back in his chair, letting his mind drift to that night in the library. They had gotten a study group together but hadn't been very productive. It turned out that they all just needed a break. So instead of letting research, papers, and deadlines dominate the conversation, they sat around the old wooden table, carved all over with initials and hearts - young college love at its finest - and just talked. He told them about his brother - missing in action and what it had done to his mom. He had surprised himself by talking about it at all, but it felt good to get it out with a group of guys that could understand. Sometimes, he wondered if it would have been better for the telegram to have said KIA instead. He thought his mother holding onto so much hope might actually be making things worse.

Harry talked about his wife - married just six months - and how he felt like the luckiest man alive. He couldn't wait to be a dad and put the war behind him. Paul thought about how that was one of the things he loved most about his friend. He was never afraid to say what he really felt. Everyone knew he didn't want to go to war. Not that he didn't agree or didn't feel it was right, but because he didn't want to give up the goodness he had at home. His eyes lit up when he talked about his new bride and their plans for the future. It made Paul wonder what else Harry had been through to know well enough not to take a single day for granted.

The conversation had eventually turned back to their studies. At the late hour, you would think they had been out at the bar and not the library, the way exhaustion was hitting them. They packed up their books and notes and made their way into the dark night, laughing and carrying on. Jack was the first one to bring up the morning's English class. He was well aware that English was not his strong suit, and Professor Dillard's dry presentation didn't help him much. It was then that Paul had made the awful joke, walking down the large, rounded concrete steps of the library building. The guys had all stopped in their tracks and turned around to look at Paul, the last in the group, pushing the heavy metal door closed. He turned from the door and looked up to see his pals all staring at him and briefly wondered what he had just said until, all at once, they fell to the grass, already wet with dew as the air continued to cool, and howled with laughter. He wasn't quite sure if they had found his joke that funny or if they were laughing at him instead, but it didn't matter. He looked up at the clear night, stars high in the sky, and thought it would be worth it if they were caught out late.

He laughed to himself thinking about it. They had a well-earned break that night, and he knew he'd remember it long after the war had passed - eighty years old, rocking on his front porch.

Today, however, instead of Professor Dillard walking through the door, Paul was surprised to see Colonel Rumberg. He sat forward, the legs of his chair scraping loudly on the tile floor as he scrambled to his feet. Colonel Ira Rumberg was a formidable figure, but Paul considered him a good boss. The former football player towered over most other men, standing at over six feet tall. His muscular stature made him look like he might burst out of his uniform. Paul had a helluva lot of respect for the man. He had already been in England, commanding a training program there. Paul could guess what his presence here today meant for him and the rest of the soldiers standing at attention all around him.

Colonel Rumberg went to the front of the classroom in a few long, confident strides, looking around at the men quickly composing themselves in front of their superior officer, surprised by his visit.

"At ease, boys," he said, motioning for them to take their seats.

Paul's eyes were trained on the Colonel. He admired the easy confidence with which Colonel Rumberg carried himself. Surely, it came from years of experience, something Paul didn't yet have in the Army, but he wished he could exude some of that same calm steadiness. Instead, he found himself bouncing his knee, an uneasiness settling over him in anticipation of what Colonel Rumberg was here to tell them.

Rumors had been circulating throughout the barracks for several months, heightening in the last few weeks. Some of his fellow classmates had brothers already overseas who had been getting their letters - all saying the same thing - get ready to join us over here. Most of the guys couldn't wait to be sent to the continent. Paul wasn't as eager. He may have been just as angry as the next guy, but he was less than thrilled at the idea of having to fight. He was mortified to feel the start of a cold sweat breaking out down his back. Despite the warnings, the whispers, and knowing this was bound to happen, Paul found he was not prepared.

How do you prepare for this, he thought to himself. Realizing he had been staring past Colonel Rumberg at the empty blackboard behind him, he tore his gaze away and focused on the Colonel, for once wishing it was Professor Dillard standing before them instead. Colonel Rumberg gripped the podium as the men took their seats.

"While I'm sure you can all guess why I'm here today, it is now official. The ASTP is being, well, let's just say it's being greatly downsized." Paul thought he saw a flash of something cross the Colonel's face, but it was gone before he could put his finger on what it was. "Each of you will be making your way into an Infantry division."

There were a few glances at one another as he continued, "You will have one week's leave to do with as you choose. My recommendation would be that you go home and put all thoughts of the future out of your mind. Enjoy the time with your families. Your mothers, fathers, siblings. Friends, loved ones. Those are the memories, the relationships that will carry you forward when the days are long and tough, and you feel like you can't stand another minute."

He slammed his hand onto the podium, and Paul swallowed the lump forming in his throat, not breaking eye contact with his superior officer. His head was spinning. One minute, he's waiting on Professor Dillard, finishing up an "I'm fine" letter to his mother, wondering how on earth he'll stay awake through an hour of droning torture. Now, he's being sent to what will undoubtedly be true torture. He tried to focus only on what was before him - one week at home. One week in his own bed. But his anticipation of a good night's sleep wasn't enough when he looked over at his pal, Harry. His normally red complexion was sheet white, and he looked as though he might lose his breakfast. Paul wasn't the only one feeling queasy about the sudden change to their future. He tried to give Harry a reassuring smile, but Harry's eyes snapped back to Colonel Rumberg as he continued.

"When your one week is up, you will reconvene at Camp Blanding. A word of advice? Pack plenty of extra T-shirts. It's damn hot there. No doubt you'll be sweating through them." A few groans could be heard throughout the classroom but were quickly stifled as Colonel Rumberg stepped away from the podium. "You'll receive your official paper orders shortly." With that, he made his way to the door, making brief eye contact with each soldier seated before him as he went. With his hand on the doorknob, he turned and added, "Oh, and boys? Welcome to the 66th." He nodded and stepped from the room, the resounding click of his freshly shined shoes echoing down the hall.

As soon as the door clicked shut, the room erupted. Twenty-two men pent up with emotion over the news that they'd soon be joining fellow comrades, brothers, and cousins slapped each other on the back, hugged, and whooped at the news. The air buzzed with excitement and anticipation. But Paul didn't feel much in the mood to carry on with the rest of the men in the room. What he was feeling was not the excitement so many of the other men were feeling. He looked around at his classmates, his fellow soldiers, celebrating their chance at the 'damn Krauts' and wondered how he could be the only one feeling so unprepared. And if he was being really honest, so scared. He sat for a moment before pulling the letter from his pocket that he had only just folded. He held it, sliding his thumb down the crease before ripping it into pieces. He stood, tossing the shredded letter in the wastebasket, watching the scraps of paper settle to the bottom before walking across the classroom. He stepped over books and chairs, dropped in haste, and put his hand on Harry's shoulder.

"Come on, Harry. Let's go on down to the lawn." Harry, still in shock, stood and followed Paul out of the classroom. They didn't say a word as they walked along the hallway and down the winding staircase, each step landing with a loud echo in the stairwell. They pushed open the large double doors to the main entrance and continued down the steps to the sidewalk leading to the lawn. It wasn't a great day for a walk around the school grounds, but neither seemed to mind the cold drizzle or the mist that hung low around the trees. They walked for a while, keeping on the paved walkway that wound throughout the campus. On a sunny day, they'd have passed a dozen GIs out on the lawn, enjoying a break between classes. Today, no one else was out walking to the pond at the far end of campus. Paul shuddered against the wind that had picked up. He scooped up a few rocks to skip across the pond.

It wasn't until he'd thrown his fourth rock that Harry finally said, "I've got some things I need to give you."

Paul turned to his friend. "Yeah, sure, Harry. I'm headed to have some of my uniforms pressed if you want me to take any of yours with me before we have to head out." They often shared laundry duty, but he was confused as to why his friend was suddenly concerned with his laundry when all he could think about was trying not to spiral into a funnel of dread.

"No, it's not my clothes this time." Harry hesitated. "It's just…you know…if…" He trailed off again. Paul kept skipping rocks, knowing his friend was trying to sort things out just as much as he was.

"Yeah, so, if I don't come back, there's some things I'd like you to give to Edith."

With his arm pulled back, Paul stopped mid-throw. He looked at his friend.

"Harry…" He'd had those same thoughts…what if? But he'd shoved them down, forced them from his mind because, well, what was the use? It wouldn't do him any good to worry about anything except what was happening right now. *Easier said than done,* he thought. But Harry…Harry was different. With his red hair and freckles, he'd burn in the shade and had probably never even been in a school fight. He was too good. Most of the guys here were. That's exactly why they *were* here. Things must really be getting bad if they were wanted on the front lines. Again, Paul tried not to think about it.

"Harry, come on. You're going to make it home. Don't talk like that."

Harry wasn't convinced. The color had started to come back into his face, though that was more from the wind than from Paul's reassurance.

"Come on, Paul, we both know I'm not built for war. Look at me. I can hardly stand *this* blasted weather. A little wind and rain, and I'm ready to throw in the towel. At least you've got that farm strength." He turned to look at his friend. "I'm serious, Paul. If I die...I need you to send some things to Edith. Maybe even check in on her when you get back."

Paul hesitated. He had to admit neither he nor his friend were your stereotypical soldier. They were the brains - not the brawn. It seemed, at least for now, that their brains had taken them as far as they could go. Their days stateside were numbered. But he was saddened by his friend's bleak outlook. He wished he could shake him into believing in himself a bit more.

Paul clapped his friend on the shoulder and gave it a squeeze. "Let's get outta this rain," was all he managed to say. Paul eyed his friend, afraid he might push the issue. But he knew that, like him, Harry would prefer to stay warm and dry as long as he could. The library, school, even church - especially church - all sounded good right about now, but instead of making a motion to move in out of the rain, Harry shifted the conversation to Paul.

"So, what'll you tell your Ma now?"

Paul blew out a breath. He looked over at Harry's questioning gaze.

"I don't know," he answered. And it was the truth. He really didn't know how he'd tell his mom this news, even if they all knew it was coming.

"Tell her not to worry."

"You think I should lie to her?"

"Do you really want to tell her the truth?"

The guys had always razzed him about all the letters he'd write to his mom. But the truth was, he couldn't bear to put her through another sleepless night like his brother did. He never wrote. Never. Not one letter. And then… just one. They didn't need to look at it to know what it said. To know what it meant when the officers knocked on the door. It was another reason he had been so thrilled to get into the ASTP. He'd be stateside, away from the 'real' war. His mother didn't have to worry while he was at University. But to lie? Could he really lie to her when the truth could come knocking on her door?

Chapter 3

*U*nder any other circumstance, the beauty of spring in full bloom as she walked down Main Street in her little hometown would have brought a smile to Anna's face. Today, however, she didn't even see the dogwoods or the last of the tulips poking their heads out before the weather turned too hot. Instead, she was stomping her way to Dr. White's office for her two p.m. appointment. *Surely, he will see the steam radiating off of me if I don't get it together,* she thought. The stomping hadn't quite quelled her frustration as she'd hoped it would. She supposed she was no longer a child, and an outward tantrum wouldn't do the trick. She slowed her steps and took deep breaths until she felt she was calm enough to approach Dr. White's office.

Why her mother found it necessary to meddle, she'd never understand. But, here she was, about to go inside for an interview she had not asked for, an interview for a job she knew she would not be taking, an interview her mother had insisted upon for a job in which Anna would serve as dear old Dr. White's nurse. Or, as far as she could tell, an overqualified secretary. She could think of nothing worse than seeing her degree go to waste. *The nerve of that woman,* Anna thought. *She knows I want to leave. She knows I cannot take this job. It is just like her to make this more difficult.* She blew out a breath, hoping to rid her frustration with it.

She stopped on the sidewalk in front of Dr. White's. It was a small white house converted to the family practice that Anna and her family had been going to since she was a child. The outside had recently been painted, and a lovely new ramp was installed to accommodate the many elderly patients Dr. White cared for. While he occasionally made house visits, the only doctor in town found himself busy enough in the office, running a full schedule each day. It was no wonder he had been looking for help.

She climbed the steps next to the ramp just as a young boy with sandy blonde hair sticking up every which way came barreling up the ramp with a wagon in tow. Sitting in the wagon was a little girl with the same blond hair and freckled nose, her face tear-streaked and red from crying.

"Oh, my, what have we here?" Anna looked between the two children. The little girl hiccuped, trying not to sob, as the boy regaled the story in significant detail to Anna.

"Mama is going to be so mad. I swear I was watching her the whole time! She was just riding her new bicycle in the driveway, and then boom! On the ground she goes before I could get to her. I swear it was an accident."

Anna watched him, hiding her amusement. Memories of

her and her brother finding themselves in similar situations came flooding back to her, making her smile and ache with worry for him all at the same time.

"Ok, ok, take a deep breath, buddy. We'll get her fixed up, not to worry." She smiled at the little girl as the boy yammered on.

"I tried everything to get her to stop crying, but she just wouldn't. I'm sorry ma'am. I just had to bring her to Doc White's, I didn't know what else to do." The boy stopped pacing long enough to pin Anna with a stare. "So can you help me, I mean her, can you help her, or what?"

Anna chuckled and bent down beside the little red wagon. The girl looked at her with bright, watery eyes. She could see no visible signs of injury, save for what might be a skinned elbow hiding beneath the towel she clutched tight to her arm. She smiled at the little girl.

"Mind if I take a peek?" The little girl held tighter to the towel.

"It's ok, you don't have to show me. But I promise," Anna made an 'x' over her heart, "I won't hurt your arm. How about you just show me how brave you are? Can you do that?" The little girl nodded her head, sucking her bottom lip in to keep from crying.

"Ok, then. Can you show me your big, strong muscles and bend your arm up for me?" She copied Anna.

"Good job!" Anna praised. "Now, how about you straighten it all the way out. Can you touch my hand over here?" She straightened her arm, tapping Anna's fingers, the towel falling away as she did to reveal an angry scrape, bright with blood and dirtied from her spill on the ground. Anna was relieved to see the pair of children were more scared than hurt.

"You're a very brave young lady. Why don't we head inside and let Dr. White take a look at that scrape? I bet you'll be back on your bicycle in no time." She winked at the girl as she stood to open the door. The little boy, who had stood quietly bouncing on his toes while Anna inspected his sister, grabbed hold of the wagon handle and began to pull his sister the rest of the way into the building. Anna stopped him with a hand on his shoulder and bent down toward his sister again.

"Do you think you can be really brave one more time and walk inside? The wagon should probably stay out here." She eyed the wagon's muddy wheels, fairly certain that Dr. White wouldn't be too happy about having tire tracks left on his floors. Thankfully, the little girl reached for Anna's hand with her good arm and hopped down out of the wagon.

The empty waiting room smelled of antiseptic and the potpourri Mrs. White kept in glass bowls on the counter. The soft rumble of Dr. White's deep voice came from down the hall.

"Hang here just one minute," she said to the children. The little boy nodded, leading his sister to a wooden bench to sit while they waited. Anna rounded the corner, walking behind the front desk piled high with folders and papers strewn in all directions, looking like they hadn't been dealt with in many months. She continued down the hall, following the doctor's voice.

She hesitated outside the closed door of the exam room. She hated to interrupt, but she really didn't feel right cleaning up the little girl's wound without first clearing it with Dr. White. She rapped lightly on the door, and a chair scraped across the wooden floor in response before the door creaked open, and Dr. White poked his head out. He smiled kindly at Anna, though the dark smudges beneath his eyes told her how exhausted he really was.

"Anna," he said, relief in his voice.

"I'm sorry to interrupt," she said. "There's a couple of children in the waiting room."

Dr. White nodded. "I think I have an idea of who they are." He scratched at his gray beard, hiding a smirk behind his hand.

"Oh, you do? Well, if it's okay with you, I'm happy to bandage up a little scrape on the girl's elbow and send them on their way."

Dr. White smiled. "Sure, sure." He motioned to the empty exam room across the hall. "I think you can find your way around in there," he said, his voice hopeful.

"Yes, sir, I'm sure I know where just about everything is by now." She smiled at the kind old doctor before she headed back to the waiting room to fetch the children while the doctor disappeared behind the door to finish with his patient.

～～

"You're hired." Dr. White sat in his chair across from Anna. She had made quick work of cleaning up Molly's elbow while her brother Sam looked on in awe. His eyes had gone wide when Anna asked if he'd like to place the big bandage, and he'd stuck his tongue out in concentration as he carefully followed Anna's instructions. She'd sent them on their way with a high five for the boy, and a hug for the sweet little girl, and an admonishing 'Be careful!' By the time Dr. White was ready for their meeting, the children were halfway down the block, wagon wheels squeaking noisily and leaving a trail of dried mud as they went.

Anna laughed. "You haven't even interviewed me."

Dr. White smiled. "I saw and heard everything I needed to know in the way you handled the Barrett kids. They're in here at least once a week, dragging that dreaded wagon halfway down the hall before I catch them and send it back outside. Mrs. White will be very happy to know you've saved her from a muddy floor this week."

"Trouble must find them quite often," Anna said.

"Mhm. Something like that." The doctor looked thoughtful for a moment. "There's more to nursing than just medicine and first aid, Anna. And you've got it. You already know that. I can see it. The connections you make with the people you're treating. That's just as important."

She let the doctor's words sink in. He was right. She knew it was what made him the beloved town doctor. And she knew it was why she'd always wanted to be a nurse. More than bandaging wounds or taking blood pressure, she genuinely cared about people. And she enjoyed talking to them, connecting with them.

"You're absolutely right, Dr. White. Which is why I am so terribly sorry for having wasted your time this afternoon, but I cannot accept your offer." Her words tumbled out as she tried to stave off the embarrassment she felt at taking up the doctor's time.

"And I apologize on my mother's behalf for scheduling this appointment. She knows I want to leave, but she prefers to live in denial." Anna stopped herself before saying too much to the kind doctor. *Kind but not so confidential,* she thought. If she wasn't careful, she'd have her dirty laundry aired before the town.

He sat back in his chair and steepled his fingers on his desk. A slow smile spread across his face. "You're going to make a wonderful nurse, Anna. Our country will be lucky to have you serving alongside our soldiers."

Surprised, Anna looked down at her hands, feeling her cheeks flush. When she didn't say anything, the doctor continued.

"I'm going to be honest with you, Anna. I knew you were hoping to leave. Your mother told me she feared as much when she came to ask for this interview."

Anna looked up. "I'm sorry. Do you mean to say that you knew I'd say no to this position?"

The doctor chuckled. "Well, it was worth a shot at having you agree to a job here. Lord knows I could use the help. But I had a feeling your mother was grasping at straws to get you to stay. I can't say I blame her. I'd probably do the same if I thought my daughter was willing to sacrifice her own comfort and safety for the war effort."

Anna stood, suddenly needing some air. She shook the doctor's hand and thanked him once again for his time, scrambling out the door and making a left out of Dr. White's, practically running down South Street, the opposite direction of home.

~

The old porch swing creaked with each forward motion. She sat on the railing, picking at the peeling white paint, lost in thought while listening to her grandfather's rocking and the tap of his thumb on his knee, no doubt in time to a song he'd soon start whistling.

"Penny for your thoughts, AB?" Her grandfather's question pulled her back to the front porch, the gentle breeze picking up, blowing her hair across her face as she looked up at him. She smiled at the use of his nickname for her. AB. Short for Anna Banana. Her smile grew as she remembered how she had scolded him once she turned thirteen. She was too old to be called Anna Banana. So, instead of giving it up altogether, he shortened it. And she loved him for it. It was their thing, a secret silliness they shared, even now, when life felt so heavy.

Her thoughts tried to tumble out when her eyes met his. Wrinkled at the corners, her grandfather's kind eyes had always comforted her. She had already told him a bit about her interview, but she hated to burden him with the rest of her worries.

"I know you don't want me joining, either..." she trailed off.

"Whoa, now, don't go lumping me in with your mother."

Anna let out a snort. It was no secret that her grandfather and her mother rarely saw eye to eye. But on this, she found it hard to believe they didn't agree.

"Oh, come on Gramps. I know how you feel about me joining the army. My whole life, you've told me the army is no place for a woman. You surely can't deny that." She narrowed her eyes at him.

"Don't think you can scare me off with that look, AB."

He wagged a finger at her before he continued.

"But...you are right. I did say that. And I do know that it's going to be harder than you can even imagine. Especially now. But I also know you're a damn pistol, and when you've made up your mind, there's not a soul who can change it. So," he paused and looked thoughtful before a sly smile took shape on his face. "Unlike your mother, I will support you. That's what I am here to do. That is what I have always been here to do. I'm not here to tell you I know better because I don't. It's your life, AB. You need to live it."

Anna looked away, down the front path, feigning a sudden interest in the weeds cropping up between the cracks of the concrete walk. She waited until she felt like she'd hidden her tears well enough to jump down off the railing and join her grandfather on the swing. They rocked in a steady rhythm as she rested her head on his shoulder. He patted her knee like he had done so many times before. This, she knew, was what she'd miss most. She said a silent prayer that she did, in fact, know what she was doing. How could she know if this was really the right choice?

As if he could read her mind, her grandfather shifted to put his arm around her and squeezed her tight.

"It'll all be okay, AB. It'll all be okay."

She hoped he was right.

They rocked in silence for a few minutes more, her grandfather's feet planted on the porch, propelling them forward and back. Curled up beside him, Anna tried to focus on everything around her. This was a memory she wanted to be able to pull up whenever she needed it. The smoky vanilla scent she had come to associate with her grandfather, the sound of the neighbor starting up a lawnmower. The gentle breeze on her face with each forward motion of the swing. She didn't want to forget any of it. She squeezed her eyes shut, trying not to let fear and doubt creep in. *It would be so much easier to stay*, she thought. Easier, maybe, but she was no coward, and knew deep down she couldn't stay.

BEYOND the SURFACE

Her mother's idea of contributing to the war effort may have been to tend to the most beautiful and thriving victory garden in town. For Anna, it just wasn't enough. Not when she had given her all to a nursing program. She had taken advantage of the free program, at first, to get some time away from her mother's hounding each day, but it had turned into something more for her. What started as just something to do had become something she loved, and she wasn't going to give up on that feeling when she felt the pull to do more. Sure, she could stay in town and be useful in some way. Her mother had already secured her a job at Dr. White's. And while Dr. White was a perfectly good doctor, running a lovely, busy family practice, Anna had no interest in staying. She had all of this new knowledge she was desperate to put to good use.

"So, tell me everything," her grandfather said. She tilted her chin upward to look at him. He had a twinkle in his eye and a smirk on his face as if to say, *I've got all the time in the world*, and she was glad for it.

"Well," she began, "I don't think I've even processed it all myself. It's happened so fast."

"Let's process together, then."

"Okay, then." She smiled. She felt like the luckiest granddaughter in the world. She blew out a breath and started.

"It started last week…"

Her grandfather leaned in.

"Mother and I had the fight of all fights. She had gone down to Dr. White's and asked him to give me a job." She shifted on the swing, sitting cross-legged with her back against the arm to better face her grandfather. "I was mortified! The embarrassment of having *mommy* go asking for a job. As if I couldn't do it myself if I wanted to." Anna rolled her eyes.

Her grandfather chuckled. "I take it you did not want to."

"Of course not! And the worst part was she *knew* I didn't want a job there! I love Dr. White just as much as the next person but…" She trailed off and closed her eyes. When she opened them, her grandfather was watching her, waiting for her to go on.

"She said I was being an 'ungrateful brat.' Can you believe that? She called her daughter an ungrateful brat!" She stopped and looked at her grandfather. He cringed. They both knew how hot her mother's temper could be and just how stubborn she was. While Anna was glad she hadn't inherited the bad temper, she knew she'd certainly gotten her fair share of stubbornness. And although it really was nothing to laugh at, her ability to let things roll off of her angered her mother even more.

Laughing, Anna continued. "Do you know what she did, Gramps? She slapped me! That woman slapped me right across the face." Picturing it all over again gave her the giggles. She tried to fight it, but her grandfather started laughing, too, tears forming in the corners of his eyes, and soon they were uncontrollable, howling out on the porch swing. Hardly able to compose himself, no longer rocking in any kind of steady rhythm, bent over, clutching his side, Gramps finally righted himself. "You didn't laugh like that when she slapped you, did you?"

"Gramps, I couldn't help it! You know I laugh when I'm nervous. Plus, we both know I can't keep a poker face." And the two of them started all over again in a fit of laughter until they were gasping for air.

"Oh, I can only imagine the look on your mother's face."

Anna wiped the tears from her face. "It wasn't one of my finer moments. She stormed out into the orchard, and we haven't spoken since. After I went to Dr. White's, I walked into town and saw the ad in the pharmacy window. Gramps, I just knew it was a sign. I mean, it was an actual sign hanging there in the window, but it was also a *sign*. I am meant to do this. This is the one part of my life that I've never felt more clear on, and even though she tries to muddle my thoughts and guilt me into staying, my mind is made up."

She thought maybe Gramps would say something, but he just kept watching her, letting her talk through it all.

She continued, "I took the poster down from the window and walked back to the counter. I must've been quite a sight because Mr. Porter asked me if everything was alright. I showed him the poster and asked him if he knew where the nearest Red Cross recruiting station was, and he said he was pretty sure it was on Main Street in Richmond, just one town over. I couldn't believe it. Can you believe it, Gramps? Surely it was another sign! Anyway, he told me Ginny was at home and could take the car if I needed a ride. I gave him a big hug and practically ran all the way to Ginny's." She sat for a moment, catching her breath and pondering over the fact that her best friend's father was more supportive of her decision than her own mother. She shook her head.

"Now, hold on a minute. You mean to tell me this was all a week ago and you and your mother haven't talked since?" Gramps couldn't hide the surprise…and disappointment from his voice.

Anna just nodded. She really could be just as stubborn as her mother. But if she were honest with herself, she might've been taking the easy way out. She was too tired to argue any-more, so if the alternative were to just not speak at all, for now, anyway, that's what she was doing.

Gramps let out a whistle. "I sure am glad I don't live under the same roof as the two of you."

Anna snorted and wrinkled her nose. "It's not easy, Gramps. Poor dad." Anna's father, much like her grandfather, had quickly learned not to get between the two women.

"Well, anyway, I grabbed Ginny. She grabbed the car keys, and we went on over to Richmond. She was happy to have an 'adventure' as she called it, and I was happy to have her with me. I had the ride there to get nervous, and I needed her support. Turns out, it was a breeze! I had all my credentials. It was just a matter of verifying that I had my degree. Of course, they still need to do the usual checks - height and weight, and all that nonsense, but Gramps, I'm in. I'm not just saying it, hoping for it to happen. I'm really going. Can you even imagine all the places I'll see?" She looked up at her grandfather. A wave of emotion she hadn't expected to see passed over his face as he pulled her in for a hug. He rested his chin on the top of her head.

"I can imagine, AB. I can imagine." The laughter had gone from his face, and she got the feeling he was holding back from what he really wanted to say.

He pulled her back, holding onto her arms and looking into her eyes. "You're going to be an incredible nurse, AB. Just do me a favor. Try to remember that all these places you've dreamed of seeing since you were a little girl...remember they're going to look different right now. It might not be a dream realized, and I don't want you to be disappointed. Actually, I don't think you're going to have time to feel disappointment. Just…remember that. Take care of yourself. No one will do that for you."

She knew she had no idea what she was getting herself into, and to her grandfather, she probably sounded more than a little bit naive. She had never been away from this small town for any length of time. She just kept telling herself it was better than staying. And she didn't know what her future held or where she'd be in five months or even a week. She did know that one morning, she sat down in a classroom, started her first nursing course, and had stood up at the end as a different person. She knew that for her mom, the gardens, baking cakes, and rotary clubs filled her up. Those were the things that brought her joy. But for Anna, she found no fulfillment in staying home. She had no desire to marry and keep a house. Not yet, at least. She wondered if maybe one day she would. For now, the thing that lifted her soul was healing people. It was knowing she helped someone in need in a way that felt far more powerful to her than fundraising or growing carrots. It was the thought that she could help someone who might sit down before her and stand up a different person. It might sound like a tall order for a nurse to fill, but she'd be damned if she didn't try.

Chapter 4

*P*aul climbed down the train's steps, duffel bag slung over one shoulder. He was glad to be out of the cramped, stale air of the compartment, even if it was now replaced with the smell of burning diesel. The train sounded, puffing even more of the sooty smoke, and Paul turned to watch it pull slowly out of the station, the noise of the metal rails screeching and clacking as it gained speed. He stood watching the train disappear down the tracks, feeling no need to rush. He had written home - only because he thought it better than showing up without warning - but he still felt an uneasiness about seeing his folks. He knew what he'd see on his mother's face, and he hated that he'd be adding to her heartache. She'd been through enough, and he prayed the Lord would spare him if only to keep his mother from having to grieve over two sons lost.

He began his walk through the station, nodding at a few GIs waiting on the long wooden bench inside. He pushed open the door and let his pack slide down his arm to the ground as he thought about what he'd do next. He hadn't planned for a ride home, so he stood for a moment, letting the sun wash over him. He let his eyes close, happy to be back in the warmth of his hometown. He hadn't quite gotten used to the dreary, cold months in Missouri. He opened his eyes, grabbed his bag, and started through the parking lot. His childhood home was only a few miles from here, and after being cooped up first on a greyhound from campus and then on the train here, he welcomed the idea of stretching his legs with a walk. He figured he'd better get used to it, anyway.

He crossed the street, passed the old bus station, and headed into town. He thought about whether or not he should make a stop at Eddie's. He decided that, yes, he could certainly do with a fountain treat or maybe a chili dog before he walked any further out of town. He approached the ice cream shop with its red and white canopy hanging overhead and matching curtains in the windows, and caught sight of a familiar car parked out front. It wouldn't have been unusual for dear old dad to have satisfied an afternoon sweet tooth. He hesitated, thought about continuing on ahead, then, annoyed at himself, he swung the door wide. *What am I so worried about*, he thought.

The smells of chocolate and sweet cream, followed by the sauteed onions and cheese, were the first things to register as he took in the familiar layout of his favorite shop. He took a seat at one of the nineteen stools, stretching the length of the counter. He had often run up and down as a child, counting each stool, wondering why there were nineteen. Not twenty, not eighteen, but nineteen. He chuckled at the silly innocence he had had counting the stools at the bar. He had always loved counting things, even when it drove his mother nuts. He'd count the buttons in her sewing kit and the cracks on the sidewalk, making up math problems and solving them as he went. He liked things to be organized and even - probably why the nineteen stools seemed to bother him so much. It was also probably why he had done so well in the army so far, though he had learned to loosen up a bit. He couldn't go around counting sidewalk cracks as a grown man. Occasionally, he'd catch himself counting his steps, but he told himself it didn't hurt anything to keep track now and again.

He glanced down at the menu while he waited. He really didn't need to look, knowing he'd be getting two chili dogs with the works, followed by a fountain soda of their choice. Despite his love of organization, he enjoyed a surprise now and then, even if it were as simple as a soda flavor.

"Well, well, well, look what the cat dragged in." Paul turned at the teasing voice behind him. He grinned as he swiveled his stool around and hopped down, his sister standing before him with a matching expression. He pulled her into the biggest bear hug he could, careful not to squeeze his nephew, perched on her hip. When he stepped back, he reached for the baby and swung him around in a circle before cradling him into a hug of his own. Giggles bubbled up out of him, and Paul looked at his sister and smiled.

"Gosh, he's getting so big. Look at you, birthday boy!" Danny had his first birthday last month, and Paul had beat himself up over missing it. He ran his thumb over the boy's forehead, glad his nephew hadn't forgotten him.

"Oh, Paul, I can't believe you're here! Why didn't you call from the station? I'd have picked you up." His sister gave him that motherly look she seemed to have developed overnight. He supposed it was to be expected now that she had a baby of her own. They settled back onto the bar stools and Paul looked out the window.

"You mean to tell me that Pop lets you drive his car?" Disbelief flooded his face, but his sister's wry smile told him he was right. He let out a whistle.

"Does he inspect every square inch of it when you pull into the driveway?"

"Nah...I think he feels bad now that I've moved in with them. He's loosened up quite a bit."

They looked at each other, silent understanding passing between them.

"Evie..."

His sister shook her head and held up a hand as she watched her brother bounce Danny on his knee.

"It's fine, Paul. Really. I wasn't sure at first, but it's the best thing for everyone right now. With Sean away and Jamie..." She trailed off. They hadn't yet figured out how to talk about their brother without fighting back tears. Paul often forgot that not only had his sister lost her big brother, but her husband had been overseas for four months. He tried not to let her see the pain on his face - she hated it when people pitied her. Evie dug around in her bag, pulled out a teething biscuit, and placed it in her son's chubby fingers. If she had seen anything cross Paul's face, she didn't let on.

"Danny keeps mom busy, and even though she swears she doesn't want to pick up after a baby," Evie did her best impression of their mother as she continued, "because 'she's finished raising hers,' I can tell she loves it. So. That's that. It's good, Paul. I promise."

She patted Paul's shoulder. "It's really good to see you, Paul."

"It's good to see you too, Evie."

The waitress walked through the swinging doors from the kitchen and over to Paul and Evie. Grateful for the interruption, Paul picked up his menu with one hand, keeping a grip on Danny. The little boy hadn't quite figured out what to do with the biscuit yet, but Paul had a feeling he'd soon be covered in drool and baby food. He knew Danny would do a number on his uniform, but he didn't care. He had a week to think about anything but his uniform or the army, and he planned to enjoy that time with his nephew as much as his sister would let him.

He looked up to find his sister and the waitress staring at him. He guessed he'd gotten lost in his thoughts again. "I'll have the.."

"Let me guess," said his sister, "the chili dog, extra cheese, extra onions, and a fountain drink, surprise me."

Paul grinned. "Actually, it'll be two chili dogs, thank you very much."

Evie laughed. "Not much has changed, huh?"

The waitress took their menus and made her way back to the kitchen with Paul's order.

"So, what's new around here?" Paul asked, looking around.

"Oh, you know. What you see is what you get. Not much changes in this old town. Just more boys being drafted and less of them coming back. It's a bit depressing, but you already know all that. I'm just glad I've got Danny to keep me busy. He sure knows how to keep my mind from growing idle. If he wasn't such a chunk, he'd probably be walking by now." She looked at her son. Just as Paul had predicted, there was drool and baby food forming a paste on the pant leg of his uniform. Danny had one hand gripped around the biscuit and another holding fiercely to Paul's finger.

Paul laughed. "He's got some grip on him."

"You're telling me! Lucky you've got such short hair. I swear I've got chunks missing the way he grabs on." She reached into her bag, searching for a tissue or napkin. "Sorry, Paul. It doesn't take him long to make a mess."

"Don't worry about it, Evie. I don't mind."

Paul's order came out, and Danny's eyes went wide. The waitress chuckled. "Isn't he a cutie? He looks hungry, too."

Paul popped a fry into his mouth and turned to his sister.

"You on your way anywhere? I don't want to keep you if you've got things you need to do."

Evie whacked her brother on the back of the head. Paul ducked, but not fast enough.

"Ow, Ev, what was that for?"

"You have got to be kidding me. Thinking I've got something better to do than be right here with you," She shook her head.

"Just didn't want to keep you held up, is all." Paul rubbed the back of his head.

"Don't make me smack you again. Like I said, there's nowhere else I need to be."

"Well, if it isn't Paulie O'Reilly." Mr. Kelly, the owner, rounded the counter, his round red face alive with laughter as he shook Paul's hand. Evie reached for Danny, and Mr. Kelly pulled Paul into a hug.

When they pulled back, the older man held onto Paul's shoulder a moment longer, letting go only when the jingle of the bells hanging from the door alerted them to another customer. Mr. Kelly resumed his place behind the counter.

"Business good?" Paul looked around at the booths filled with people.

Mr. Kelly waved his hand. "I'm still here, anyway," he said. "How are you doing, son?"

His serious expression made Paul nervous. He reached for his nephew, hoping to dodge the question. When he looked up, Mr. Kelly watched him, waiting for an answer. Paul shrugged.

"As well as the rest of 'em," he said. Mr. Kelly nodded. Danny slapped at the counter with one chubby fist, making them laugh.

As Paul finished his last bite, Danny started to fuss. He smiled down at his nephew.

"Perfect timing, kid."

"He needs his nap. You mind if we head home?" Evie stroked a hand over her son's head.

Paul pulled out his wallet as his sister picked Danny up off his lap and headed for the door. He could hear his nephew wailing even after the door closed behind them. *Boy, he sure could throw a fit*, Paul thought. He laid a few bills on the counter and stood to leave.

Mr. Kelly grunted. "What's this?"

"Paying for my lunch," Paul said.

Mr. Kelly shoved the money back across the counter. "Get that outta here," he said. "Your money's no good here."

"Oh, come on, Mr. Kelly. That's no way to keep business booming."

Mr. Kelly snorted. "The hell it isn't. I take care of all the boys here. You're not the only special one," he joked. Paul laughed and took the bills from Mr. Kelly's outstretched hand.

"Thank you, sir," he said.

Mr. Kelly nodded. "Make sure you come back around when you get home."

Paul shook Mr. Kelly's hand once more and followed his sister out to the car he had seen on his way in - the one he couldn't have imagined his sister being allowed to drive. And here she was, getting her son in and taking the driver's seat like it wasn't anything at all. He shook his head and got in on the passenger side. He was happy to have this time with his sister. Long gone were the days of bickering and picking on one another. It was nice to be able to chat with her and enjoy one another's company. A grin overtook him as she skillfully backed out onto the road and proceeded toward their childhood home. He was glad he decided to come back for his furlough. Not that he really thought he wouldn't, but part of him had wondered if it would be easier on everyone if he'd gone straight to training. He was afraid one week at home might make leaving again that much harder.

Turning up the long drive, Paul looked around and decided to put those heavy thoughts aside, at least for now. He knew he couldn't avoid the inevitable forever. Right now, he enjoyed seeing the fields on both sides of the driveway growing up for hay season. The wildflowers his mom and Evie had planted when they were kids still bloomed in random patches all the way up the gravel drive. She was right; not much had changed. The farmhouse still needed a fresh coat of white paint. It stood at the end of the field, looking just the same as always. Evie cut the engine, and everything was quiet.

"Where's the dogs, Evie?"

She gave her brother a sly smile. "Ah, well. That's one change, I suppose. Daddy let Ranger in the house. Claims he's been bothering the neighbors at night, but I don't buy it one bit. And then let's see…" She looked around to the right, down the hill toward the barn. "Freddy's probably down in the barn. He's made friends with the horses, and you know, he still hates the heat, so when he's not laying in the breeze on the porch, he's usually down there."

Paul was still stuck on the fact that his Pop let the dog in the house. "I'm sorry, sis. I think I misheard you. You mean to tell me Pop not only lets you drive his car, but he also lets the dog sleep in the house?"

Evie chuckled. "No sir, not just sleep in the house. That dog is in there all day and all night long. He's become a regular house pet."

She started to carefully get a sleepy Danny out of the car. Paul thought about the changes in his father. He wondered what was really going on with their old man. Was he really just trying to help Evie out during a tough time, or was he going through his own tough time? He tucked the thought away to think about after he saw his old man and could judge for himself.

From the front steps, Evie called out. "You comin' or what?" Danny's head hung heavy on her shoulder, and Paul felt like a dud for not thinking to help his sister.

He hopped from the car and ran up the steps two at a time.

"Wait," his sister whispered. But it was too late. Paul had yanked open the screen door only to let out a giant Labrador, too excited to control his rear end, which was shaking with delight. Before Paul had time to react, the dog was on its hind legs, front paws on his shoulders, tail wagging. Evie tried to avoid being hit with Ranger's frantic tail as she sidled past, holding onto her sleeping baby's head, covering his eyes as best she could so as not to wake him. She looked back toward Paul, who mouthed '*sorry*' as she headed up the stairs to her old bedroom. Her parents wanted her to take two rooms upstairs, one for her and one for the baby, but she had refused. They were fine in one room together, she swore. She hadn't wanted to take up any extra space, already feeling like a burden being back at home at twenty-five.

Downstairs, Paul had been knocked to his knees by the old dog, still prancing and whining all around him. His mother appeared from the kitchen, stopped in her tracks, her hand flying to her mouth.

Paul grinned up at his mother from his spot on the floor, still trying to control Ranger. Grabbing the dog's collar, he managed to get to his feet. "Hey, Ma," he said.

"Paul Finnegan O'Reilly," his mother said when she finally removed her hand from her mouth. Paul cringed at hearing his very Irish full name. No one had ever used it except his mother, and usually only when she let that Irish temper fly. He let go of Ranger, hoping the dog might calm down, and opened his arms toward his mother. "Hey, Ma," he said again, folding her into a hug.

He had thought so much about what it would feel like to come home, and yet he still wasn't prepared for his mother's emotional reaction. She clung tightly to him as if she hadn't known if she'd ever see him again. He had written home to let her know he was coming, but he supposed it was just what mothers did - got all blubbery when their *babies* came back.

He finally managed to get one arm unwrapped and walked with her to the kitchen, his other arm still around her back in case she needed the extra support. He couldn't remember a time when his mother ever needed extra support - she was always strong enough for everyone - but then again, she'd never lost a son to war before, either.

The kitchen, situated at the back of the house, had a door perfectly in line with the one in front so that on warm summer days, they'd open up both doors and feel the glorious cross breeze that offered some reprieve from the sticky humidity. Today, though, the door was closed, and the little radio played quietly in the corner. The sink was full of bubbly water, and the drying rack was half full of dishes ready to be wiped and put away. He walked over and washed his hands, the beginnings of fatigue setting in after a long day of traveling. He reached for a drying cloth just as his mother tried to snatch it away from his hands.

"You get yourself settled in upstairs. I'll finish these."

"Nah, Ma. I'm okay. Let me help." Paul was raised better than to leave the kitchen when there were dishes to be dried.

She looked as if she might argue, then let go of the towel and dipped her hands into the soapy water, retrieving a plate to be scrubbed. They worked in silence for a while, Paul feel-ing awkward and not knowing what to say to break the ice. He hadn't exactly told his mother the truth in his letter home, and he was sure she was smart enough to figure out what was hap-pening. He just didn't really feel like getting into it the moment he got home.

Evie appeared and grabbed the towel from him. He put his hands up in surrender and backed away from the sink while the two women got to work in a rhythm that suggested they had been doing this together for a while. Paul opened a cabinet, pulled out a can of coffee, and got to work making a pot. It was nearing three o'clock, and if things had stayed the same around here, he thought he'd see his father for his afternoon cup any minute.

The sound of boots on the back steps told him he was right. He looked up to see his father trudging in through the kitchen door.

"Hey, Pop." Paul greeted his father in the same way he had his mother, trying to sound much more nonchalant than he felt.

"Paulie Boy!" His father's eyes lit up, and in two great strides, he had wrapped Paul up in a bear hug, clapping him on the back with his giant mitts. Paul felt himself relax. It felt good to be in his father's presence, almost like he wasn't carrying the weight of the world on his shoulders. Or maybe it was the feeling that he could gather up some of his father's strength to use for himself, not wanting to let his dear old dad down. Wanting to make him proud. If he kept his thoughts set on that, maybe he wouldn't feel like such a chicken.

His father pulled back, framing Paul's face with his hands and looking at his son. "So, how long are you here for? Where to next?"

Leave it to his father to get right to the point. He knew the drill. Paul blew out a long breath and glanced at his mom and Evie. His mother was draining the soapy water while Evie put away the last clean dish, both pretending not to listen.

"Well, Dad, I've only got a week here. Next stop is Camp Blanding down in Florida, then after that I suppose it'll be on to the front lines." Paul turned to sit at the wooden table in the corner. He and his father had worked together to build the bench that ran in an L shape along the wall. He ran his hand down the wooden seat, avoiding his mother's reaction. Of course, he had to look up when she placed his cup of coffee in front of him.

"Thanks, Ma." She nodded and brought three more cups to the table.

"What happened to the program you were in, Paulie?" she asked as she joined him at the table.

"It's being downsized. Or so they say. I think they're getting rid of it altogether, but they don't want to say it outright. All I know is they must be desperate, wanting all of us brains on the front lines." He was trying to poke fun at his intelligence and make light of a dark situation, but it fell flat. He looked from his mom to his dad and finally to Evie, who was swiping at some imaginary crumbs on the table in front of her.

His dad cleared his throat and gave him a smile that didn't reach his eyes. "Well, we'll enjoy this week with you, son." He looked at his wife and took her hand, swallowing it up in his giant one. "It'll all be alright, Marie. We'll all be alright."

Danny let out a wail from the upstairs bedroom, and his mother seized the opportunity, scraping her chair along the floor as she rushed out of the kitchen. Evie covered her face with her hands. Paul slumped back against the hard wooden bench and looked up at his dad.

"She'll be alright, Paulie Boy. Don't worry yourself about things here. You keep your head on right, and you'll make it back home just fine."

Paul nodded and gave a weak smile. His father's reassurance did little to ease the storm he felt brewing inside his stomach, and he was pretty sure it didn't have anything to do with his mother's strong coffee. His thoughts went to Jamie. He'd had his head on right, too, but it didn't seem to matter. He hadn't made it out alive, as far as they knew. They were still waiting to find out exactly what had happened to his brother. *God only knows what's in store for me,* Paul thought.

Chapter 5

ANNA
JUNE 1944
FORT GEORGE G. MEADE,
MARYLAND

Anna looked around the train station outside of Fort George Meade. It was a tiny depot, no bigger than the house she grew up in. In fact, it looked as though it had been a house at one point. A long wooden porch wrapped around the building that looked like it had been pieced together with leftover scraps of wood to serve as a platform. A set of steps in front and another in back were the only way in and out. With the way the place was swarming, she was glad to not need a ticket and decided to go around the building to the parking lot by way of a grassy area to its left. She stopped to admire the few flowers that had been planted around the flagpole. She knew someone would meet her to show her the way to the barracks, but as she looked around at the passing uniforms, she wondered how she'd find him. She spotted several women in nursing uniforms huddled together and decided it would be best to join them. As she approached the group, a young GI stepped in front of her.

"Heading to Fort Meade, Ma'am?"

"Yes, I am. Are you bringing me there?"

Ignoring her question, the GI, forehead beaded in sweat, looked down at his clipboard.

"Name, unit, and rank," he demanded.

"Anna Mitchell." She didn't want to admit she hadn't a clue what her unit or rank was.

The soldier looked at her, waiting for her to continue.

Anna sighed. She could feel her hair beginning to curl at the base of her neck in the warmth of the sun.

"Well, I'm sorry to say but I haven't the foggiest what my unit or rank is. I don't believe I've been assigned either of those things."

She could hear the group of nurses to her right begin to chuckle and she looked over to see them with their hands over their mouths, watching her squirm under the glare of the soldier. She pursed her lips and gave a small wave, feeling a bit embarrassed. *Who doesn't know their rank and unit?* She thought.

"Ma'am, you mean to tell me you've been sent here with no idea where you're actually going?"

Anna could feel her face getting hot, but she was sure she wasn't wrong. She'd remember an important detail like that. She glanced over at her fellow nurses, hoping they'd help her out. A red-haired woman bounced over and winked at Anna.

"I think we know where she's going," she said. She linked

her arm with Anna's and led her toward the other nurses waiting nearby. They turned back to see the GI, head buried in his clipboard, pencil scribbling away.

"What was that all about?"

The women laughed. "The poor boy was thrown to the wolves. Don't worry, he asked us the same questions, and we gave him the same answers. He's gotten himself in a panic without a clue what to do with us."

Anna's eyes went wide.

"What do you mean? We're in Fort Meade, aren't we?" Anna turned like she'd go back to help him, but the woman's arm remained firmly linked through hers, keeping her in place.

"Yes, yes, of course. We're in the right place. His orders were to get the names, ranks, and units of all the nurses arriving today. He's afraid he'll be handed it if he doesn't get this assignment right."

Anna considered this. He did look terrified. *Poor kid*, she thought.

"So, what are we supposed to do, then?"

"We're just waiting for the rest of the nurses coming in today," she said.

"I'm Gretchen." The red-haired woman unlinked her arm from Anna's to offer her hand.

"I'm Anna. It's nice to meet you." She shook Gretchen's hand.

Another woman stepped forward.

"Louise." The two women shook hands. Gretchen walked over to the last nurse in the group.

"This is Eleanor, though in the last two hours we've been sitting here, we've nicknamed her Elle," Gretchen said. She smiled at her new friend, who scowled back at her.

"No, *you've* nicknamed me Elle," she replied.

Anna chuckled. "It's nice to meet you, *Eleanor*," she said.

Eleanor yawned and sat down on a bench behind them. Anna sat down beside her, needing to rest her feet. She had just bought new shoes - the perfect pair for a nurse on her feet all day, according to the store clerk - and they were making her feet throb. After a full day of travel, she couldn't wait to get them off.

"Anyone else a bit nervous?" Louise looked around at the group of women.

Anna gave a small nod, happy to have something other than her aching feet to think about. Thinking about how nervous she was wasn't much better, but she was glad to know she wasn't alone. For a split second, she had thought about lying, but she knew her shaky voice would have given her away. She hoped these women would become her friends, and she wouldn't let her pride stand in the way.

"Hopefully, we'll be at the front soon," said Eleanor.

Anna looked at her, stunned. She knew what she'd signed up for and where they were going, but she couldn't say she was excited to be on the front like Eleanor seemed to be. Anna looked up at Louise, who raised her eyebrows in surprise.

"Well, if we have to wait here much longer, I might just give up on the whole thing," Gretchen complained.

Louise laughed. "Better get used to it. Haven't you heard of the unofficial Army motto?"

Anna shook her head.

"Hurry up and wait," Louise and Eleanor said in unison, saluting.

"We've been here two hours already. I'm starving and ready to put my feet up," said Gretchen.

They watched as their trunks were loaded into a GMC army truck.

"I don't see why we have to sit here and wait when they've got the trucks here. Can't we just hitch a ride with them?" Eleanor said loud enough that Anna was sure the soldier had heard her complaint.

He strode over to them, smirking as he tucked his pencil behind his ear.

"Well, ladies, it looks like you're right. No reason to sit and wait. We'll be on our way now."

Relief flooded their faces as they grabbed their duffel bags and headed toward the truck, now loading the last trunk.

Anna hung back from the rest of the girls.

"Shouldn't we ask the truck to wait in case another train comes in with other nurses?" She thought that was a perfectly good suggestion, but from the look on the GI's face, he did not agree.

"Oh, I didn't say we'd be going on the truck," he called out to the others who had run ahead.

Anna turned to look at him.

"Why wouldn't we be going on the truck?" she asked.

He laughed, actually laughed, a hearty, joyous sound like he had just told the funniest joke he'd ever heard, and they had missed the punchline.

The nurses looked at one another, not amused in the least, and sauntered back toward Anna.

Gretchen cleared her throat.

"Um, everything ok?"

The GI wiped his eyes and regained his composure.

"We won't be going on the truck because your training starts now. You're learning how to march."

"Excuse me?" Eleanor looked as though steam might come out of her ears. "You mean to tell me we just got here after hellish train rides, sat for two hours for no reason at all, and now we are going to be *walking* to the base?"

The soldier's smile faltered only for a moment.

"Actually, I said you'd be marching, not walking. Get used to it. You're in the Army now."

He turned on his heel and started for the sidewalk, not bothering to see if they were following. There was no other choice, really, unless they decided to risk a running jump into the back of the giant truck that was now pulling away.

"Who does this kid think he is anyway? He can't be more than nineteen with that baby face." Eleanor puffed as they picked up their pace. A group of nurses Anna hadn't yet met stayed close behind their escort. *They look just as young as he does,* Anna thought. She wondered if she and her new friends were going to feel like the old ladies of the group, judging by the few other recruits she'd seen so far.

"How far is it to the barracks, anyway?" Gretchen called out.

The soldier shouted over a passing car. "Oh, just about five miles." He kept up his stride, not giving any indication of slowing down.

"He has lost his damn mind," Eleanor groaned.

Anna glanced around, trying to take in the town she'd be calling home for however long the Army decided to keep them there. If she had to walk five miles, she might as well do some sightseeing along the way. They passed by a stately firehouse and a group of red brick houses situated along a semi-circular driveway. *Aren't they adorable?* she thought. Each one was well maintained and exactly like the next, with white trimmed windows matching the pillars on each side of the front door. Even in the warmth of the June sun, she could picture them in the winter, a blanket of white snow contrasting the bright red of the brick, chimneys puffing smoke, green wreaths adorning the doors. She wondered where she'd be come Christmas.

"Seems like a cute place to live," she mused out loud.

Gretchen nodded her agreement.

"Too bad we'll be too busy to enjoy much of it."

"Hey, Boy Scout," Eleanor called out to the soldier.

Anna and Gretchen looked at each other, eyes wide, mortified.

"Elle…are you crazy?" Gretchen whispered.

"Aw, I'm just messing with him, gotta keep him on his toes," she replied.

He turned on his heel and glared at Eleanor. She glared back.

"You care to tell us what all these buildings are since you're so keen to torture us with this five-mile walk?"

"I'm fairly certain you can read," he said. "Perhaps you can't since you don't know your rank or unit…"

He turned back around and continued on. Eleanor stuck her tongue out at his back. Anna stifled a laugh.

"So much for learning to march," she said.

"Hey, don't let him hear you complaining. Walking this far is bad enough; we don't need to march the whole way," said Anna.

They came to an intersection in the road and were led down the lane to the right where they could see rows and rows of small white buildings on either side. Further ahead, the buildings became larger, some with pillars in front and ornate carvings along the roof. Even from this distance, Anna could see the steps leading up to giant double doors on the building straight ahead. The smaller buildings were kept in good repair, though they were plain. Their wooden exteriors had all been painted white with matching clay-colored roofs.

Making the turn down the road, the GI stopped suddenly.

"Ok, ladies," he said to the group of nurses, "since we've actually been on base since we left the train station, it's time we started marching." He looked toward Eleanor and grinned.

"Ha! I knew you were messing with us. Five miles! And to think we'd have followed this Boy Scout for five miles!"

He just laughed and turned around, marching ahead. The girls continued to walk.

"Left, left, left, right, left. I wasn't kidding about the marching," he called out.

They stopped and watched as a line of soldiers crossed in front of them, marching in perfect unison.

"Well, it can't be too hard," Gretchen said.

They continued on, attempting to march and getting thoroughly mixed up. Anna laughed. She knew her left foot from her right, so why was this so difficult?

"If I can skip, I should be able to march, shouldn't I?" she looked at the rest of the nurses. None of them was marching with any particular skill. She clapped her hand over her mouth and tried to stifle the laughter that threatened. She could only imagine what they looked like to passersby or those watching from the windows of the buildings they passed. *Oh boy,* she thought, *what a first impression we must be giving.* It didn't take more than Gretchen catching her eye for the two of them to fall into a fit of giggles right in the middle of the main drag. Eleanor tried to continue ahead of them, maintaining her focus on her feet, but she, too, couldn't fight the hilarity of their situation. Maybe it was travel fatigue, maybe it was their nerves bundled up tight, whatever it was, they couldn't stop the laughter pouring out of them. Hanging on to each other's arms, they tried to straighten themselves between breaths.

"Ok, ok, we can do this. Just don't look at me!" cried Gretchen. But as she attempted to march ahead of Anna and Eleanor, she fell into a skipping pattern, bouncing on her toes, sending both girls into another gale of laughter.

The GI, either oblivious to their struggle or choosing to ignore them altogether, continued to march them down a narrow lane lined with identical buildings on each side. From this angle, they could see that the buildings weren't as small as they had looked from the main road but rather were long and narrow, with several doors down the length of them. Anna thought they looked like little motels - little, unattractive, uninviting motels.

They stopped at a door with a small plaque that said Unit C-17.

"Home, sweet, home," the GI said, checking his clipboard again.

"Let's see…Ms. Mitchell, Ms. White, Ms. Reeves, and Ms. Duncan. You're here in C-17." He gestured to the door in front of them. "And you three ladies," he pointed to the other nurses and then across the lane to the building opposite. "You're right across the lane in D-17.

Gretchen walked up the two steps to their new room and tried the door.

"You'll be needing these," the GI said, dangling several keys from his fingers.

Eleanor snatched them from him. She gave him a wry smile.

"So, Boy Scout, what's your name anyway?"

The question had caught him off guard, and the smirk fell from his face. He cleared his throat, and Eleanor laughed.

"Cat got your tongue? Alright, I guess I'll go on calling you Boy Scout then."

He shifted on his feet, looking uncomfortable.

"It's Matthews."

Anna and Gretchen watched the awkward exchange with amusement. Anna doubted if Eleanor had any real interest in the boy, but her friend did seem to enjoy making him squirm.

Eleanor dangled the newly acquired keys in the same way he had just done as she walked past him.

"Alright then, Mr. Matthews, sir, thanks for the escort."

She unlocked the door, and the three girls tripped over each other, trying to get inside. Anna closed the door, and they looked out the window, watching the soldier shake his head and walk back down the lane.

Gretchen gave Eleanor a smack on the arm.

"What is wrong with you? Messing with that poor kid!"

Eleanor laughed.

"Oh, please. It was all in good fun. He messed with us first. That *poor kid's* not gonna know what hit him when he gets over there."

Anna blew out a breath.

"Makes me nervous for him."

Eleanor looked at her.

"You better forget about being nervous for anyone. We're all headed in the same direction. It won't do you any good to worry about anyone just because they look too young and innocent to be here." She paused. "We're all too young and innocent to be here."

"You're right," Anna said. "It's hard to shake the nerves, but you're right; it does no good."

They were quiet for a moment, watching troops march down the lane past their building.

"How in the heck do they do that? Make it look so darn easy, too. It's just not right," said Louise.

Anna laughed.

"Of all the things I thought I'd struggle with, marching was not one of them."

Eleanor made a face.

"Honestly, it's the dumbest thing we have to learn. Who ever heard of a nurse marching to her patients? I can just see us now on the frontlines, being called for help. 'Sorry, we'll get to you as soon as we can march on over.'" She rolled her eyes and tossed her bag on the nearest bottom bunk. "Don't these look nice and scratchy," she said, pulling back the rough gray blanket.

Looking around the room, Anna found it was about as bare as you could get. Two sets of bunk beds lined the far wall, one small nightstand between them. In the corner stood a small cupboard. She opened up the doors to reveal a few metal hangers. They'd all be sharing the space to hang their uniforms. She closed the doors and turned back toward the little window beside the door. Glancing outside, several GIs were unloading trunks and carrying them toward their door. Anna jumped up to hold the door open wide as they shifted the trunk to fit through the narrow space. Two men carried the first trunk in, with another two on the truck unloading the next one.

"Ladies, where does this one go?" This GI had a grin on his face even while he struggled to hold up the heavy trunk. He was clearly not rattled by a room full of women, unlike his younger comrade, who had led them to their building. Anna craned her neck and held the door open with one foot while she checked for a name. She pointed to the far bed. "Gretchen, looks like it's yours."

The men dropped the trunk at the foot of the bed with a thud and walked out to gather the next one. When each bed had its rightful trunk, the GIs filed out the door without so much as a wave. Reaching for the door, the last one out turned to the girls. "Chow is at 6pm, you don't wanna be late. Oh, and lights out at 9pm." He flashed them a smile and pulled the door closed behind him.

Gretchen flopped down on her bed and fanned herself dramatically. Eleanor rolled her eyes.

"You better get used to all the men around. Don't be giving us a bad name swooning over every man you meet."

Gretchen sat up. "Oh, please. Can't a girl have a minute? Swooning, really? You call that swooning? I call it enjoying the view. I wouldn't dare embarrass myself." She elbowed Eleanor in the ribs. "But there's no harm in noticing."

Chapter 6

"Hey, girl," Paul crooned as he rubbed his hand down the horse's nose. Her sleek coat shined in the light coming through the slatted barn window in her stall, and he stood reveling in the beauty of his horse. He pressed his forehead to hers. He had missed her while he was away, and he'd never tire of seeing her strength and grace when she moved, the connection and depth in her eyes unmistakable. There was no other place he'd rather be than home on the farm, and down in the barn was one of his favorite spots. He enjoyed doing the work passed down through generations of O'Reilly men.

His father approached, a saddle slung over his arm, and opened the stall next to Paul. When he did, a beautiful chestnut brown horse poked her nose out, rubbing his father's arm playfully.

"Looks like she's ready to ride."

Paul looked up.

"Me too. One more go before I have to head out." His father's eyes searched his face before he turned and saddled up his horse.

They kept a slow, steady rhythm as they headed out of the barn. There was nothing like being in tune with such a gentle giant as Bess. Paul thought back to when his father had first gotten her. He was about fifteen and struggling, as most fifteen-year-old boys do. At a time when he could've gone off and rebelled against the world, he liked to think Bess had saved him, if a horse was capable of saving a person. Much the way his father had saved Bess from an abusive farmhand on the other side of town, she had saved Paul from a lot of the stupid things teenage boys could find themselves in. Instead of finding trouble, Paul had come home each day, determined to bond with the skittish horse. His efforts had paid off, and they forged a relationship he knew would hurt to lose one day.

He looked out, adjusting his hat down low over his eyes. The fields seemed to go on forever. It was hot, and they were in desperate need of rain, the dirt puffing up in little clouds with every step of the horses' hooves. They rode in silence for a while - another thing that Paul loved about being out here - the understanding that passed between him and his father without a word needing to be said.

Today, they planned to move one hundred or so cattle to a field in front. And while his mother wasn't thrilled at the idea of cows eating her petunias, they'd run out of any other options. It was the last section that hadn't been burnt to a crisp by the sun and drought, and it still had green grass to offer.

His father was the first to break the silence between them when he pointed across the fields and out to his left at an odd-looking patch of sky.

"Looks a bit dark over there, huh?" Paul's gaze followed where he pointed.

"Mmm...Hopefully, just some rain clouds rolling in."

"I don't know." His father pulled on the reins and stopped his horse. Paul slowed but continued a few more paces, squinting against the sun. His dad was right: it didn't look like rain clouds, but what else it could be, Paul didn't know. The sun was still high in the sky, the clouds a stark contrast to the heat beating down on them now. Paul lifted his hat to wipe the sweat that had formed under the brim.

"Doesn't look much like a rain cloud to me. I think we should head back."

Paul was surprised at his father's extra caution but decided it best to heed his warning.

"Pop, you've not been wrong about much out here, so if you think we need to head back, we head back. What do you think it is?"

The strange clouds continued to swirl in the distance, moving fast and picking up speed every second they watched. They were much darker than storm clouds, and the ominous way they swept the distant sky of its color, despite the bright sun, made Paul uneasy. Bess, sensing Paul's nerves or knowing they were in danger, let out a whinny and dug her hoof into the dirt. Paul rested his hand on her neck.

"It's okay girl, it's okay."

With his father still behind him and his focus on his horse, he was unaware that the clouds had started encroaching on them and fast.

"Let's go! Now!" His father's shout startled him, but Bess was ready. Paul took one look behind them to see the clouds were upon them. It was a storm but not the kind they'd been hoping for. He'd never been unlucky enough to be caught out in a dust storm until now. The air around him grew thick and gray, and he couldn't see his father ahead of him. He didn't know if they were going in the right direction. All he could do was relinquish control to Bess and pray she'd get them to safety. He leaned as far forward as he could, burying his face in her mane, and his hands, without having time to grab the reins before she darted off, were wrapped tightly around her neck. He kept his head down, and his eyes closed away from the harsh pelting of the dirt in the air.

Bess began to slow her gait. Paul risked a glance up long enough to see his father, handkerchief covering his mouth and nose, poised to slide the barn door shut behind him. Bess knew the way back to safety, even without his guidance, not that he thought she needed it. Inside the barn, he hopped down on shaky legs, heart pounding as he stroked his horse's neck - as much to calm him down as it was to calm her.

His father whistled and tilted his hat back. "Almost made it my whole life not havin' to experience that."

Even from inside the barn, dust made its way through the cracks of the windows and doors. They could hear the frantic *tick tick tick* of the dirt flying in the air, hitting everything around.

"Glad you're ok, son." His dad clapped him on the shoulder. "Coulda been a lot worse for us."

Paul smiled. "Yeah, I'm all good, Pop. Though for a second there, I thought there might'a been some kinda bandit waiting for me in the barn," he teased, yanking on the end of the handkerchief still tied around his father's face.

"Yeah, I see you're just fine," his father muttered, giving Paul a shove.

~⌣~

"Paulie Boy."

Paul looked up in time to catch the keys his dad had thrown from the porch. He was on his way down to the car to load up his things. Not that he had much to bring, but he knew he'd need his arms free when it came time to say goodbye.

"What are these for?" Paul asked. He looked up at his dad from his spot on the lawn. At just over six feet, his father could be an intimidating man. But what Paul saw in his old man these days was a little less rough around the edges. Evie was right; he had softened. And not just in the way of letting his kids drive his car - though Paul certainly appreciated the thrill of getting into that 1937 Chevy Master - or letting the dog sleep in the house. Paul could see it in the ways he interacted with his family, especially with Danny. He had been reluctant to admit it at first, but his sister's moving in with them seemed like the best thing for everyone. He never thought he'd see the day when his dad would retire early in the day instead of breaking his back till sundown - 'there's always something that needs to be done around the farm' - but he was glad for it. His parents deserved to take a break and enjoy life a little more. He was just sad he wouldn't get to stick around to see more of it.

Danny came crawling around the side of the house, Evie not far behind, watching him make a beeline for Paul. She caught up to him and swung him up onto her hip while he did his best to wriggle free. Climbing the steps, she sat him down on the porch with a stack of wooden blocks. Paul took the steps two at a time, laughing at the sight of Danny, shoving a block into his mouth to gnaw on.

"Must be getting some teeth in, huh, little guy?" Paul said.

"It seems like it all happens at once," Evie remarked. "The teeth, the crawling…It's incredible how fast they get once they figure out how to use those little legs!" She reached down and gave her son a gentle squeeze, and he squealed in delight.

They both turned at the sound of the screen door banging shut behind their mother, with her hands full of leftovers and freshly baked cookies wrapped tight.

"Let me help with that, Ma," Evie said.

Paul sat down in a rocking chair, listening to the Andrews Sisters singing *'don't sit under the apple tree with anyone else but me…'* no doubt his sister's doing. He had enjoyed seeing his sister and his mother get under each other's skin, bickering about the music being played or the latest fashion. He wasn't sure how his father was surviving with the two of them under the same roof but he assumed that's what the barn was for.

Danny began to fuss, bored with watching the grown-ups from his view on the floor. Evie picked him up and swayed to the soft sounds of the radio coming through the screen door, hoping to assuage him for just a few moments more.

"I should get him up to our room for his nap."

Paul wanted to snuggle the little guy once more before he left but didn't want to interrupt his sister's routine with her son. Instead, he stood and wrapped his mom up in a hug and kissed the top of her head. He might not have been the most athletic, but he had inherited his father's height and what Harry liked to call his 'farm strength.' His mother stood, her arms around his back, her head easily tucked under his chin. He looked behind his mother, counting the wooden boards that made up the siding on the house to keep from crying. *Do not make this harder on her, dammit,* he thought. She swayed to the music, and he let her dance.

"Remember those dance lessons in the living room, my how you fought me on that," she sniffed.

Paul laughed. "How could I forget?"

She tightened her arms around him until he could hardly breathe. "Paul Finnegan, you come back home, you hear me?"

Paul swallowed the lump in his throat. It wasn't a promise he could make, and she knew it.

"I'll drive ya down to the station, Paulie," his father said.

Paul smiled. He appreciated his father's interruption. His mother let him go, pulling a tissue from inside her sleeve.

"But Pop, I've got the keys," Paul reminded him, dangling them between his fingers.

His father chuckled.

"I suppose you do. Well then, I guess you'll be doing the driving." He went in for another bear hug from his father, knowing they'd likely be saluting down at the train station. *Dear God,* he silently prayed, *get us all through this.*

Evie tried to slip back into the house while Paul said his goodbyes. She opened the screen door, but Paul was too quick, grabbing it before it could slam shut behind her.

"Mind if I try to put the little rascal down for his nap?"

Evie looked as though she might say no. Tears welled in her eyes as she passed Danny into her brother's outstretched arms. She swiped the tears from her face.

"I thought I could disappear upstairs before I started this nonsense." She sniffed. "We sure are going to miss our Uncle Paul, aren't we buddy?" She rubbed Danny's back, trying to soothe him into settling down, though he was perfectly content in Paul's arms. He turned with his nephew to head out onto the porch.

"How 'bout we sit back out in the warm breeze, little guy?" He looked back at his sister, giving her his best puppy dog eyes. "I promise I'll put him in the crib if he falls asleep." She swatted him on the arm as they stepped outside.

Their parents had moved onto the wrought iron sofa, which, like the house, was also in need of a fresh coat of paint. Paul took a seat in one of the rocking chairs, enjoying his nephew's fidgeting. His father cleared his throat. "Paulie Boy...as much as I don't want to see you go, it's probably about that time."

"Pop, I think I can spare a few minutes more."

He rocked in a steady rhythm, hoping he could, in fact, get Danny to sleep. He hated to leave his sister with a cranky baby, and he knew he was being selfish. He couldn't help it. Not when his wandering mind questioned when he'd get another chance to rock his nephew out on his parent's front porch. Even if he did make it home, Danny'd have grown so much that he probably wouldn't remember his uncle in a year. He wanted to commit this moment to memory. He closed his eyes, taking it all in. The happy gurgling coming from Danny, the creak of the old wooden rocking chair, the morning breeze that he knew would turn sticky and humid later in the day. He began to hum to his nephew. The tune of *Danny Boy* was always at the forefront of his brain when he was around his nephew, and it seemed appropriate. Singing the first few verses quietly, Danny looked up at Paul, one chubby fist stretching out to touch the side of his face. He was no Bing Crosby, but Paul did his best to let his emotion carry him through the song, not worrying about how he sounded.

> *"Oh, Danny Boy, the pipes, the pipes are calling*
> *From glen to glen, and down the mountainside,*
> *The summer's gone, and all the roses falling,*
> *It's you, it's you must go and I must bide.*
>
> *But come ye back when summer's in the meadow,*
> *Or when the valley's hushed and white with snow,*
> *And I'll be here in sunshine or in shadow,*
> *Oh, Danny Boy, oh Danny boy, I love you so!*
> *But when ye come, and all the flowers are dying,*
> *And I am dead, as dead, I well may be,*
> *Ye'll come and find the place where I am lying,*
> *And kneel and say an 'Avé there for me;*
> *And I shall hear, though soft you tread above me,*
> *And all my grave will warmer, sweet be,*
> *For you will bend and tell me that you love me,*
> *And I shall sleep in peace until you come to me!"*

He finished the last refrain with Danny sleeping soundly, his head against Paul's shoulder. He stood, careful not to rouse his sleeping nephew, and walked across the porch. Before he could get to the door, his sister stood, nose red and eyes shining with tears. She held out her arms. Paul shook his head.

"I promised I'd get him in the crib."

By the time Paul had pulled into the train station lot, his hands were sweaty and he wanted to make a hasty goodbye to his father. His nerves were taking hold, and the last thing he wanted was for his father to think his son wasn't man enough to face his responsibility.

He parked the car, and both men got out. His father grabbed his duffel bag and began the walk toward the station.

"Hey Pop, you don't have to wait with me. I know you gotta get back to the farm."

His father gave him a sideways look.

"My to-do list will be there when I get back."

Paul blew out a breath. "Well, you don't have to carry my pack for me."

His father just smiled and kept walking. They had made it with plenty of time to spare, as Paul had predicted. He was glad to have spent the extra few minutes with his nephew. But, the longer he had to wait, the more his stomach twisted. How easy it would be to let the fear take hold. Boy, a man could spiral if he sat too long with his thoughts. He glanced over at his father, settling onto a bench to wait with his son. Paul sat beside him. He watched as his father reached inside the collar of his shirt and pulled something over his head, handing it to him.

"Pop...I can't take this." His father had worn the brown

scapular for as long as he could remember. He'd had his own, too, his grandfather having given each of his grandkids one. But taking the one from his father felt different. His family had long believed in the promise it provided - the grace at the hour of one's death, the reminder to emulate the heart of Jesus - the likeness he saw in his father and the way he chose to live each day.

"Of course you can. And you will. I've worn it a long time, Paul. It's your turn. Let it protect you." He hesitated. "Let God protect you. That scapular, it doesn't have any magical powers, son. We both know that. But it does carry a reminder of our faith. That reminder has made me a better man. Has made me turn to God when I wanted to turn away. Remember that when the doubt creeps in. Believe me, you will question everything you know when you're trudging through the muck, feeling like the depression of that war will kill you if the enemy doesn't."

Paul felt the tears welling in his eyes despite his greatest effort to stop them. He hated saying goodbye, knowing he'd not be back until the war was over. He turned to his dad and gave him an awkward hug as they sat side by side on the bench. He no longer cared about proving how brave he was. He was scared as hell, and he knew his dad could see right through him. He'd soak up these last few moments feeling like a kid again under the protection of his father. When he climbed those train steps, then he'd be brave. At least he hoped he'd find some courage by the time he got to Camp Blanding.

Chapter 7

ANNA
JULY 1944
FORT GEORGE G. MEADE,
MARYLAND

*S*he smoothed her freshly pressed uniform down her thighs, trying to wipe away more nerves than wrinkles as she waited for class to begin. It was a cold classroom with cinderblock walls painted a pale, faded blue. A blackboard hung on the front wall, and tall windows let in the bright morning sunlight. Posters had been placed around the remaining walls - diagrams of skeletons, muscles, and organs. Anna looked from one to the next until she came to the last one - the male anatomy - and quickly turned away. She felt a sudden blush creep up her cheeks, and she became annoyed with herself. *Get a grip, Anna,* she thought. She was no prude, having completed rounds and seen all parts of the human body when treating patients.

Despite her experience, she felt the doubt creeping into her thoughts. Her mother's disapproving words taunted her. She'd finally mustered up the courage to tell her mother she was leaving. She'd told her the day before, after several pep talks, and had braced herself for her mother's reaction. She had prayed she'd built the wall around her heart high enough that her mother couldn't tear her down. Even still, the disappointment and disapproval in her eyes had been more painful than the sour insults rolling off her tongue. Anna could still play the entire encounter in her mind, making her wish she had just left without saying a word. She was foolish to think she could have mended fences before she left.

"What makes you think a sickly little thing like you could be a war nurse? You couldn't take care of a damn cat if you tried," her mother's vicious voice rang in her head. She closed her eyes at the memory, hoping to shut out the thoughts of her mother. She'd made her choice, and her mother had made hers when she told Anna not to bother coming back.

The wooden door slammed shut, and Anna opened her eyes to a smallish woman entering the classroom, gripping a clipboard. A pair of thick black glasses hung around her neck by a silver chain. Her uniform was impeccably tailored, and her hair coiffed in a perfect bun. Anna's stomach did a nervous flip as she rose from her seat, along with the rest of the women in her unit, to stand at attention.

"Alright, knees, here we go," she whispered under her breath.

She hoped the head nurse wouldn't see the shake in her hands. She gave herself a pep talk. *You are competent and intelligent*, she thought. *You deserve to be here. You are here to serve your country. Those boys need you.*

Lieutenant June Campbell strode into the room straight to the blackboard and began scrawling across it without so much as a glance at the ninety-six women waiting patiently behind her. When she had finished, she took a step backward, reviewing her work, hands placed firmly at her hips. She turned to face her students.

"Ladies, welcome to Fort George G. Meade. Please make note of your schedule written behind me."

Anna scribbled down the schedule as fast as she could, careful not to miss anything her new boss was telling them.

> *0615 hours - Fall out of bed*
> *0700 hours - Fall in for mess*
> *0800 hours - School - two subjects / one hour each*
> *1020 hours - Drill/calisthenics/sports*
> *1200 hours - March to mess*
> *1250 hours - School - five hours of instruction OR outdoor hike/drills*
> *1800 hours - Mess formation - change from uniforms to dress uniforms*
> *2000 hours - Study Hall OR cleaning/housekeeping*
> *2200 hours - Taps - Lights out*

"You will be completing courses in Manners for Military Women, Uniform Regulations and Care of Clothing, Military Sanitation, Company Administration, as well as Physical Training and Drills. You will be up early, you will march to your classes, and you will turn in late. We will be packing as much training into our short time here as possible. Friday evenings are for GI parties." She paused as the women looked around at one another, excited at the possibility of a party every Friday night.

"I assume you are not yet familiar with a GI party, but you will soon find out. You will do your washings on Saturdays, and Sundays will be for church services in the morning and ironing uniforms in the afternoon.

"I am your superior officer for the duration of your time here. Any issues should be reported directly to me. Though I do not anticipate any problems." Her words sounded like a warning to heed, and Anna had no intention of finding herself in trouble with Lieutenant Campbell.

"As you have all earned yourselves the rank of Second Lieutenant, it would be wise to remember that you are considered an officer in the Army now. That means you are not to fraternize with enlisted soldiers, and you are to conduct yourselves in such a way as to uphold the values and morals of not only the Army but also, a woman."

~

After their first meeting with Lieutenant Campbell, the days passed quickly, and the women marched around Fort Meade as best they could, though not exactly in the formation of the soldiers they passed around the base. They passed Lieutenant Campbell, who gave them a curt nod, her lips pressed into a thin line as she watched them try to salute and maintain their forward march.

"How could someone so tiny be so intimidating?" Anna wondered once they were deep in the woods, hiking up the overgrown path she'd come to look forward to each afternoon.

Gretchen laughed. "I wouldn't want to cross her."

Eleanor snorted. "I guess you'd better put blinders on then. You wouldn't want to get caught fraternizing."

Gretchen gasped in mock surprise and gave her a shove.

"Maybe we should practice out here in the woods where we don't have to die of embarrassment."

Gretchen was joking, but Anna thought the idea wasn't half bad. They still hadn't mastered the art of marching.

They stopped as they approached mile marker three, letting them know they were more than halfway through their afternoon hike. Now that they had walked this path a dozen times, Anna was sure she didn't need the mile markers to remind her where they were anymore. It was one of the things that had surprised her the most since being at Fort Meade. She had discovered hidden strengths she never would have uncovered if she hadn't taken the leap and landed here. She tried to remind herself of that fact as often as she could, especially on the tough days. Sometimes, the girls would roll their eyes at her, telling her she sounded like a postcard or a motivational brochure, but most days, she really believed what she told herself. And she was proud of what she had accomplished so far.

She didn't really need the breaks that they took at each mile marker the way they had when they first started training, but she didn't mind taking a moment to turn her face toward the sky. These days were grueling, and she'd give anything for a softer bed or a silkier pillow at night, but she was settling into the barracks life quite well.

Except the marching. She laughed out loud, thinking how foolish they looked when it came time to practice those drills. For women who could easily make their way across a dance floor, they were sorely frustrated when they couldn't hack it on their marches.

Eleanor started walking ahead.

"Oh, no. Nope. We've been tortured enough. I'll continue to enjoy my hike in peace, no marching involved; thank you very much."

Anna snorted and jogged to catch up.

"You know, we haven't been forced to practice as much this past week, now that I think about it."

"Maybe they've finally decided to take some pity on us and realize we're hopeless in that department," Gretchen replied. She and Louise were following behind, with several other nurses making their way even further down the hill.

Eleanor turned back.

"Doubtful. There's probably something worse coming for us before we get outta here."

Anna just shook her head. Eleanor liked to think she was a realist, telling it like it was, but Anna thought she was a bit more of a pessimist. Gretchen had been trying to persuade her to loosen up, though Anna didn't think she'd ever let loose. The pursuit of finding the optimist in 'Elle' had thus far been for naught. Eleanor wouldn't budge.

As they passed mile marker five, the barracks came back into view with rows and rows of bunkhouses and office buildings. The rest of the women began to split up, each going in the direction of their units. Getting to their unit meant passing by a fenced-off area filled with tents set up for the German and Italian prisoners of war that had been shipped in. Anna tried not to look in their direction. She was afraid to make eye contact with the enemy - she preferred not to put a face to the men who took part in killing their boys. A shiver went up her spine despite the heat of the afternoon sun that had her drenched in sweat.

She picked up her pace, focusing instead on shedding her heavy boots and uniform. On the days they were required to hike, they had coerced the captain into letting them shower in the evening rather than the morning, the one luxury they had been granted here.

Getting closer to their building, the three women broke into a mad dash to be the first inside. They raced to grab their change of uniform and towel to be the first one down the lane to the end building where the showers were housed. Anna, who was not very competitive, let Eleanor and Gretchen duke it out. She and Louise stayed behind to grab a drink of water or, in Louise's case, write a quick line home. Some days they still had time to shower before dinner, but she didn't mind if she showed up to the mess hall looking sweaty and disheveled, anyway. She had no one to impress but herself.

Nearing the bathhouse, they heard Gretchen's squeals.

"Eleanor! Don't you dare take your sweet time in there!" She gave up the fight and stomped out to where Anna and Louise stood, waiting their turn for an empty stall.

"You know, I don't think she even cares about freshening up before dinner. She just does it to get my goat." She blew out a breath, sending a stray ringlet of hair into her eyes.

Anna laughed at the pout on Gretchen's face, "You're probably right."

"Well, I'll show her." Gretchen pulled a pin from her hair and turned on her heel, stomping back into the bathhouse.

"What are you doing, Gretchen?" Louise was the most timid of the bunch and had worry written all over her face.

Gretchen turned around and put a finger to her lips. Inside were several shower stalls, all with towels draped over their doors, showing they were occupied. Most of the women clicked the locks to ensure their privacy, but they were easy to unlock with the use of a skinny hairpin. Gretchen stuck her pin into the lock and popped it open. Anna and Louise watched from the main door, hands over their mouths, eyes wide - Anna's with amusement, Louise's with horror - as Gretchen snuck into the stall. Each shower stall had a small area to place clothes and toiletries with a curtain beyond that to close off the shower and keep the water within the little cubicle. With the shower curtain closed, Eleanor wouldn't have seen Gretchen as she reached in, grabbed her bundle of clothes, and ran back out. She gave Anna and Louise a thumbs-up as she flew past them and ran back outside.

The two girls looked at each other, then turned and dashed out after her. They didn't have to run far to find Gretchen leaning against the side of the building, hands on her knees. When she saw her friends, she raised up Eleanor's clothing in triumph, laughing between gasps of air.

"Oh no. No, no, no." Louise was horrified.

"Gretchen, what have you done?" Anna asked. She knew exactly what her friend had done but stared in disbelief.

"Isn't…it…obvious?" Gretchen puffed out.

"Well, yes, but I think I'm just in shock that you actually did it!"

Gretchen began waving Eleanor's clothes around like a victory flag. Louise groaned.

"At least she left the towel."

Gretchen threw her head back and laughed her way down the road to their bunkhouse.

"You're not seriously taking them all the way back?" Anna called after her.

"Oh yes, I am!" Gretchen yelled back.

The door to the bathhouse burst open behind them. An angry Eleanor came charging down the steps clad in only a towel, hair bonnet, and her shower slides. She clutched at her towel with one hand and her bonnet with the other as she ran after Gretchen, shouting a number of threats along the way.

"You have got to be kidding me! You have got some nerve! There will be payback!"

Gretchen, within a few feet of their bunkhouse and trying desperately to escape Eleanor's wrath, tripped over her own feet, tumbled head-first onto the dirt path, and landed seated in the middle of the road. Anna and Louise had just caught up to her, Eleanor not far behind, and they all just stared at one another. Anna was trying hard and failing to contain her laughter, fully aware of Eleanor's anger. But the more she looked at the two of them, the more the ridiculousness of their situation got the better of her. Eleanor in her towel, Gretchen covered in dirt sitting in the road like a child. She looked at Louise, and they erupted into peals of delirious laughter, eventually sitting themselves in the dirt next to Gretchen. Eleanor stood over them, hands on hips, lips pursed to keep from laughing. She grabbed her clothes out of Gretchen's grip, who was too spent to fight, and stormed into the bunkhouse, leaving them sitting in the dust.

Friday morning came faster than they would have liked, the day hot and muggy when they woke. The girls were not so lucky as they had hoped in escaping marching drills for the remainder of their time at Camp Meade. Instead of heading to their usual classes, the Captain gathered all ninety-six nurses and marched them down to the field where they practiced drills and calisthenics.

"They cannot be serious. Calisthenics at this hour of the day. It's barely 7 a.m." Gretchen touched her hair, which she had taken extra time to curl the night before. She had barely pulled off her silk bonnet before the Captain had arrived. "So much for my perfect coif," she pouted.

"They can do what they darn well please, haven't you learned that yet?" Even Eleanor, who seemed always ready for anything thrown at her, had been caught off guard this morning.

Gretchen rolled her eyes. "Aren't you just a peach this morning?"

The drill sergeant stood before them, apparently enjoying their foul moods and banter, grinning despite the moody group of women.

"Ladies, today is the day you will master marching in formation." He waited for the collective groans to stop before he continued. "Tomorrow will be a final inspection. This may seem trivial to you." He hesitated, the smile gone from his face, replaced with a gravity that came when faced with the reality of why they were here. "And it likely will be, compared to what you'll be heading into. But this is the Army, and this is basic training. You will master these skills before you may move on."

Anna's stomach sank. They hadn't taken this part of training seriously. He was right about that. Her cheeks flushed with embarrassment. Not so much because of her inability to march properly, but for thinking somehow they'd be allowed an exception. How silly she had been to think that just because they were nurses, they'd be given a pardon for two left feet. She straightened her spine, prepared to do everything she could to get it right today. She would not be left behind for the stupidest reason she could think of. She'd just die if she had to go home and tell her mother she couldn't cut it because she failed 'Marching 101.' She started sweating just thinking of the possibility.

"All right knees, you can stop that shaking now and hold me up," she whispered under her breath.

By the time the bell rang out for the evening chow line, the girls were sweaty and exhausted, and their moods were largely unchanged from the morning. The sun setting below the mountains had left them with a chill after sweating all day in the heat, and when Anna had thought she'd had quite enough, the wind began to pick up. Her eyes watered and her nose began to run. She wished she could reach into her trousers for her handkerchief to blow her nose, but she didn't dare break formation. She had made a promise to herself this morning, and even if that meant letting her nose run down her face, even if her thighs burned from the unrelenting up and down, up and down, she'd finish what she started. She wondered if they'd be forced to miss dinner at the rate they were going. Her stomach growled in protest as the drill sergeant walked down the row of nurses, and she squeezed her eyes shut, hoping he hadn't heard. She didn't want to present with any sign of weakness, even if it was perfectly normal to be hungry after today's torture.

"One last practice," the drill sergeant called out. "March to chow." He looked at Anna and winked. Relieved, the women performed a near-perfect march to dinner after hours of following orders. "Left, left, left, right, left." Anna thought she'd be hearing those commands in her sleep.

They ate in silence, too hungry to converse, filed out of the mess building, and marched to their row of bunkhouses, where they fell out of order and flopped onto their beds. They were ready to turn in for the night after their day of drills, even with their hair still stuck to their foreheads from the sweat that had dried. Instead of crawling into bed, they spent the evening scrubbing their quarters, aching limbs be darned, as they prepared for inspections the next morning. They split up the tasks, scrubbing the floors with turpentine, and then scrubbing with soap and water on hands and knees. They took turns relieving one another so they could stretch their backs. They now had aching hands to add to the list of maladies they'd endured today. Just before midnight, they sat on their trunks, shining their shoes and stifling yawns.

"And here I thought a Friday night GI party meant dancing and music, not cleaning from top to bottom." Anna pulled herself up and began to change out of her sweaty uniform. She nudged Gretchen, who looked like she'd fall asleep sitting upright on her trunk.

"I'll never be fooled into another GI party, that's for sure," Gretchen said as she climbed under the covers.

They were awake again before dawn to make their beds with the perfect six-inch fold and six-inch gap between pillow and sheet. Too nervous to eat, they stayed in their bunk, waiting for the Colonel to come. They didn't dare to sit down for fear of wrinkling their uniforms or the freshly made beds. The normally chatty group was quiet, peeking through the window every few minutes until they saw a group of officers making their way down the units in their row. Standing at attention when the Colonel entered, Anna hadn't realized she was holding her breath until the door closed, and they were alone again. Gretchen blew out a sigh and shook out her arms. "Sheesh, that was terrifying."

"What happens now?" Anna wondered.

"Now, we go see what's left of breakfast," Eleanor answered.

～

Chapter 8

*P*aul had thought about his father's words all the way to Camp Blanding. The train ride gave him plenty of time to reflect as he felt the small medallions attached to the brown fabric between his fingers. His father had worn a scapular since he could remember. He'd never thought much of it, but his father had always sworn it offered him a protection he couldn't explain. He never liked being without it. Paul slipped it over his head and tucked it underneath his shirt, just as he had seen his father do so many times, one brown rectangle in the front and one in the back. He tried not to feel guilty that his father was now without it.

The train began to slow, and he looked out the window. He had hoped to rest on the ride, knowing full well that rest would soon be hard to come by, but his thoughts and worries kept him awake. Instead, he watched the passing scenery, feeling a bit like he was in a daze, still in disbelief about the direction his life was now going. If he made it through the training here, and who was he kidding, everyone would be making it through whether they liked it or not, he'd be off to Europe. He wondered how hard the physical exertion would be for him. He was used to physical labor - he grew up on a farm, after all - but he wasn't sure what the Army's idea of 'rigorous' training was. Sure, he had survived boot camp once before, but that wasn't in preparation for going overseas to fight in the war. He had a feeling this go around wouldn't be like the basic training he was used to.

He gathered his pack and stood, ready to stretch his legs as the train came to a stop. He looked out the train window as he waited his turn to amble down the narrow aisle. The place was buzzing with GIs. He looked around, hoping to see someone he knew, knowing it wasn't likely. The friends he had made in the ASTP had come from all around the country, and he doubted if they'd all be grouped together again. He doubted if he'd ever see many of them again.

He pushed his way through the crowded platform and out to the front of the station, where several convoy trucks were idling. A soldier standing beside the last one in the line waved him over. "We got room for one or two more, son; hop on in the back. I'll throw your bags up to ya."

Paul did as he was told and climbed into the back of the waiting truck. Several other soldiers were already crammed in, their bags resting between their feet or piled on their laps. Paul found a sliver of a spot in one corner and tried to make himself small enough to fit. Comfort would soon be a thing of the past, so he tried not to worry too much about the men on either side of him, grimacing as he tossed his pack beneath his feet. It had been hot down on the ground, but up here, in the confines of this truck with twenty other GIs packed in, the heat was nearly unbearable. Paul felt sweat rolling down his back already and wondered when they'd start moving. *Hurry up and wait*, he thought to himself. *Ain't that the Army slogan?* They continued to wait with the sun beating down on them, Florida's afternoon heat relentless. They'd be cooked sardines before long. The last GI finally climbed aboard the back of the truck, his red hair unmistakable. Relieved to see his buddy, Paul tried to jump up, but he'd been suctioned to the bench, held in by the soldiers on either side of him. Instead of standing, he called out.

"Harry, pal!" His friend turned to him, a grin on his face.

"Hey, thanks for waiting," he joked.

The man next to Paul chimed in. "You two need us to scoot over so you can give each other a big smooch, too?" He laughed at his own joke. Paul chuckled and nodded at Harry, who took his seat in the small space left for him in the opposite corner.

The ride to the base, though fairly short, offered no relief from the heat, as any breeze picked up along the way was accompanied by the dust from the dry dirt road. Paul kept his head down most of the way, tucking his nose into his shirt to keep from inhaling the filthy dirt and exhaust fumes. By the time they got to their barracks, the men were not only slick with sweat but tinged with a gray hue from head to toe.

They marched toward what they'd soon find out was the quad, an area in the middle of the base, surrounded by small hut-like buildings that served as their barracks. They were greeted by

a portly General with a strong southern accent and a no-non-
sense attitude. Paul didn't think he'd ever forget the first words
he heard. Waiting for all the men to fall into line and stand at
attention, he strode up and down the front row, hands clasped
behind his back.

"We are not here to die for our country. Kill the enemy and
let him die for his. You are here as a trainee because your country is engaged in a life-and-death struggle with one of the most
powerful and ruthless combinations of powers the world has ever
known. Our enemies are tough, cruel, and highly trained. Their
defeat is essential before this world can become a decent place in
which to live. The defeat of the enemy can not be accomplished
by amateurs or half-trained men. During the seventeen weeks of
intensive training, you will find the work hard, the hours long,
the going tough in spots, as it should be. If, however, you concen-
trate your energy and determination on your work, you will become an alert, confident, skilled soldier, prepared to function as a
member of a combat division. In the serious business of training,
strive with all your might to master every detail of the instruction each day. If you are shooting at a bullseye and you're outside
the 10-ring, remember that shot only whistled by your enemy's
ears and alerted him; you haven't hit him yet. If you were careless
about tossing a grenade into a simulated window, consider that
you left the enemy sniper in the room free to kill your buddy on
the other side of the street. Your officers and non-commissioned
officers are vitally interested in your progress and will assist you
in a complete understanding of each phase of instruction. Learn
your lessons well during your training period and avoid having
your mistakes marked by a cross on the battlefield."

The General strode away, flanked by an officer at each side, leaving the men in stunned silence. Paul knew the reality of war, or at least he thought he knew. But hearing it put so plainly had shocked him to his core. He could picture himself and any number of his fellow GIs, his comrades, in any of those situations. A pit formed in his stomach at the thought that any careless move on his part could mean life or death for a friend.

Paul lay in bed, a veil of darkness covering him. It was early, earlier than he'd have liked to be awake. Not wanting to wake his bunkmates, he lay on his back, taking in the stillness. He felt for the scapular under his shirt. It wasn't often that he was inspired to talk to God - not that he didn't believe - he just went about his days not questioning things, just...believing. He wondered now if that would be enough. Should he have worked on his faith more before now? He supposed his father had been right - all of the unknowns were raising questions he hadn't had to think about before. *Will I survive? Will I kill another man? Will I see my friends and comrades be killed?* He knew the likely answer to two of those questions. He continued to wonder, letting the questions float through his mind in rhythm with his breath. *Will my faith be enough to carry me?*

When his thoughts began to feel too heavy a burden to bear, he got up to walk off his worries in the crisp morning air. He quietly tucked the sheets of his cot, pulled on his uniform pants, grabbed his boots, and overshirt. He tiptoed out of the barracks into the dim light of the moon. The sun hadn't yet risen, but he could see the fiery red beginning to make its appearance in the distance. With nowhere to go, he stood outside, letting the cool air wash over him. He forced himself to focus only on today.

Worrying about the future won't get you very far, he thought. He tried to rein in his nervous energy, breathing deeply and wondering instead about what his nephew might have in store for his sister today. He smiled to himself and began to walk up and down the lane in front of his barracks. He thought about his sister's letter, how proud she sounded when she told him Danny was finally toddling along. He'd be running before she knew it, and he chuckled when he pictured Evie chasing after him.

When he realized he was counting his steps, he stopped walking and stood in front of his hut, hearing the sounds of the men inside beginning to wake. Harry appeared behind him, clapping Paul on the shoulder.

"Couldn't sleep?"

"Nah, got tired of my feet hanging off the end of the cot," Paul joked, though there was truth to his statement - his feet did hang uncomfortably off the end, causing his toes to end up with pins and needles. He'd tried curling up on his side, but after their physically demanding schedule during the day, he woke with aching hips and knees when he wasn't outstretched.

Harry chuckled. "I hear ya." They stood amicably, watching the sun rise behind the buildings on base. Paul looked over at his friend. He still found himself surprised at the change he had witnessed in Harry since they'd left the ASTP. The calisthenics had really paid off for his friend, at least when it came to his physical fitness. Harry had gained muscle and strength, and he no longer looked too lanky for his tall frame.

"What are you staring at?"

Paul laughed. "Just admiring how much my little boy has grown up in such a short time," he teased.

Harry snorted and grabbed Paul in a headlock. Paul, surprised by his friend's quick maneuver, hardly had a chance to fight back but managed to escape Harry's grasp.

He rubbed the back of his neck, eyeing Harry, a smirk on his face.

Harry shook his head. "You think you're real funny, Paulie Boy."

Paul looked around, thankful no one else had heard his nickname. It was bad enough that Harry had seen his father's letter, now he knew his friend had seen the name his father used for him.

"Aw, come on, I'm kidding. But you really have bulked up, you know. I'd say you're looking ready to roll into battle."

Harry rolled his eyes. "Doesn't matter how big I get. I'd rather not. It won't save me from a bullet or a bomb or whatever else these damn Nazis have in store for us."

Paul mulled this over. "Maybe not, my friend. But it might mean you're better able to handle the cards we're dealt, anyway. You've always joked about my farm strength. Well, now, you're right there with me." He gave his friend a shove, hoping to lighten the mood. Lately, he found it too tiring to get down into the doldrums too often. Not that he'd be turning into a class clown any time soon, but he was starting to appreciate the ability to not take things too seriously. The whole reason he'd woken early and come outside was because he was thinking too much. He had quickly learned that he needed to conserve all of his energy, mental and physical, for whatever the day and the drill sergeant had in store for them.

The rest of their unit filed out of their bunk, and they fell into formation for the march down to breakfast. He eyed Lake

Kingsley as they passed, wondering if they'd get a chance to put a line out today. They were lucky to be allowed to use the lake, but more often than not, they were too exhausted to do much with the little free time they had. Some of the guys would muster up the energy to walk into town, check out the local businesses and have some fun. Paul never had much interest in leaving the base, so he'd walk down to the Post Exchange, grab a beer, and sit by the lake. He was waiting for the day he saw a big gator come walking up out of the lake. He didn't think it'd ever happen, but still, it would be a fun story to tell.

"Morning, Men," General Herman said as he approached them after they had eaten. "Hope you got a good night's sleep. Today's a big day." He smiled an ominous smile, one that said they were not going to like what they were about to do.

"Today is the day for your Tank Test. I think you're all ready." His eyes roved up and down the rows of soldiers in perfect formation. "You've worked hard. This is the final test in proving your courage and determination along with your trust in one another."

"Sir, what is a Tank Test, sir?"

Paul was surprised to hear Jack ask the question they were all wondering the answer to.

General Herman addressed Jack directly, inches from his face.

"You will lie face up in a ditch while a Sherman Tank drives over you. The true test of whether or not you are fit to be part of the Black Panther Division."

～

Chapter 9

ANNA
AUGUST 1944
FORT GEORGE G. MEADE,
MARYLAND

"*L*adies," Lieutenant Campbell beamed. "I wanted to be the first to congratulate you on your hard work. It's been a pleasure to work alongside each and every one of you." She paused, looking up and down the rows of women seated before her.

"This training hasn't been easy... and I'm afraid to say, it's not over just yet."

Several women groaned, and Lieutenant Campbell chuckled. It was an early Saturday morning, and the air was warm inside the classroom they were gathered in. The nearly one hundred nurses filled the desks that lined the large room.

Its once bright white walls were now a dingy gray that matched the dusty floors. No special arrangements had been made for the women before they arrived several months ago, and while they could often be heard wishing for a silk pillowcase or a hot bath, they actually did prefer it this way. They had learned and trained alongside the men, proving themselves worthy of their positions. They didn't need special treatment simply because they were women, nor did they need the men thinking they couldn't handle some of the same rough conditions. While they may not have been able to keep up with the men in their exercises or drills, they didn't need a flowery powder room or down-filled pillows to lay their heads. The exhaustion that settled in at the end of a physically demanding day did not discriminate against scratchy sheets and hard cots.

"I have no doubt each of you will be of great service to our soldiers when we land on the continent in a few short weeks," Lieutenant Campbell said.

The women looked around at each other, sharing knowing smiles and tired yawns. The matching black smudges beneath their eyes outwardly reflected the last few months of rigorous training. Anna couldn't believe the amount of physical exercise she had endured, nor could she believe it had been almost six months since she'd first met Lieutenant Campbell and the ladies sitting around her now. She felt like she might collapse if she had to run another mile. She could do without ever having to crawl through the mud again, though, she knew she would if she was told to. She had pushed herself even when she didn't know if she could finish. And all the times she had wanted to quit, her fellow nurses and friends had been there cheering her on - or in Eleanor's case, telling her to 'get her ass moving.' Her friend's vulgarities had shocked her at first, but she'd gotten used to, even enjoyed, not knowing what might come out of her mouth next. She glanced at Eleanor and smiled. Her friend stuck out her tongue in return. Anna pursed her lips, trying not to laugh. She was definitely the firecracker of the bunch. Anna guessed what everyone said was true - in this situation, you make fast friends. You had to if you were going to survive.

"Now, many of you have been asking when exactly we will be leaving. Even more of you have been wondering if you'll have time to go home before we depart." Anna's eyes snapped up to Lieutenant Campbell. She had most definitely not been one of the ladies wondering about going home. In fact, she had hoped there wouldn't be time at all to do so. The guilt she felt over not seeing her grandfather and her father, too, warred with her feelings over facing her mother. She tried to tell herself she'd done her best to keep in touch with her family - her grandfather had written several times, and her father, though not a man of many words, had also written once or twice. She hadn't heard from her mother. Not that she'd made any effort to write to her, either, but she had thought that maybe her mother would have softened after this time apart. At least for Anna, this canyon between her and her mother had started to seem silly. Sure, they had their differences, and yes, her mother had been cruel with her words, but were they really that different? Anna had to wonder. They were each doing what they felt was right. What was so wrong about that? She sighed, knowing her mother would not see it the same way. To her, the only right way was her way.

"I'm happy to say you will have next weekend to say goodbye to family and friends, should you choose to use that time to go home. For many of you whose hometowns are much too far, you will stay here until we leave for Boston."

Anna made a snap decision to stay the weekend rather than chance a quick trip home. But she was happy for several of the nurses whose family homes were close enough to allow for a visit before they moved on to Boston. They knew that Boston meant the harbor, and the harbor meant leaving for England. Anna closed her eyes against the nerves starting in her stomach. *One day at a time,* she reminded herself.

"Now, back to your last assignment. I will be with you every step of the way, so believe me, I'm not thrilled about this any more than you are. But it is necessary for our preparedness in combat."

❦

"Oh, for heaven's sake!" Anna wasn't one to complain. She could count on one hand the times she had outwardly shown dismay at any of their training thus far. She knew she'd essentially signed her life away to the Army for the duration of the war, even when she wanted to quit. But every time she thought things were starting to get easier - or perhaps that her skill and abilities were improving - the goal post moved, and they were forced to do something even more unthinkable.

"Absurd, isn't it?" Gretchen mumbled through her gas mask. They were preparing for their ten-mile hike - complete with full gear and gas masks.

"I know we need to know how to use all this stuff," Louise said, adjusting her steel helmet, "but really, ten miles with all this on?" She patted the pistol belt and tried to adjust it to prevent it from sliding down her waist.

First Lieutenant Campbell didn't look thrilled either, but as she had promised, she was right there with them. As they continued to dress, she made her rounds, giving reassurances to her girls.

"I will be with you every step of the way, ladies. We'll get through it just fine, and we'll come out stronger on the other side."

Anna knew that she was trying to make them feel better about what they were about to march into, but her placations did little to calm her nerves.

They approached the location for the starting point of their hike, by now an organized unit keeping pace with one another. Anna was happy to say she had at least found her rhythm and had gotten used to marching everywhere. There was one weight off her shoulders. *At least I know I won't get kicked out for having two left feet,* she thought. Now, she had a new worry to occupy her mind. *How will I last in the hot sun for ten whole miles weighed down with all this gear?* The women had borrowed fatigues from several soldiers on base as theirs had not yet arrived. She wondered if they'd even need them once they were transferred overseas. They were to be fitted for new nurse uniforms before they left, but they weren't much better. The white skirts were highly impractical, and Anna couldn't imagine being on the front lines with them. They had started their training in those uniforms and quickly realized they were impossible during drills and pretty much every other activity on base. The nurses had taken a liking to being able to wear trousers, and she hoped they'd be able to continue on wearing them. She cringed at the thought of wearing pantyhose in this heat.

The women in the unit fell into formation, waiting for their next orders. The morning sun warmed her face, and while it felt good to tip her chin up to the sky, Anna knew she'd be cursing the heat before the day was through.

The General strode front and center. The women stood at attention, a motley crew of nurses dressed in uniforms several sizes too big, in some cases. Anna could have sworn she'd heard the General chuckle on his way over, but there was no evidence of amusement on his face. That man showed no emotion. She wasn't sure he was even capable of feeling anything. *I hope that's not what the Army does to me,* she thought, then laughed. *I am far too emotional to ever appear that hardened.*

"Ladies, as you proceed in this march - and yes, it is a ten-mile *march* - you will be faced with the Air Corps running practice drills above you."

Anna's gaze drifted skyward. *He can't be serious.*

"As they practice their bombing skills, you have this opportunity to practice ducking and running for cover."

Anna nearly laughed at the General's choice of words. *We have this opportunity? Why, thank you for allowing me the chance to avoid getting hit with a bomb,"* she thought. She closed her eyes before the superior officer could see them roll.

"This practice will be made more difficult with the gas mask and equipment and the…well, the ill-fitting clothing may prove to be an added hindrance." He grimaced, shaking his head. Private Matthews, the young GI that had escorted them on their first day, approached his side.

"Private Matthews is here to demonstrate how to prevent giving yourself a concussion with your gas mask when you run for cover."

Matthews fitted his gas mask over his face and ran down the

rows of nurses. The general gave instructions as he ran. "When avoiding a bomb, you'll need to run for cover. To avoid concussion or injury to your neck, you must throw back your gas mask, fall to the ground, elbows out so they catch your fall, and keep your head from hitting the ground." He stopped and looked on as Private Matthews showed the women how to fall on their elbows. It looked quite painful to Anna, and she cringed, watching the impact on his arms when he fell to the ground. If ever there were a time when she'd long for a hot bath, it would be after today.

The General walked up and down the rows of nurses, checking their field packs and equipment. Anna looked down, hoping she'd remembered to put everything on correctly. She affixed her gas mask over her face, wincing when she felt how little fresh air she had. *And I'm not even out of breath yet*, she thought. She replaced her steel helmet on her head and waited for the final order to begin their march.

At the end of the field they'd be marching through, she could see a tower high above the woodline. Before she could wonder what it was for, the sound of gunfire not far off rang out around them, echoing through the empty field.

The General chuckled, "Sounds like they're eager to get started."

Anna groaned quietly, the sound muffled behind her gas mask.

"Fall in," the General ordered, "Forward march."

They marched to the bottom of the hill, stopping when they came to a muddy trench stretching the length of the field, as far across as Anna could see.

Gretchen let out a string of curse words beside her, and Anna bit her lip. She didn't want to wade through the mud, either.

An explosion to their left made Anna jump, and she lifted her face to the sky, holding her gas mask in place. The air corps pilots were flying above, making giant circles, then disappearing behind the trees. The drone of the engine warned her that they'd be coming back soon.

"Forward march!"

The women hesitated in front of the ditch until Lieutenant Campbell took the lead, plunging waist-deep into the mud pit. The rest of the nurses followed suit, sinking into the muck one after the other. Anna waded through the thick mud, trying to settle the panic she felt climbing up her throat. She could feel the dampness seeping through her pants, the mud so thick she could hardly take a step forward.

Trying not to hold onto her friends, she took in slow, steady breaths while she got her bearings. It didn't take long for her to figure out that her panicked, erratic breathing only made things worse inside the mask. A few of the women were pulling at each other haphazardly, stumbling over one another and not making much progress. Anna kept to herself, glancing at the sky and hoping the planes would at least give them a chance to free themselves of the mud before raining down on them again.

"Slow and steady," she murmured to herself. She neared the edge of the trench and clawed at the earth with her fingers until she was close enough to prop herself up on her elbows and climb free of the mud. As soon as she stood, the drone of the engines above her became louder and louder. She followed Lieutenant

Campbell in a fast march across the field. Weighed down by her pants and boots filled with mud, she nearly cried when Lieutenant Campbell threw back her gas mask and hit the ground. Anna did the same, ignoring the pains that ripped through her elbows when she landed. They continued forward on their bellies, nearing closer to the tower she'd seen at a distance. Several soldiers looked down on them from above, shouting orders she couldn't comprehend. She continued to crawl forward, stopping only when their shouting became too frantic to ignore. She looked up at the tower, one soldier waving wildly at her. She looked to her right and realized she hadn't been crawling forward at all but rather too far to the right, very nearly into the mines that had been set up for practice drills. She'd been so focused on getting to the end - *the sooner this is over, the better*, she thought - she hadn't looked up long enough to see where she was going. She redirected, spotting Eleanor running to her left and clambered to her feet, matching strides with her friend.

"Just think, only eight more miles to go," Eleanor huffed, her voice muffled through her gas mask.

Another explosion rattled Anna, and she looked up seconds before the Air Corps circled over them again. She threw her gas mask up over her forehead and her body down to the ground.

"Why do we not have elbow pads?" She shouted over the rumble of the planes.

"What?" Eleanor shouted back.

"Pads! For our elbows!" Anna rubbed one achy elbow. She felt like giving up, lying in the grass and surrendering. Instead, she kept crawling, this time keeping her eyes on the soldiers watching them from the tower. It felt like hours by the time she finally reached the edge of the field, only to find another trench filled with mud on the other side. She blew out a frustrated breath, looking down at her pants and boots, already caked with a layer of dried mud. An arm reached up from the trench and grabbed at her ankle, pulling her forward. She lost her balance and fell into the mud head-first. Surfacing from the muck, she swiped at her face, looking around for the culprit. Gretchen squealed, trying to get away but stuck to the spot where she stood. Anna shook her head and pushed against her friend, using Gretchen to propel herself forward to the other side where she could climb out.

When the last woman rose up from the muddy trench, they stopped to catch their breath. They had been unaware that the Army band was waiting behind the trees, and they marched out now, coming to a stop before them, instruments ready to play.

"What on Earth?" Louise lifted her gas mask off her face to wipe the mud from the outside while the band began to play.

"Oh, you beautiful doll, you great big beautiful doll!"

"Oh, they think they're real funny." Gretchen rolled her eyes.

The band could hardly get the words out around their laughter, but they continued on, singing the words to the old ragtime song.

"Let me put my arms around you, I could never live without you.
Oh! You beautiful doll, you great big beautiful doll!
If you ever leave me how my heart would ache,
I want to hug you but I fear you'd break..."

Anna laughed. She had to admit they looked a bit like a comedy routine. The soldiers in the band were grinning from ear to ear. Even the General, who had been waiting for them, had a smile on his face.

Somehow, they made it over the rest of the hike, only slightly battered and bruised.

"Well, I know I was killed at least a dozen times out there today," Gretchen said, pulling out her sandwich.

"We're going to be hurting tomorrow," Anna said. She hoped these preparedness drills were the extreme and not the norm once they were in their assigned locations overseas.

"Tomorrow? I'm already there," Louise replied. She pulled off her boots and socks to reveal angry red blisters across her pinky toes.

The women were scattered around a small lake - the one perk of this grueling day. Some were already wading into the water, others sat on the rocky shore eating what rations they had packed. Eleanor was the first to finish her food and made a mad dash into the water, splashing the other girls sitting nearby as she went.

"Come on, girls! It's refreshing!" She laughed happily as she called out to them, flipping onto her back and floating even further out. Anna approached the water's edge and dipped her toes in, holding her pants up around her knees, dried mud cracking and falling off when she did.

"You're crazy, Eleanor. That water is freezing! I'm not walking back to base in a drenched uniform! I'm already soggy enough," she said, pulling her sweaty shirt from her back. It was bad enough having her clothes cling to her from sweat. She didn't need wet pants sticking to her all the way back. Eleanor just shrugged and went back to swimming as if she hadn't just marched ten miles.

Louise came to stand beside Anna. "How does she have the energy? I'm wiped."

Anna shook her head, shading her eyes against the sun with her hand. "I'm with you there."

After their walk through 'Death Valley,' as Gretchen had coined it, the women were given the weekend off. It would be their last weekend at Fort Meade before leaving for Boston. They completed their usual Friday night GI party - probably the least thorough cleaning yet with their sore muscles from the hike the day before.

Eleanor sneezed and blew her nose in her handkerchief as she came in from dumping the bucket of dirty water they'd used to scrub the floors.

"Elle, you don't sound so good," Gretchen said.

"I'm fine. It's just the dust stirred up from cleaning," she replied.

"Mhm. There's no way you'd have caught a chill after all that swimming yesterday..." Anna teased.

Eleanor shot her a look and sneezed once more.

Louise yawned. "Well, I don't know about you, but I'm ready to call it an early night," she said.

They turned in early, hoping to regain their energy by morning.

Changing out of their dirty uniforms, Gretchen paused. "Anyone else a bit concerned that First Lieutenant Campbell told us not to return these fatigues to the men we borrowed them from?"

Anna climbed into bed and pulled the scratchy covers up to her neck. The sun was just starting to set and they were all in bed before the Taps had even played, something that had never happened before.

She yawned. "I don't even want to think about what that means for us."

~⌒~

In the pitch black of the night, Anna was awakened by a rustling sound near the cupboard in the corner of the room. She rolled over, grabbed her flashlight from the bedside table, and sat up in bed. She flicked it on and saw Eleanor crouched over, digging through her things.

"Eleanor, what are you doing," she whispered.

Eleanor turned, and Anna gasped, clapping a hand over her mouth.

"Just getting some Vicks. I'm terribly congested," her friend said through a stuffy nose that made her sound like she was underwater. She looked like she was still half asleep.

"Eleanor…I don't think you found the Vicks," Anna began. She opened the nightstand drawer and pulled out a compact, handing it to Eleanor. She shined the light so that her friend could see herself in the tiny mirror. Eleanor shrieked. "What in the world is all over my face?"

"I think you may have used the ink bottle," Anna whispered as she sat cross-legged on her cot, horrified at the black smudge all over Eleanor's face.

Gretchen started to stir, and Eleanor attempted to hide herself, scrubbing at the ink stains with the inside of her shirt.

"No, no, no, she cannot see this. She'll never let me live it down," Eleanor hissed, rubbing furiously.

"Can't let me see what?" Gretchen sat up, groggy with sleep.

Anna wasn't fast enough to turn off her flashlight, still illuminating Eleanor's face, now splotched with ink and turning red from her futile attempt to remove it. Gretchen coughed.

"What in God's creation happened to you?"

Eleanor groaned and climbed back under the covers, too exhausted and too sick to care how her face looked anymore. Anna explained about the Vicks, and Gretchen laughed even harder.

"Oh my, this is too good. Inky Elle!" Gretchen howled as Anna tried to shush her. "Don't wake Louise, too," she warned. They settled back into their beds. Anna listened as Gretchen tried and failed to contain her laughter, blowing out air in little puffs. She smiled in the dark, her lips pursed to keep from laughing along with Gretchen. She really did feel bad for her friend, who was already feeling so miserable, but she had to admit it was quite comical. She shook her head, wondering how they seemed to keep finding themselves in these outrageous situations. She started to drift off again, still feeling more tired than she'd ever felt in her life, and heard Gretchen whisper 'Inky Elle' once more. She knew things would be interesting in the light of the morning.

Anna closed her eyes and smiled in the dark. She'd never been this happy. The work was hard - sometimes so hard she thought she'd give up - but she marveled at how even the hardest parts of training had so far been bearable because of the women she was sharing it with. She'd made the right choice, even if her muscles ached in protest.

"My last bit of information for you is this - I have been moved from my position."

Their weekend furlough had come to an end, and they were all back at Fort Meade, awaiting their orders to move out, packed and ready to go at a moment's notice. Reconvened in the classroom once more, they listened to their First Lieutenant's next directions.

Several of the girls were audibly upset. They had built a relationship with Lieutenant Campbell, and in the midst of so much uncertainty, losing your superior officer to a new assignment was devastating. She raised her hands, calling for them to quiet.

"If you'd let me finish, ladies. I did not mean to alarm you. I will be traveling with you to England, however, not as your First Lieutenant." She paused and smiled. "I am now your Captain."

The girls cheered, offering their congratulations as she called for them to settle down. She called out several names, Anna and Gretchen among them. "Please stay so that I may have a word with each of you. The rest of you may go. We'll be heading to the train station shortly."

As the rest of their comrades filed out of the classroom, Anna looked over at Gretchen. "What do you think it could be?" Gretchen mouthed. Anna just shrugged. She was beginning to get used to the unknowns that came with this life. She no longer had expectations - on that, her grandfather had been right.

When the rest of the nurses had gone, Captain Campbell approached the twenty or so girls still seated before her.

"As you now know, I have been promoted to Captain. And it is with great honor that I am able to notify you all of your promotions as well. In addition to your time in nursing school and in service, you all have done an exemplary job during your duty here thus far. I am pleased to announce to you all that you now hold the rank of First Lieutenant." She smiled brightly, examining the faces of each of the nurses, a mother bird checking in on her young, ensuring they were just as pleased with this news as she was to give it to them. Anna smiled from ear to ear. She couldn't wait to write home. If this didn't convince her mother that she was meant to be here, she didn't know what on Earth would. She frowned when she caught Gretchen's eye and realized her friend didn't look as happy about her promotion. "What's wrong?" She whispered.

"Eleanor is going to have a fit," Gretchen said. Her eyes were wide with worry, and she chewed on her bottom lip. Anna's elation ebbed as she thought about her friends, back in their bunkhouse by now, waiting to board a train to Boston. Gretchen was right. But instead of agreeing with her, she tried to give Eleanor some credit.

"She's a good friend underneath her tough attitude. She'll be happy for us." But even as she spoke the words, Anna wasn't convinced, either.

It was an awkward wait after they had been dismissed from Captain Campbell and had walked back to their room. Gretchen had been right. Though Eleanor tried to hide it, she was visibly upset at their promotion. Anna could understand her frustration. She had worked just as hard as they had, and she had no answer for her friend as to why she was passed over this time. Avoiding the growing tension in the room, Anna focused her attention on writing a letter that was long overdue.

Dear Mother,

I hesitate to be the first to break this unspoken silence that has permeated our relationship. And while you have no doubt been taking great pleasure in your valuable contribution at home, I have also been enjoying my way of contributing in the war effort. And so, before I leave the United States, I felt it important to make my case one last time. Truthfully, I don't know why, as I will likely be met with your continued silence, but I feel I must get you to see that I do not begrudge you of your choices. I only wish that you would not begrudge me of mine.

You see, my dear mother, I have come to realize what I suppose I have always known but perhaps have not been able to properly convey to you. I admit our stubborn and Irish-tempered ways have often stood in the way of our hearing one another. I do hope you will be able to listen now.

While I DO respect and admire (yes, Mother, I do admire you despite what you might think) your decisions to stay home and do the things you do, I cannot disguise myself simply to make you happy. I can see that you are truly happy and content in your garden and in your kitchen and in your wonderful efforts in town - in the life you and Father have built. I admire the joy and fulfillment your soul feels knowing the choices you've made fill you up. But should I pretend to love the same things you love...Mother, I would never get to feel the soul-stirring happiness you have found. Do you not want your daughter to pursue the same passion with which you've filled your life? Just because our joy comes from different things doesn't make them the wrong things.

All I ask is that you try to understand that what I'm doing and where I'm going has ignited a fire in me that I hadn't known existed.

I love you, Mother. Please understand that I cannot apologize for my decisions just because they are different from yours.

Please give my love to Dad, and I send a kiss for my dear Grandfather (though it may pain you to do so).

Anna

P. S. I've been promoted to First Lieutenant. I hope you'll be proud of me eventually. But even if you're not, it's okay, I'm plenty proud of myself.

Anna sealed and sent the letter before she could lose the nerve. *To be a fly on the wall when Mother receives it,* she thought. But as she handed off the envelope, she left with it any anticipation or yearning for a response. She had said what she needed to say, and her mother's reaction held no bearing on her moving forward. She saw it fitting that as she left her letter behind, she'd also packed up her few things and would soon be boarding a train for Boston, leaving yet another version of herself behind, too. She could hardly believe that she'd be sailing across the Atlantic, the life she'd once thought she was destined for left far behind her.

Chapter 10

Hey Ma,

Seems like I barely blink and we're off to another base. I guess soon I won't be able to tell you where I am. It hasn't come to that quite yet, and I'm sure you'll soon see on the postage that I'm moving again. Hard to believe we've finished our training in Florida - thankful for that! The heat, phew, was brutal - near 100 degrees every day. I thought the Texas heat had me ready, but I was wrong. I suppose I didn't often find myself hiking twenty-five miles with full gear on when I was home.

I write this as my dear pal Harry sleeps on the train next to me. Next stop is Arkansas - hopefully, we'll get a break from the heat, though it doesn't seem likely this summer. Anyway, I worry a bit about Harry. He misses his wife terribly. Say a prayer for him, if you would. He's a great friend, and I'm glad for his company here.

If you're wondering, training has been good – at least I feel more confident in my abilities so I suppose there's something to all this training nonsense anyway. Don't worry Ma, the General here said we'd be like a well-oiled machine by the time we were done, and I have to say I think he's right. I'm sure we'll be ready as ever by the time we head over.

Give little Danny a kiss from his dear old Uncle Paul.

Harry snored in the seat beside him, his pack tucked behind his head as a pillow. Paul was too restless, as usual, to find sleep. Camp Blanding had nearly killed them all, though he'd never tell his mother that. It was true – he did feel more confident in himself and his unit. Weeks of drills and calisthenics and simulated battles had honed their skills and molded them into the beginnings of a refined unit. He was sure that the next leg of their training would prove even more beneficial to them all, even if it was near torture. At least if they continued with the twenty-five mile hikes, it wouldn't be in the Florida sun. He blew out a breath thinking about that day. He had slowed his pace, keeping alongside Harry, and had nearly fainted, his face redder than he'd ever felt it. Harry looked as though he'd have a permanent sunburn - it was no wonder he was now in a deep sleep. Harry may have gained physical strength, but he was still letting his fear take the wheel. It made Paul nervous for his friend.

He looked over and said a silent prayer, just as he'd asked his mother to do. *Dear God, take care of Harry. Help him find strength in you, Lord. Help him to feel your guiding presence and make it back home to Edith. Please, Lord.* He thought about adding a P.S. *Please do the same for me,* but this was for Harry. God must've been sick of hearing his desperate pleas by now.

"No man of mine will be killed in action due to a lack of training or knowledge," General Kramer screamed into the faces of the soldiers standing at attention before him. "Is that clear?" His face was red, his thick neck protruding with angry veins, looking like they might burst any minute.

A resounding "Sir, yes, sir," echoed back at him from the hundreds of men newly arrived at Camp Robinson.

"If you thought you'd arrive here and have a picnic lunch, I suggest you think again. This," he stomped his foot on the ground, "is where you will become worthy of the Black Panther patch." Paul nearly chuckled. It seemed all the Generals had taken the same notes. Each one regurgitated the same old lines. It was *their* way that would make these men worthy. It was *their* training that would really prepare them. *Nothing's going to prepare us*, Paul thought.

The General continued his tirade. "This is where you will become a combat team ready to take on the enemy. Picture those damn Krauts coming at you during drills. Get angry." He fisted his hands as he spoke. "Use it as fuel. You'll need plenty of it while you're here. Reconvene at 2400 hours." He marched away, hands still balled into fists, his face only slightly less red than it was when he was screaming.

"Phew, that new General is intense, huh?" Paul and Harry were lying down in their barracks, determined to move as little as possible before having to start drills at midnight.

Harry gave a half-hearted nod. "I thought he had to be joking, starting us out at midnight. Seems screwy to me. We'll all be half alive by then."

Jack walked in, his shirt drenched in sweat, a football under one arm, and flopped onto his cot. "You boys ain't been runnin' around out there." He tossed the football over his head and caught it. "It's brutal." He wiped his forehead, beaded with sweat. "I say startin' at midnight sounds like a dream to me."

Harry snorted. "Some dream that is."

Paul rolled over to his back and stared at the ceiling. He hoped he'd be able to tame his restless mind enough to get a few hours of sleep.

"Sounds like we're in for a hell of a nightmare here. Hard to believe, just last week, we were complaining about being in Florida. Not lookin' much better here, though I'd thought we'd been through the thick of it. Guess I was dead wrong."

"Eh, we'll be fighting them Nazis soon enough, be grateful for this," said Jack.

"Maybe so," replied Paul. *With any luck, this damn war will be over before we get there,* he thought, closing his eyes. He didn't think he'd ever get used to sleeping in all these different places. He felt too vulnerable to really drop off into a deep sleep. The best he usually got was a few hours of fitful sleep. He supposed it was a good thing - he'd always be ready to go. But damn, he'd give anything for a good night's sleep.

Three nights in a row, the men rose just before midnight and trained until the sun came up. On the last night of jungle combat drills, the heat and humidity was nearly unbearable. Heat storms rolled through, the sky brilliant with lightning. Cracks of thunder startled the men with no sign of letting up.

"Thought we'd get a break from this sticky air tonight," Paul remarked.

"Ha. It's only making it worse," Harry replied, looking up to the sky. *Always the pessimist,* Paul thought. Though he had to agree, the air really did feel heavier than ever. He didn't think his shirt would ever dry, and at this point, he had no idea whether it was wet with sweat or the rain pouring down on them.

When the Captain appeared to tell them they were moving out, Paul swore you could hear the collective sigh of relief from each man out there. They marched to Building 3, a large garage, to clean ordnance equipment. Not exactly a vacation, but Paul would take this monotonous task over sitting all night in a thunderstorm.

By the time the sun rose the next morning and the men shuffled into their bunks, Paul's fingers were stiff from cleaning parts.

"Thank the good Lord, it's Friday," Harry mumbled as he fell, face first, onto his cot. Within minutes, he was snoring. Paul took off his boots and prayed for sleep.

~

The weekend brought with it a welcome break. By Friday afternoon, those who had completed their three days in the woods were given passes to head into town. Paul stayed back, still too tired for a night out. He had no interest in exploring a town he planned on never coming back to.

"I'd rather spend my free time writing to Edith," Harry said. The two men walked down the lane to the Post Exchange and bought a beer each. On the walk back, Paul thought about how glad he was to have a pal like Harry here with him. They didn't say much as they neared the barracks, the sun dipping below the horizon, leaving a haze that hung low in the sky, the early part of the evening settling in around them. The quiet comradery reminded Paul of his father. He smiled, both from thinking about his Pop and how Harry felt like a brother to him. *Hell, we spend all this time together. I guess he kind of is my brother,* Paul thought. He looked over at Harry, who was now settled onto his cot, a beer in one hand, pen in the other, scratching out his letter to Edith. Paul just shook his head. He didn't mind these quiet evenings, but he wouldn't share his thoughts with Harry. They may have been close, but he wasn't that pathetic.

Saturday morning, General Kramer stormed into the barracks before the sun had risen. The men leapt to their feet, scrounging around for glasses and uniforms, taken by surprise at the unexpected visit.

"I see you thought you'd have today off. You've been mistaken." Paul swore he saw the General crack a smile through that permanent scowl. "I'll see you all outside and in formation in five minutes." He turned on his heel and slammed the door on his way out.

"What in God's name…" Jack looked more than a little hungover. Paul looked around at the rest of the group and was glad he'd chosen not to join them last night. They looked like they'd be paying for it today.

"I thought we had the weekend off," complained Harry. He sat at the end of his cot, pulling on his boots.

A baby-faced GI named Glenn groaned from his cot in the corner. Paul walked over and chuckled. "You're looking a bit green, Glenn. How much *did* you have to drink last night?"

The soldier in the cot next to his piped up. "He's never been drunk before. Convinced him he had to experience it. Before going overseas. Thought we were off today. Bad idea." He spoke in clipped sentences, swallowing hard between words, trying not to be sick, then fell back against his pillow.

"You don't look so hot, either." Paul whistled. "You boys are gonna have a hell of a time out there today."

Paul walked down to the infirmary after a long day of dodging shrapnel from the live mortars that had rained down on them. What had started as an unexpected Saturday of drills had turned into a ten-day maneuver. They'd had no time to prepare, haphazardly throwing their gear together and marching out into the woods. Paul assumed that was intentional. They'd completed their ten days, having covered over fifty miles. All he really wanted was a hot shower and to climb into his cot. *Nothing like sleeping outside to make me actually miss that dreaded cot,* he thought. It had been miserable, battling with other regiments along the way - the ultimate test of mental and physical strength. The men had learned new tactics as they hiked the terrain, becoming more and more aware of what they needed to look for when out in the forest. He'd come out of the woods with the rest of his unit feeling dirty and exhausted but more prepared than he'd expected. He couldn't say he enjoyed it, but he could understand it, at least.

He turned down the hall of the small hospital and signed in at the nurse's station.

"I'm looking for Harry Peterson."

"He's down the hall. Count three curtains," the nurse pointed.

Paul nodded. "Thank you, ma'am."

He reached the third curtain and stood outside momentarily as he looked around. *Do I just peek in?* He wanted to knock, but each patient was separated by only a curtain, and he didn't see anywhere to rap his hand.

"Knock knock," he called out, before pulling back the curtain slightly.

Harry was sitting up in bed, still in his dirty fatigues.

Paul walked inside the room and stood at the side of the bed.

"You know, if you wanted to get out of the last day's maneuvers, I'm sure there are less painful ways to do it," Paul joked.

"Ha..ha.." Harry had been stitched up, the bloody gash across his left cheek now cleaned and covered with a large bandage.

"You joke," he continued, "but I'm telling you, Paul, sometimes I wish there was something wrong with me so I could get out of this hellhole." Harry leaned back on his pillow, looking away from Paul.

"Come on, Harry, don't talk like that."

His friend didn't respond.

"You can't think like that. It coulda happened to anyone. It was just an accident. You couldn't have avoided it. No one in your shoes could have." He tried to reason with Harry.

Harry snapped his head back to look at Paul. "But it wasn't anyone. It was me. I was the only one to take a piece of shrapnel to the face. Don't you get it?"

There was anger in his voice, and Paul wondered, too, why it had been Harry. He chalked it up to just being one of those freak accidents, but he ached for his friend, who was already struggling to keep his head above water and muster the strength to continue each day. He sat at the foot of the bed, searching for the right words. They never came. Harry fell asleep while Paul sat with him until the nurse came back around.

"You're good to go, soldier," she said as she pulled the curtain open wide.

Harry grimaced and sat up slowly.

"Back to reality," he said and strode past Paul and out of the hospital building, not stopping to wait for his friend to catch up. Paul shook his head as he jogged down the sidewalk.

"Harry, come on, wait up. We're going to the same place."

Harry stopped in his tracks and turned around. "You sure about that? Because I'm pretty sure we're not ending up in the same place."

"What are you talking about, pal?"

Harry blew out a breath and ran his hand through his fiery red hair. "You're good, Paul. You've adjusted to this life. I haven't. It's just not in me. I'll never feel like this is anything more than just a forced position. I don't want to be here. I won't make it back. We won't be 'going to the same place.' You understand?"

Paul looked at his friend. He wanted to help him, but he had a feeling nothing he said would be enough.

"Listen, Harry, I know you've convinced yourself you're no good here, and you won't make it out alive, but I think that kinda attitude is doing you more harm than good."

Harry scoffed and turned to walk away. Paul grabbed his arm. "Just listen to me. You think I want to be here? You think I want to go kill some Germans and watch my buddies be killed? No one does. You're not the only one. But the only way we'll make it out alive is if we tell ourselves we will. This negative bullshit has gotta stop. I'm worried about you. Please. We're gonna make it out, ok? We have no other choice. That damn cadre thinks us ASTP guys are a bunch of pantywaists. Prove him wrong. You're not leaving Edith. Do your best for her."

Paul hadn't realized he was yelling until he looked around to see a group of GIs staring as they marched past. Harry looked like he'd crawl under a rock if he could.

"I don't want to leave Edith," he whispered, crumpling onto a bench with his head in his hands.

Paul sat down next to him.

"I know you don't," he said.

My Dearest Little Sister,

I am so close to home - in Arkansas now. And yet, still so far away. I guess I'll continue to feel further and further if all goes as planned. Pretty soon, we'll be on the east coast, heading further and further east, if you catch my drift... Don't worry about me, though. I'm doing just fine. I've got to tell you a bit about the last week here. Don't tell Ma, okay? I already sent her a letter, too.

It's all going good, really. I can't complain - I mean, I could, but what good would it do? My buddy Harry, on the other hand... he's got a bit to complain about. Poor guy has had a rough go of it. We were nearly done with a ten-day march - fifty miles if you can believe it! They were firing live mortars all around us - told us they wouldn't get close enough to do any harm. But poor Harry, he got too close or they fired too close, who knows which. He ended up with a piece of shrapnel to his face. Had to go on down to the hospital for a cheek full of stitches. He's pretty down about it and I can't say I blame him. He says it's a sign of what's to come, and I told him to shut up with that nonsense. If you don't mind, could you say a quick prayer for him?

Anyway, sorry I don't have much good news to report. Tell me all about my sweet little nephew when you write next. I miss him something fierce.

Hugs for Danny (and you too)

Paul

Chapter 11

ANNA

OCTOBER 1944

BOSTON, MASSACHUSETTS

*D*earest Grandfather,
    I am currently traveling in a Pullman sleeper car, if you can believe it! I'm thankful to have an officer's rank, as I've heard the regular troop trains are quite uncomfortable and stuffy. We have our own little compartment, enough space to fit three of us nurses with three bunks, one on top of the other. It's cramped, but nothing we aren't used to by now. During the day, we fold up the middle bunk and have a little bench seat to better accommodate us. We have a kitchen car somewhere in the lineup, and we get our meals delivered to us. It's not the best, but it's been a welcome break. After we waited several hours at the station, the food tasted spectacular. A hearty breakfast with eggs, bacon, and coffee. We could hardly believe it!

    I'm grateful for the other nurses here. What a gift it is to have them to share this experience with. I couldn't imagine going it alone.

I hope you are in good health, and don't worry too much about me! Love you, Gramps!

AB

PS - I'm not going to New York! Can you guess where?

Anna yawned and stretched her legs out in front of her. Any minute, they'd have breakfast delivered to their compartment. Though it was cramped, it had been a welcome reprieve from the barracks at Fort George Meade. Having their meals delivered had been a surprise she could get used to - rather than having to march to mess. She looked out the window at the passing scenery. They moved along so fast she could hardly focus on the distant mountains. Everything was painted a blue-gray hue, the fog hanging low in the air, clouding the landscape.

Gretchen and Louise sat beside her on the bench seat, writing letters home. They'd had so much free time on board the train they didn't know what to do with it. They passed the hours by writing letters and playing cards. Gretchen had attempted to socialize amongst the soldiers in other train cars a few times. She had taken to her seat after getting *the look* from Captain Campbell that said she'd be wise not to continue down that road.

The porter came with their breakfasts, and the girls tucked their letters away, anxious to dig in. They'd be arriving in Boston today, and they knew there was a long day ahead of them.

"I wonder where we'll be staying," Anna said. They hadn't been given much information about what their time in Boston would be like, except that it would be the last stop before they climbed aboard a ship bound for England.

"One of the guys in the car behind us said we're probably going to end up at Camp Myles Standish. That's where they're headed, anyway," Gretchen answered.

Louise looked at Gretchen, her fork halfway to her mouth. "What?"

"How do you do it?"

"Do what?" Gretchen asked, batting her eyelashes.

"You can get anyone to tell you anything. It's incredible, really," Louise said.

Gretchen gave her a sly smile. "I'm just friendly, that's all."

"Mhm," grunted Louise.

~

They filed into the Station Hospital and were ushered to the third floor. After sitting for so long on the train, Anna was glad to stretch her legs with a walk up several flights of stairs. In the hallway, metal chairs lined the wall, and they were directed to sit and wait to be called in for their physical examinations. Anna and the other nurses reluctantly sat down. She was wrought with nerves, pent-up energy, and worry. She couldn't stop bouncing her knee up and down. Gretchen sat on one side of her and Louise on the other. She wished Eleanor would have come in their group. It didn't feel right without her, but she had chosen to stay back and wait with the next group. She was still keeping her distance. Anna looked over at Gretchen. Her normally jubilant friend had not been herself lately. She hid it well, and Anna wondered if anyone else had noticed the change in Gretchen. She knew her friend was still upset over Eleanor's reaction to their promotions. Just as Gretchen had predicted, it had changed their close-knit dynamic. *Ridiculous, really,* Anna thought. She was beginning to feel annoyed over Eleanor being such a spoilsport. And over something that was completely out of their control. She was tired of walking on eggshells when Eleanor was around. *Things will change once we're in England,* she thought. *She'll realize how silly she's being.* Anna failed to convince herself, but she hoped they'd at least be able to work well together.

The door at the opposite end of the hall from where they'd come swung open. An older nurse held open the door with her foot and squinted down at her clipboard. Her gray hair was piled high on her head, and her uniform looked like it had been fitted to her about thirty pounds ago.

"Ms. Anna Mitchell," she called, her voice echoing down the long hallway. Anna wiped her sweaty hands down the front of her uniform and rose from her seat.

"Yes, ma'am."

She followed the stout woman through the door and down another bare hallway, the incandescent bulbs flickering overhead. The sterile hospital halls made Anna feel like she was heading to an interrogation rather than a physical examination. Save for the squeak of the old nurse's shoes on the white tile floor, Anna didn't hear a sound. *Strange for a busy hospital,* she thought. In the exam room, Anna tried to fill the awkward silence. She had gotten so used to being the nurse she had forgotten how odd it felt to be the patient.

"Quiet day today?"

The nurse laughed. "Oh, goodness, no. We've got you nurses on the third floor because it's closed for renovations. You go on down to the first or second floors, and it won't be anywhere near as quiet as it is up here. Alright, dear, let's go ahead and take your shoes off and step up onto the scale.

Anna stepped onto the scale and waited while the nurse found her weight.

"One hundred fifteen pounds," the nurse announced. "You're a tiny little thing," she said, then added, "not like me," and patted her stomach. She chuckled. "I'm trying to retire before I have to buy any new uniforms."

"Oh, I can understand that," Anna said. "I can't imagine the cost right now. I'm very thankful the military provides our uniforms."

The nurse nodded her agreement. "Go ahead and change into this gown while I step out and get the doctor."

Anna nodded politely, a sudden wave of nerves sweeping over her. She shouldn't have had any worry over today; she knew she was perfectly healthy, but everything about this process tied her up in knots.

She removed her skirt and blouse, folding them neatly to avoid wrinkles as best she could. She draped the gown over herself and sat down on the exam table with her feet dangling over the edge. Looking down at her toes, she nearly laughed at the absurdity. She felt like a child sitting there swimming in a giant gown with her feet off the floor. She thought of her childhood visits to Dr. White's office. *I don't think I'll be getting a lollipop on the way out today.*

～

Anna sat outside the main entrance to the hospital after completing her examinations. Not only had she been tortured with a very thorough physical by a doctor with a cold stare and few words, she'd also suffered through a dental exam, eye exam, chest x-ray, and a smallpox vaccination. After four hours inside the hospital walls, she was glad she'd eaten every last bite of her breakfast on the train. Her stomach grumbled. She was ready to find dinner. She had promised Gretchen she'd wait to go to the officer's mess just across the street, so she watched the traffic and the passersby on the street in front of her, the nearly setting sun casting a golden glow that was too glorious to ignore. She tried to put the miserable experience out of her mind, but she still felt like a pincushion.

Gretchen came barging through the double doors and ran down the steps, Louise on her heels.

"That was the worst experience yet," she exclaimed.

Louise came alongside her. "I'll take drills and calisthenics any day as long as we don't have to go through *that* again."

Anna nodded. "I feel like every last inch of me has been thoroughly inspected. Hopefully, tomorrow's fittings will be a breeze compared to what we just went through."

"Ugh, I don't even want to think about it. Come on," Gretchen said. She tugged Anna up from her spot on the concrete steps. "Let's eat and forget about today. I'm absolutely famished."

More official business beckoned the nurses the following morning. With less than forty-eight hours before they left Boston, a sense of urgency filled the air all over the barracks. That same urgency, however, did not hasten the process of getting their identification paperwork and photographs. Anna and Louise had arrived at the Administration Building just after breakfast. They were still waiting in a small lobby area while the clerk typed up their papers as it neared eleven o'clock.

"I wonder how in the world Gretchen was able to get herself a hair appointment with such short notice," Louise said.

Anna pushed her hair back out of her face, only to have it land right back where it was. She tucked it behind her ears. "That woman can talk anyone into anything."

Louise laughed. "That's certainly the truth."

"I'm beginning to think I need to have Gretchen squeeze me in for an appointment, too," Anna laughed, frustrated by her uncooperative hair.

"Oh please, your curls are gorgeous," Louise replied. "This pin straight mop, on the other hand."

Anna admired her friend's soft blonde locks. "The grass is always greener, I guess. I'd have given anything as a girl to not have to fight the frizz." She lifted up the back of her thick, unruly hair and fanned her neck. The sun was unusually hot for late October which had given way to a halo of frizz that framed her face.

The two women spent the rest of the day hurrying from one administrative building to another, only to be told to wait some more. They were fitted for new uniforms - shipping out to England with winter soon approaching meant heavier layers and new boots - given their identification papers and were finally free to go in the early afternoon. By the time they made it back to their hut, Anna and Louise were spent.

Gretchen came barging in right behind them, red-faced and sweaty, her fresh hair sticking to her cheeks. She was carrying a giant watermelon and had several newspapers tucked under her arms.

"What in the world?" Anna said, taking the watermelon from Gretchen.

"Where did you find a watermelon this late in the season?"

"An old man was selling the last of his produce just a few blocks from the hair salon. It's such a warm day, and it looked so good, I thought we'd have some fun!" Gretchen could always find a reason to have some fun.

Eleanor sat up from her cot to join them, something she hadn't done since their promotions. Anna smiled at her, an awkward moment passing between them before she finally looked at Gretchen.

"What's all the newspaper for?" Eleanor took one off of Gretchen's trunk and flipped through it.

"Well, we don't have any giant knives to cut it open, so this could get messy," she said as she took the rest of the newspapers and spread them over the floor of their hut.

Eleanor took the pages from her newspaper and helped Gretchen lay them out. Soon, nearly the entire hut was covered in newspaper pages.

Gretchen stood with her hands on her hips, satisfied with their work. Then she took the watermelon from Anna and held it over her head.

"Gretchen, what…" Before Eleanor could finish her question, Gretchen had let the watermelon go, smashing it on the floor. It burst open, and a juicy mess began to pour out over the newspapers. The girls were on their knees, clawing at the watermelon, breaking it apart, and doling out handfuls to one another.

Gretchen paused, a giant chunk of watermelon in her hand. She looked at Eleanor and grinned.

"Don't even think about it," Eleanor warned. Anna and Louise sat motionless, afraid of what might transpire.

Gretchen took the watermelon and threw it at Eleanor,

where it splattered in her hair - juice, seeds, and the pink flesh dripping down her face.

"Oh, you shouldn't have," Eleanor said, licking the juice as it ran down her face and over her lips. All at once, there was watermelon flying, Eleanor was laughing, Gretchen was covered in a sticky mess, and Anna sat watching, happier than ever. Leave it to Gretchen to break the ice with something as ridiculous as a watermelon fight. By the time they'd gotten through the watermelon, the newspapers were shredded, and the mess was everywhere. They sat looking around them.

"We've got our work cut out for us tonight," Anna said.

"It was worth it," Eleanor replied. Gretchen beamed at her and leapt up, wrapping her in a giant hug. Eleanor struggled to get up and out of Gretchen's embrace, but Anna and Louise piled on, too, keeping her held to her spot on the floor.

"It's good to have you back, Elle," Gretchen said, squeezing her even tighter.

"Don't call me Elle," Eleanor grumbled.

"I hate to spoil this party..." Anna started, "But are you really okay, Eleanor?"

They separated from one another, sticky with watermelon juice, and sat cross-legged on the newspaper. Louise got up to fetch a garbage bag, and Eleanor blew out a breath. She scooped up a piece of the rind and began breaking it into pieces, avoiding Anna and Gretchen's eyes. Finally, she looked up.

"I got promoted today." She tried to keep a straight face, looking down at the mess they'd made to avoid making eye contact, but she couldn't hold back the grin that formed. Gretchen hugged her once more.

"I don't know why they didn't just do it with the rest of us," Anna said. "It's not like you don't deserve it."

Eleanor sighed. "I guess it was just about the number of days in service or some nonsense."

"Well, either way, I'm happy for you. We all are."

She looked down again, scooping more watermelon rind and helping Louise fill the garbage bag.

"I was such a jerk, girls. I know it wasn't your fault. Thanks for forgiving me."

Gretchen snorted. "Who said we forgave you?" She kept a straight face, looking Eleanor in the eye.

Eleanor looked at Gretchen from her spot on the floor, hands full of wet, sticky newspaper, surprise etched on her face. Gretchen threw her head back and laughed. "Gotcha," she said, giving Eleanor a gentle shove.

"Don't make me throw this at you," Eleanor said with a smirk.

"Oh, no you don't." Louise stepped between them, handing Gretchen a garbage bag. "I'm wiped. Let's get this mess cleaned up."

～～

They set sail on October 31, the moon nearly full in the sky - a fitting backdrop for the evening of Halloween. Anna walked up the gangplank, nerves swirling in her stomach. She gazed up at the enormous ship. She'd never been this close to a troopship before. She had admired the boats in the harbor during their few days in Boston, but to actually be boarding one now...*intimidating is an understatement,* she thought.

She smiled at the officer waiting at the top and fumbled with her identification papers. Her fingers shook when she handed them over. He checked his clipboard, handed back her papers, and ushered her aboard. She tripped on the edge of the gangplank that met the ship's deck and threw her hand out to catch the railing just before she fell forward. Her face burned with embarrassment. *Way to go, AB*, she thought, rolling her eyes at herself. Hundreds of people gathered at the harbor, some waiting to board and others to wish them well on their departure.

Hour after hour, they waited, watching as the officers changed posts, still directing the endless line of soldiers and nurses waiting to board.

"This place is crawling. Looks like a bunch of ants down there from way up here," Gretchen marveled. "I feel like the queen looking down on her subjects." She gave a pageant wave before Eleanor slapped her hand down.

"Quit it," she said.

Gretchen rolled her eyes. "Loosen up, Inky Elle," Gretchen teased. Eleanor scowled.

Anna just watched, overwhelmed at the enormity of the convoy they were a part of.

By the time it looked like they might finally be leaving the harbor, the sky had darkened, and night was fully upon them. The buildings they had seen so clearly only a few hours before were now only twinkling lights. The street lamps had flicked on hours ago, and Anna strained her eyes, hoping to still see the swarms of people meandering on the pier. She could just make out the silhouettes of those still hanging over the pier's railings, shouting their farewells. And then, they were moving. The ship lurched backward, then steadied as it navigated out of the harbor.

Anna stood on deck, the four women linking arms. They were swallowed up in a sea of soldiers and fellow nurses, all gathered to watch the fading Boston Harbor. With the moon illuminating overhead, they could see the harbor lights and the crowd of well-wishers vanishing from sight. Their cheers of farewell were drowned out by the drone and creak of the ship, engines firing, metal grinding, as they eased out into the open water, flanked by several other troopships also making the two-week voyage.

They remained on deck, even after they could no longer see the lights of Boston, looking in the direction of the land they'd only hours before been standing on. Anna thought she might collapse with overwhelm if it weren't for Gretchen and Louise on either side of her. A few soldiers began to mull about, looking for the stairs that would lead them below deck. Eleanor turned to go, too, but a voice pulled her back. Somewhere within the crowd, a soldier began to sing.

'God Bless America, land that I love
Stand beside her and guide her
Through the night with the light from above'

A chill ran up Anna's arms as she listened to the soldier's sad melody, his voice haunting and beautiful - the words too fitting for tonight. A few people began to join in, and soon, the entire deck of the USS West Point was singing the most heart-wrenching version of 'God Bless America' that Anna had ever heard. She could hardly get the words out over the lump in her throat, tears streaming down her face.

Chapter 12

PAUL
NOVEMBER 1944
CAMP SHANKS, NEW JERSEY

Joe, a native New Yorker and the smoothest talker Paul had ever heard, ran into their hut waving an envelope.

"You're never going to believe what I've got in here, boys."

They had been getting ready for a night out in New York City. There was no real plan except to see the sights and find a place for dinner. Paul yanked up his dress pants, tucked his white t-shirt in, and looked up at Joe. He was as giddy as a school kid.

"Whatcha got?"

Joe opened the envelope and pulled out several tickets, fanning them around dramatically.

"None other than five tickets to the Paramount Theater for tonight's show." He could hardly keep the pride from his face as the guys gathered around him.

"Get out," Paul said. He rushed over to see if Joe was serious. Even Harry, determined to remain miserable in his cot for the duration of their stay at Camp Shanks, had been impressed. He rolled over onto his side to face Joe.

"Woo-wee," said Jack. "How on Earth did you manage to snag these?"

Joe grinned. "I owe my sister big time. She stood out in line for hours. It's going to be jam-packed - at least, that's what she heard. It's worth it. Did you see who's headlining?" He flipped the tickets around and pointed. "Frank Sinatra."

Paul whistled. "I didn't think this night could get any more exciting. Small town Texan like me out in the big city. And I thought that was enough, now we're going to see Frank Sinatra." He paused. "Hey, Joe, what do we owe you for those tickets?"

"Nah, don't worry about it, Paul. It's on me. I just want one good night before we ship out."

Paul clapped him on the back. "That's awfully nice, Joe, but I have to repay you somehow."

"Forget about it," he said.

"Well, I sure will enjoy tonight, but I won't forget about it. I'll pay you back one day. You can count on it."

"Come on, Harry," Paul urged. "When will we ever get another opportunity like this? We're talking Frank Sinatra. How could you say no to that?"

Harry lay on his cot while the rest of the men finished getting dressed in their best uniforms. There was no way Paul would miss out on the chance to see Frank Sinatra. Heck, he'd have gone just to walk around New York City. He tried all he could to reason with Harry, but if his friend wanted to stay holed up in the musty hut, well then, so be it.

Paul adjusted his tie and gave it one last ditch effort, punching Harry on the arm.

"Wouldn't Edith want you to enjoy yourself before you ship out?" He hoped that the mention of his wife might snap him out of his slump.

Harry blew out a breath and rolled onto his other side. Paul could tell he wanted to go, but he insisted on punishing himself for reasons Paul couldn't understand.

"All right…I didn't want to have to do this, pal." Paul nodded at Jack and Glenn, who had been waiting by the door. The two men walked over to stand next to Paul.

"Ok, boys, how should we do this?" Jack grinned and grabbed a hold of one of Harry's ankles. Surprised, Harry kicked and flailed until he broke free, sitting up on his cot.

"What the hell? What are you guys doing?"

The three men standing over the bed looked back and forth at each other. "I say we just dump the whole cot," said Glenn, the goofy grin on his face making Paul laugh.

"Don't even think about it," Harry said, grabbing each side of his bed.

"Listen, I told you I didn't want to have to do this…but you've left us no choice," Paul said at the same time the three men hoisted the cot. In one swift motion, the cot was on its side, and Harry was on the floor.

"Looks like you're outta bed, pal. Might as well get dressed and come with us."

Harry grumbled and said a few expletives under his breath as he got to his feet. Paul thought he might flip his cot over and climb back in bed, in which case he'd have left him alone. Instead, Harry surprised everyone and started to dress.

"Alright! I knew you couldn't say no to good Ol' Blue Eyes," said Jack.

~

"How about we head on down in the direction of the theater and find a bite to eat?" Joe checked their tickets. "Show starts at 8. Plenty of time to grab dinner as long as we stick nearby." He looked around, trying to think of the best place to eat near Times Square.

They'd just gotten off the train from Camp Shanks and were following behind Joe, expertly navigating them through the crowds of Grand Central station. Paul was in awe of the grandeur of the famed station. He wished his family were here to see how incredible it was. He turned around in a circle, taking it all in before realizing Joe was halfway out the door. He dashed to the exit and was struck once more. He opened the door to the monstrosity that was New York City. *This sure ain't Texas,* he thought. He'd seen views from the train on the way in. There was nothing like standing in the middle of it, the buildings soaring high overhead, the people rushing by on the street, the noise - everywhere you looked, there was commotion. Joe never stopped walking. He two-stepped across the busy intersection, entirely unphased by the honking horns or the roar of the engines waiting their turn.

"Man, you're a real city-slicker, aren't you?" Paul said, catching up on the other side of the street.

"Ha! I guess I am compared to you, Texan."

Paul's heart pounded in his chest as he tried to avoid collision with fellow pedestrians, keep up with Joe while playing it cool, and pick his jaw up off the streets of New York. The bright lights of the Paramount Theater came into view as they continued down Broadway. He glanced at his watch. Just after seventeen thirty hours. The line to get in had already started. The giant signs advertising Frank Sinatra 'In Person' were plastered everywhere. Paul read the signs as they stopped in front of the Paramount Theater building. "Our Hearts Were Young and Gay" and "Frank Sinatra, Eileen Barton, Richard Paige and his Orchestra" were hanging high above them. A line of bobby-soxers had already started to form. They could hardly contain their excitement, squealing every time the doors opened in hopes it might be Mr. Sinatra himself walking right out the front doors. Paul smiled. He imagined his sister, Evie, could've been any one of those girls when she was a teenager.

"I don't know about you, fellas, but I'm not standing in line listening to that for the next two hours." Joe picked up the pace, passing the theater and continuing down Broadway.

"You got a place in mind?" Paul and the rest of the guys followed close behind.

Joe smiled over his shoulder, a big, broad smile like he was letting them in on a secret. "Trust me, you're gonna love it," he said.

Paul thought they'd love any place Joe brought them. They were so in awe of everything around them - cabs screeching to a stop, the bustle of people jostling past, the friendly waves and 'thank you's' to the men in uniform. Everywhere you looked, the streets were buzzing with GIs, excited for one last hurrah before shipping out.

Chasing Joe for several blocks, Paul breathed in the crisp Fall air. It was tinged with the smell of exhaust and cigarette smoke, and what he was pretty sure was fried onions. He nearly collided with Joe, who had stopped on the corner of Broadway and 48th Street in front of a building adorned with more bright signs and flashing lights.

Paul read the name aloud. "The Latin Quarter." He looked around at the outside of the building the nightclub took up residence in. It was a smaller space than the buildings that towered around it - lower to the ground at least - with arched windows all across the upper level. "You sure we can get food here?"

"Positive," said Joe. He swung open the door and strode inside. It was dark, and Paul waited for his eyes to adjust to the smoky room. Joe snagged them a table near the dance floor as if he owned the place. Now that Paul thought about it, Joe carried that natural confidence everywhere he went. An ornate set of stairs led to a small stage just in front of their table. A red velvet curtain hung from one end to the other, hiding the busy backstage from the crowd.

When a waitress came by, Paul was quick to put in his order. "Joe's drink is on me," he added. "Thanks for being our tour guide tonight, city slicker."

"I got his second drink," said Jack.

"Third!" Harry and Glenn took dibs at the same time.

Joe laughed. "How much you fella's think I'm going to drink tonight, anyway? I still have to get you back to the train, don't forget." He smiled and looked at Harry like he'd just had an idea. "I've got Harry's first drink," he said. "Let's see if we can loosen you up a bit."

Harry rolled his eyes. "Here we go."

They bantered with one another until the waitress reappeared, balancing a giant tray overhead. She stopped in front of their table and began unloading their plates of food. When she had finished, she gave them a grin. "Enjoy, soldiers," she said and sauntered away with the empty tray held high.

"I wonder what act they've got going on here tonight," Paul said as he popped a French fry into his mouth.

"Chorus Girls," Joe said around a mouthful of pasta.

Paul looked around the nightclub. The tables had all filled up, and people were still pouring in, standing against walls or squeezing in at the bar. The walls were black, the lighting dim, and it was even smokier now than when they'd first arrived.

An announcer from somewhere Paul couldn't see started introductions, and women began filing out on stage. The red curtain remained closed, serving as their backdrop. Music began, a song Paul hadn't heard, and the women glided down the steps right toward their table. Paul sat, captivated at the skill and finesse they exuded. They shimmied past, one after the other, until the last girl paused long enough to hook her finger under Paul's chin and give him a wink. She walked away, his friends whistling and slapping him on the back. He continued to watch as they took their positions on the dance floor and the music picked up. Harry, despite looking a bit uncomfortable, seemed to also be enjoying himself, if his foot tapping on the black and white tile floor were any indication.

Paul sipped his drink and looked across the table at his friend, drink in hand, grinning from ear to ear. As the first song came to a close, the Chorus Girls moved back to the stage and opened up the dance floor to the crowd. They watched as Jack smooth-talked his way into a dance with a girl on the other side of the dance floor. Harry glanced over at Paul and tipped his glass toward him.

"Sorry, I've been such a heel. I hate that I'm bringing you down," he called out over the music.

Paul shook his head. "Forget it, Harry. You don't bring me down." He pointed toward the dance floor at Jack who was now spinning the young woman around in time to the music.

"He's sure got some moves," Paul laughed.

"Hey, I'm serious, Paul. I'm going to be better from now on."

Paul eyed his friend. "Nah, you won't. That's just the alcohol talking."

Harry threw his head back and barked out a laugh. "I appreciate your honesty, pal."

Paul shrugged. "It's okay, Harry, you've got something better than all this back home. I get it. Just do me a favor?"

Harry nodded.

"Just enjoy tonight, okay?"

Harry smiled and drummed his fingers on the table. "I'll do my best," he replied.

They'd polished off their dinners and were on their second round of drinks when Paul nudged Joe. "What time do we need to head out of here to make our seats in time?" He was enjoying himself, but he'd rather not miss a performance by Frank Sinatra while he still had the chance.

"After this number, we'll make a break for it."

The music softened, and Paul took that as their cue to exit. Leaving their napkins and empty glasses, they stood to leave.

Paul gave a small wave to the girl who had winked at him when he saw she was watching him from on stage. She blew him a kiss without missing a beat. Paul walked out of the nightclub with a silly grin on his face. *Man, a country boy sure could get swallowed up here*, he thought.

They walked back to the Paramount Theater, where the screaming girls from earlier were now inside, rife with anticipation. Joe handed over their tickets to a man in a three-piece suit standing at the door. He grabbed all five tickets, tore the tops off, and handed them back the stubs.

"Up the stairs to the left. Middle balcony. Section E. Check your seat numbers."

They darted off in the direction of the stairs. Paul hadn't felt this much excitement - he stopped to think about it - ever, actually.

They found their seats and, too anxious to actually sit, Paul walked up to the front of the balcony and craned his neck to look above and below at the crowd filling the theater. He thought if he reached out, he'd be able to touch the excitement in the air, the vibration coursing through the building itself. Looking down, he saw the crowd filled with men in uniform. He was surprised at how many women were also in uniform.

Looking at the group of nurses in the audience below him, he thought about Evie and wondered if she'd have joined up if it weren't for Danny. He thought about both of his siblings, Evie at home taking care of her son, worrying about her husband, and Jamie...*God only knows where he is*, Paul thought.

The joyfulness of the crowd was infectious, though Paul's thoughts had turned inward. He couldn't help but smile at the excitement all around him, couldn't help but be here in this moment with the friends he'd made through the grueling hours of training. And at the same time, he couldn't help but wonder at the way things turned out. *Why me? Why am I the one standing here and not Evie or Jamie?*

Harry pointed down at the stage where the orchestra members had started taking their places. The men took their seats and waited for Frank Sinatra as the crowd clapped over the few first test notes from the band.

Paul could hardly believe it when the curtain finally swung open, and there stood Frank Sinatra himself. All other thoughts left him, and he was on the edge of his seat, right there with everyone else in the theater.

"Howdya do? Look who's here," Mr. Sinatra said, his blue eyes sparkling under the stage lights. He flashed the crowd a smile, and they roared. The ladies jumped up out of their seats, and the men tried to play it cool as if it was no big deal to be seeing Frank Sinatra at the Paramount Theater - until Eileen Barton sauntered on stage. The pair said their hellos, and she waved out to the crowd while the orchestra kicked up and soldiers all around the theater whooped and whistled their appreciation. The lights faded to black, a single spotlight shining down on the performers as they began their duet. Paul and the rest of the guys in his group were on their feet, clapping and whistling, all their cares forgotten. Any worry or fear over their futures paused as they got lost in the music.

When they poured out of the theater hours later, the city streets were still crawling with activity. Everywhere around him, Paul could hear people talking about the show. He was right there with them, the exhilaration washing over him. Evidently,

Harry had allowed himself to get caught up in the moment, too, as he walked up between Paul and Joe, draping his arms around their shoulders.

"Where to next?" He grinned.

Joe laughed. "Well, well, well, how about that. A couple drinks and a little Frank Sinatra is all it takes to loosen up our pal, Harry."

They walked down Broadway, joking and laughing, as if they had all the time in the world. Paul looked down at his watch. As much as he didn't want to spoil this feeling, he knew they had to face reality.

"Hey, anyone know what time the train leaves for Camp Shanks?"

"I think it said 11:05," Jack said.

"Joe, it's 10:45. Are we gonna make it in time?"

"Now you sound like you need another drink," Joe said. Paul really hoped he wasn't seriously considering going to another bar. They'd already be getting in after curfew, a risk he was willing to take for tonight's incredible experience, but he wasn't interested in missing the train back. Paul laughed it off, but relief flooded him when Joe clapped him on the back and said, "Yeah, we'll make it."

They kept their easy pace, walking toward Grand Central, reminiscing over their favorite parts of the show. The city was lit up, flashing signs and a palpable fervor that Paul guessed could probably be found anywhere you ended up in New York City. He let himself relax, replaying the performance with the rest of the guys. They came to an intersection, and he watched as Joe looked down the street one way, then the other, and broke out into a sprint. Paul, Harry, Jack, and Glenn took off after him like little ducklings, not wanting to get lost in the big city.

"What the hell, Joe?" Glenn called out from the back of the pack.

"Sorry, boys, we gotta hoof it." He turned around and flashed them his signature smile without slowing down. "Unless you feel like sleeping on the streets tonight."

They clamored into Grand Central, and for once, Paul was grateful to be wearing his uniform, which meant they didn't have to stop and wait in line for a ticket. They didn't stop running until they reached the platform and saw the train was still idling. They hopped across the gap, one after the other, onto the waiting train car. The train hissed and popped as the doors closed and the train prepared to leave.

"Phew, that was close," Paul said, flopping down into an empty seat.

"Nah," said Joe, "We had plenty of time."

The half-hour train ride went by in a blink. Paul buzzed from the thrill of the night. They pulled into the station, climbing down to walk to their barracks just before midnight.

"Here we are boys, Last Stop USA."

Chapter 13

ᏅᎬᏅ

ANNA
NOVEMBER 1944
LONDON, ENGLAND

ᏅᎬᏅ
---

*A*nna smiled as she pulled out her grandfather's letter. In the backyard of the house she was billeted with, she sat down on a lawn chair that had seen better days. She didn't care what it looked like as long as she could enjoy the fresh air. *And dry land,* she thought. She unfolded the letter and a newspaper clipping fluttered to the ground, landing at her feet. She scooped it up and looked at an image of President Roosevelt. She read the print underneath the photograph.

'*President Franklin D. Roosevelt addresses 40,000 supporters at Fenway Park, Boston on November 4. His final campaign speech well received after performance by Mr. Frank Sinatra.*'

She wondered why he had sent the article - *President Roosevelt gives a good speech,* she thought, *but what was so important that he mailed it?* She traced his familiar handwriting with her finger.

Anna Banana, my dear,

I imagine you are halfway across the ocean as I write this. I'll keep it short - not by choice - the arthritis says I must. Anyhow, I thought you might've been in town for the president's speech. Maybe I'm wrong, but you said you were not in New York City, so I'm taking a guess at where you are...

Love you AB. You keep your head up and stay safe.

Gramps

Anna tucked the letter in its envelope and held it against her chest. She marveled at how clever her grandfather was. They had not been allowed to share their location before they started for England, so she'd simply said 'not NYC' in her last letter. *Leave it to Gramps to know exactly where I was,* she thought. She looked at the newspaper clipping again, now understanding why he'd sent it. *Too bad we were already on board the West Point crossing the Atlantic by the time President Roosevelt had been in Boston on the Fourth,* she thought.

Her grandfather's was the first letter she had received since arriving in England. It may not have contained much, but she treasured the note from him. Her heart ached for his comfortable sofa that somehow always put her to sleep, his glass container of sun tea sitting on the top step of the porch, always perfectly steeped.

She sat in the old chair in the backyard of this new place and tried to ignore the nerves firing in her stomach. There had been so much change in such a short time that she thought she'd never get rid of that nervous feeling. It was like a shadow shrouding her everywhere she went. Acclimating to the uneasiness that was a way of life here had so far been the biggest thing to get used to. She closed her eyes and pictured her grandfather. She swore she was conjuring him up, the breeze on her face just like the one on his front porch swing - though quite a bit colder - the musky vanilla scent she'd come to associate only with him.

She opened her eyes and nearly jumped out of her skin.

"Oh! Hello, I'm sorry, I didn't hear you come out here. I hope you don't mind my using the patio set. You have a beautiful backyard." She rambled on, embarrassed at being startled.

The owner of the house gave her a kind smile. Anna could see the laugh lines that had formed and thought how happy he must have once been. Now, she could see that though he had a kind, inviting smile, there was a sadness about him. She wondered what this war had taken from him. Her grandfather had been right; England didn't look anything like she'd expected. It almost appeared like a barren land, especially in the small towns they had passed through to get here, some of them bombed completely to the ground.

The man sitting across from her was a bit younger than her own grandfather, but in contrast to the vibrancy of her grandfather, he looked tired and worn beyond his years.

"It's no problem at all, ma'am. I'm sorry to have startled you. I can get these chairs cleaned up tomorrow morning. They'll be much more usable once they've had a good scrub." He looked around at the four chairs and the glass table in the middle. "We used to come out here for times of celebration - birthdays and what have you." He waved his hand as if he could wave the memories away. "There hasn't been much to celebrate in a while." He smiled at Anna, then added, "Except being alive - and what greater gift is there than that? Sometimes, in the darkness, I forget what a wonderful thing it is just to be alive."

Anna tipped her head up to the sun and leaned back in her chair. The smell of vanilla and smoke made her sit up, opening her eyes once more. She watched as the man took a puff of his pipe. He gave her a strange expression, held out his pipe, and looked for something funny he had missed.

Anna tried to explain.

"A moment ago, I had been reading a letter from my grandfather. I could have sworn he was sitting right here with me," she said, smiling. "It turns out that you two must have the same taste in pipe tobacco."

~

The following morning, Anna woke early again, the air around her cool in the upstairs bedroom of the house. The only heat source was a small vent in the floor for the hot air from the stove downstairs to rise through. She lay there in the strange new room in the strange new house in a strange new country. Claustrophobia crept up her neck. She hadn't slept well since they'd boarded the ship from Boston. *Occupational hazard,* she thought. The lack of sleep did nothing to calm her frazzled nerves, and she suddenly needed fresh air. She was glad she had packed her warmest robe in her small collection of belongings. She wrapped it around her now, tying it tightly at her waist, and tiptoed out of the little room. She closed the door on her friends, still sleeping soundly.

Anna wound down the wide wooden staircase that told of happier times, the handrail worn with use. Several steps creaked on her way down, and she cringed, hoping not to wake anyone. The inside of the home resembled the outside - what had once been a grand home now sat in disrepair, and what once had been an inviting, comforting place now appeared hollow - devoid of warmth. Anna crept down the hallway, the remnants of cheer and liveliness within like a ghost quieted by a world at war.

Anna paused to look at the single small photograph hanging above a slim table in the hallway beneath the stairs. A beautiful woman about her age smiled up at Mr. Perkins while a young girl looked up at the two of them, an expression on her face telling of mischief running through her. She wondered where the two girls were now. Part of her was afraid of the answer. She reached up and touched the frame, then quickly pulled back when the house made a creaking noise somewhere below her. She continued down the hallway, past the den, and into the kitchen at the back of the house.

It was no surprise that there were no lights on - Captain Campbell had enforced the importance of maintaining the blackout. She had assured them they were safe out here in the country, but Anna still feared they could become a target for any Germans flying overhead. She was just fine with feeling her way around in the darkness. Though, she couldn't deny that doing so in a new place did make her a bit jumpier. The moonlight peeked through a crack in the curtain covering the window over the sink, giving her enough light to reach the back door.

She was in awe of the great home she was staying in, considering herself lucky to be in such a lovely accommodation, even if it wasn't in its greatest splendor. She wished she could have seen it before the war had left its mark. With a kitchen this big, she pictured a staff preparing meals for the family. Now it sat empty, though quite clean, save for the layer of soot covering the counters from the coal stove glowing in the corner.

She unlocked the wooden door, taking care not to jingle the little bell that hung against the floral curtain over the window. *Don't creak, don't creak,* she thought as she gently pulled the door open just enough to squeeze outside. She walked through the wet grass in her slippers and sat down in the garden. She wiggled her toes against the cold dew that had soaked through. She hugged her arms around her waist - it was colder than she'd anticipated, and her breath came out in little clouds in front of her. Sitting out here in the overgrown garden, it was hard not to think of her mother, and she wondered if she, too, were sitting in her garden halfway around the world. The thought gave her comfort despite her best effort to feign a disinterest in her own thoughts of her mother. Out here in the still of the early morning, she allowed herself to be vulnerable, to feel the connection she tried so hard to deny. She realized she wasn't so unlike her mother. She mused at how she was drawn to the outdoors in much the same way as her mother. She may not have wanted a hand in her mother's garden, but she did prefer to be out in the open air over cooped up somewhere indoors. There was nothing like being on a ship in the middle of the ocean to make her realize she hated being confined. She'd spent most of that time staring out over the rail at the wild sea, the waves crashing and the wind blowing her hair across her face.

The back door creaked open, and Anna turned to see Mr. Perkins struggling to balance a teacup in each hand.

"Oh, Mr. Perkins, let me help," she whispered and jumped up, trudging through the wet grass. He fumbled with the door-knob and nearly dropped the teacups before relenting and handing one cup to Anna.

They sat in silence, sipping their tea in the darkness, the glow of the moon having gone from the sky, the first hint of sunlight coming from the east.

"So, we meet again out here," said Mr. Perkins, his voice gravelly with sleep. He smiled in that congenial way that made Anna's heart ache for her own grandfather. She wondered if she could adopt Mr. Perkins as her honorary English grandfather while she was here.

She smiled back at him, her face half-hidden by her teacup. "Thank you for this," she said, tilting the teacup in his direction. "It's the best I've had since my grandfather's back home."

"Ah, it seems he and I would get along quite well."

She nodded in agreement. "You remind me very much of him."

"I am glad. It must be difficult for you American nurses coming here and staying with a strange old Englishman." He chuckled. "But we are very happy you are here to help. This is the least I could do," he made a sweeping gesture with his hand, "to open my home, to help in this small way. Otherwise, it would sit here and remain empty, like me." He looked down into his teacup. Anna cocked her head to the side and studied him. She could see the pain in his eyes that he tried so hard to hide. She was ashamed to admit that it made her afraid to ask him about the photograph on the wall. She didn't know if she could handle hearing his story.

He continued on anyway, and Anna braced herself as she listened. His voice was filled with grief as the sun came up behind him, the soft golden glow of just a few minutes ago now a blazing fiery red between the branches of the bare trees.

"At one point, we had four generations living within these walls." He nodded toward the house. Anna curled her legs beneath her, trying to keep warm. She held her teacup between her hands, warming her fingers.

"It was a very full house with my wife, my daughter, my granddaughter, and my great-grandbaby," he said. "I'd do anything to be tortured by living with all of those women again." A sad smile played across his face. He looked at the house, a heaviness blanketing him as he told her about the life he once had. Anna wasn't sure she was the right person to offer him words of condolence. *What do I know about grief this deep?* But something held her there; she didn't know exactly what - maybe his resemblance to her grandfather, or perhaps the sadness in his eyes, the way they remained half-lidded as if it was a burden just to open them to a life where his family had been taken from him.

She traced her finger over the outline of flowers that adorned her cup, too chicken to meet Mr. Perkins's eyes. He spoke anyway.

"We had gone into London." He closed his eyes at the memory and sighed. "I wish we hadn't," he whispered.

Chapter 14

*P*aul walked up the gangplank and onto the *George Washington* in a long line of GIs and officers bound for England. He watched from the rail as men continued to board in a procession that seemed to go on forever. He stood there watching until the last soldier boarded the ship, and they started their slow push out of the harbor.

"Guess I can't go AWOL now," Harry said, coming alongside Paul and leaning over the railing, mirroring Paul's stance at the back of the ship.

Paul chuckled and checked his watch, just before 7am. They were finally watching the Statue of Liberty and New York City's skyscrapers slowly fade from view.

"I suppose not," he replied. It was a somber morning, the early sun reflecting off the water as they strained to see the shrinking buildings dotting the horizon. Paul turned around, resting his back on the rail. In front of them lay only the giant fleet of ships traveling in their convoy, and beyond that, nothing but water. An occasional bird flew overhead, swooping down toward the deck of the ship, tempted by the smells of cooking grease and spoiled food. Paul wondered how long they'd hang around before they, too, would fly back home to dry land. He hadn't known what to expect out in the middle of the ocean, and he tried not to think about the fact that he'd be stuck out here for almost two weeks before he'd see any sign of land again.

He didn't know how long they stood like that, the sun beating down on their backs, the cold November breeze on their faces stealing away any warmth it provided. *Is this what it will feel like from now on?* he wondered. The warmth of home was stolen by the cold front of war as the ship steered them closer and closer to the front lines.

"Hey, did I ever tell you how I met Edith?"

Paul looked over at his friend. Moments before, they had held back tears watching the Statue of Liberty fade away.

"No, Harry, I don't think you ever did." He looked out over the railing. The shock of being on board such a large ship had compounded when they got so far out into the sea that they couldn't see land anymore. He squinted his eyes against the sun and tried to convince himself he could still see a shadow of Long Island.

"Nah, never mind. I don't want to bore you with that old story." Harry's hands were wrapped tightly around the railing, his knuckles white.

Paul faced his friend and rested a hand on his shoulder.

"We got all the time in the world right now, my friend. I'd love to hear that story."

Harry gave him a sad smile and loosened his grip on the rail.

"It's a good story, anyway." He trailed off, lost in thought, reliving the memory before he could tell it out loud.

"I had walked into this little diner, and this cute waitress came by to give me a menu." He shook his head, a smile on his face. "Paul, I'm telling you, she was perfect. Still is perfect, to me anyway."

Paul smiled and watched his friend, so filled with joy at the thought of his wife that it made Paul long for someone like that. It'd likely be a few years before he returned to his small-town life and could think about settling down, though he was surprised that Harry's meet-cute tale wasn't making him break out in a nervous sweat.

"I managed to make a fool of myself in those first thirty seconds," Harry said.

"It took you that long, huh?" Paul laughed when Harry gave him a shove.

"I told her I was going to marry her. Hadn't even put my order in for lunch and there I was, practically ordering her instead. But I swear I knew she was the one from the moment she walked by. Crazy, right?

"Love at first sight, pal. Crazy for me, maybe. For you? I believe it. Sounds like it worked out pretty well for ya."

"That's not even the worst of it," Harry continued, a goofy smile plastered on his face.

Paul couldn't help but grin back at his friend's animated storytelling. He was glad to have taken his mind off of the present.

"You know how the guys get into a bit of gambling here now and again? Well, I happened to have won by a landslide and went back that weekend to take her on a date. She'd already eaten but agreed to take a walk with me instead. We talked for hours.." Harry drifted off, thinking of time spent with the woman he loved.

"That sounds wonderful, Harry. I'm really happy for you, my friend," Paul said. He felt the breeze turn colder as the sun dipped below the horizon. He hoped Harry would be ready to go below deck soon. He'd had enough of the ocean spray in his face.

"That's not all!" Harry was on a roll now, and Paul didn't have the heart to cut him off.

"I wanted to take her out the next weekend, too, but I hadn't been quite as lucky. I was dead broke. But I couldn't stand her up, so I took her out again and just hoped maybe we'd go for a walk. But Edith had other plans. She purposely hadn't eaten so she could join me for dinner!" Harry's eyes went wide, and he slapped the rail. Paul chuckled.

"So what happened?"

"I fell even more in love with her, watching her polish off two whole dinners by herself. I had nearly forgotten that I had no money until the bill came. Edith, ever so polite, insisted she pay her own way since I had told her I wasn't hungry and had only ordered a soda. Normally, I'd never have allowed it but I was so relieved that night. I had been sweating bullets!"

Paul and Harry laughed, their joyous sound swallowed up by the vast open sea. They stood quietly for a few moments longer until Paul felt he couldn't stand it anymore.

"It's a bit nerve-racking out here, isn't it." He'd never been away from land before. Hell, he'd never been away from the farm for this long before and it made him uneasy. He wasn't sure if it was seasickness or homesickness that was hitting him or maybe both all at once. *Reality had to hit sometime*, he thought. He closed his eyes.

"I think I need to lay down for a bit." He hoped that closing his eyes below deck, where he couldn't see the ocean for miles in every direction, might make the fear dissipate. *I'm just tired*, he thought. *Just a normal reaction to stress. Just need to get some sleep.*

They found the stairway down to their bunks. He counted each step on the ladder and kept counting until his feet had brought him to his cot. Stacked three high, he laid down in the middle bunk while Harry climbed to the top. He followed the steady rhythm of his breathing and continued counting. *In one, two, three, four, out four, three, two, one.* He tried to ignore the sounds around him - the drone of the engines, the banter of the GIs not far from where he lay.

He shifted in his cot, more uncomfortable than the ones on the train to New York. Their quarters below deck were cramped and dark. There was very little light, and a dank smell permeated the air. Paul thought it smelled something between stale urine and salty snails, worsening his already sour stomach.

"Hey, Paul?" Harry whispered down from the top bunk.

"Yeah?"

"Thanks for listening." His voice was barely audible above the din of the ship.

"Don't mention it, pal." Paul reached up and slapped his hand against the side of the bunk.

Thanksgiving in the middle of the ocean was an experience Paul hoped not to have more than once in his life. It was bad enough being away from home on his favorite holiday, but the storm that rolled through made matters even worse. He spent most of the morning with thoughts of holidays past, traditions his mom and dad had always upheld, even as he and his siblings had grown up and gone their separate ways. If the stench of thousands of men trapped in a poorly ventilated vessel hadn't been so overpowering, he might've even been able to conjure up the smells of the feast being prepared in the kitchen of his childhood home. He pictured Evie, sitting at the table with little Danny fidgeting on her knee, breaking apart the bread for stuffing while his mom busied herself chopping onions and carrots, Pop at the sink dressing the turkey. He smiled, hoping they were having a more enjoyable holiday than he was.

Dinner on the ship was taken in shifts, the best they could do under tight quarters. But when it came time for Paul to take part in the Thanksgiving spread, his stomach was already lurching with seasickness thanks to the choppy water and stormy winds. Add to that being trapped below deck due to the bad weather, and his stomach protested at the mere thought of food. His good manners insisted he partake in the celebration, and so he attempted a plate of turkey and what he hoped was stuffing. He had nearly finished his plate when he saw Harry running for the ladder, and his own stomach began to grumble. Paul followed Harry's lead and rushed up the steps to the top deck, which was closer than any toilet. He passed several men running for the head or in the most dire cases, grabbing their steel helmets.

Colonel Rumberg stood on deck, looking over the rail when

Paul approached, tinged with green. He looked over at Paul and grimaced.

"Don't puke into the wind like those poor saps." He nodded to a couple of GIs at the rail, wiping their faces with handkerchiefs. All Paul could do was nod and hope for the best. He didn't have much choice in the matter - his stomach rolled again. He succumbed to the seasickness that had been plaguing him for most of the day. When he was fairly certain he'd emptied his stomach, he turned around and slumped against the railing, the wind cold on his clammy forehead.

Colonel Rumberg lit a cigarette and smirked. "Happy Thanksgiving," he said.

Paul groaned, "Yeah, Happy Thanksgiving, Colonel."

Chapter 15

ANNA
DECEMBER 1944
LONDON, ENGLAND

A month had passed since they'd first arrived in England. Anna was adjusting to the busy schedule - awake before the sun, uniforms on, out the door to the hospital for long days, and with any luck, back home before dark. Unless she was working the evening shift, Anna preferred to go straight home to Mr. Perkins's. While many other girls enjoyed nights out, Anna was still too nervous to take any chances. She was here to do her job, and she'd do it well. Gretchen liked to tease her about being so uptight, but she wasn't ready to loosen up. She wasn't sure she'd ever be ready.

From inside the hospital, Anna heard the distant siren, warning of buzz bombs, a sound that still gave her the chills. It took everything in her to continue on in her duties, checking her patients, not freezing in fear. She figured she'd get used to it eventually, so she kept a smile on her face for those boys stuck in bed and never showed a sign of what was really going through her head.

She checked the time on the clock above the door.

"One last patient coming in before shift change," Captain Campbell called out. Anna looked to see a soldier being rushed in, anguish on his face. She ran over, ready to assist.

"Hey there, soldier," she said, smiling brightly, looking into his eyes. He looked up at her with puppy dog eyes filled with fear and pain. "Don't worry about a thing. You're in good hands. We'll get you feeling top-notch in no time."

He closed his eyes then, and Anna touched his cheek. "Not time to sleep yet, my friend. Stay right here with us."

She worked quickly as he went in and out of consciousness, flinching when she removed the gauze that had been applied in the field. Another nurse brought her a basin of water and a cloth, and Anna cleaned the wound. It was deep, with tissue and bone exposed. She knew the doctor would likely need to operate, but because they were so short-handed, she'd clean the wound and keep the young man comfortable until he could be seen.

A scream rose up out of the soldier when Anna dabbed the open wound. She'd gotten used to the screaming and cursing and didn't flinch anymore. Captain Campbell draped a cold cloth on his forehead. "This is the worst part," she said, watching Anna as she worked.

The soldier in the bed next door offered his hand to the young man to hold onto. "Trust me, I know, it's no picnic," he said, nodding down at his foot, wrapped in a fresh white bandage.

Anna continued cleaning, pulling out the metal fragments she could easily reach. She pulled back a layer of skin that would likely need to be removed and nearly gagged at the maggots wriggling underneath. She kept her composure, looking up at Captain Campbell, who nodded, giving her the go-ahead to continue cleaning the wound. She took a deep breath and dug deeper, pulling the white, grub-like larva out. Her face scrunched up in concentration, and she was glad to have Captain Campbell staying late to assist in keeping the poor boy as still as possible while he writhed on the bed.

"How are we doing down there, Lieutenant Mitchell?" Captain Campbell was refreshing the towel she had lain across the soldier's forehead. His screams were beginning to subside as he slipped in and out.

"Almost done, I believe, Captain. Just checking to make sure I didn't miss any of those little suckers."

The soldier lifted his head in alarm. "What little suckers?"

"Lay back, soldier, you're doing just fine," she said, a smile plastered to her face. Hoping to ease his worry, she began to make small talk. "Where are you from?"

He looked like he didn't believe her and wanted to keep looking at what she was doing, but he leaned back, too spent to keep his head up any longer. He closed his eyes, and Anna thought he might not answer. *He knows the game,* Anna thought.

"New York," he finally answered.

"Ah, a city boy, huh?"

"No, actually. It ain't all New York City, ya know." She was glad to have gotten him talking, taking his mind off of what she was doing to his leg. She continued as gently as she could, debriding his wound as quickly as her hands would let her.

"Is that so?" she replied.

"Yeah, I grew up on a farm upstate. Never even been to the big city until it came time to ship out. I was just as struck by the Statue of Liberty as the guy next to me."

Anna smiled. How alike they all were, in the end. Each one of them had come here, voluntary or not, and watched the land they called home disappear in the distance. They had seen more in the last month than they ever thought they'd see in their lifetimes. She prayed she could hold onto hope without the bitterness of war taking hold and squeezing the life out of her like she'd already seen in so many of the people she encountered.

When she was satisfied with her work, she began to loosely bandage him, knowing the doctor would need to remove any dressing she applied. Enough to keep it clean and covered and to keep him from seeing the depth of his own wound. She said a silent prayer that he'd keep his leg as she wrapped the gauze around it. She pulled out the bottle of penicillin she carried in her front pocket and measured out the dose. She hoped this 'miracle drug' would be the miracle this young man needed to get him back on his feet.

"Alright, my friend, you're all set for now. Time to rest until the doctor can see you." She smiled down at him. "The Red Cross girls should be around soon if you're up for a donut or a coffee, though you might want to stick with your water for now," she suggested, pulling the little white cup closer to him.

"Thank you, nurse," he said.

Anna laughed. "I appreciate the thanks after what I just did," she said.

Gretchen and Eleanor were waiting for her outside the hospital when she walked out into the cool evening air. She'd passed

Louise on her way in for the night shift, and the two nurses shared a quick hug as they went in opposite directions. They'd been like ships passing in the night lately, barely able to catch up with one another. Even when they were on the same shift, they were so busy running from one patient to the next that they'd hardly mutter two words before falling into bed at the end of the day.

"I figured you'd have gone on home by now," Anna said when she reached the cobbled walk.

"We thought we'd all walk home together," Eleanor said. "It wasn't too bad when we first came out."

"Sorry I ran late. One more came in just before I left. Captain Campbell let me take the lead, so I couldn't say no."

It was a mild day for December, though the chill in the air felt like snow would be coming. Anna buttoned her coat higher on her neck and pulled on her gloves as they started down the road toward home.

Home, she thought. How funny it was that she thought of it as home. She supposed it was a good thing - having a place she felt safe in was a luxury she hadn't expected.

Eleanor blew out a breath. "I wonder if we'll ever see the sun while we're here."

"Mm. I suppose I've gotten used to the gray," said Anna, "but it would be nice to have a bit of cheer before it snows."

They rounded the bend and started uphill toward Mr. Perkins's house. Anna was glad for the walk home. Her feet were sore and aching, and the air was cold on her face. Still she welcomed the fresh air after being cooped up in the hospital, where the smells only varied between rotting flesh and antiseptic. She loved the work and the soldiers she cared for, but some days, she began to feel like a caged animal by the time her shift was over.

Gretchen stopped suddenly, digging around in her bag. Anna and Eleanor turned back and waited for her to catch up.

"What are you looking for now? You don't need to reapply your lipstick, Gretch, we're going home to bed." Eleanor bounced on her toes, cold and impatient.

Gretchen waved her off. "No, no. It's not my lipstick. You reminded me - all this talk about the gloomy weather. I found this flier this morning. Where is it…" She continued to scrounge through her belongings.

"What on earth do you keep in there, anyway?" Eleanor, forever practical, couldn't understand the need for a purse when their uniforms had perfectly good pockets.

"Just shush! Ah! Here it is." Gretchen pulled out a crumpled paper and cleared her throat for emphasis.

'The boys of Company I are at it again.
They're reeling and rocking and filled with vim.'

Eleanor rolled her eyes. Gretchen continued, undeterred.

'They're giving a party to celebrate, and would like to have you for a date.'

Gretchen waggled her eyebrows, and Anna laughed. She had a feeling she would not like where Gretchen was heading with this. So far, she hadn't ventured many places outside of the house and the hospital, and she had no real interest in going anywhere else. Though most of her fellow nurses and doctors and many of the local girls she'd met seemed perfectly comfortable going about their lives, going to dinner, dancing, taking the train to London, Anna wasn't ready. The sirens warning them of buzz bombs still made her jump, and she'd much rather not be in an unfamiliar place when she had to go running for safety. She was happy to stay at Mr. Perkins's house, sitting out in the garden on the days that weren't too cold or chatting with him in the kitchen while he cooked dinner.

Gretchen kept reading as Eleanor and Anna eyed one another and started walking again.

'So put on your party clothes and come on down and we'll show you how to go to town.'

Neither Anna nor Eleanor said anything when Gretchen had finished reading. They reached the back of the house and entered through the kitchen, the smell of cooked onions making Anna's mouth water. She realized she hadn't eaten since breakfast that morning.

"Hellooo, don't you get it? You're talking about needing some cheer. Well, here it is." Gretchen waved the flier in their faces.

"Gretch, I was talking about the sun. You know, a little sunshine would be nice. The sun would cheer us up a bit," said Anna.

Eleanor nodded her agreement. "Right. I'm not going to some GI party."

"Oh, come on," pleaded Gretchen. "This is exactly what we need. We've been here a month already. We need a night out. Plus, we'll be surrounded by well-trained soldiers, no safer place than that." She winked at Anna.

"Please," snorted Eleanor, "what does that have to do with anything? I'm still not going."

"We need to meet people here. We're going to be here for God knows how long. You can't go on like this. It's not healthy." She stuck her bottom lip out in a pout.

Anna laughed at her attempts to convince them they needed this party.

"When is it anyway? We're probably working that night," said Anna.

Gretchen smirked. "As it happens, it's tomorrow night." Her smirk turned into a full-blown grin, and Anna groaned. Gretchen knew they were all off tomorrow night. Even Louise, who'd been pulling all-nighters, would finally have a night off. Captain Campbell had arranged for them to have an evening together, a rarity before things got even busier, she had said. They'd planned to find a quiet place to go out for dinner to celebrate having survived one month overseas.

"What better way to celebrate?" Gretchen said. "I won't take no for an answer." She put her hands on her hips as if they'd be intimidated into agreeing. Eleanor stuck her tongue out at her.

"I bet the boys of Company I will love that sass," Gretchen teased. Anna couldn't help but laugh when Eleanor popped her tongue back in her mouth and scowled.

"I am not here to impress any boys," Eleanor said and marched off through the house, stomping up the stairs.

"But what if they're men?" Gretchen called after her.

Mr. Perkins rounded the corner and joined the two girls in the kitchen.

"What's got her in a twist?"

Gretchen chuckled. "She doesn't want to attend a party we've been invited to," she said, handing him the flier.

He perused the paper, laughter in his eyes. "Well, they sure are a clever bunch, aren't they?"

"Sounds like fun to me," Gretchen replied.

Hoping to avoid more of this conversation, Anna walked over to the stove to investigate the pot simmering on the back burner.

"Smells delicious." It seemed to Anna that their being there had been good for Mr. Perkins, too. When they'd first arrived, there was barely any food to scrape together, not that she'd expected to be fed. They got meals at the Officer's club or at the hospital, but now, Mr. Perkins was cooking nearly every meal for them and took great pleasure in having them break bread with him whenever they could.

"Ah, thank you. It's not much, just a simple stew, but it warms the soul on a rainy day like today."

He stirred the soup, and Anna turned around, coming face to face with Gretchen, her hands still firmly on her hips.

Anna's eyebrows shot up. "What?" She feigned innocence, but her friend saw right through her.

"Don't think you can change the subject, AB," Gretchen said. "You haven't said one word about tomorrow night."

Anna hesitated. She couldn't come up with a single excuse as to why she couldn't attend.

"Gretch…you know…we've been so slammed at the hospital…I just thought I'd use the day off to actually rest."

"We can rest when we're dead, AB. We deserve to have some fun."

Mr. Perkins snickered from his spot at the stove.

Part of her, the part that had led her here in the first place, the adventurous spirit that she'd tried to tamp down, told her that Gretchen was right. But the practical side, the side that had been awoken to the destruction of war - the sirens and buzz bombs and wounded men pouring in through the hospital - that side of her wanted to crawl under the covers and hide from the world every chance she got.

The two stood there, staring at one another. Anna wouldn't have called it a standoff exactly, but she didn't want to back down, either. It was easy for Eleanor to just say no and storm off, all broody and glass half empty. For Anna, though, the people pleaser in her hated to let anyone down, even if it came at the cost of sacrificing herself. She supposed it was one of the things that made her a great nurse and a pretty good friend. But it was also what drained her and made her want to stay in bed in the first place.

Gretchen turned to Mr. Perkins. "What do you think? Shouldn't she go? As hard as Anna works, she deserves a break, right, Mr. Perkins?" Anna rolled her eyes at Gretchen's change in tactic, but Mr. Perkins couldn't be so easily coerced into their argument.

"Oh, no, no, no," he said, holding his hands up in surrender. "I know better than to get in the middle of an argument between two women." He smiled. "Don't forget, I had a house full of them once." Gretchen's expression softened when he brought up his family, and the three of them stood in awkward silence.

"Dinner will be ready in about ten minutes if you're hungry," he finally said as he backed out of the kitchen. "I'll just go see if Eleanor would like to join us." He disappeared down the hall to the upstairs.

Gretchen was not ready to give up on Anna yet. "AB. Even Louise is going. And you know how dog tired she'll be after running the midnights all week."

Anna walked over to the little wooden table and draped her coat on the back of a chair before dropping down into it. Her feet had had enough standing for one day. She sighed, exhaustion settling over her.

"Gretchen, I'm just not ready," she admitted.

Gretchen pulled out the mismatched chair across from her, the legs scraping loudly on the tiled floor.

"I know, AB," she said, understanding in her eyes. She grabbed Anna's hand. "But you'll never be ready, let's be honest." She pinned Anna with a look that said *just try to deny it*, and Anna laughed. Gretchen was determined. She really wanted to go to this party.

"Seriously, Anna. What's to worry about, anyway? It's just a little bit of fun. I'll die of boredom if we don't go."

There was the Gretchen Anna knew and loved. "So dramatic," Anna teased. "You know, that's exactly what I *am* worried about." Gretchen arched a brow. "I don't think your idea of fun is the same as mine," Anna said.

Gretchen gave her a sly smile. "Oh, please, darling, I'm not that bad," she said, playing up an absurd drawl.

Mr. Perkins and Eleanor walked into the kitchen then, Eleanor joining them at the table while Mr. Perkins went about getting bowls and spoons, pretending not to listen to the girls chatter.

An idea popped into Anna's head, and she snapped her fingers.

"I'll go," she started, and Gretchen beamed with excitement. "If Eleanor goes," Anna finished. Gretchen's excitement turned to disappointment, like the air being let out of a balloon.

Eleanor made a face and crossed her arms like a giant X. "No way," she said, "Absolutely not."

"Oh come on, Elle," Gretchen pleaded. "Let your hair down for once."

Eleanor flipped her short hair. "It's already down, thank you very much."

Gretchen rolled her eyes and whined, "Come on girls, why are you making this so difficult?"

The girls stood to help Mr. Perkins carry their bowls to the table. The room was quiet as they savored the stew he had made.

Gretchen wiped her mouth with her napkin. "Alright," she said, a slow smile spreading across her face. Anna should have known she wouldn't give up that easily. "I've got a deal for you."

Eleanor, her mouth full, motioned for her to go on.

"You both go to the party. If you don't have a good time, I'll do your washing for a week."

Gretchen looked back and forth between the two. Anna looked at Eleanor. Her fate for tomorrow night now lay in Eleanor's hands. From the look on her friend's face, she had a feeling she'd not be getting the quiet night she'd hoped for.

Eleanor sat, chewing her potatoes and thinking about Gretchen's offer. She really did hate doing the washing; that was no secret. Gretchen was using that weakness to her advantage, but both girls were too stubborn to back down.

She looked over at Anna. "Sorry, Anna," Eleanor began. Gretchen clapped her hands together. "This should be easy," she said to Gretchen. "One miserable night out and not having to do laundry for a week. Thanks in advance, Gretch." Eleanor smiled like she'd already won, and Mr. Perkins threw his head back and laughed, enjoying the banter between the women.

"Don't be so sure, Elle," Gretchen said. "Those Company I boys are *filled with vim,*" she crooned, tossing the flier in Eleanor's direction. "Anything more than a polite smile and the deal is off." She raised her eyebrows and waited for Eleanor to agree.

"When have you ever known me to smile politely?" Eleanor shot back.

Chapter 16

Gretchen squealed. "This is going to be so much fun!"

They were gathered in their little upstairs bedroom. Louise was curled up in bed, catching up from her midnight shift the night before. Anna sat against her pillow, writing a letter home, feigning deep concentration to avoid being tortured by Gretchen. Eleanor was getting the brunt of it, being held hostage 'in the name of beauty,' as Gretchen called it. She'd been plucked and dabbed, and her hair had been set in curlers, after which Gretchen had reapplied even more powder.

Powder puffed up out of Gretchen's compact, and Eleanor sneezed. "Really, Gretchen, I didn't agree to all *this*." She waved her hand from her head to her feet. Gretchen ignored her and pulled a red lipstick out of her never-ending bag of cosmetics. Eleanor covered her mouth with one hand and jumped off the trunk she'd been sitting on.

"No, absolutely not. I draw the line at red lipstick."

Gretchen tried to come closer, but Eleanor evaded her once more. Anna risked a glance. She was struck by Eleanor's beauty. She had to hand it to Gretchen; she knew what she was doing with a makeup brush.

"You look stunning, Eleanor," Anna said, standing to admire her friend.

Eleanor blushed and sidestepped Anna's compliment. "Yeah, yeah, lipstick on a pig and all that," she said, obviously uncomfortable with the attention. Anna knew she'd hate having all eyes on her, but she wanted her friend to know how incredible she looked.

"I'm serious, Elle, you're gorgeous." Anna squeezed her hand while Gretchen watched with pride.

"She's right, you know. You don't even need the makeup. Pinning your hair back out of your face was enough, but I knew you'd never let me doll you up again, so I had to make the most of it!"

Eleanor scowled. Anna seized the opportunity to tiptoe back to her bed. She was too late. Gretchen took hold of her arm and spun her around.

"Not so fast. You're next."

She directed Anna to the trunk to sit. Anna groaned. She'd never been one to get herself dolled up to go out, nor did she want to sit and be stared at so intimately, even if Gretchen had become one of her closest friends. She appreciated beautiful clothes as much as the next girl, but she'd never taken an interest in makeup or glamor. She tamed her frizzy strawberry blond curls to the best of her ability, and beyond that, she couldn't be bothered.

"You know, this is the perfect way to make sure Eleanor and I don't have an ounce of fun tonight."

Gretchen looked at her, not understanding.

"Dress us up and make us feel even more uncomfortable than we already do." Anna winked at Eleanor, smiling in agreement. Gretchen hesitated for a moment, curlers in hand, then shrugged and continued on. In minutes, Anna had a head full of curlers sticking out every which way. Gretchen had bobby pins stuck between her lips and a look of deep concentration that made Anna fearful of what she was doing.

Eleanor nodded to the half finished letter on Anna's bed. "Anything from your mom?"

Anna shook her head. She'd told her friends a little bit about her mother and how awful things had gotten before she left.

"She sounds like a snob to me," Gretchen said, pulling the pins out of her mouth.

Eleanor elbowed her. "Gretchen, you can't say that about someone's mother."

"Why not? It's the truth. I'd say it about my own mother if it were true."

Anna opened her mouth to defend her mother - *why is that my first reaction?* - then closed it again. She thought about it for a moment. *Is my mother a snob?* They weren't wealthy by any means, just your run-of-the-mill working class family. But she supposed money wasn't the only thing behind being a snob. Her shoulders slumped forward, and Gretchen pulled on her hair, making her sit up straight again.

"It's ok, Gretch. I think you might be right. I just don't know what to do about it."

"There's nothing you can do, Anna," Eleanor said. "Besides not letting her get to you."

Anna nodded. "Easier said than done," she said. "I just for once hoped she'd tell me she was proud of me," she admitted. She tried to touch her hair, and Gretchen swatted her hand away.

"Oh well," she shrugged, "I've got you girls now."

"And we're proud enough," Gretchen said.

"You're damn right," said Eleanor.

They were quiet for a while. Gretchen focused on Anna's hair, Eleanor trying not to muss hers.

"It seems silly, doesn't it?" Anna said, breaking the silence.

"What does?" Eleanor tilted her head, looking at Anna.

"I don't know," Anna sighed, "Such a silly reason to argue - over a stupid garden. Every time I think about it, it sounds even more ridiculous. I'm angry at her because she loves her plants, and she's angry at me for *not* loving them." She nearly pulled out the pins digging into her scalp out of frustration.

"Leave the hair alone," Gretchen said, swatting Anna's hand again.

"Listen, people have argued over less," Eleanor said.

Anna snorted. "Like what?" She loved her friends for trying to make her feel better, and she knew she was being difficult, but thinking about her mother and the damage that had been done had put her in a foul mood.

"Peanut butter and jelly," Eleanor said, laying back on her bed and staring up at the ceiling.

"Peanut butter and jelly?" Anna repeated.

"Yep. How do you make a peanut butter and jelly sandwich?"

"How many ways could there be? Two pieces of bread, peanut butter on one, jelly on the other, put 'em together, presto," Gretchen said.

Eleanor sat up, touching the back of her hair, which had flattened out from lying on it. "Well, that's where you'd be wrong then. My folks have argued for years over the right way to make a peanut butter and jelly sandwich."

"What's the other way?" Anna was curious now.

"Peanut butter first, jelly on top, then the bread."

"What?" Gretchen laughed.

"How can jelly go on top of peanut butter? It'd slide all over the place," Anna said.

Eleanor shrugged. "Tell that to my Pops. There are some things you just can't change in a person. It's sandwiches for my dad and gardens for your mom. And I'm sure each of us has something we're stubborn about, too."

"So wise," Gretchen teased.

Anna mulled this over while Gretchen finished curling her hair. She blew out a breath, tracing circles around the rivets on the trunk while she waited. Maybe Eleanor was right - it didn't have to be so black and white. Maybe she could bridge the gap with her mother in spite of their differences.

<hr />

"I can't believe I agreed to this," complained Eleanor, yanking at her skirt.

Gretchen bounced ahead, her copper hair shining in the glow of the setting sun.

Anna hung back with Eleanor. "I could be curled up on Mr. Perkins's couch with a cup of tea and a book off one of his shelves right now," she sighed.

Louise elbowed her. "Oh, come on, not you, too.".

Anna shrugged. "I didn't enlist for the parties."

Gretchen scoffed and turned back around. "None of us did, honey. But why not take advantage of it while you can?" She waggled her eyebrows and linked arms with Louise, dragging her further ahead.

They could hear the band from out on the sidewalk, and Anna blew out a breath.

Captain Campbell breezed past. "Coming in, ladies?" She held out the door for the two women.

"I guess it's now or never," Anna said.

"I'd prefer never," Eleanor grumbled.

Captain Campbell chuckled and headed for a table to their right, where several women were already seated with their heads together, chatting and laughing.

Eleanor and Anna stayed near the entrance, taking it all in. Gretchen and Louise disappeared into the crowd, looking for a willing dance partner. They stayed there until the door opened behind them, and a group of nurses edged their way in, forcing the two women further into the hall. Tables and chairs lined the perimeter, a large dance floor taking up most of the room in between.

Eleanor took hold of Anna's hand and guided her to an empty spot against the back wall. "Maybe no one will notice us back here," she said.

Anna laughed. "I don't know that I can stand here all night in these shoes," she replied, lifting a leg to show off her heels. She put her foot back down and looked up, making eye contact with a soldier across the room.

"Well, we'll grab a table back here when one opens up. More people are bound to move to the dance floor soon."

"Unless they're like us," Anna said, tearing her gaze from the soldier who was still staring.

"If they were like us, they wouldn't even be here," Eleanor replied.

The only reason they'd gotten stuck coming was because of their silly bet with Gretchen, which Anna wholly regretted now. It wasn't worth the painful shoes or the discomfort she felt standing in a room full of men and women trying to drown their feelings away. As if the world outside would fall away. The war didn't stop just because a few soldiers decided to throw a party, and she had a hard time reconciling the two.

She felt the beat of the music vibrate through her chest and trained her eyes on the band, avoiding any more eye contact with the soldier across the room, though she could feel him watching her. She had to admit, they were good. She tapped her foot despite herself.

Gretchen and Louise wound their way through the crowd, carrying two drinks each. Anna waved to them and started in their direction.

"Figured I'd get you two started with something to drink," Gretchen said, handing one to Anna.

"Actually, her exact words were 'let's get them loosened up,'" Louise laughed. She handed her extra drink to Eleanor.

"Please," Eleanor snorted, "It's not loosening up we need."

"Well then, what is it?" Gretchen challenged. "I think you need to relax and have a good time."

"I think we have plenty of fun," Anna said, coming to Eleanor's defense.

A table opened up, and she led the way, each step in time to the music. She looked over at the dance floor, happy couples and small groups of friends spinning merrily about. It would be so easy to let herself get lost in the night instead of holding back. She'd gotten so used to making herself small, to staying focused on doing the next right thing, she worried that any distraction, even for an evening, could change the direction of her already uncertain future.

She sat beside Eleanor and looked up, letting her gaze wander again to the soldier on the other side of the room. He was tall, with sandy blonde hair trimmed short, the scruff of a five o'clock shadow further accentuating a strong jaw. He gave her a small smile, and she felt butterflies kick up in the pit of her stomach. She looked away again, tapping her fingers against the side of her glass, pretending she wasn't affected by him.

"Well, girls, I can't sit here all night," Gretchen complained. "I'm off to mingle." She stood at the edge of the dance floor and looked back at their table, blowing them a kiss before making her rounds. Anna laughed. She admired her brazen friend.

Eleanor nudged her shoulder. "Zip it," she said, which made Anna laugh harder. Eleanor rolled her eyes. "Fat chance we'll win this bet if you can't wipe that smile off your face." She crossed her arms over her chest and slouched back in her chair, her mask of unapproachable aloofness plastered on her face.

"Sorry, Elle," Anna said, pursing her lips to keep from laughing.

Eleanor glared at her. "Very funny," she said.

"What?" Anna feigned innocence, knowing full well Eleanor hated the nickname.

"You're doing my washing if we lose the bet, that's what." Eleanor cracked a small smile at the idea.

"You know what, that's a deal," Anna said, watching her friend's eyebrows shoot up in surprise. "It's too much pressure. You know I laugh when I'm nervous."

She sipped her drink, tapping her foot to the music. She would never tell Gretchen, but the longer she sat there, the more she began to enjoy herself. The happiness in the hall was contagious. *Maybe it's not a matter of one or the other*, she thought. She'd felt as though she couldn't possibly enjoy herself because of the war going on right outside. But what if that wasn't right, either? She wondered - what if it was a beautiful thing that they could gather together to find some semblance of joy *despite* the war going on. What if she didn't have to feel like such a martyr because of what she saw in the hospital and in the field? Couldn't she feel a profound happiness regardless of where she was? She was lost in thought, thinking about the answers to the philosophical questions running through her head, when the soldier she'd been watching stepped into her line of sight. He cleared his throat at the same time that Eleanor elbowed her.

She looked up, startled, and noticed the flecks of green in his eyes before anything else. He smiled at her, and she willed her cheeks not to flame red. But between the warmth of the hall, the drink she'd had, and the handsome man looking down at her, she was sure she looked nothing short of a ripe tomato.

"You have the greenest eyes," she blurted out, closing her eyes in embarrassment. She felt Eleanor chuckle and looked down at her feet, wondering if she could climb under the table. When she looked back up, his eyes were still pinned to her, amusement on his face.

"Are these seats taken?" He ignored her obvious embarrassment and gestured to the two empty chairs across from them. She shook her head, afraid to open her mouth for fear of what else might tumble out. Eleanor scowled beside her and kept her arms firmly crossed around her waist. Anna noticed she hadn't so much as sipped her drink and thought maybe Gretchen was right. Maybe they did need help loosening up a bit.

She glanced over at the soldier across from her, and he stuck out his hand.

"I'm Paul," he said. "And this is my pal Harry." He pointed to the red-haired soldier next to him, who gave her a half-hearted wave and looked back down into his glass. *He looks nearly as miserable as Eleanor,* she thought.

She took Paul's hand in hers, his warmth radiating up her fingers. She couldn't say it was an electrical jolt or even a fairytale spark, but there was something to be said of the comfort she felt when his large hand encompassed her small one.

"Anna," she replied. Eleanor nudged her. "Oh, and this is Eleanor. She'd rather not be here," she added.

Eleanor rolled her eyes. "Really, Anna?"

She grimaced. "Sorry," she whispered.

A hint of a laugh played on Paul's face. "Is that so? She hides it very well," he said. "Almost as well as Harry here."

Anna pursed her lips. They sat in awkward silence for a few moments more until Paul stretched his hand across the table again. "Would you like to dance?"

She hesitated, glancing at Eleanor, torn between letting go and leaving her friend alone. She looked up at him, and his smile faltered for a moment before he recovered and asked again.

"Just one dance? I promise your friend will be just fine here with Harry - he's happily married and just as miserable to be here." He grinned, and Anna covered her mouth, hiding the laughter that threatened.

She lifted her hand from her lap, still contemplating what to do. She was waiting for Eleanor's approval before she accepted his hand, but before she could get her friend to look at her, Paul closed the gap between them and drew her hand into his. Eleanor finally looked at Anna, and she shrugged, half an apology and half nervous anticipation, as Paul led her onto the dance floor.

A slower melody began to float over them, and he wrapped his arm loosely around her waist.

"I swear I didn't plan this," he said, nodding toward the band.

She smiled and bit her lip, letting him take the lead across the floor. He surprised her with his graceful movement and she looked down at their feet between them, hoping she wouldn't step on his toes. He tipped her chin back up with his finger.

"So, where are you from, Anna with the blue eyes?" She felt her face flush, but she was determined not to feel foolish. She straightened her back and looked him in the eye.

"Actually, I have to be honest with you, Paul," she started. "You seem like a very nice man." She watched uncertainty fill his face before she continued. "It's just that I'm supposed to be helping my friend win a bet tonight, and then you came along and…" she trailed off.

Paul chuckled. "You say that like it's a bad thing."

When she didn't answer, he urged her to continue. "What kind of a bet are we talking about?"

She smiled. "Our friend Gretchen," she pointed to the woman making her way around a table full of GIs, "made a deal that if we had a terrible time tonight, she'd do our washing for a week."

Paul laughed and spun her around the dance floor. "I appreciate your honesty," he said, then grinned. "And I'm sorry you'll have to lose that bet tonight."

Anna's eyes widened. "Excuse me?"

"Well, I may be overstepping here, but I know I'm not having a terrible time tonight." He paused, searching her face. "And I don't think you are either."

She looked up at him, keeping her eyes on his. She wondered what it was that had brought them together and if she'd ever see him again after tonight. "You're right," she agreed. "I'm not."

~

"Don't you look like the cat who ate the canary," Louise said, laughing at Gretchen.

Gretchen danced a little circle around Eleanor. "Seems to me the two of you," she pointed from Eleanor to Anna, "had quite an interesting evening."

Eleanor scoffed. "Seems to me you couldn't keep your hands off any man willing to dance."

Anna stayed quiet. She'd give herself away if Gretchen turned the interrogation her way. The truth was, she *had* enjoyed herself. She looked down at the ground, wet from the misty, cool night, and smiled at the memory. For the first time since they'd arrived in England, she'd felt relaxed and was happily exhausted as they neared the station.

Captain Campbell had left with them, escorting them home, and she led the way toward the steps leading underground just as the sirens started. Anna cringed. *So much for getting through a night out,* she thought. She'd almost let herself forget they were in the middle of a war, with thoughts of Paul spinning her around the dance floor clouding her vision.

People on the street started running to the station entrance, seeking shelter from the impending buzz bombs. They began to run too, Anna struggling to keep pace in the heels she rarely wore.

"Come on ladies, let's get in before it gets too crowded," Captain Campbell called over her shoulder. Worry and dread filled Anna. *This is what I get,* she thought, *this is what I get for playing pretend tonight.* She was upset and distracted when the heel of her shoe caught on the uneven stones. She didn't see the pothole until it was too late, and she stepped into it, her ankle giving out and sending her tumbling forward. She felt her ankle twist, and then she was in slow motion, her hands stretching out in front of her, not soon enough to keep her from falling to the ground. Gretchen and Louise collided with one another as they skidded to a halt beside her. Anna looked down at her ankle. The heel of her shoe had broken and was hanging off to one side.

"Anna! Are you okay?" Gretchen bent down to help her up, and Louise got on her other side.

Anna struggled to stand, her ankle throbbing with pain. She squeezed her eyes shut as her friends tried to get her to her feet. With pain ripping through it, she knew her ankle would be too swollen for its shoe in a matter of minutes.

"I twisted my ankle. Darnit!" She sat back down on the ground. "I can't put weight on it."

Captain Campbell and Eleanor, realizing they had been separated from the group, turned around and raced back. The wail of the siren punctuated Captain Campbell's every word.

"Ok, ladies, let's get her up. We need to get to safety, now."

Louise and Gretchen got on one side, Captain Campbell and Eleanor taking the other. The four women easily hoisted Anna to her feet, and she draped her arms over Louise and Eleanor's shoulders so she could hobble toward the station.

They sat on the floor against an empty wall nearest their departing train. Gretchen carefully took Anna's foot and put it in her lap, keeping it elevated.

"Best we can do for now."

Anna nodded. She could feel her heartbeat pulsing through her ankle. *How am I going to get up for my shift in the morning?* She covered her eyes with her arm and sat back against the cold brick wall. *I wish I'd have stayed home,* she thought, but even as the thought crossed her mind, she knew it was a lie. She'd had a wonderful time with Paul. *Take this as your sign, Anna.* She shouldn't have gotten so caught up in having a good time.

"Where does it hurt?" Captain Campbell looked at Anna's ankle. It had nearly doubled in size.

"Ha," Anna said. "Do you mean where doesn't it hurt?"

Gretchen attempted to pull off her broken shoe. Anna cried out in pain.

"No! Leave the shoe on," Anna pleaded. "I won't be able to get it back on for the rest of the trip home, whenever that might be." She looked around at the crowded station, the sirens still blaring from outside.

"Honey, you can't put weight on it anyway. Don't you want to relieve that pressure?" Anna looked down at her ankle. Gretchen might be right. The swelling and the tight shoe made for a painful combination, but Anna was stubborn, and the thought of being vulnerable without her shoe on made her more upset than the throbbing inside the shoe.

She put her head in her hands. Eleanor rubbed her back. "It'll be ok, Anna. We'll get some ice on it as soon as we get back."

Gretchen nodded. "And I've already found the cutest little shoe shop. We'll get this fixed in no time."

Anna gave her friend a half-hearted smile. "I'm not really worried about the shoes, but thanks, Gretch. I'm more worried about my shift tomorrow." She looked up at Captain Campbell and panic set in.

"Well, ladies," Captain Campbell started. "I suppose this isn't the greatest time to tell you this..." She crouched down beside them. "We've received new orders and will be leaving for Cherbourg in one week."

"Oh my goodness," Anna said, rubbing her leg. "What if I'm not better before we're supposed to leave?"

"Don't even think about Cherbourg. It's a week away. We'll have you healed up by then. As for tomorrow, I'm giving you orders to stay home and keep your foot elevated." Captain Campbell hesitated. She looked at her watch and around the crowded station, then to where the train should have been departing. "Since it's already so late, I think I'll be staying the night at Mr. Perkins's. I can make sure he is well aware you are not to get up for any reason."

Anna rolled her eyes. Captain Campbell had gotten to know each of her nurses, and she knew Anna would have a hard time sitting around all day.

Louise patted her knee. "How about we take our minds off of our current situation." Anna raised her eyebrows in question. "Care to share who that nice looking soldier was twirling you around the dance floor tonight?"

Gretchen's eyes lit up, and she waggled her eyebrows. "I bet that's why your heel broke right off your shoes," she teased. "All that dancing took its toll."

Anna groaned. "I was just being polite..," she said, trailing off.

Eleanor snorted, and Anna shot her a look. It was for her that Anna had been hiding her smile all evening. Eleanor pursed her lips and went back to watching people piling into the station, looking for an empty place to sit.

"Mhm," said Gretchen. "Likely story."

Anna yawned. "I'm just in too much pain to even think about dancing," she lied, leaning her head back against the cold wall.

～〰～

Chapter 17

*T*he morning sun streamed through the enormous windows in Mr. Perkins's living room. Anna stretched out as she woke, gradually opening her eyes. She bolted upright when she realized she was not in her own bed upstairs but rather on a floral sofa that had been made up as a bed with sheets and blankets and a pillow beneath her head. She rubbed her eyes and started to stand.

"Oh, no, you don't," Mr. Perkins said at the same time that Anna put her weight on both feet. The previous night's events came flooding back to her when a jolt of pain shot through her ankle. She collapsed back onto the sofa with a groan. *I do not have time for this,* she thought. She was already aggravated, and she hadn't been awake for five minutes. *Why did I wear those stupid heels?* She stared at the ceiling and blew out an angry breath. Mr. Perkins came over to her with a cup of tea.

"Captain Campbell mentioned you might not be too thrilled to be laid up like this."

"She did, did she?" Anna softened toward the older gentleman when she looked up to see his eyes filled with concern. She shook her head.

"I should have known they'd make you babysit me all day," she said.

He chuckled. "You're lucky to have such wonderful friends," he said. "Makes being here a bit easier, I'd imagine."

She nodded her head in agreement. He was quiet for a moment, then added, "I know it's been easier for me having you girls around."

Anna looked at him, and devastation hit her like a ton of bricks. *We're leaving soon,* she thought. It was on the tip of her tongue, but she couldn't bring herself to say the words. She cleared her throat, unsure of *what* to say.

He gave her a sad smile. "Wipe that look of pity off your face," he joked.

Anna frowned. "Mr. Perkins...," she began, but he waved her off.

"I know, I know. Captain Campbell has already informed me that our days together are numbered," he said.

"She did?"

He nodded. "You're off to Cherbourg. They need you there more than this old man needs you here," he said.

Anna stayed quiet. If she were being honest with herself, she'd become dependent on Mr. Perkins. All of the comforts of home he'd provided to them had made it feel less like a war zone and more like...well...home. *But,* she thought, *my comfort comes second to the soldiers who need me.* She'd repeat it as many times as she needed to remind herself.

"I wish I could stay," Anna whispered. "I hope you don't mind, Mr. Perkins…but I've sort of come to think of you as my British grandfather."

He beamed at her. "I'm honored," he said. He looked thoughtful and then added, "Of course, that means you'll have to keep in touch…" He hesitated. "And perhaps even pay a visit to an old man when this dreaded war is over."

Anna stood and hopped on one foot over to where he was sitting in a worn easy chair by the fireplace. He tried to protest, but she shooed him away. She steadied herself with one arm on the back of the chair and wrapped the other arm around his shoulders, bending down to give him a peck on the top of his bald head. He patted her hand with his own.

"How about some breakfast?" he said.

Mr. Perkins forced Anna back to the couch to rest after she'd been hopping around the kitchen after lunch, trying to help him clean up.

"Enough, enough, you're hovering," he said and directed her to the sofa where she'd already sat too long with her own thoughts.

Louise breezed in, her cheeks flushed like she'd just been out running in the cold December air. She carried several bags in her arms, one of which she held out to Anna.

"What's this?"

Louise set her bags down and tucked her wind-blown hair behind her ears.

"I had today free, so I took your shoes to that shop Gretchen told us about."

Anna was stunned. It hadn't even been twenty-four hours, and her friend had already gotten her shoes fixed.

"Louise!" She was ready to protest with all the reasons she shouldn't have gone and done that. Instead, she looked up at her friend with her newly fixed shoes in her hand and began to cry.

"Oh, Anna," Louise said, sitting down on the edge of the sofa. "It was supposed to make you happy, not make you cry."

Anna shook her head. "I am happy," she sniffed. "I don't know what's gotten into me lately. I never cry." She wiped at her eyes and composed herself. "Thank you," she said and engulfed Louise in a giant hug.

"Well, I got to do some Christmas shopping while I waited for your shoes, so it was really a win-win."

Anna leaned back against the arm of the sofa, and Louise adjusted the pillow under her ankle, keeping her foot up high.

"How's it feeling today?"

"Not great, but I'll make do. I can't bear to lay around like this much longer," Anna said.

"Oh, good," Louise replied. "Because I got to chatting with the gal at the shoe shop. She's about our age, and her folks own the place. What a sweet family they are! When I was just about to leave, they invited me for a day of 'Christmas Cheer.'"

Anna tilted her head. "What exactly do they do on their day of cheer?"

"Marjorie said they mix up a special pudding that brings good luck. Decorate, of course, eat food, sing carols. It sounds like exactly the kind of thing we need before spending Christmas God knows where in France." Anna shuddered at the thought. God knows where was right. She could only imagine the kind of living arrangements they'd have once they were closer to the front lines.

"That sounds really nice, Louise," Anna said. She thought about it for a moment. *I wonder how we could bring some of that cheer to Mr. Perkins. Maybe he knows that pudding recipe.* She picked at a strand of loose string on the quilt that covered her legs.

"Well, then, why do you say it like you don't want to go?" Louise arched an eyebrow.

Anna looked up. "Oh! No, it's not that. It's just, I figured they'd only invited you. I mean, they haven't even met the rest of us."

Louise patted her hand. "Don't be silly. They invited all of us. If I'm going, all five of us are going."

"Five?" Anna wondered who the fifth person might be. Perhaps Louise was thinking of bringing Captain Campbell along, too.

"I couldn't very well leave Mr. Perkins at home by himself while we're out finding holiday cheer," she said.

Anna smiled and squeezed her friend's hand.

"Ugh, but what about this stupid ankle?" She didn't think she could deal with another train ride the way she felt today.

"What about it? I'll carry you if I have to." Louise smiled, and Anna laughed at the image of Louise carrying her piggy-back.

By Saturday morning, Anna was ready to pull her hair out from boredom and being cooped up in the house. She loved Mr. Perkins and everything he'd been doing to make sure she rested and let her ankle heal - 'strict orders from Captain Campbell,' he kept saying - but she was ready to get back to work. She *needed* to get back to work. She hated missing out this past week. Captain Campbell had checked in Monday morning and ordered her out of work for the rest of the week. She'd seen right through Anna's act when she couldn't help but wince in pain with every step she took.

Today, she'd been up before the sun and was eager to get back into a routine. She'd wrapped her robe tightly around her, buttoned her overcoat up to her neck, and hobbled her way down the steps to sit out in the garden. Her breath came out in little puffs in front of her face, and she was pleased with herself for having gotten out there at all.

She hadn't told her family about her injury. It was a minor setback and she'd soon forget all about it. By the time they'd get her letter, she'd probably be in Cherbourg. *Cherbourg*. Since she was a little girl she'd dreamed of seeing France. The Eiffel Tower, of course, but everything she'd read about French culture had fascinated her. She wondered what Cherbourg would look like now.

She thought about her grandfather's advice and tried not to let herself get excited. She'd heard the soldiers - those willing to talk about what they'd seen - and it had always been the same. France had become unrecognizable. Destruction had become the new norm. It was inescapable. She shivered, watching the sun peek through the bare trees, and decided to head back inside. Today was the big day - they'd be experiencing a day of British Christmas preparations. She had to admit, she was excited to learn new traditions to bring home with her.

She busied herself in the kitchen, making tea and toasting brown bread. She had no idea where Mr. Perkins continued to get such things, but she enjoyed them. She poured the hot water with visions of herself in her kitchen, pouring coffee and frying eggs for...who? She wondered. She let her imagination carry her and hummed a Christmas carol while she worked. When she'd finished getting the tea ready, she stood and looked out the window over the sink. She pictured her own backyard through the kitchen window, complete with spring flowers in full bloom, children playing in the grass, and a man chasing after a little boy toddling along. She smiled at the happy picture in her mind. She had never thought she'd be ready for the life of a wife and mother, but she didn't cringe at the idea that began to take hold. She closed her eyes, trying to feel what it would be like to be someone's wife, a child's mom. Who's wife? Who was that man chasing the children?

Paul. Her eyes shot open the moment she pictured his face. *Nonsense,* she thought. *I dance with the man one time, and my brain has us married. I really do need to get out of this house.* She spun around to see Mr. Perkins in the doorway watching her.

He smiled. "Good Morning," he said. "You're up early today. Who's Paul?" He didn't miss a beat.

Anna's eyes widened, and her eyebrows shot up into her hairline. Embarrassed, she handed him a teacup. "What are you talking about?"

He nodded his thanks. "You were looking out the window and said the name Paul." He was not going to let her out of this one. "Sounded all dreamy, if you ask me." His eyes crinkled in the corners when he smiled that mischievous smile.

"Who sounds dreamy?" Gretchen came staggering in, still bleary-eyed from sleep, and took a teacup from the counter. She looked between Anna and Mr. Perkins. Before Anna could get her mouth to connect with her brain, Mr. Perkins spoke up. "Well, Anna did. She said 'Paul' while she was staring out the window." He mimicked her voice, waggled his eyebrows, and Anna couldn't help but laugh. *Meddlesome old man,* she thought.

"Oh, really?" said Gretchen, a bit too smug for the early hour.

Louise and Eleanor trailed in and sat down at the table. Louise stifled a yawn.

"What time did you tell Marjorie we'd be at her house?" Anna ignored Gretchen's inquisitive eyes, happy to distract her friends with talk of their plans for the day, putting all thoughts of Paul and her startling picture of a future with him out of her mind.

Mr. Perkins turned out to be an animated tour guide the entire way to Marjorie's house. He was full of knowledge and history and made the cold, dreary walk from the station much more enjoyable. Anna linked arms with him, and between her pathetic hobble and his arthritis, they both tread gingerly. She wasn't sure who was holding whom as they ambled along, but she enjoyed his company and was thrilled to see him so happy.

They walked up a path, gravel crunching beneath their shoes, toward a little cottage at the edge of the woods. They were welcomed into a whir of people, alight with the spirit of Christmas. Marjorie came bustling out to greet them, kissing Louise on each cheek before introducing herself to the group.

"Come in, come in," she urged, ushering them further into the warm house. Anna breathed deeply, the smell of cinnamon and firewood filling the air around them.

"It smells incredible," Anna remarked. She unbuttoned her coat and draped it over her arm.

Marjorie smiled. "I can't wait to show you our family recipes," she said. "My mother and father insisted we welcome as many soldiers as we could this year. It's the least we could do to show our thanks for having you here. Plus," she added, "my American cousin is here. It's such a special time."

Anna stopped pulling her scarf from around her neck. "Surely you couldn't fit many more than the five of us," she said. *Relax,* she thought, *it couldn't be. There are thousands of other soldiers in town.*

Louise cleared her throat. "That's right, you did mention some other soldiers might be here tonight." She smiled innocently at Anna, an unspoken apology in her eyes.

"The more the merrier," said Gretchen, obviously pleased with this new information.

They followed Marjorie and the aroma of warm bread and sugar to the kitchen. It was much larger than Anna would have guessed from the outside. Mr. and Mrs. White were bustling about, flour and eggs and mixing bowls being passed back and forth. Mrs. White stopped to greet their newest guests.

"Merry Christmas!" Her gray hair was pulled back into a tidy bun at the nape of her neck, and the red apron tied around her waist was streaked with flour. She held a bowl and wooden spoon and never stopped mixing the sticky batter inside.

"Thank you for having us, ma'am," Louise said. "How can we help?"

Mrs. White laughed, her whole body shaking with merriment. "First, we eat and drink and be merry," she said. "Then we'll make the Christmas pudding." Her eyes glimmered in the soft light streaming through the kitchen's bay window.

Laughter rang out from another room, and Marjorie led them through the kitchen to the back of the house. It opened into a great room, warmth radiating from a wood stove roaring in the corner. Several others were already gathered around the room, enjoying the spread laid out before them. Anna noticed the Christmas tree sitting bare opposite the fireplace and thought about the tree her parents would have back home. She wondered if they'd put one up at all this year.

"Please, sit, make yourselves at home, and we'll decorate the tree as soon as Mum and Dad get things in the oven and come in to join us," said Marjorie.

Gretchen, the least shy of the group, was already on her way to interrupt a trio of soldiers seated on a sofa with their backs to them. Anna hung back, and Eleanor stayed with her. She looked back toward the kitchen and thought about checking in on Mr. Perkins. She heard his laughter loud and clear and smiled. *I guess he's just fine,* she thought.

"Anna," Eleanor started. Anna turned to look at her friend. "What's wrong, Elle?"

Eleanor rolled her eyes at the nickname. "Nothing, no, nothing's wrong. It's just, well, I thought you should know I've been seeing one of the guys from the Company I party. Well, not really seeing, so much as, just, well, writing letters."

Anna felt her mouth drop open before she could stop it. Eleanor grimaced.

"It's just, the bet is over, and it was silly anyway. Plus, Gretchen's never going to do our laundry," she said. "And I don't want to waste any more time trying to pretend I don't want someone to make me happy. I don't want to be alone forever, you know?"

They stood there together, watching the rest of the room buzzing with Christmas cheer. Anna was stunned at Eleanor's honesty but happy for her all the same.

"It means a lot to me that you'd tell me, Elle. You really didn't have to, you know."

"Oh, I know," said Eleanor. "But, I was hoping it might, I don't know, motivate you to do the same. I mean, if I can open up to someone…anyone can." She laughed at herself, but Anna knew it had taken a lot for her to confess her feelings. She just wasn't sure she was ready to do the same. She preferred her tough exterior. She'd have preferred it even more if it hadn't begun to crack.

Eleanor blew out a breath. "Okay, that's enough of that. Let's go have fun." She walked away without another word, and Anna watched her friends mingle. She propped herself up against the wall, taking the weight off of her ankle when it started to throb.

"Merry Christmas." She knew the voice that had come up behind her without having to turn around. A warmth spread through her, and she couldn't deny the happiness she felt when she turned around and came face to face with Paul. How familiar he felt even though they'd only met one other time. She didn't believe in love at first sight - *childish*, she thought. There needed to be depth there that one meeting couldn't possibly provide. How could one meeting possibly tell you everything you needed to know about someone's heart?

She made the mistake, then, of looking into his eyes. Paul smiled at her, his eyes crinkling in the corners and making her feel even weaker than she already felt with only one good foot.

She smiled back at him. "I had a feeling you'd be here," she told him honestly.

"Is that so?"

She nodded. "How'd you meet the White family?"

"Well, actually, I hadn't before today. But Jack is Marjorie's cousin. She told him to bring along any friends he'd like, and I'm lucky enough to be one of them."

"Is that so?" She repeated his question back to him. "So he's the American cousin she mentioned."

Paul chuckled. "I was hoping I might see you again. I guess you could say it was meant to be, don't you think?"

"How so?"

"Do you know how many American soldiers are in England right now? Any old Joe could've shown up here today. And any nurse, too, for that matter. Instead," he hesitated. "It's me and you."

Anna didn't respond right away. She tried to keep her feelings locked up tight. "Well, you and me and everyone else here," she said, gesturing to the room full of people.

He narrowed his eyes at her in disagreement but was undeterred. "How about we sit?" He nodded toward the sofa that Glenn and Eleanor had just stood up from. They headed toward the piano, with Eleanor looking entirely more smitten than Anna could have ever imagined. She shook her head and smiled.

Paul reached for her hand but stopped. "Is that a no? We can stand if you prefer."

"No, no, it's not that," Anna said, looking up at him. She saw uncertainty swirling in his eyes. *Do I affect him the same way he affects me?* She felt dizzy at the idea. "I'm just shocked that

Eleanor let someone knock down all those walls she's put up," she said. Then added, "And so quickly."

They sat down on the sofa and enjoyed listening to Glenn play 'Silent Night' while Eleanor sang along.

"I guess that's the nature of things here," Paul said.

"What do you mean?"

"I can't help but think that we feel things more deeply than we would have back home." He accepted two glasses from Marjorie and handed one to Anna. She sipped it, and the warmth of the steaming apple cider spread all the way from her throat to her stomach.

"Everything is heightened here," he continued. "Everything happens faster." He looked over at Glenn and Eleanor and back to Anna. "I suppose that goes for love, too."

She looked down at the glass in her hands. *You wanted depth,* she thought to herself.

She rubbed her ankle, avoiding his gaze, but just like the night of the Company I party, he was persistent.

"Tell me something about yourself, Anna."

"Hm…like what?"

"Anything at all," he said.

She laughed. "You don't give up easily, do you?"

He frowned. "Would you like me to?"

Her eyebrows shot up. "No, no…I'm sorry. I'm not really used to this kind of thing." She pointed between the two of them.

"What kind of thing is that?"

She blew out a breath. "Are you always this exasperating?"

He chuckled. "Well, if you ask my sister, yes."

"You have a sister?" Anna deflected, happy to talk about anything other than herself.

"I do. Her name is Evie. She's a couple years younger than me. She's got the cutest little boy, Danny."

She watched him light up at the mention of his nephew.

"Her husband is over here somewhere," he continued, and his brow furrowed. "Wish I could say I knew where. She moved back in with our parents after…" He stopped short and shook his head. "Look at me, chewing your ear off about my family when you were supposed to tell me more about you."

"I enjoy seeing you talk about your family. Your whole face lights up," Anna said.

Paul smiled. "They are a good bunch."

They sat quietly then, listening to the music and enjoying one another's company. Their shoulders brushed together on the small sofa, and Anna didn't mind the contact.

Jack came bursting in, struggling with a box nearly the width of the doorway. "Christmas decor," he announced. Marjorie clapped her hands and helped open the box. "Dig in, everyone," she said. "Please, help us decorate the tree."

Anna made no attempt to move. Paul nudged her shoulder. "You going to hang some ornaments?"

She hesitated. "I think I'd better sit this one out and rest my ankle."

"What's wrong with your ankle?"

"Just a little sprain," she replied, wishing she hadn't said anything at all. "Not a big deal," she added.

They trimmed the tree and sang carols around the piano, passing plates of food back and forth. Anna didn't think she'd seen so much food since she'd arrived in England. After a few sips of Irish coffee, her cheeks were pink, and she was enjoying the afternoon with her friends. Gretchen and Louise danced their way around the piano, giving an occasional wink or raised eyebrow to Eleanor, who had planted herself next to Glenn on the piano bench. Anna smiled at their antics. Mr. Perkins had made himself at home in the kitchen with Mr. and Mrs. White, and Anna was grateful to Louise for including him today.

Mrs. White appeared in the doorway, her hands clasped together, watching the fun and admiring the decorated tree.

"I hate to break up the lovely time you are having," she began, "but we're ready for the main event." Her eyes twinkled with mischief, and she crooked a finger, telling them to follow her.

They filed into the kitchen, where a large wooden table stood in the middle of the room. Several bowls had been lined up with spoons for mixing laid beside them.

Anna walked as carefully as she could, not wanting to draw attention to herself. She tested her ankle, putting weight on it as much as she could without causing too much pain. Paul guided her, holding her elbow until she was close enough to the table to hold onto the edge.

"Has Jack told you what we're doing?"

"Not a word. He said Mrs. White would have his behind if he ruined her surprise."

Anna chuckled, watching Mrs. White's excitement.

"Alright, ladies and gentlemen," she began, taking her place at the head of the table, Mr. White at her side. "Please empty your wallets."

They looked around at one another, stunned at her request.

Anna looked at Marjorie, standing at the other end of the table, stifling a laugh. Mr. White wrapped his arm around his wife. "My dear, I think a better explanation of *why* you'd like their coins would be in order."

Mrs. White looked at the confused faces and burst out laughing. "It's...for...the...pudding," she managed between gasps.

She was even more confused, but Anna decided to go with it. "I'll need to go grab my purse. I left it with my coat," she said and started to step away from the table.

Paul touched her arm. "I've got it," he said.

"Oh, thank you, but it's no problem," she replied, determined to maintain some kind of distance.

"Anna, please?" He gave her a pathetic look, and she smiled.

"Sure, thank you, Paul. I'll have you paid back before we leave tonight."

"Don't worry about it. Consider it a Christmas gift," he said and flashed her a grin.

She plastered a smile on her face. She knew she was being stubborn, but she was trying desperately to keep her walls up as long as she could. "We'll see," she answered.

"Alright, now that we have everyone's coins, we'll make the pudding. We add the coins for good luck to whoever finds them in their dessert on Christmas Day," said Mrs. White.

"Ah, that sounds lovely," said Louise.

"How fun," Gretchen said, clapping her hands. Anna noticed her friend's cheeks were quite red and thought she might need to slow down. She reached across the table and took Gretchen's glass, pretending she'd wanted a taste, then kept it near to her, out of Gretchen's reach. Gretchen shot her a dirty look, but Anna smiled sweetly, pretending not to see the daggers shot in her direction. Gretchen could be mad all she wanted. It was worth it to avoid her friend making a fool of herself.

Paul put his arm around Anna's waist, and rather than protest, she allowed the warmth of his hand to move across her back. It was only their second time seeing one another, and she'd hardly call them dates, but she wanted to lean into him instead of push him away. He felt like...*home*, she thought. She remembered the image that had conjured up in her thoughts earlier, of Paul as her husband, chasing around *their* children in *their* yard, and she stiffened. He must have felt it because he rubbed her back gently and placed a few coins on the table in front of her. She stepped forward, letting his hand drop, and picked up one of them and turned it over.

"It's a 1922 Peace Dollar," he said.

"Don't you want to keep this one? It looks brand new," she replied.

"I suppose it very nearly is. My grandfather gave it to me, and I've kept it in my wallet for years."

Anna turned to face him. "Paul," she said, "don't you want to keep it?"

He shrugged. "What if someone else needs good luck?"

"I can easily go get some coins from my bag," she said. "You shouldn't give away your grandfather's coin. It's important."

"I'm not giving it away. I'm paying it forward. Today is a special day." He winked at her. "Someone else might need it more than me."

I'm in deep trouble, she thought. "Tell me about him."

"Who? Gramps?"

She nodded.

Paul scratched the back of his head. "He passed right after I joined up," he said.

Anna reached out and touched his hand. "I'm sorry, Paul. I didn't realize. You don't have to talk about it."

The rest of the guests were busily mixing the pudding, chattering on, but to Anna, it was just her and Paul. All of the background noise fell away when she focused on his face. She watched him turn the coin over on the table, his brow furrowed in concentration. He looked at her and smiled, and she noticed the dimple in his left cheek.

"It's okay," he replied. "No one's ever asked me about him before. He was a gruff old man," he laughed. "But he loved hard in his own way. I learned everything I know about farming from watching him and my dad."

"So you're a farmer?"

"Well, I grew up on a farm. I don't know if I'll keep on farming after this, but who knows. It feels like that's a lifetime away right now."

Anna nodded. She understood that feeling all too well.

He tucked his hands into his pockets and rocked on his heels. "So, what about you, Ms. Anna? What do you do back home?"

He dropped the coins into a bowl full of pudding and began to stir. "Actually, come to think of it, I don't even know where home is for you."

Anna laughed. "I don't think I do, either."

Chapter 18

*A*nna stood on the windy Southampton pier, shivering against the cold mist coming down as they watched the water slapping against the pilings. She looked up at the Leopoldville, high above them in the water.

"I don't think I'll ever get used to the size of these things," Anna said.

"They sure are intimidating," Louise agreed.

Eleanor shrugged. "Better this than a rowboat," she said. "We wouldn't stand a chance in this weather. At least we know we'll make it to the other side on this beast."

Anna nodded but didn't feel any better about the trip to Cherbourg. She'd heard about the German submarines, their torpedoes, and entering into accidental mines. She couldn't help but feel tense about the day-long crossing. *Duty calls,* she thought, reminding herself of why she was here. She'd go where she was needed. *Plus,* she thought, *it's France.* She tried to drum up her childhood memories of a little girl infatuated with all things French. That, mixed with the stories she'd overheard soldiers telling one another while they lay in the hospital beds - bombs and Nazis and buildings destroyed - had her wrought with worry. Her stomach twisted as they waited to board the ship. *All this waiting,* she thought, blowing out a frustrated breath. She'd rather just get on with it than stand here waiting. It only gave her brain more time to entertain her growing list of worries.

By the time she walked up the gangplank and actually stepped foot on the Leopoldville, she had convinced herself she should have said some kind of a final farewell to her loved ones. She had written home, telling her grandfather of the wonderful Christmas celebration and the traditions Marjorie and her parents had shared with them - with the exception of *whom* she shared that day with and *why* she'd really found it so enjoyable. She'd also left out the part about moving to Cherbourg. Knowing he'd get her letter so close to Christmas, she hadn't wanted to worry her grandfather. *I'll just write another as soon as we land, she told herself. After a safe arrival.*

What if we don't make it across? Panic gripped her.

"Gosh, I guess I should have told Paul I was leaving," she said, biting at her lip.

Gretchen whacked her on the arm. "You didn't tell him?" The incredulousness in her voice made Anna feel even more guilty.

"We only saw each other twice," she said, trying to defend herself.

ANNA DECEMBER 1944 SS LEOPOLDVILLE, ENGLISH CHANNEL

Louise patted her arm. "You really like him?"

If Anna's cheeks hadn't already been chapped from standing out in the wind, she'd have been red with embarrassment. "I suppose I do," she admitted.

"It's okay, Anna. I told Glenn we were heading to Cherbourg. I'm sure he'll tell Paul." Eleanor's reassurance only made her feel worse. *Even Eleanor had told Glenn.*

She wasn't sure why she hadn't told Paul. It had been on the tip of her tongue all evening, but she just couldn't bring herself to say it. Part of her didn't want him to worry about her. *He needs to focus on keeping himself safe,* Anna told herself. But another part of her was still holding back. Her feelings for him were escalating far faster than she'd expected, and the things she'd envisioned, the future she'd started to see herself in, was not the same one it had been just a few months ago. So fearful she was of becoming her mother, she'd dug her heels in and had done everything she could to alter her course. She'd gone so far as to deny herself of a budding relationship, even if it meant she'd be hurting the both of them. Deep down, she knew. *Self-sabotage,* she thought. *What is wrong with me?*

She followed her friends and fellow nurses in an orderly walk down to the ship's dining room and tried to shove her swirling thoughts to the back of her mind. They entered into a room filled ceiling to floor with luxury. So beautiful was the entirety of the intimate room that, for a moment, she thought she was on a passenger liner rather than a troopship.

Gretchen squealed. "Can you believe this?"

They stood gaping at the tables covered in white linen, table settings made up of ivory china and shining silver. Rich curtains hung around the outside walls of the room, and waiters entered

215

from behind a set of doors at the far end of the dining room. One had a white cloth draped over his forearm and a tray filled with several glasses and pitchers of water. Another opened a bottle of wine and started turning over their wine glasses, pouring a small amount into each one.

Anna was speechless. She'd never expected this kind of service on a troopship across the English Channel. The soldiers she'd treated spoke of dirty cesspools filled with stagnant air and little room to sleep, certainly not fine dining and a three-course meal.

They sat around one of the tables, folding their white cloth napkins into their laps. "I can't believe in a week's time, we'll be celebrating Christmas," Louise said, setting her wine glass down.

"I wonder who will be the lucky one with the coins in the pudding," Gretchen said.

Anna thought back to Paul and his grandfather's coin. She still felt badly that he'd likely never see it again. *But,* she thought, *he's still in England. Maybe he'll get to spend Christmas with Marjorie's family.* A sadness settled over her, and she took a sip of her wine. She looked up to see Eleanor watching her.

"Penny for your thoughts?"

Anna rolled her eyes and laughed. "Actually, I *was* thinking about coins," she said. "But not pennies."

Eleanor frowned. "Seriously?"

Anna nodded. "I swear," she said. "Paul put a special coin into the pudding. It was a gift from his grandfather. I just felt bad that he gave it away." She waved her hand like it was nothing.

"That was very kind of him," Louise said.

"Mhm," Gretchen agreed. "He seems like a very kind person." She waggled her eyebrows at Anna. "Our girl found herself a keeper."

Anna groaned and covered her face with her hands. "Really, Gretchen? Can we talk about something else now?" Her words came out muffled between her fingers.

Gretchen feigned innocence. "What? I call it like I see it. Isn't it the truth?"

Anna could tell she wouldn't get herself out of this without giving her friend an answer. She wanted to say no. She wanted to keep denying her feelings and pretend the pit in her stomach was entirely from seasickness and not the growing knowledge that she was getting further and further away from the person she wanted to be nearest to right now. She uncovered her face to three expectant women awaiting her answer.

"It's true," she whispered, wholly embarrassed to be 'that girl.' The one who hadn't kept her eyes on the reason she was here. "I didn't want this to happen." She felt her ears go red.

Gretchen laughed. "Oh, please. You're one of the lucky ones. We all hope we'll find Mr. Right." Eleanor and Louise nodded their agreement.

"It's not a bad thing, Anna. We're all wearing our hearts on our sleeves out here. We're seeing things and dealing with things that girls back home couldn't imagine. Don't punish yourself because you think you *shouldn't* have a bit of happiness. You deserve it as much as any other schmuck."

Anna laughed at Eleanor. "Thanks, girls," she said. "Let's eat before I get sick." She was still getting used to the rock of the ship as they got further out into the English Channel. For once, she was thankful for her empty stomach beginning to protest, bringing an end to an awkward conversation.

～⌒～

My dearest Grandfather,

I'm sending you a quick note to tell you I've made it safely to Cherbourg. I'm sorry for not telling you before we left, but I hated to worry you. More to come when I have the time! Love to you all!

AB

She reread her note and shoved it in an envelope and into her bag. She'd mail it as soon as they disembarked.

She had enjoyed the trip across the Channel more than she'd expected. The hearty meals quelled the seasickness that had been brewing from the moment she'd stepped foot on the Leopoldville. She hadn't gotten sick like many of the other nurses and soldiers on board, but she was just as grateful to finally see the twinkling lights of Cherbourg in the distance.

In the early morning hours, she convinced her friends to climb up to the upper decks to watch the sunrise as the buildings of Cherbourg came into view.

Gretchen shivered. "Tell me again why I'm out of bed when it's still dark and frigid out here?"

Anna nudged her. "You'll see, Gretch. Sunrise from the water. It'll be magnificent."

"What was magnificent was that bed below deck in the officer's quarters that we'll likely never see again before we're sent to tent cities," grumbled Eleanor.

"Oh, come on, girls. I'm with Anna. Once in a lifetime," said Louise. She wrapped her arm around Anna, and they huddled together against the cold sea spray.

They stood at the rail, the noise of the engines loud as the Leopoldville steadily approached the harbor. The sky began to lighten in a brilliant display of colors that took Anna's breath away. They had left Boston in the dark of night to a tune of 'God Bless America,' and Anna had thought then that nothing could have been more moving. *But this.* Standing here with her friends, the ones that had become family in such a short time, twenty feet above the water - she hoped she'd remember this feeling forever.

She tried to memorize every detail - her friends standing as close together as they could, breath coming out in little white puffs, the warmth of the rising sun on her face, a welcome contrast to the cold air. The colors streaked vibrantly across the sky, and she looked over at Gretchen, her mouth open in awe.

"I hope I can hold onto this moment no matter how bad things get," Gretchen said.

Anna hugged her tight. "Told you it was worth it."

It was still early when the Leopoldville made it to port, and they filed down the gangplank behind Captain Campbell. An officer escorted them to an awaiting car, and they sped off to their next destination - though what that was, they were still in the dark about.

Anna's nose was glued to the window, wanting to see everything in this unfamiliar place. She watched people scurry by, their collars high on their necks, eyes glued to the sidewalks as they rushed to wherever they were going. The air was different here. In England, rumors of the war soon ending had grown at a rapid pace - perhaps the holiday excitement had been to blame. But here, the excitement was replaced with urgency. *Even the cars drive faster,* Anna thought, sliding into the car door as the driver turned sharply.

They drove deeper into Cherbourg, revealing more of the war torn city and its people. Anna watched through the window, her eyes glued to pedestrians running through the city streets, their expressions fearful, their movements harried. Piles of brick and stone lay abandoned where buildings had once been. Those that had been lucky enough to stay standing were left with jagged holes through which Anna could see the sky out the other side. She looked in horror, her heart pounding in her ears and her palms beading with sweat. She was trapped inside the stuffy car, the heat blasting through the vents, crammed between Eleanor and the door. *My God, I hope it's not much further,* she thought, tucking her hands inside her coat sleeves.

The officer slowed at a busy intersection long enough that Anna was able to read a street sign. *Place General de Gaulle.* The officer gunned the engine again. The awkward silence stretched on. *Where are we going?* Anna had hoped they'd be given a chance to settle in wherever it was they'd be staying.

Captain Campbell was quiet in the front seat, her lips pursed in distress. Was it the officer's driving or where they were going that warranted her worried expression?

Another sharp turn threw Anna against Eleanor. "Sorry," Anna whispered.

Eleanor nodded, offering an arm for Anna to right herself.

The car stopped in front of a large brownstone building. Intimidating columns and enormous arched doors paled in comparison to the ornate stonework above them.

"Theatre Cherbourg," the officer announced. The car idled in front of the theater, and Anna marveled at how it had survived the destruction surrounding it.

Captain Campbell opened her door and stepped from the car, motioning for them to do the same. The officer stayed in the driver's seat, shifting into reverse, ready to take off again. Captain Campbell walked briskly up the cobblestone path.

Anna looked up in wonder at the building before them. Three intricate stone carvings adorned the spaces above the doors.

"Corneille, Boieldieu, Moliere," she read.

"I'd venture to guess they haven't had their plays performed here in a while," Eleanor said.

"Thank Hitler for that," Louise replied.

Anna shivered. She hated hearing that name.

"Ma'am," Gretchen said, just behind Captain Campbell, "What are we doing at a theater?"

Anna wasn't naive enough to think they were here for enjoyment, but she *was* curious why they were there. She silently thanked Gretchen for always asking the questions she was thinking.

"No fancy plays today, I'm afraid," Captain Campbell said. "The empty theater is being used by the United States and British military. We're attending a training seminar." She swung open one of the enormous doors, ushering them inside. Another officer was waiting for them in the lobby. He looked down at his watch.

"Right on time, I see."

"Yes, sir," Captain Campbell replied.

He turned on his heel and walked through another set of doors, barely stopping to hold the door before it came back in Captain Campbell's face. He led them to a row of seats near the back of the theater.

Louise covered her mouth and pointed. "Look how adorable."

A group of small children stood in a row on stage, their teacher unaware of their new audience. The nurses filed into their seats, watching the children's rehearsal. They couldn't have been more than ten years old. The littlest of the bunch looked like she was four, with pigtails and rosy cheeks.

"Oh, dear," said Gretchen. "Do you think they're orphans?"

Anna had noticed their shabby clothing, and her heart ached for them. She covered her mouth and held back tears at their sweetness as they began to sing, prompted by their teacher. She couldn't understand the words, but the melody was familiar - a Christmas song she knew she'd heard somewhere.

The officer marched down the aisle toward the teacher. She didn't so much as glance in his direction. When the littlest performers became distracted, she motioned for them to continue. Irate, the officer stepped even closer to the woman, invading any personal space between them until she couldn't ignore his presence anymore.

Anna rose from her seat. "What on Earth is he going to do to that poor woman?"

"Anna, please take your seat," Captain Campbell said. A warning more than a request, Anna complied, glued to the scene on stage.

The officer, inches from the woman's face, waved his hands and gestured wildly. She stood her ground. When he had finished, she turned to face him, matching his yelling, only in French.

Gretchen sighed. "Even when they're angry, their language is beautiful."

Eleanor snickered. "Good for her," she said. "She's not backing down."

They were all quietly rooting for the French teacher defending her students.

Several minutes of arguing ensued before the officer slinked down the aisle like a dog with its tail between his legs to the back of the theater. The teacher collected herself, smoothing her hair and continuing to direct her students in their Christmas carols.

"We'll have to wait until they are through practicing their pageant," he seethed from behind them.

Anna was quick to answer. "It's no bother to us," she replied. The words slipped out before she could catch them. Evidently, she surprised everyone else, as their heads snapped to her with wide eyes.

"What? They're just little children, for goodness sake." She couldn't stand to see this man on his power trip. Isn't that how they'd ended up here in the first place?

They watched the rest of the show in silence, giving the children their undivided attention as if they were big-name stars up on that stage. Anna would have paid to see their innocent little faces sing their hearts out.

After the final song, the children bowed and waved to the nurses. Anna was the first to stand and clap as loud as she could. If she had been any good at whistling, she'd have done that, too. Eleanor, Louise, and Gretchen joined in, stomping their feet and cheering for the children, whose cheeks had turned pink from the attention. Captain Campbell remained seated, but Anna could see from the corner of her eye that her feet were tapping and her hands clapped ever so slightly as though she wished she could take part in their serenade. She risked a glance back at the officer. His lips formed a thin line, and he still looked like his blood pressure might cause him to explode. Anna turned back to the children and smirked. *Serves him right,* she thought. Who could be so cruel to a group of poor children? But she knew the answer to that question, and it sent a chill through her at the thought.

The children filed off the stage one by one, blowing kisses as they went. The nurses caught their pretend kisses, and they giggled with delight. Their teacher helped them down the stairs and led them through the theater, glaring at the disgruntled officer as they passed. Anna wished she could high-five her, but the best she could do was make eye contact and nod, gaining a small smile in return.

"Now, shall we get on with this training?" Captain Campbell stood, trying to keep a neutral facade between the angry officer and her nurses.

The officer rose and cleared his throat as the nurses took their seats.

"You are here to learn about avoiding landmines." He grimaced, looking in the direction of the closing door. "A much more important subject than children's nursery rhymes."

Anna bit her tongue and closed her eyes to keep from rolling them. Gretchen gave her a nudge with her knee. It was all she could do to keep from laughing at the foolish man standing before them.

Chapter 19

PAUL
DECEMBER 1944
CAMP PIDDLEHINTON,
ENGLAND

*T*he promise of a quiet Christmas just a few days away leant itself to an air of excitement all around the base. Paul and Jack lugged a sad little tree into the mess hall tent and propped it up in the corner. Several GIs gathered around, hanging gum wrappers and empty cigarette cartons from its spindly branches. Harry sat and hammered a tin can into the shape of a star and placed it on top.

They all stood back to admire their handiwork.

"Not quite like the ones back home, but it'll do," Paul said.

One of the officers started singing 'Silent Night,' and several men joined in, joy and sadness colliding in their voices - grateful to be alive yet missing home at Christmastime. They had been in England for almost a month and were growing bored and restless - though no one dared complain this close to Christmas. They were happy to stay here if it meant a peaceful holiday. *And anyway,* Paul thought, *rumors are picking up left and right that the end of the war is near.* He could only hope.

He sat down to finish his letter home.

My Dearest Little Sister,

How are things shaping up on the homefront? I can picture the old farmhouse all decorated, candles in the windows. I sure am homesick thinking about Christmas here. England is nice enough, but it's no Texas. I don't think we'll be in this spot much longer, but who really knows? We're all getting a bit restless waiting around, but I certainly don't mind staying here through the holiday.

Harry rented a taxi to take me and some of the other guys around London. He borrowed a camera from Jack's cousin Marjorie. We spent a nice day with her and her parents, making Christmas pudding. That was a great time, too. Anyway, we went into London and had some fun seeing all the sights. I'll see if I can get any extra photos to send to you. Harry's putting together a little album for his wife with whatever supplies he can get his hands on. He hoped he'd get it out in time for Christmas, but he ran out of time. Even still, I think it's a great idea.

Well, that's about it around here. Hope little Danny has a wonderful Christmas. I wish I could be there to see him open up his presents - I sure miss that little rascal! Can't wait to spoil him rotten when I get home. Missing you all and praying for Jamie, too. Still haven't heard anything to report.

Love to you all and hugs for Mom and Pop,
Paul

The mail officer burst through the mess tent, lugging a bag full of packages and holiday mail. The men gathered around, hoping for goodies from loved ones back home. Harry walked away with a box from his wife. "It's a sweater," he said. "It's always a sweater." Paul chuckled and reached for a small box addressed to him. He tore into it, excited to see what his mother might have sent over. He crossed his fingers that it would be his favorite chocolate chip cookies.

"Don't you want to wait till Christmas morning," Harry asked, tucking his own package under his arm, unopened.

"Nah," said Paul, "who knows where we'll be by then." He unwrapped a red and blue knitted scarf and picked up the note that was tucked inside.

'I took up knitting to calm my nerves. It's awful, I know. Give it to a needy kid.

Love ya, Evie'

Paul chuckled and wrapped the scarf around his neck. "It's not so bad, Evie," he muttered. He reached into the box again and pulled out a tin. He'd barely popped the lid when the rest of the guys gathered around him. Paul elbowed them away.

"Savages," he joked. He peeked inside and stole two chocolate chip cookies before passing the tin around. He knew it would come back empty. He took out an envelope with his mother's delicate cursive on the outside and tucked it into his shirt pocket. He'd read it later when he had more privacy.

"You hear anything from that gal you met at the party?" Harry asked.

Paul frowned and shook his head. "Nah, I don't think I'll be hearing from her."

"What? Why not? I thought you two hit it off real well," Harry replied.

Captain Gangwere appeared at the tent's entrance, saving Paul from having to answer. He jumped up to stand at attention. The GIs in charge of the Christmas meal emerged from the kitchen, impatient to get back to their cooking.

"At ease," Captain Gangwere ordered. Paul clasped his hands behind his back and clenched his jaw. The holiday cheer that had filled the musty mess tent dissipated immediately.

"It's time to go. Be ready by eighteen hundred hours for the train to Southampton. We'll be in Cherbourg for Christmas."

The men looked around at one another in disbelief as the Captain left the tent. No one moved. *We're leaving two days before Christmas*, Paul thought.

"What the hell?" said Harry.

"Been here waiting for weeks, and they can't even wait two more days to move us." Jack lit a cigarette and took a long drag. Paul looked toward the kitchen where the guys who'd worked so hard all morning preparing a meal for the entire camp were scratching their heads, wondering what to do with all the food. It would likely end up wasted. Paul blew out an aggravated breath when he realized any hope of Anna coming for the Christmas party tonight was now out the window. *I'll probably never see her again*, he thought.

Harry clapped him on the back, and they filed out of the mess tent. They'd have to pack up and clean their bungalows before they left Camp Piddlehinton. Paul kicked at the dirt, annoyance weighing him down - at the change in events, but mostly at himself. His disappointment over losing a chance to see Anna made him feel like a dope. He threw himself onto his cot when he walked into their bungalow. The uniform he'd hung out to dry that morning was still damp.

"Great, now I get to cart a wet uniform in my pack," he grumbled. "I'm sure that'll smell great by the time we get to France."

Harry sat down on the cot beside him. "I wonder if they'll let us eat that dinner before we leave."

Jack snorted. "Yeah, that sounds just like something the Army would do for us."

Glenn walked into their bungalow just behind them. "Yep, I heard the kitchen guys pitching a fit. Captain's orders to toss all the food and get the place licked clean."

"Ain't that some shit," said Jack.

"Shortages left and right, and let's just let it all go to waste. Makes sense to me." Paul hadn't let much get to him since they'd gotten here, but this really got him hot. Between the rumors of the war ending soon, the promise of the Christmas season, the girl...Paul had been a fool for letting his hopes get so high. He sat up and hung his head in his hands, elbows on his knees.

"Man, what an idiot I am," he said.

"Nah, don't let it get to you," Glenn said, "We're all pissed."

Harry chuckled. "I don't think it's the move so much as it's the girl," he teased.

"What girl? Who's got Paul's panties in a twist?" Jack grinned and punched Paul on the shoulder.

He ignored his friends and grabbed his pack from underneath his cot.

"Pretty sure lover boy here was hoping to see a certain nurse at the party tonight," Harry explained.

"Is that what you're mad about? Well, I've got news for you; those girls are already headed to Cherbourg," said Glenn.

Paul's head snapped up. "What are you talking about?"

"They might even still be on a ship. I'm not sure. All I know is they were leaving right after the White's Christmas party."

"How do you know that?"

Glenn's face flushed, and he looked embarrassed. "I, uh, I've been keeping in touch with Eleanor."

Paul shoved his friend and laughed. "That's right, I forgot Anna said Eleanor had been talking to you. How'd you get her to talk anyway?" Paul remembered the first night he'd met her and how angry she'd been. He thought he'd seen steam coming out of her ears when he'd taken Anna for that dance. He'd been so wrapped up in Anna he must not have noticed Glenn talking to Eleanor.

Glenn shrugged. "I didn't. Not really. We just bumped into each other on the way out of the dance. I was tired and didn't feel like sticking around any longer. I tried to slip out, and I walked right into her. She was standing outside the door. I guess she'd thought about leaving but didn't want to go off by herself."

"So Anna's already in Cherbourg? What are the odds?" *Imagine that*, he thought. *We're both sent to Cherbourg*. He finished tying up his pack and placed it outside the door with the rest of his belongings. When he walked back inside, he gave Glenn a small shove.

"What's that for?"

"I just can't believe a shy guy like you got Eleanor to talk, that's all."

"What's that supposed to mean?"

"I don't mean anything by it," Paul said. "Just that she looked down right miserable when I first met her."

Glenn grinned. "Nah, that's just her tough exterior. She's not so mean as she looks."

Paul laughed. "Good to know," he said.

They started moving the cots to scrub the floors before leaving. An idea formed in Paul's head, and he dropped the cot and snapped his fingers. "Hey, Glenn?"

"What's up?"

"You said you write to Eleanor pretty frequently, right?"

"Well…yeah…I suppose so, I mean…not all the time…just, you know…here and there."

Glenn fumbled over his words, but Paul ignored his obvious embarrassment. He was only thinking about how he could connect with Anna.

Do I write her a letter, send it with Glenn's, and hope Eleanor passes it on? He considered this idea, but what if Anna was put off by her friend reading a letter intended for her? *Should I ask Glenn to find out where they're staying in Cherbourg and surprise her with a visit?* That was another risky plan. *What if I'm not in Cherbourg long enough to pay her a visit? Or worse…what if she doesn't want to see me?* It had been several weeks since they'd spun around the dance floor together. They'd gotten more time together at the White's house, but as the days passed, he'd felt less confident in their connection. Hell, she hadn't even told him she was leaving. Maybe the spark was all in his head. *What if my feelings are one-sided?*

"Um, Paul?" Glenn was watching him, waiting for an answer.

"Right, I, uh," Paul stammered, rubbing the back of his neck, trying to make a decision. "I was wondering if I could send a letter in with your next one to Eleanor." *There,* he thought, *the least vulnerable choice.*

"Wait..." Glenn started. "Why?" He looked at Paul, his hands clenching into fists at his side.

Paul's eyes went wide, and he put his hands up in surrender when he realized the mistake he'd made. Harry and Jack chuckled as they watched Paul squirm.

"No, no...let me explain. What I meant to say is, could I include a letter for Eleanor's friend, Anna."

Relief flooded Glenn's face, and he smacked Paul on the back of the head. "Sorry, pal," he said. "I jumped to the wrong conclusion. Guess I'm more of a goner for this girl than I thought."

Paul laughed, relieved that Glenn hadn't clocked him before he had a chance to explain.

"Sure, yeah, of course, you can send a letter with mine. But I could just give you the address she sent me, and you can write to Anna, no?"

Paul felt like an idiot for not thinking of that himself. "You sure they're still together over there?"

"Pretty sure," Glenn said. "Eleanor mentioned how happy she was to still have her friends with her. I'm guessing Anna is one of them."

Paul nodded. "Alright then, I'll give it a shot."

"Oh, but, uh, don't tell Anna what I told you about Eleanor being happy - she'd kill me," said Glenn.

Paul chuckled. "Not a word," he said.

⌒

They marched out of Camp Piddlehinton without a trace left behind, bound for the train to Southampton. Their Christmas Eve dinner had been tossed in the woods, save for one turkey the Company K men had roasted over a fire they'd made outside their barracks in an open field. They'd used their straw ticks and rotated it as best they could, but the result didn't look appetizing enough for Paul to give it a try. He'd rather go hungry than risk what looked burnt on one side and raw on the other.

They marched through the small towns, full packs on their backs and all of their belongings stuffed any way they could fit them. Most of the company officers had given up on keeping their men in formation. They'd been marching the cobbled streets for hours and had resorted to dragging their bags behind them. Paul didn't care about the damage his pack or his things inside it might incur over the stone roads, so long as it saved his back from having to carry it another mile.

Families living in the houses along their route came outside to watch the soldiers passing by, waving their thanks and offering prayers for the 66th Division men.

"Were we supposed to take our patches off?" Paul spoke quietly to Harry.

"Beats me," he replied.

"Seems odd we're telling everyone which division we're in and what direction we're headed."

"I just do what I'm told, my friend," Harry said and yanked his bag further down the street.

A truck approached, slowing down as it reached the line of

soldiers, and Paul looked hopeful. Surely they'd be picked up and driven the last mile.

The truck maneuvered around them and kept going. Paul cursed under his breath.

"Same old song and dance," complained Harry when they'd finally reached Pier 38 in Southampton and waited to board the ship. Officers had given up on reprimanding their men to stand at attention. Paul was relieved when Captain Gangwere grew just as impatient as he felt and put his men at rest.

"Hurry up and wait," Paul agreed. He slipped down to the ground, using his duffel bag as a seat. He was tired, hungry, and, like everyone else, covered in dirt from the dusty road and the soot-filled train.

Glenn and Jack wandered over to them, hands full of coffee and donuts.

Paul perked up at the smell. "Where'd you get all that?"

Glenn nodded toward the other end of the pier to a Red Cross cart that Paul hadn't noticed.

"I'll go back with you for another refill," Glenn said, shoving the last of his donut in his mouth.

"Harry, you coming?" Paul nudged him. He was using his duffel bag as a pillow, stretched out over top of it.

"Mm." Harry sat up, limb by limb, and ran his hand through his hair before replacing his cap on his head. "What good do they think we'll be sending us in as replacements after making a trip like this?"

"The coffee helps," Glenn said, helping Harry up.

They stood on the pier, eating and slugging coffee, looking out at the massive Leopoldville.

"It doesn't look too organized," Paul said, watching the thousands of soldiers running from one end of the pier to the other. A group of paratroopers walked up the gangplank, disappearing inside the Leopoldville.

"Hey, I thought it was just the 66th going across," Harry said.

"Beats me," said Jack.

"It's one hell of a ship," Glenn said.

"I don't know if it's gonna make it to the other side," Joe joked.

"Good Lord, don't say that," Harry replied.

Glenn shrugged. "I mean, look at it."

Jack elbowed Joe, a mischievous grin on his face. "Where are we going in this tub?"

Joe laughed and raised his cup of coffee overhead. "To the bottom!"

Harry shook his head. "You guys are sick."

They lined up, waiting to board the ship with their gear in piles all around them. Captain Gangwere passed them, his face red with rage.

Joe whistled. "I wonder what that's all about."

A minute later, they were ordered to move back out of the way while the paratroopers that had just gotten on filed back off the ship.

Paul looked around. "What in the world?" he muttered.

Captain Gangwere's voice echoed down to them. "You think you can just herd my men onto your damn ship without a second thought? My men aren't cattle to be prodded through a lineup.

They are soldiers, for God's sake. They deserve more respect than this half-assed setup you've got here."

Paul stepped forward with his ID in hand. He was beginning to see why Captain Gangwere was so angry. There was no log, no checking that all the men in one unit were together or which units had already been boarded. The man hardly looked at Paul's ID before ushering him forward.

Confusion continued below deck when they climbed down a wooden ladder to reach the hold they'd been assigned.

"What the hell," Jack said. "There's nowhere to sleep."

Duffel bags, rifles, and equipment lay in heaps anywhere men could find a spot to drop them, and wooden tables took up the little remaining room. Captain Gangwere searched around the compartment, opening a door in the rear to find a pile of hammocks that had been hidden inside. He yanked them out in heaps, dropping them at their feet.

"Figure out how to make good use of these," he said. While the men took turns grabbing the hammocks, the captain started moving the equipment out of the way and into the closet.

Paul took a hammock, tried to open it, and promptly gave up, throwing the tangled mess back on the floor. "I think I'll just lay on one of the tables."

When the ship was fully loaded, an announcement came over the loudspeaker, ordering all troops to report to the top deck. Once there, they were given their emergency stations and told to wait.

"What exactly are we waiting for?" Joe looked out over the railing after they'd stood there for forty-five minutes without any further instruction.

"I've had about enough of this," Captain Gangwere said, giving his men the okay to go back below decks.

Paul chose to stay out on the top deck despite the dropping temperature. He held onto the railing while the Leopoldville navigated away from the Southampton Harbor.

The ship passed one lighthouse and then another, where they were joined by the rest of their convoy.

"Nab Tower," Jack said, pointing to one of the lighthouses, "and St. Catherine's Point," he pointed to the other stone tower.

"How do you know this stuff?" Joe asked.

Jack shrugged. "Marjorie is really into history," he said. "I think that one is the oldest medieval lighthouse in England."

"Alright, well, if the history lesson is over, I'm going down below," Harry said. "It's too cold up here."

They filed down the ladder, one behind the other, until they were fully engulfed in the suffocating air below. The stench burned Paul's nostrils.

"Good God," he said, "I'm not going to last long down here."

Chapter 20

PAUL
CHRISTMAS EVE 1944
SS LEOPOLDVILLE,
ENGLISH CHANNEL

*P*aul stood on the top deck of the Leopoldville. Despite the biting wind, he'd convinced his friends to come back up with him. It was cold - too cold to be up there - but the alternative below decks was even worse. His stomach lurched just thinking about the stench of raw sewage mixed with whatever slop they'd been served for dinner, lowered down in buckets through the openings between each deck for them to scoop out into their mess kits or bowls that looked like they hadn't been washed since the ship was built. He couldn't stay down there if he'd been ordered to.

They sang half-hearted Christmas carols until they gave up on that, shivering and miserable on Christmas Eve.

"I'm going back down," Jack said.

"Come on, Paul," Glenn agreed. "It's below zero out here."

Paul rolled his eyes. "It's not that cold," he said. The wind picked up then, blowing his collar up higher on his neck.

"It *is* that cold," Harry said.

"Well, it's better than the foul air down there," Paul replied. "I can't do it." He was bound and determined to stay on top until they landed at Cherbourg.

"To each their own," Jack said, and started to walk away. "Once I fall asleep, I won't smell a thing."

Paul laughed. "Who could get to sleep on this old junk? We don't even have any beds."

No beds, no working bathrooms - which explained the awful smell. Paul had witnessed dozens of men too seasick to even make it to the head, never mind that it was completely backed up. His stomach rolled at the thought of having to go back down there in that.

"Just one more song," he pleaded. He looked around at the faces of his friends. "It's Christmas Eve, guys."

Jack relented and walked back to join him.

"One more," he said. "That's it."

Paul smiled. "Gee, thanks," he teased. "I'll even let you choose which one."

Jack rubbed his chin. "Hmm…"

Paul looked out into the sea while his friend thought. The sky had darkened, making the water below look black.

"What the…"

Harry followed Paul's gaze. A giant silver bullet streaked through the water, heading straight for the hull of the ship. Paul felt like he was watching in slow motion, bracing for the impact of what he assumed could only be a torpedo.

"Holy shit," Harry exclaimed. "What the hell is that?"

They watched over the railing, helpless to stop as the torpedo made contact with the starboard side of the Leopoldville.

Paul braced for an explosion that would send them all overboard, rocking the entire ship. Instead, the initial hit did little more than knock the men into one another as if they'd hit a rough patch of water. But they knew what it was. He looked over the rail in disbelief.

"What do we do?" Glenn whispered.

"Get to our 'abandon ship' station," Paul replied. There was nothing else they could do. "I'm sure they'll get us off before anything else happens." He nodded in the direction of Cherbourg, the lights twinkling in the distance. The lights, which moments before, they'd whooped and cheered to see. It had been a welcome sight after having been in darkness when blackout orders had gone into effect. As little as a cigarette burning on deck had been banned - anything could give them away to the enemy. *And yet, here we are,* thought Paul. *On a sinking ship on Christmas Eve.* He took a deep breath. *They won't let it sink,* he thought, just as the lights on deck turned on, illuminating the ship in the dark night.

"That's great," Jack said. "Let's just let them know exactly where we are."

"I'm going back down quick," Harry said suddenly.

Paul grabbed him by the arm. "What in the hell for?"

Harry wrenched himself free. "I've gotta get the sweater Edith made for me. And my pack."

"I'll go with you. I'm going to need more cigarettes. This could take a while," said Glenn. Both men acted as though they hadn't just witnessed a torpedo hit the ship they were standing on.

"Guys, you can't go down there," Paul said.

"Oh, come on. You said yourself they won't let us sink. Besides, look how close the Harbor is. We could swim it if we had to," said Glenn.

"Are you crazy? You think it's cold out here on deck, but you're gonna survive a swim in that water?" Paul couldn't believe they weren't taking this seriously. "You have no idea the conditions down there, but you're going to risk it for a sweater and some cigarettes?"

"We'll be right back, Paul. Calm down. Look, no one's running around in a panic. We're fine."

They took off, leaving Paul and Jack standing on deck. Paul looked over the side again. A jagged hole tore through the bottom part of the ship - F Deck in the number four hold.

"Jesus, you could drive a truck through that hole," Jack said.

"There's no way this thing is staying afloat," Paul replied.

"You think those guys are okay down there?"

The loudspeaker system crackled. 'All men on deck. No men are to go below deck.' It was the first command they'd heard in English since they'd boarded. Paul looked at Jack, deciding what to do.

"Should we go look for them?"

"I don't know what to do. They want us on deck, but what do we do? Just stand here and wait?"

Paul frowned. "No, I can't. We need to go find them and get them back up here."

They ran toward the stairs to go below from C deck into their hold, following the steps Harry and Glenn would've taken only a few minutes before them. Paul stopped at the top where the stairs should have been, the wood splintered and mangled with no way to make it down. They raced further down the deck of the ship to the next staircase, leading to the mess hall, but this one was destroyed as well. Paul started to lose hope of finding their friends. They looked around for any other access when the ship creaked, steel beams snapping under pressure, sending rivets flying through the air around them, popping like gunshots. A steel door leading below deck was left mangled in front of them.

"Help me push it open," Paul said to Jack. The two men shouldered the door, putting all of their weight into it until it opened enough to see through. Jack shined his light through the crack, barely big enough to climb through. The mess hall was pitch black, the only light coming from another soldier's flashlight. Jack called down into the dark void.

"Hey! Anybody down there?"

"Yeah, we're down here. We're trapped. The stairs were blown apart," the soldier with the flashlight answered.

"Can you get to the door over here?" Paul edged into the mess hall, Jack shining the light for him. He held onto a steel bar while Jack moved the light across the room, looking for a way to help the men stuck below them.

The soldier's light shined up at them, and he shouted back. "The water's up to our knees. I got a line of men behind me and a hole where the stairs used to be. There's a steel ladder over there," he swung his flashlight to the only ladder left. "But we can't get across this giant hole." He swung his flashlight back down to reveal a black hole, the sound of rushing water coming up from inside.

Several men became impatient, going around the soldier to attempt a leap to the ladder.

"Jesus, Mary, and Joseph," Jack murmured when the man missed the rungs and fell, screaming into the hole.

"Shine your light around the edge of that hole," Paul said. "Hey, I think you can make it around if you're careful," he called down. "Stay close to the wall, and we'll get you pulled up over here."

"Alright, I'll go first, make sure it's even possible." The soldier with the flashlight carefully edged his way around the snarled steel. When he got close enough, Paul reached out and pulled him to safety. He disappeared through the door. The line of soldiers that had been waiting patiently let loose, anxious to get out of the rising water.

"Let's hope the guys are somewhere in this lineup," Jack said.

Paul nodded, pulling another GI to safety. "That's what I'm hoping for. If they got into our compartment and couldn't get back up, they'd have to come this way."

They lifted man after man up and out of the mess hall until the last one crept across, his hands shaking when he reached out for Paul's.

"Dammit," Paul said when Jack shined his light down into the empty mess hall.

"I guess we just go back to our stations. Maybe they'll be there by now."

Paul nodded. He didn't want to give up searching for Harry, but with no way of getting into their compartment, he didn't see any other choice.

Captain Gangwere dropped to his knees in front of their Abandon Ship Station and began to pray. Paul watched several men back away from him, embarrassed by his outward display of faith. Paul drew nearer to him, instead. He knelt down and joined him, bowing his head. *Lord, protect us,* he pleaded. *Lord, provide me with wisdom and certainty in the face of the unknown so that I may be useful to my fellow comrades. Use me for good, Lord.*

The ship groaned, lurching forward, and Paul threw his hands out in front him. The engines sputtered and knocked several times before they ground to a stop.

Soldiers were milling about on deck without any sense of urgency. *They really don't think we're in any trouble,* Paul thought. By now, after seeing the mess hall left in shambles, watching the crew members hurrying past, ignoring the GIs and officers that tried to get their attention, Paul knew they were in more trouble than they were being told. He walked past several groups of American soldiers, following a couple of crew members. He was going against the only order they'd been given since they boarded - to wait at your station for further instruction. But instructions weren't coming, and he was tired of waiting. An announcement sounded over the loudspeaker, and relief flooded Paul. *Finally,* he thought, followed by an immediate frustration when 'Make way for the crew, make way for the crew,' was the only thing he heard. Nothing about how urgent their situation was. Nothing about lifejackets or lifeboats or the condition of the ship.

He caught up to the two crewmen just as they were cutting the ties holding one of the only usable lifeboats.

"What the hell are you doing?" Paul walked up behind the two men. One was throwing their belongings into the boat while the other climbed in, motioning for several more crewmen to do the same. They all ignored him, working feverishly to get away.

Paul wrenched on the man's shoulder to get his attention. He pulled away, the look on his face a warning. Paul stayed planted beside him, standing in his way until he got an answer. He hadn't seen any other crew members, and he was determined to find out what was going on, even with a language barrier. The man turned back to Paul as the boat started to lower. He was frantic now, pointing and shouting something Paul couldn't understand. He shoved a bird in its cage into Paul's hands before he had a chance to reject it. The absurdity of holding a damn parrot in the middle of a sinking ship while the crew saved themselves and said, 'To hell with everyone else' fueled a fire that burned him up inside. The man climbed into the boat and gestured for Paul to hand him the bird. Paul looked into the man's eyes, his anger simmering. The Congolese man yelled what Paul could only assume were profanities - the man wanted his bird. Paul wanted to scream at him, tell him what cowards they all were. He lifted the birdcage, the parrot squawking madly inside. He had every intention of tossing the damn thing right into the sea. With the cage raised high, he swung it outward, past the lifeboat, while the crewman screamed wildly, grabbing for the cage.

Something stopped Paul then, and he dropped the cage into the boat with a loud thud. He turned his back to the traitors and walked back toward his company's Abandon Ship Station.

"Paul!" His anger dissipated at the sound of a familiar voice.

"Harry! Oh, thank God! I thought you were trapped in the hold."

Harry walked toward him, his pack on his back. "I got back up before the ladder gave out. I got separated from Glenn and Joe, though. I couldn't find them. The lights all went out, and I was lucky to feel my way to the ladder. The water is rising fast, Paul."

Paul nodded. "I know. We tried to look for you in the mess hall. It's bad. They must have a rescue boat coming."

They walked back toward their station. Harry patted his duffel bag. "At least I saved Edith's scrapbook," he said.

~⌒~

Chapter 21

PAUL
CHRISTMAS EVE 1944
SS LEOPOLDVILLE,
ENGLISH CHANNEL

On the top deck of the Leopoldville, Paul watched the ship list more and more in the choppy waters. Soldiers lined up at their emergency stations, waiting for their orders until they could no longer stay upright. They had to move further up the ship away from the water creeping up the deck. Paul couldn't wait any longer. The HMS Brilliant came alongside, maneuvering as close as it could get. He stood watching, counting. He counted the waves, timing the up and down of both ships. He and Harry looked on as men leapt from the sinking ship to the Brilliant one by one. Men in full gear with overcoats and steel helmets weighing them down. In their haste, they hadn't thought to lighten their load. Harry was white with panic. Paul, despite his racing thoughts, remained calm.

"Harry, we're gonna have to jump."

Harry groaned. "I told you, Paul. Didn't I tell you?"

"Not now, Harry. We're gonna get off this death trap if you just shut up and listen." He didn't mean to be so blunt with Harry, but the ship was sinking. They would be trapped if they didn't take matters into their own hands. The line moved in an orderly fashion, and only a handful of men were openly panicking. The rest remained so calm it was almost eerie. No officers in sight, no orders, no direction. *Are we supposed to just stand here and go down with the damn ship?*

"First things first - lose the overcoat." Paul was already out of his and yanking his life vest back over his head.

"You're crazy. It's freezing out here, Paul."

"Harry, if you keep that coat on you're gonna sink the second you hit that water. Better to be cold up here than frozen at the bottom."

Harry conceded and took the coat off, then pulled his life vest on. "I'm keeping the pack, though," Harry said, pulling his bag back onto his back over the life vest.

"Untie your boots." Paul bent down to undo his laces.

"Great, cold and barefoot," Harry said, following Paul's lead.

They moved up in line.

"I figured out the best time to jump. So when I count down and tell you to jump, just do it, okay?"

He clapped Harry on his padded back. Harry just stared ahead, his eyes following the men lined up to jump before him. He gave Paul a weak nod.

They stood behind the rail, just one soldier ahead of them now. Paul caught the conversation between the two soldiers in line behind him while they waited.

"I know, I tried to get Colonel Rumberg to come up, too."

"I saw him go back down below deck. Said he'd keep going till there were no men left to save down there. I told him if he keeps going under, he's going to be the one needing the saving."

Paul turned around.

"Sorry, but did you say Colonel Rumberg went back down below deck? Not in the hold where the water's rushing in?"

The soldier nodded. "Yes, sir."

"Where did you last see him?"

"Near E Deck," he pointed behind them. "Closer to the explosion."

Paul yanked on the back of Harry's life vest just as he was about to step up onto the rail. They lost their place in line, but Paul didn't care.

"I thought you said we're jumping," Harry said.

"We are," Paul answered. "But not here. I have an idea."

They hung back as the soldier ahead of them attempted the jump to the Brilliant. Paul squeezed his eyes shut. He knew the soldier had mistimed his jump. He didn't need to see it to know the sounds of the young man falling between the two great ships as they smashed together in the violent, churning sea. Harry's face went from white to green as they looked overboard to see the English Channel swirling and streaked with blood.

"Dear God," said Harry, mortified at what they'd just witnessed. He wouldn't be the last soldier Paul saw get crushed between the Leopoldville and the Brilliant before the night was through.

Paul pulled at Harry again, snapping him out of the shock of men dying around them.

"Come on, I'm going to get you off this damn tub."

He ran toward the center of the ship, tripping on his loosened bootlaces as the ship lurched further into the sea.

"Why are we going back down there?" Harry panicked.

"Just trust me," Paul called over his shoulder. "I haven't steered you wrong yet, have I?"

They came out on C Deck, three floors down from the top. They were nearly even with the deck of the Brilliant now, instead of twenty feet higher like they were at the top of the Leopoldville.

Harry came up behind him. "Shit, Paul, you're a genius."

"I don't know about all that, pal. But we need to hurry." He looked behind him at several men with the same idea nearing their spot by the railing.

Harry climbed onto the rail and looked down at Paul, standing behind him.

"You'll remember to send that letter to Edith, right?"

"Just shut up. You're not gonna die today, Harry." But he nodded anyway, reassuring his friend.

Harry took a deep breath and faced the Brilliant.

"Alright, Harry. You ready?"

Harry steadied himself. "You think I'll ever be ready for this?" He looked down at his feet, ensuring he wasn't stepping on his laces. Paul looked up at Harry, whose teeth had started chattering with cold or maybe fear. He looked out at the waves. The Leopoldville went down, the Brilliant separated and went up. With the two ships at their farthest distance from one another, Paul screamed.

"JUMP!"

He said a silent *Thank you, God,* that Harry didn't hesitate. He easily closed the gap between the two ships as another wave sent them crashing together, just in time for Harry to land hard on the deck of the Brilliant. Paul watched from the Leopoldville, waiting to see Harry pick himself up. He scrambled to his feet and leaned over the rail of the rescuing ship. Paul backed away from the rail. The soldier behind him eagerly took his place and climbed on the rail, ready to jump. Paul timed his jump and called out to him at the exact right moment. Harry stood at the rail of the Brilliant, waiting while Paul helped the rest of the soldiers make it safely across. And yet, Paul still did not make the jump.

When there were no more men to direct, Harry leaned halfway over the Brilliant's railing, yelling to Paul.

"PAUL! PAUL! WHAT THE HELL ARE YOU DO-ING?" A crewman on board the Brilliant grabbed Harry's legs before he spilled overboard and threw him backward. "What the hell are *you* doing?" Paul heard him say to Harry.

Paul cupped his hands over his mouth and shouted back. "I can't leave Colonel Rumberg down there. I'll see you on shore in a bit."

He took a few steps backward before turning around and breaking into a sprint, dodging fallen debris and equipment sliding down the listing deck of the ship. He ran, Harry's cursing and swearing ringing in his ears, in search of Colonel Rumberg.

An officer Paul didn't recognize shouldered him as he tried to run past, "What the hell are you doing?" *That seems to be the question of the day,* thought Paul.

"Going down to see where I can help," Paul said.

"This ship is sinking, son," the officer said. "It's time to help yourself now."

"Oh, I know," Paul said and swung his leg down onto what was left of a ladder leading to the deck below. The officer shook his head and kept moving, following the rest of the men in his company.

The rushing water was louder the further down Paul climbed. He dropped down to the next deck and searched for an opening to take him even deeper into the bowels of the ship. Every step took him closer to the men trapped by the torpedo's explosion.

He found a hole and crouched down, shining his flashlight to look for something he could grab onto. The ladder had been blown apart, and the only piece left was the top rung, swinging loosely from the ceiling. *That's useless,* he thought. He lowered his legs down through the hole, supporting himself with his upper body. He inched further and further until the jagged floorboards dug into his fingertips. He could see the beam of a flashlight illuminating the rushing water. It was closer than he'd realized. He got as low as he could before his fingertips gave out, landing with a thud and rolling onto his side. He rubbed his hands, riddled with splinters, and said a prayer of thanks that he hadn't fallen straight through the platform and into the rushing water.

He heaved himself up off the ground and followed the direction of the flashlights. The water crept into his boots as he sloshed closer to the worst part of the wreckage. When he stopped, he swore he could hear cries for help, muffled by the gushing water and the ship's groaning. Several men stood over a small hole in the hold that looked barely big enough for a child to fit through.

"What have we got?"

The saturated soldiers turned to Paul, surprised someone else had been able to reach them. No one had gotten this close to the torpedo's destruction. Those that had tried were swept away by the rising water or blocked by the bulkheads intended to keep the water contained to one compartment.

"Rumberg pulled us out and won't quit until he's got everyone he can grab."

Paul looked down. "He went through that hole?" The metal was sharp and jagged. Not to mention Colonel Rumberg's six foot two, two hundred-fifty pound frame. Paul stood there in disbelief. One man shined a flashlight, and Paul looked down, struggling to see into the raging water that was growing higher every second they stood there. And then he saw him. Colonel Rumberg was treading water, struggling to hold up a nearly unconscious soldier. He was losing strength, and if any more water rushed in, they'd be at the top with little room to breathe. He found it hard to believe that Colonel Rumberg would make it back out. Paul looked around, but there didn't seem to be any other option.

"He can't hold much longer. We need to help him." The ship creaked and they steadied themselves, feeling it list even more.

"No shit. Any ideas, genius?"

Paul looked up, shining his light and pleading for a way out. He didn't have any ideas. Beneath the blown-apart wood he spotted a steel ladder, still intact and reachable if he jumped. He stood underneath the ladder and jumped, grabbing onto the bottom rung and pulling himself up with his upper body until he was high enough to pull his legs up, too. He poked his head out onto the next deck. From up here, he could see just how badly the ship was listing. They didn't have much time before they went down with the ship. A pile of tangled rope caught his eye, and he reached for it, snagging one end and pulling it as hard as he could. He dragged it back down the ladder.

He knotted the rope and lowered it through the hole.

"You're a regular cowboy, aren't you?"

"Actually, I am," he said. "Born and raised and proud of it." He smiled at the man, then directed his attention to Colonel Rumberg, circling in the water.

"Grab the rope! Loop it under your arm," Paul shouted down. "Let us pull you up!"

Colonel Rumberg shook his head between the waves of crashing water. The soldier he'd been holding onto was now entirely unconscious, a dead weight that Rumberg struggled to keep above water. His efforts were futile when he could barely keep his own head up.

"Please!" Paul wasn't above begging. Their time was running out. Another wave crashed over the two men, sending them underwater. Paul cursed when neither one reappeared right away. Colonel Rumberg finally surfaced but had lost his grip on the soldier, now gone beneath the water. Defeated, he relented and searched for the rope. He struggled to stay above water, and when he reached for the rope, he could hardly pull it over his head.

Paul and the other soldiers pulled the rope - an easier feat in his mind than in reality. Soaking wet, Rumberg felt more like five hundred pounds, and it took several attempts before they could take hold of one arm to pull it up through the hole. Every wave sent the Colonel floating - first, farther from them, then upward, slamming his head into the metal above him.

On the third attempt, they wrestled him through the sharp edges of the hole, his uniform torn to shreds. Blood pooled around him, and the water advanced on them with a vengeance. The four men got him to his feet and headed for the ladder.

"How the hell are we going to manage this?" They looked up the ladder.

"It's the only way out," Paul said.

"I'm afraid he's going to tumble back down on us the higher we go," said another soldier.

Paul started up the ladder. "I'll go up and pull from the top," he said over his shoulder.

"I ain't dead yet," Colonel Rumberg rasped. He used the little remaining energy he had to help himself up the ladder, Paul grabbing his arm as he got closer, the men behind him pushing. He collapsed on the deck, his chest heaving in and out. Paul knew they weren't done yet.

The ship gave another groan and lurched forward, sending loose debris sliding down the deck toward them. Paul grabbed a piece of splintered wood before it collided with them and sent it sideways down the ship. Colonel Rumberg's breathing slowed, and his eyes were small slits.

"Alright, Colonel," Paul said, trying to keep the fear out of his voice. "Up and at 'em. We've got more work to do before you can rest."

Colonel Rumberg grunted and rolled onto his side, revealing a puddle of blood that had pooled beneath him. He lifted his hand, working to sit up, when Paul saw it. Three of his fingers had been cut clean off, fresh blood running down his arm. *Jesus, Mary, and Joseph,* Paul thought. *How is this man still functioning?*

Paul tore the sleeve off of his shirt and wrapped the Colonel's hand as best he could. At this point, there was no infirmary left, and any patients that had been there were long removed in an attempt at safety. Paul thought about the group of orderlies that had carried one GI on a stretcher to the awaiting Brilliant. He had watched in horror as they swung the stretcher out over the water, gaining momentum, and tossed the wounded man onto the deck of the Brilliant. He had gained new injuries in the fall, no doubt, but the alternative would have been much worse.

"It was wrapped before I went back down," Colonel Rumberg mumbled. "Guess it ripped off somewhere in the water." He looked at his hand like it was no big deal and rose to his feet on wobbly legs. Paul helped steady him as best he could, but he worried about what they'd do once they hit the water.

They climbed up one more deck, moving farther from the worst part of the wreckage. Paul felt sick knowing that there were still men trapped down there. Men they couldn't reach. And time was running out. He pulled himself to the railing and climbed over the side. Silence fell over the ship, and he looked back at Colonel Rumberg. The engines stopped, the emergency lights flickered out and, still, no Abandon Ship order came.

Soldiers crowded into the highest part of the ship, the only part still above water. They held onto the railings, each other, anything they could grab onto to keep from sliding down into the water.

Paul looked back down over the side of the ship. Lifeboats had never been deployed. Men were crawling down the nets hanging on the side of the ship and pushing themselves off into the icy English Channel, as far away from the suction of the sinking ship as they could get. The water continued to rise, which, Paul realized, was not the water rising at all. The ship was sinking deeper into the sea. Wooden debris and steel beams snapped under the pressure of the sinking vessel, sending rivets and shrapnel flying in every direction. Where just hours earlier, men had stood on deck singing Christmas carols, cheerful in their anticipation of arriving in Cherbourg before Christmas morning, violent waves now crashed over the open deck.

The Brilliant had long since pulled away, leaving the remaining men stranded. The lights of rescue boats in the distance gave Paul little hope. The ship was sinking fast - faster than the boats could get to them. He weighed his options. He could scale down the nets like he'd watched several men do already, or he could let go of the railing and slide down into the water, down the deck of the Leopoldville. *Either way, I'm going swimming*, he thought. The latter option ran the risk of getting trapped beneath the ship or being hit by its debris when it finally gave in and started its descent to the bottom. Which, judging by its near vertical position and the consistent creaks and pops echoing from deep within its interior, would be only a matter of minutes.

A panic-stricken officer addressed his men. "Lose your helmets," he cried. "They'll become anchors in the water."

Soldiers left and right ripped off their steel helmets, tossing them into the sea. Paul looked down into the water.

"Stop!" he shouted. "You're going to kill them!" Soldiers already floating in the Channel had become the unintentional targets, hit in the head from twenty feet above.

"Ah, shit," said one GI, dropping his helmet on the deck of the Leopoldville. Paul watched it roll down the length of the ship, disappearing when it reached the water.

"Colonel," Paul said, "we either climb down," he nodded toward the nets, "or we jump."

Colonel Rumberg looked weaker than when he was trapped in the rising waters. His wet uniform clung to him, and Paul watched his hand tremble when he let go of the rail. "I'll take my chances right here, I think."

Paul shook his head. "No way, sir. If the suction doesn't pull you under, all this loose debris will kill you first."

Colonel Rumberg shrugged. "Not much fight left in me." The Colonel shivered and closed his eyes against the biting wind.

"Bullshit," said Paul. Rumberg eyed him. "With all due respect," Paul added, "I'm not getting off this tub without you."

Colonel Rumberg blew out a breath. "You're a real pain in my ass, you know that?"

Paul grinned. "That's what I'm here for, sir. This piece of shit is going down. Let's get the hell off of it."

The colonel took a deep breath and hoisted himself over the railing, finding a foothold at the top of the net. Paul followed him over, keeping the distance between them close. He knew the colonel didn't have much left in him, and he didn't want to let him out of his sight. They climbed halfway down, fighting with the thick rope and the swell of the sea. Without warning, Colonel Rumberg pushed off, letting go and kicking his feet, untangling himself from the net and landing backwards into the freezing water. Paul hurried to do the same before the choppy water separated them. The shock of the cold water made him gasp for air, but instead, he swallowed a mouthful of oily water. He tried to swim, determined to stay with the colonel, but another wave crashed over his head, disorienting him.

The water was black, and the sky matched it. *What a way to die,* he thought. *Hypothermia first, then drown out here in the pitch black.* It wasn't that he was afraid of the dark. He had wandered around the farm under the cover of darkness plenty of times. But out here, this was different. He'd never felt so vulnerable as he did then, searching for something, anything to hold onto.

He joined in with the other voices of agony, then. He prayed loudly and desperately along with the men crying out for help. The sea was full of soldiers begging for God or their mothers, crying senselessly out of fear and shock. Paul thought he could have cried then, too, if it wouldn't have used so much of the little energy he had left. Just thinking about the boys that were lost on board - most of them *just babies* - he damn near lost it.

He tried to flip over onto his back, hoping to float, but came up coughing and sputtering when the waves engulfed him once more. He started treading again, still searching for something he could grab onto. He could see Colonel Rumberg struggling just a few feet away and tried to swim to him again. The lights from the approaching rescue boats illuminated the men in the water. Hundreds of soldiers bobbed like apples, their screams quieted by the cold. Paul felt like he'd been submerged in the icy water for hours though it couldn't have been more than a few minutes. He wondered how the hell so many men were staying afloat.

How were they keeping their heads above the relentless waves? He drifted close enough to one GI and realized he wasn't floating or conserving his energy. He was dead. They were all dead. Every single one of them that floated past had their screams smothered by death's silence.

A wooden plank floated by, near enough that he could reach out with his fingertips but far enough that he had to fight to grab on. When he finally pulled his arms over it, he fought the current with everything he had to reach Colonel Rumberg.

"Colonel," he cried. Another wave crashed over his head, and when he surfaced, he was only a foot from the officer. "Grab on," he said, coughing out more dirty seawater.

Colonel Rumberg reached out with icy, stiff fingertips, too cold to hold onto anything. Paul managed to snag his sleeve and hauled him closer. Both men gasped for air, fatigued from the rough wind and the unforgiving sea. Paul tried to time his breaths against the waves lest he swallow more water, but there was no predicting the angry swells. There was no rhythm, no rhyme or reason to the violent Channel waters.

Another GI floated past, too weak to reach for the board. Paul grabbed him and pulled his arms up onto the wood, and the three of them clung to their only hope for survival. They were far enough away from the wreckage that they weren't a target for desperate, frantic men who would pull them under the water in an attempt to save themselves. They didn't need to fight their comrades for a place on the board. They were close enough, Paul hoped, that a rescue boat might see them, still far enough not to be run over. They took turns lifting their torsos onto the board - any attempt at relief from the frigid water.

Paul watched the rescue effort. Screams of men still alive, begging for help when a rescue boat neared, echoed through the empty night. He was helpless and exhausted and ready to give up. The freezing water was too much to bear for too long. He was sure he must have been dozing in and out of consciousness because when he looked behind him to where the Leopoldville had been, the ship was gone. Nothing except the last of the floating debris and the hundreds of soldiers bobbing up and down remained.

Colonel Rumberg lay across the board, unconscious. A searchlight swept over them, and Paul could see the colonel's eyes were closed. He heaved a giant exhale, and his grip on the board loosened. Paul's hands, cramped with cold, were of no use to him now.

"Rumberg," he said. "Come on, Rumberg, there's a rescue boat coming."

No response.

"Rumberg," he said again, panic rising up inside of him.

"Dammit, Rumberg, answer me," he cried. He tried to get his legs to work, to move him closer to the Colonel but his legs were too frozen. He was at the mercy of the tide taking him wherever it wanted.

"Come on, Colonel," Paul whispered. It was too late. Colonel Rumberg's arms slid from the board, and his lifeless body splayed face down in the sea.

"No, no, no, no," Paul cried. His lips trembled with cold. If he had an ounce of energy left in him, he'd have swam to Colonel Rumberg and lifted his body back up onto the wooden board. He didn't deserve to sink to the bottom of the Channel.

He didn't deserve to die. *Why? Why? Why? After he saved how many men stuck inside that death trap? This is how he dies? It's not fair!*

Everything around him faded out of view. The soldier still on the board with him struggled to stay up, his teeth chattering uncontrollably.

"God in Heaven," Paul said, looking up at the dark sky. "Where are you?" No stars could break through the dense fog that settled around them. *So this is how it ends,* he thought. He had no more fight left in him. Not when a hero like Colonel Rumberg was gone. *I'll go too,* he thought. He laid his head down on the board and wept. The salty channel water mixed with his tears as his body heaved in giant sobs. He no longer cared about keeping his head above water or keeping his mouth closed. He coughed and sputtered, growing weaker with every mouthful.

Images of his loved ones flashed through his mind, and he welcomed the distraction. His mom, first, then his dad, Evie, and Danny Boy - *Christ,* he thought, *another telegram will kill them.* He thought about his brother, still missing. *Will I see you soon?* Sadness rolled through him, grief consuming him as he thought about all the things he'd miss out on. *Anna.* All of the things he'd hoped to do with her. Take her for ice cream. Horseback riding. *Bringing her home,* he thought. *I wanted to bring her home.* The realization hit him like a punch to the gut, and he began to pray out loud.

"Dear God, please. I beg of you. If you save me tonight, I swear to you I will do good. Please, God, there has to be a reason for this. Let me live long enough to figure it out because right now I feel like giving up, but I don't think you want me to. Please, God, give me strength enough to make it out of this water. Help me believe in your goodness because right now I'm having trouble seeing it." He didn't know what he was saying or if it was coherent at all, but he knew this was not how he wanted to die.

"Amen," groaned the soldier next to him. "Same here."

Rescue crews were too far away and couldn't get much closer without the risk of running over the hundreds of soldiers in and out of consciousness in the water. Paul laid his head down on the wooden board, resolved in the fact that there was nothing else he could do. He had tried and failed to save his colonel. Colonel Rumberg was the one who had started Paul out on this journey. That day in the classroom flashed through Paul's mind - the day that had sealed his fate - when he'd dreaded another English lesson, only to have Colonel Rumberg show up instead. That's how it was. The colonel was always there for the hardest, most pivotal moments of Paul's military career. He guided his men well. Paul often thought if he could just emulate Colonel Rumberg's confidence, his ease, his bravery, then he'd make it out okay. But now…who would he turn to if he made it out of here alive?

At least you saved Harry, he reminded himself. *I can die knowing Harry will make it home to Edith.* He closed his eyes, wondering where his friend had ended up - if he had reached Cherbourg or was still out here on one of the vessels idling around looking for survivors. He hoped he'd gotten off the Brilliant on its first trip back to shore.

Paul lifted his head to look around. Gone were the screams of the remaining men fighting to keep their heads above the water. They, too, had been silenced by the sea. Some had lost hope, too weak to call out, and others had lost it all, disappearing beneath the surface of the Channel. Paul laid his head back down, resolved to whatever God's will for him might be. Too much had been lost already to think there was any hope of being saved. He felt himself slip away, the rhythm of the waves lulling him. In and out of consciousness, he didn't know how long he laid there, but the feeling in his feet was gone, and his fingers were so stiff he knew he couldn't hold onto the board much longer.

Chapter 22

ANNA
CHRISTMAS EVE 1944
CHERBOURG, FRANCE

*C*aptain Levine stood in the opening of the tent they considered the lounge where nurses and officers had congregated to celebrate the holiday. Anna had been introduced to the surgeon the day before, and she glanced up to see him looking around the room, a grim expression on his face. She set down her glass and approached him.

"Captain Levine," she said, "Merry Christmas."

He looked down at her, his expression unchanging. "I'm looking for Captain Campbell," he said.

"She should be back momentarily," Anna said. "She just stepped out."

"I need all available nurses as soon as possible," he said, eyeing the off-duty group and the drinks they were enjoying. "It doesn't appear as though many of you will be equipped to handle yourselves tonight."

Anna drew back, surprised at his judgment. "Sir, we're perfectly capable of performing our job duties should we be needed." She swept her hand across the room. "What you see here is a few friends enjoying a rare night off and the promise that tomorrow's holiday holds."

Captain Levine gave a curt nod. "Yes, well, tomorrow will never come for hundreds of our men trapped on a sinking ship right now."

Captain Campbell approached from behind. "What men are trapped?"

The surgeon stepped out to face her. "A troopship has been torpedoed in the English Channel," he said. "We need to get to the docks as quickly as we can. I need as many nurses as you can spare."

"We'll be ready when you are," Captain Campbell replied. The surgeon eyed her as if he didn't believe they could live up to his expectations.

"Now, then," he said, testing her. She nodded and whistled into the tent. The laughter and singing stopped.

"All of my nurses, come with me, please."

The women immediately left their drinks and conversation and fell into formation, forming a line at the tent's entrance behind Anna.

"What's going on, boss?" Gretchen asked.

Captain Levine didn't wait for her to answer, marching out of the tent.

"A troopship has been torpedoed," she repeated the information Captain Levine had shared.

Eleanor looked at Anna. "The boys were due over here soon," she said.

"They were?" Anna was ashamed to admit that although she'd thought of him often, she hadn't written to Paul yet.

Eleanor nodded and seized Anna's hand.

The two Captains climbed into the front of the ambulance idling on the dirt road. Anna, Gretchen, Eleanor, and Louise scrambled into the back. The women had become a well- oiled machine and immediately got to work checking their equipment. The speed of Captain Levine's driving and the bumpy roads sent them bouncing off their seats. Anna held tight to the pack on her lap to keep her kit from flying across the back of the ambulance.

"How far are we from the harbor?" Captain Campbell asked.

"Fifteen miles," Captain Levine said. The way he was driving, Anna estimated they'd be there in five minutes - if they made it at all.

They pulled up to the harbor, and Anna looked through the front window. Men ran toward the docks, and others checked the incoming cars.

"Dammit," Captain Levine said, slamming his hand on the steering wheel. They were stuck in a long line of trucks trying to reach the docks. He rolled down his window as a soldier approached.

"What the hell is going on?" he demanded. "I've got to get down there."

"Sorry, sir, it's protocol," the soldier said. "We have to check every vehicle. You never know where a Nazi might be hiding out."

"There's no damn Nazi's in this ambulance," he said. "We're here to save our men."

The soldier held his hands up. "Just doing my job," he said.

"And preventing me from doing mine," Captain Levine

grumbled. The soldier opened the back, poked his head around, and closed it again, pounding the back of the ambulance. "Good to go," he shouted over the roar of the engine.

Captain Levine gunned it then, parking them so close to the water that Anna thought she'd be able to step right out onto the docks. Captain Campbell hopped out of the ambulance, following the angry surgeon.

"Ladies," she called out, "stay put until I know where you're needed."

Eleanor rolled her eyes. "Oh sure, just wait around while the men take care of business," she said.

"You don't think they were on that ship, do you?" Anna bit her lip, trying not to think the worst. *Dammit,* she thought, *I knew I should've stayed away.*

Eleanor shrugged. "I really don't know." Worry etched her face, and the four girls held one another's hands until Captain Campbell came running back.

"No equipment," she huffed. "There's too many men getting off the rescue boats. We won't have time to treat them all. Check them over, load up the ones that need a hospital, and keep moving to the next." She turned back to the water. "It's not good, ladies," she said. "Say a prayer for them. They'll never be the same…if they survive at all."

Eleanor and Anna looked at each other before they jumped down out of the back of the ambulance and ran after Captain Campbell.

A delivery of blankets and litters arrived just as they stepped up onto the docks. There was no organization that Anna could see, just droves of men being herded off the rescue vessels one after another. She began sorting the men as they came out - immediate attention went to Eleanor or Louise to be loaded into an ambulance. Those on the verge of shock but otherwise uninjured went to Gretchen for her skill in flirtation and light-hearted conversation to keep them distracted. Anna tossed blankets at shivering men as they walked past.

As soon as they emptied one boat, another one arrived. Anna didn't think it would ever end.

"How many men were on this ship?" Before anyone could answer her question, Captain Campbell shouted down to her from the rescue boat that had just docked.

"Anna, I need you here. Eleanor, Gretchen, Louise, get on any available ambulance. You're needed in the hospitals. Now. They're completely overrun."

Anna gave her friends a quick wave. "Good luck," she said.

"You too," Gretchen answered, taking off down the dock.

Anna ran down the dock and climbed aboard the enormous boat.

"Over here," Captain Campbell waved.

Anna held in a gasp at the sight of a baby-faced soldier. His clothes had been ripped to shreds, and his head hung limply against Captain Campbell.

"Captain…" Anna began. At a loss for words, she looked at her superior officer for what to do next.

"I don't know, Anna. But he's got a heart beat so we're going to do whatever we can. First is getting him off this boat."

Captain Levine came upon them then. Anna recognized the same shock she'd had on his face at what he saw. The soldier's stomach had been blown apart, his intestines hanging outside of his body. *How is he still alive?* It was the unspoken question amongst them all.

"Alright, let's get him in an ambulance."

"But how?" Anna didn't mean to question his authority, but she had no idea how they could possibly move him.

"As best we can," he said. "I need a litter now," he called out into the cold night to anyone around.

Two GIs came running with a stretcher in tow. They laid it on the ship's deck next to the wounded soldier. Between the two of them and Captain Levine, Anna watched as they carefully slid him from Captain Campbell's side onto the litter.

The two soldiers picked up each end, and Anna helped Captain Campbell up off the floor.

"Anna, ride with him to the hospital," Captain Levine ordered.

She nodded and followed behind the soldiers down the dock to a waiting ambulance.

They arrived at the Field Hospital after a ride that felt like it could have been the last one of her life. The ambulance had driven like a madman, and she'd held on for dear life in the back, watching the young soldier slip in and out of consciousness, groaning with every bump and turn until they'd unloaded and had been taken into an operating room.

"Hey there, soldier," she smiled. "How old are you?" He looked up at her with bright, watery eyes. "Nineteen just the other day," he beamed.

"Is that right? Well, happy birthday," She held his hands to keep him from feeling around his stomach while the doctor assessed his injuries.

"Exploded his intestines," the doctor muttered while he worked. Anna frowned and talked over him, keeping the young GI engaged and distracted. The doctor and the operating room nurse worked at what they could in any attempt to keep him comfortable. Anna doubted they could fix anything that remained. She knew it was unlikely he'd survive, and yet, she played pretend, smiling and chatting, keeping him calm in what might very well be the last moments of his life.

"So, nineteen, huh? You have a sweetheart back home?"

His pale cheeks turned pink, and he almost smiled. "Nah, not yet. Probably a good thing now, anyway." He grimaced, then let out a scream when the doctor reached into the mangled mess hanging out of his stomach.

"We'll need more," the doctor demanded, and the operating room nurse ran for more anesthetic.

Anna smoothed a hand over his forehead. It wasn't often that a floor nurse was allowed to stay for surgical procedures, but in the chaos, no one had questioned her position at his side.

"Where do you call home?" She kept her eyes trained on his, not looking down at his waist so he wouldn't follow her gaze and go into shock at the extent of his wound.

"Alabama," he said, gasping at the pressure of the doctor's attempts to put things back together. "Small town in Alabama."

Anna nodded. "Bet you're not used to this cold, icy winter, then."

"No, ma'am. It's not so bad, though." He was struggling to respond and cried out again.

"Can you call the priest? My mama will be comforted to know there was at least a priest here when I died."

Anna looked at the doctor. He looked up from the boy's gaping wound and gave her a curt nod, confirming what she already knew. There was no way to put what remained of his intestines back together. Too much damage had been done in the explosion. He'd likely not live through the night. Though she normally did not allow herself to get too attached to her patients, she hesitated to leave his side.

"You're doing just fine, soldier. Don't worry about a thing," she lied. "Hey, you never even told me your name."

"Matthews, ma'am," he huffed.

Matthews, she thought, *Why do I know that name?* Recognition dawned on her. "Why, PFC Matthews, I do believe you escorted me and my friends to our bunk on our first day at Camp Meade." She remembered how nervous he'd been and how sorry she'd felt for the young GI. And now here he was, dying in her arms. *The cruelty of it all,* she thought. *His poor mother.*

The doctor motioned for her to step away, and she placed his hands by his sides. "I'll be right back," she told him.

"There's nothing we can do," Dr. Shaffer said. Anna nodded, fighting the tears that threatened. She couldn't cry over them all.

"I've given him a sedative that should take effect shortly. Enough to keep him comfortable through the night. I don't see him making it more than a few hours," the doctor said.

She looked at the floor. "Please, can you send the priest on your way out?" She looked up at the doctor. "It's his last request, but I'd like to stay with him."

"You should go home and rest, Anna. It's been a long night."

She laughed. "As we nurses like to say, we'll rest when we're dead, right? He needs someone there with him, doc. He's just a kid."

He gave her shoulder a squeeze, knowing she wouldn't change her mind. "I'll see if I can get Reverend Ole up here," he said and turned to leave.

Anna returned to Private Matthews, placing a fresh washcloth on his forehead. He was in and out of consciousness, the sedative taking effect as the doctor had predicted. She sat beside him on the bed, holding his hand and praying. She prayed through the night, alternating between his bedside and a chair the night nurse had brought in for her. At two a.m., he began to cry, and Anna jumped up from the chair. She held his hand while he called out incoherent, rambling screams. His skin had gone clammy, taking on that waxy finish Anna had come to recognize as death neared. For nearly an hour, he carried on, writhing and crying, clawing at the sheet and the dressings covering the worst of his injuries. Anna felt her heart crack open when he cried out for his mother, begging for the pain to stop. She nearly fell to her knees when his screaming finally stopped an hour later, but instead, she climbed onto the bed, cradling his head in her lap.

She was watching his shallow breathing when Reverend Olsen appeared just after three o'clock. He came to stand at the foot of the bed without a word, closing his eyes as he began to pray. Anna bowed her head, tears welling in her eyes. In the fragile early morning hours, she was helpless against the sadness that had wound its way around her heart. She closed her eyes, listening to the Reverend's whispered prayer. "Amen," she whispered, laying a hand on Private Matthews' chest. Sometime between his cries for his mother and the Reverend's prayers, his heart had stopped beating.

Anna sat, unmoving for a moment before she reached out and gently closed his eyes. She shifted his head off her lap and took Reverend Olsen's outstretched hand, stepping down from the bed. She covered the soldier with a white sheet and turned to the Reverend.

"Thank you for coming, Reverend," she whispered, looking up at him for the first time. She was surprised to find that the man standing before her was the same one from the docks earlier that evening. He'd caught her attention when he seemed to be everywhere, standing over every lifeless body that had piled up on the pier. She had grown annoyed at his constant, lingering behavior, wondering what he was doing, checking every dead soldier when they needed help saving the ones who were barely hanging on. Was he questioning their judgment? Checking for himself to make sure they hadn't missed a heartbeat? She hadn't been able to get him out of her head, and she eyed him curiously now.

He had the same somber expression she'd seen on him at the docks, and then it dawned on her. *How stupid,* she thought, reprimanding herself. *He's the Reverend. He wasn't questioning our ability. He was praying over those men at the hour of their death.* She felt foolish and hoped he wouldn't notice the flush of embarrassment across her cheeks.

He nodded. "I understand he asked for a priest," he said, "but I'm the only one around for miles right now." He shrugged and gave her a half-hearted smile.

She touched his arm. "I don't think it matters which religion one is when it comes to the end," she said. "I do believe his mother would be glad you were here."

He placed his hand over hers and looked over at the covered body of Private Matthews. "It never gets any easier," he said.

"Mm. Tell me about it," Anna said, wiping a tear from her cheek.

They walked together outside of the hospital tent. Anna knew she'd have to bring the body out and lay him on the ground outside to wait for transport. A deep sigh shook through her. She hated this part. It never felt right to lay their lifeless bodies on bare ground.

"I can't do it," she said.

Reverend Olsen looked at her with concern in his eyes and waited for her to go on.

She blew out a shaky breath. "They deserve better than this," she said, sweeping her hand across the patch of muddy, icy ground meant for the dead.

The reverend looked thoughtful. "There are a lot of things they deserve but don't receive," he replied.

"But this," she said, "I can do something about this."

She motioned for him to follow her back into the tent, where she raided a cabinet filled with GI blankets. She grabbed as many as she could and handed a few to Reverend Olsen.

Back outside, she laid them out, one after another, over the mud and melting snow. Reverend Olsen followed her lead.

She stood back. "It's not much, but it's better than nothing," she said, tears streaking down her face.

The night nurse and ward officer came out with a litter - carrying Private Matthews. Anna and Reverend Olsen helped lay him gently on the blankets. Anna knelt beside him, taking care to fold his arms inward over his chest before covering him with the sheet once more. Before she could stand, another life-less body was brought out and laid on the blanket. She arranged the soldier's body in the same way, with his limbs tucked in tight to avoid being stepped on.

She stood and gazed out over the snowy field to the hills beyond, the sun not yet peeking out behind them in the early morning. Chilled, she turned back toward the hospital tent where Reverend Olsen waited for her.

"Thank you for your help, Reverend," she said.

"You can always call for me. I'm here to help," he said, then added, "not just in times of death, you know." He eyed her, looking for her understanding.

She nodded. "I appreciate that," she said. "It's just been a long night. I could use a few hours of sleep before I come back and do it all again." She smiled weakly, and Reverend Olsen held out his arm.

"Let me walk you home, then," he said. She linked her arm through his and let him hold her up as exhaustion wracked through her. They walked slowly through the snow, avoiding the icy patches that had formed from the melting snow and trudge of boots up and down.

They crested the hill, and the abandoned chateau came into view, surrounded by the tent city they'd set up. "How beautiful this must have been," Reverend Olsen remarked.

"That seems to be a theme here," she said. "And to think, only a few years ago, this was untouched by war."

"Hopefully, it won't be that long before this is all over," he said. Anna hummed her agreement.

~

Chapter 23

⚜
PAUL
CHRISTMAS EVE 1944
ENGLISH CHANNEL
⚜

The soldier next to Paul lifted his head.

"Hey, wake up," he said. Paul opened one eye. "Is that a rope over there, or am I starting to see things?"

Paul opened both eyes and lifted his head to look. He saw the rope, too. "It's a rope, alright, but I can't see what it's attached to."

The two men looked around. The only rescue ships were too far away to have dropped the rope. It couldn't possibly be attached to something better than the wooden board they'd managed to stay afloat on. Was it worth the risk? The other man seemed to think so. He pushed off the board, launching himself onto the rope, holding on as tight as he could with frostbitten fingers. Paul wasn't sure he wanted to give up the only raft he had. He didn't have enough strength left to swim if the rope was a dead end.

The soldier pulled the rope until there was no more slack in the line, and it looked like he was actually getting pulled closer and closer to the tugboat.

"Grab on," he called back to Paul. "It could be your only chance."

Paul hesitated. His body screamed in achy refusal. He had become so stiff he was afraid to reach for the rope. He didn't know if his muscles could do what he wanted them to. He watched the soldier drift further away, the last of the rope going with him. He was scared to move but just as scared to stay, so he reached as far as he could, letting go of the board. His fingertips grazed the rough fibers of the rope, and he felt it slip away. It was no use. He was too weak and too cold. He had lost his grip strength, along with the feeling in his feet, and now he'd lost the only thing that had kept him alive. He spun around in the water, panicked, without something to pull himself up on. He'd never survive without something to hold onto.

Water washed over him, and he was helpless to stop it. He felt it fill his nose, tasting the fuel oil that had spilled out of the Leopoldville. The foul liquid was bitter in his mouth, and he coughed and sputtered under the water that suffocated him. His brain told him to fight, but he was powerless against the sea. His body was too frozen to do anything more than let God and the sea decide his fate.

The next wave pulled him back above the surface, and he managed to cough the water out of his lungs enough that he could breathe in the salty air. His nose and eyes burned, and his vision was blurry. He could no longer see the soldier that had kept him company. He looked around him but saw no one close enough to help. The bodies of dead soldiers bobbed up and down, the moon casting its amber glow over them. Paul closed his eyes. It was too much.

"How do I know when it's time to give up?" He asked out loud. With no one to hear him, he hoped his own voice might somehow fill the void, to make him feel less alone, less afraid.

Something grabbed him from behind, and he kicked and flailed, fearing another soldier was trying to save himself by using him as a raft. He had witnessed too many soldiers sacrificed by their own comrades, pushed down and unable to resurface.

"Easy there, slugger." Paul came face to face with a burly sailor grabbing at his arm. He threw a rope around Paul's head and struggled to get it down under his shoulders. "You're not giving up today, my friend," he said, before swimming through the choppy waves to the boat. Paul somehow hadn't heard the approach behind him. The sailor climbed up the ladder on the back of the boat before a group of crewmen started hauling Paul up the side.

"I can't help you. I'm too weak," Paul said.

"We got it, mate," said the sopping-wet sailor. He added his weight to the line, and they raised Paul high enough that two more crewmen could grab hold of him. One caught his arm, and the other took hold of his leg. Together, they rolled him onto the deck, where he landed with a thud. He stayed where he was, unable to move, thankful to be out of the water.

"Lucky we found ya, mate," one sailor said.

"Yeah, gotta thank the fellow below deck. He told us you were still out there. We watched you take in that last swell. Didn't know if you'd pop back up."

Paul lifted his head and gave them a weak nod. There was so much he wanted to say but couldn't. He was too exhausted to express his gratitude.

Someone covered him in a brown, scratchy blanket and rolled him further down the deck.

"Sorry, soldier, gotta make room for more," a voice said before sending him down a set of steps. He didn't think he'd have ever been so glad to be numb all over - he didn't feel a thing when he thumped down the steps, landing in the boiler room. Even the warmth from the boiler couldn't make his teeth stop chattering, or his body stop shaking. He lay at the bottom of the stairs, moving only to get out of the way of the next poor soldier to get rolled down. A crewman came down, shoved a glass in his hands, and ordered him to drink before disappearing back up the stairs.

It took several attempts to get his shaky hands to his mouth without spilling. When he managed to connect the glass to his lips, he welcomed the burn of whiskey warming his insides. What he didn't welcome was the burning he felt as it came right back up, and he vomited all over the floor. The smell of the oil he'd swallowed in the water made him nauseous, sweat beading on his forehead despite his cold, wet clothes clinging to his body. He pinched his eyes shut and counted his breaths to keep from heaving again. He didn't think he made it beyond five before he slumped over and passed out.

When he woke again, they had reached the shore, and the ship's compartment was filled with men that looked just like him - bundled in blankets thrown over their wet clothes, expressionless eyes, their bodies damn near lifeless. He stood to climb the stairs and stumbled over his feet when he tried to lift them, numb to the bone.

The lights on the docks were blinding after hours in the dark compartment, and he squinted his already swollen eyes against the glare. He staggered onto the dock and looked around - for what? He didn't know. He had kept the blanket around his shoulders and pulled it tighter when the wind hit his wet clothes. The glow of a fire caught his eye, and he moved slowly in that direction, forcing his limbs to keep going, one foot in front of the other, though he ached all over. Several soldiers were already gathered there, and he sank down onto a wooden crate and stared into the glow of burning k-ration boxes. No one talked. He sat there, mesmerized by the flames, until he caught himself swaying. He felt like he was still treading in the middle of the Channel, waterlogged, everything around him fuzzy and muffled. He shook his head back and forth as if the water would somehow dislodge. He remained in that hazy state, similar to the twilight before falling asleep, only he wasn't asleep, not even close. He was wide awake and cracked open to the horrific realization that this wasn't a dream at all.

An officer, red in the face and with a look of sheer overwhelm, approached the group huddled around the fire. Paul could barely muster half a nod in his direction. *I hope he doesn't expect me to stand at attention,* Paul thought. *He'll be picking me up off the ground if he does.*

"Boys," he said. "Any of you need transport to the hospital?" Paul stared into the fire, unmoving. He could have probably used a hospital visit. He hadn't yet regained feeling in several of his toes, but he knew there were men in far greater need. He leaned forward with his head in his hands. He felt like crying. He could have sat right there and sobbed. So much had been taken out there in the water. So much they'd never get back. He didn't think he'd ever recover. *Doctors can't do anything for this,* he thought. He looked around at the men mulling about the docks, soldiers being loaded into ambulances, and still more pouring out of the rescue boats.

He thought about the men in his unit. *Harry,* he thought. *I wonder where Harry is.* He thought back to when he'd last seen his friend. Everything was a blur after that. He must have blacked out at some point. Several chunks of time felt too hazy to recall. He replayed the images he could remember and felt his palms go sweaty even as he shivered under the blanket. He looked down at his bare feet - *when did I lose my boots?* he wondered. And then he pictured Colonel Rumberg's lifeless body floating away from him. A sudden dizziness overtook him, and he felt a hand on his shoulder. The officer's voice sounded far away.

"Any of you not injured, load up in the truck." Paul was vaguely aware of him pointing to a forty-and-eight box truck idling near the dock.

More muffled talking, "You'll get dry at Hotel L'Atlantique for the night; we'll figure the rest out tomorrow. Try to get some rest."

Paul tried to stand with the other soldiers walking toward the truck, but his legs were too heavy to move. He stumbled and sat back down.

"Son, are you ok?"

Paul opened his mouth to respond, but nothing came out. He tumbled off the wooden crate, the officer's hand slipping from his shoulder, and everything around him went black.

〜

"Well, look who we have here. If it isn't lover boy himself."

Paul recognized the voice as one of the nurses he'd seen when he first met Anna. "Hey there, nurse. Long time no see." He tried to lift his head off the pillow but dropped back again, too weak to hold himself up.

"How ya feeling?" Gretchen checked his pulse and eyed him all over, a smile glued to her face.

"Better than most, I'm sure," he said, looking away.

Gretchen's job was to take care of her patients, and he knew part of that was keeping their spirits high. But nothing could have lifted his spirits just then. Half his comrades were dead, sinking to the bottom of the Channel with the Leopoldville or floating lifeless to shore. *That damn rusted piece of shit*, he thought. He closed his eyes, wishing he could shut out the anger roiling inside him.

Gretchen stayed by his side despite his best efforts to ignore her. He hoped she'd move on to her next patient. Instead, she sat on the edge of his bed.

"Anna's still down at the docks," she said quietly, her smile replaced with genuine concern.

He turned his head toward her and opened his eyes.

"Why?" *What a stupid question*, he thought.

"We split up when the news came in. She stayed down with Captain Campbell at the harbor, and the rest of us were sent here to help unload the ambulances."

Paul wasn't surprised. He'd only known Anna a short time,

but her determination and vivacity was easy to see. She was a woman not to be messed with, and he knew she'd never need him to save her. Even still, his immediate reaction was to do just that, even if he was stuck in a hospital bed.

"Is she okay down there?"

Gretchen shrugged. "It's Anna," she said. "She wouldn't let on even if she wasn't."

She stood then, placing a clipboard at the foot of his bed.

"You'll be alright, you know. We're keeping you overnight, maybe a day or two after that, and then you'll be back out there."

She turned to go down the line to the GI writhing in his bed next to Paul when he raised a hand to keep her there.

"You think I've got a shot with Anna?" He was probably a fool for asking when he was already at his lowest, but he just had to know.

Gretchen smiled. "I'd say so, soldier."

Relief spread through him, and he gave a small smile back.

"But I'll have your head if you tell her I told you," she added.

It was enough for him. *Hope*, he thought. He just needed a little bit of hope that it wouldn't always feel this bad. He closed his eyes and said a prayer before he dropped off to sleep.

Dear God, you spared my life for reasons I don't understand. Especially not when so many good ones didn't come out alive. All I can think is someone must still need me, God, because I don't know if I need to be here.

A tear rolled down his cheek. No matter what he did, he couldn't stop the anger from bubbling up.

Please, God, tell me why. Why the hell am I here and Rumberg's not? How about the twins? Barely nineteen. How the hell is that fair? I know life isn't fair, but dammit! I shouldn't be here either. Help me, God, help me.

He pleaded and pleaded until he fell into a fitful sleep, images of the Leopoldville in its final descent replaying over and over in his mind. Only this time, Anna was there too. He tried to swim to her, but the waves kept pushing him back further and further from her until he could no longer see her face, swallowed up in the black of night. He screamed for her, tossing in the hospital bed until he woke to something cold on his forehead.

He opened his eyes to Gretchen swabbing a washcloth over his face. He was slick with sweat, and he kicked off the sheet, feeling hot and constricted.

"Sorry, soldier, it's still just me," Gretchen said. He sat up, and she handed him a paper cup.

"Drink," she ordered him, and he took a sip. He coughed and sputtered, expecting water, surprised when the whiskey burned his throat.

"That's not water," he croaked.

Gretchen laughed. "It sounded like you needed something a bit stronger," she said.

~

Chapter 24

ANNA
CHRISTMAS EVE 1944
CHERBOURG, FRANCE

*A*nna stripped out of her dirty uniform, heavy with sadness. It had been the hardest night yet and she could only hope it wouldn't get any worse than it already was. She lay back on her cot and draped her arm over her eyes. She needed to wash her face before she dropped off to sleep, but she was too tired to walk out for water. The sun was already high in the sky, blazing through the opening in the tent. Visions of the men she'd tried to help plagued her, and she wondered if sleep would ever come easily again. As tired as she was, she dreaded the idea of replaying the night's events when she closed her eyes. She rolled over and noticed a small box with a little red bow on top sitting next to her cot.

"What's this?" She picked it up, turning it over in her hand. She traced her mother's familiar handwriting and slipped a finger under the taped edges, pulling the brown paper loose.

She sat staring at the delicate box inside, pale blue with three yellow rosettes in each corner. She wondered what could be inside, but after the night she'd had…her mind trailed off, and she sat on her bed with the box on her lap.

Everything happened so fast. She could hardly remember how she'd gotten to the docks in the first place. She thought back to before they'd found out about the torpedoed ship. The lounge, she thought, realizing for the first time what day it was. She sighed, looking at the gift box, understanding flooding her. "It's Christmas morning," she said to the empty hut. Gretchen walked in with Louise then, both of them looking just as tired as Anna felt.

"What a Christmas to remember," Gretchen said. Anna looked up at her friends. She saw in their eyes everything that she felt, too. They were weary after caring for their boys tonight. *Their boys*, Anna thought. She never thought she'd think of them in the way Captain Campbell always referred to the soldiers. But after being here, it was true. Every single soldier she'd treated was one of her boys. Every single one was someone's son, brother, husband, or father, and she treated each one of them the way she'd want her own family to be treated. Even the ones who spit on her and cursed in her face. Especially those ones - the ones hurting the most. There was no mistaking the pain in their eyes that they were so desperate to hide.

She blew out a breath and smoothed her knotted hair back behind her ears. "I bet I'm quite a sight right now," she laughed. She could still taste the salt on her lips from the wind and sea spray blowing in her face all night.

"Ha, aren't we all?" said Louise, taking a seat beside her.

Gretchen kicked off her shoes and shimmied out of her pants. She reached for her nightgown and turned back around.

"Oh! Anna, I almost forgot. You'll never guess who I took care of tonight," she said, a smile stretching across her face.

Anna was too tired to play along. "I guess I wouldn't, Gretch. Most of the people I know here are in this tent," she said, ignoring the clench in her gut.

"Your *friend* came in," she said, wiggling her eyebrows.

Clouded with fatigue, Anna nearly said, 'Okay, Gretchen,' and crawled under the covers, ready to put this particular Christmas behind her, but as her friend's words registered, Anna's eyes went wide.

She froze, her back stiff. "Who?" She tried to act as though she had no idea who Gretchen could possibly be talking about. All of her friends were here, nurses changing shifts, eyelids heavy, just like hers after the night they'd had. But she knew. Her heart knew, picking up its pace in her chest. *Paul.*

Gretchen snorted. "Oh please."

"What was he there for?" She could barely keep the tremble out of her voice. *He was there. He was on that sinking ship.* She thought she might be sick. *This damn war,* she thought. *This God-forsaken war.* She wanted to scream. *Why? Will there ever be anything sacred again? Will there be anything left that the fighting and the bombing and the sleepless nights haven't stolen?*

"Will we ever be the same again?"

Her eyes clouded with tears, and before Gretchen could answer her, Anna started to cry. She hadn't realized the tears were falling until Gretchen and Louise were upon her, crouching on the ground beside her bed, rubbing her arms, comforting her despite the questions and fears that lurked in their eyes, too.

"Honey, you need a nightcap and a good sleep." Louise grabbed a handkerchief and shoved it in her hands.

Gretchen agreed, "Yeah, so you can do it all over again in the morning."

Anna laughed through her tears. "And what if I can't?" It was barely a whisper, but it was one of her greatest fears. They'd all heard the stories - the nurses that couldn't cut it. The ones that plastered a smile to their faces but slowly died inside. The ones that couldn't handle the things they saw until one day, they couldn't fake it anymore. They became shadows of their former selves, their eyes distant and gray as they were escorted out for 'a few days rest.' Everyone knew they wouldn't be back. But no one talked about it. No one talked about how those shadows walking the hospital wards turned into ghosts - here today, gone tomorrow, carry on, nothing to see here.

She cried and cried, huge uncontrollable sobs that shook her to her core. Any other day, she'd have been mortified at her weakness. "God," she gulped, "what would mother think of me now?" She squeezed her eyes shut and cried until there was nothing left inside of her.

Gretchen rubbed her back while Louise ran out of the hut in search of something strong enough to numb the pain. By the time she came back, Anna had stopped crying, more from dehydration than because she was finished. She heaved a sigh and rested her head on Gretchen's shoulder. Louise offered her a cup, and she took it, downing it without even looking. It burned its way down, and she scrunched her nose up.

Gretchen giggled and reached for one, too, savoring the liquor in little sips.

"Scotch. In case you were wondering," Louise said. She

tipped up her cup to them before taking a sip.

Silence stretched between them, and embarrassment crept up on Anna.

"I'm such a fool," she finally said, setting her empty cup next to the mystery box she'd forgotten about. She covered her face with her hands.

"Oh please, you think I haven't buried my head under my pillow and sobbed myself to sleep a time or two?" Gretchen pulled at Anna's hands, holding onto one while Louise took the other.

"Somehow, I think you might be telling tall tales just to make me feel better." Anna sniffed. She wished she'd taken her time with her scotch. She squeezed her friend's hands.

"Thank you. I don't know what I'd do if it weren't for you girls. I can't imagine doing this without you."

"Well, I know for sure you'd never admit your feelings for one Paul O'Reilly if it weren't for us," said Gretchen, a sly smile spreading across her face.

Louise nodded. Anna looked between the two of them in disbelief.

"Really? After the night we've had? You still want to gossip about boys?" She shook her head and laid back on her cot, pushing her friends off the edge. Gretchen squealed as she jumped up and glared at Anna in mock annoyance.

"Yes," they replied in unison. "Besides, it's not just any boys," Gretchen said. "It's *your* boy."

"I don't know what you're talking about. We're just friends," said Anna, determined to deny any romantic feelings even though she'd already admitted to them on the Leopoldville. *The same Leopoldville,* she thought. The same ship that had transport-ed them just a week ago was now sitting at the bottom of the Channel.

"I need my beauty sleep." She rolled over on her side, and Gretchen and Louise swatted at her.

"Mhmm," said Gretchen.

"Just friends," said Louise, "coulda fooled me with those doe eyes you get whenever he walks in the room."

Anna laughed despite herself. Her friends were right, and she knew it. But she'd deny it to them and herself until this war was over. There was no way she'd go home broken in more ways than one. This war had already taken enough. If she didn't care about him, then at least it couldn't take him from her, too. At least, that was the lie she kept telling herself.

She had nearly fallen asleep when she rolled back over to face Gretchen, stretched out on the cot next to Anna's.

"Is he ok?"

Gretchen gave her an 'I told you so' look.

"He'll be better when he sees you tomorrow," she said with a wink.

❦

The familiar smell of antiseptic and burning coal stung her nose when she pulled open the entrance to the hospital tent. She blinked several times, adjusting to the dim lighting after walking through the brightness of the fresh white snow. Pulling off her gloves and winter coat, she walked around the back of the nurse's station, hanging them over a chair. The heat from the stove roar-ing in one corner, mixed with the anticipation over seeing Paul today, made her cheeks flush. She knew he was lying in a bed somewhere under the same roof. She picked up a clipboard to fan herself when she jumped out of her skin at the voice behind her.

"You okay this morning, Nurse?"

She laughed at herself and waved a hand, pretending Dr. Wilson's lack of personal space wasn't what made her jumpy. "Fine, fine," she said. "I just didn't see you there."

He raised an eyebrow and nodded, flipping through his notes.

"Anything new I should know about today?" She moved away from Dr. Wilson and opened the cabinet behind the desk, pulling the usual supplies she'd need for the day. Penicillin, syringes, and her log to keep track of when each soldier could have more. That was the number one request when she made her rounds, boys begging for help with the pain. With a tent full of patients, there wasn't time to check with the doctor - he'd be in and out of surgery, so the nurses took initiative - she kept the paper log in her front pocket. The nurse from the night before had written each patient's name and bay number along with the time of their last dose, and Anna would do the same for the next nurse coming later that afternoon. It was the best they could do, running from one soldier to the next.

The doctor shook his head. "It's all the same. You were at the docks last night, you saw what we've got."

I guess he didn't sleep much either, Anna thought. "Yes, Doctor. Just making sure." She sucked in a breath and edged past him. He placed a hand on her shoulder, stepping uncomfortably close.

"Anna, you'll be flying solo today. I've got three surgeries scheduled and won't be back in between." He smiled, still holding her in place.

She nodded, taking a step backward out of his grasp. "I hope they go well for you, Sir."

"I appreciate your concern, Anna." He stared at her far longer than necessary, making her squirm under his gaze until she spun on her heel and walked down the first row of patients. *Ugh*, she thought. It wasn't unusual for some of the men out here to be pushy and suggestive. But Dr. Wilson gave her the creeps. She shivered despite the roaring fire and looked back over her shoulder just as he strode out of the tent.

Anna took a deep breath and pulled back the first curtain. Butterflies swirled in her stomach when she saw Paul lying in the bed, covered to his neck, and sleeping soundly. She'd read his chart and knew he'd had a rough night, so she backed out quietly, hoping to let him sleep.

"AB?" His eyes were still closed, and she smiled at his use of her nickname. She had forgotten she'd told him about it at Marjorie's house, when they'd swapped stories about their grandfathers.

He opened his eyes and tried to sit up, groaning with the effort. She ran to his side, holding onto his arm with one hand and adjusting his pillow with the other.

"Easy there, soldier," she said "Don't be a hero." She'd meant it as a joke, but as soon as the words were out, she wished she could take them back. The light she'd just seen when he first looked at her went out of his eyes, and he looked past her now, avoiding her gaze.

"Paul…" she started, but he held up a hand to stop her.

"It's ok, Anna. I'm no hero. That much I know for sure."

"Don't, Paul. Don't do that to yourself. You can't blame your-self for what happened."

He looked at her and snorted. "For what happened? Nah. I blame the damn Krauts for that," he said. He shuffled his feet beneath the blanket and closed his eyes again. She thought may-be he'd leave it at that, the silence stretching on between them. She reached for his hand to check his pulse when he opened his eyes.

"I couldn't save him, AB. I watched him die in the water. So no, I'm no hero. I'm no one's hero. Hell, I don't know why, in God's name, I'm still alive."

She stood beside his bed, unsure of what to say. If it were any other soldier lying there, she'd have had a number of placa-tions or silly jokes to lighten his mood. But this was Paul. The man she'd sobbed over just hours before. And here she stood, tongue-tied and feeling like a jerk for saying the wrong thing.

"Paul…" She closed her eyes to keep the tears from coming. *You do not have time for this,* she thought. She would have spent all day sitting with him if she could. But she had a job to do and soldiers waiting for her.

Paul rolled to his side, away from her, and she touched his shoulder.

"I'm so sorry," she said and walked from the room.

Chapter 25

PAUL
CHRISTMAS DAY 1944
CHERBOURG, FRANCE

———— ೞ ————

*H*e glanced over his shoulder and watched her walk away. It wasn't the reunion he'd hoped for, and he could kick himself for how he was acting. He blew out a frustrated breath. She hadn't meant to strike a nerve, but he was reactive and raw from last night - his emotions like live wires on the surface of his skin.

Hell, all through the night, he'd lain awake thinking up all the ways he could convince her to marry him - the only thing distracting him from the pain he felt everywhere. *Imagine that,* he thought, *thinking she'd want to marry the poor fool she'd seen a whole two times. Three, if you count today.* He scoffed out loud and kicked the sheet off his legs, a sudden heat radiating off of him. It was sweltering in the hospital tent, though he still had no feeling in four of his toes. He looked down at his bare feet and tried to wiggle his toes, hoping he could force the feeling back into them.

A Red Cross girl came down the aisle pushing a cart of coffee and donuts.

"What can I get for ya?" She beamed at Paul while she grabbed a cup, ready to pour him a coffee.

"Nothing, thanks," he grumbled.

"Aw, come on, soldier. It's Christmas," she said. "At least let me give you a coffee and a donut." She poured him a cup and placed it beside the bed, then went back to her cart for a donut. She grabbed two and set them next to the coffee.

"Anything else you need?"

Paul scanned the items on the cart, and the realization hit him that he'd lost everything. No duffle bag, no paper to write home, no toothbrush. He had no clue where his boots might've ended up, probably at the bottom of the Channel along with everything else. He'd need a new woolen coat, and he wondered if the Army would be apt to find one for him. He pinched the bridge of his nose, hating everything and hating himself for feeling that way. The Red Cross girl waited patiently, and when Paul glanced at her, she had the same smile plastered to her face. He wondered how she could hold it for so long.

"Just a toothbrush," he finally said. It was the only thing he could think of.

"Sure thing, soldier." She reached into the cart and handed him a packaged toothbrush.

"Thank you," he grumbled.

"My pleasure," she beamed. "Hope you feel better soon." She gave him a little wave, then added, "Merry Christmas."

He squeezed his eyes shut. *Jesus, it's Christmas,* he thought. *Man, things are really screwed up.* He dropped his head back onto the pillow and stared up at the ugly tent ceiling, feeling sorry for himself. And then, thinking about how lucky he was to be lying there at all, he felt guilty for feeling sorry for himself. It was a vicious cycle of grief and anger swirling through him until he finally fell asleep.

A tray of food sat beside him when he woke up, and he wondered how long he'd actually slept. It was hard to tell what time it was inside the dreary tent.

He struggled to get himself upright, his body aching all over. He pulled the tray closer to him and reached for the coffee, untouched from earlier. He took a bite of donut first, washing it down with the cold, stale coffee.

He sat and listened. Several men cried out in pain. It became a rhythm, groans and screams, then eery silence.

I hope I didn't miss Anna, he thought, wondering when her shift ended. He cringed when he replayed their earlier conversation and tried to think about what he'd say to her to apologize for his behavior.

By the third day in the hospital, Paul was getting restless. He had no interest in going back to his unit, if he were being honest, but if the alternative was laying here like a vegetable, he'd take his chances on the front lines.

He gladly accepted coffee and donuts from the Red Cross girls as they wheeled their cart past. He'd polished off one donut before she'd moved on to the next soldier.

"Are those newspapers you've got down there?" He pointed toward the stack of gray papers at the bottom of the cart.

"Oh, yesterday's news. I've got to pitch them," one of the girls replied.

"I'll take one, if you don't mind," Paul said. Even if they were in French, he was happy to have something to look at other than the soldiers on each side of him and the dirty tent ceiling.

She smiled and handed him a paper.

"Hey, how about that? It's in English," he said.

She laughed. "Of course it is," she said.

He flipped through the pages when an article caught his eye. He thought he was going to lose the donut he'd just wolfed down. Details about the sinking of a troopship in the English Channel jumped off the page at him. 'Over 800 men dead or missing,' the article read.

He'd had no communication with any of the guys from his company. He had no way of knowing who'd made it out alive and who hadn't.

He ripped the newspaper page out and tucked it beside him under his sheet. He'd like to mail it home, let his folks know what happened, but he wondered how he could. The censors would catch it in a second and they'd already been given strict orders not to talk about what had happened on Christmas Eve. Top brass said it was to protect the troops from the enemy knowing what a great loss they'd suffered. But seeing this article, clear as day for anyone in Europe to read, he thought perhaps the Army wasn't telling the whole truth. *No surprise there*, he thought. So much had gone wrong that night, it was no wonder they'd want it covered up, buried deep beneath the tragedy of war.

A bitter bile rose up in his throat, anger that had begun to feel all too familiar rearing its ugly head again. He wasn't proud of how he felt but he was so damn angry and had nowhere to get it out. Something else the Army was great at: Ignoring what witnessing your friends and comrades dying by the dozen might do to a man. By tomorrow, he'd be back in the field, performing his job duties as if nothing had ever happened. Carry on. Fall in line. Know your place. He closed his eyes. It made him sick to think about it all.

The shuffle of footsteps approached and he blinked his eyes open. He hadn't seen Anna since Christmas Day and he was starting to worry he wouldn't see her again before he was discharged. He looked up to see Reverend Olsen step through the curtain.

Paul smiled. "Reverend Ole," he said. "It's good to see you."

The kind reverend returned his smile. "I'm glad to see you looking much better," he replied.

Paul nodded. "Good as new," he said.

Reverend Olsen chuckled. "I don't know about new," he said, "but I'd imagine you're ready to get some fresh air."

"How are you doing?" Paul eyed the Reverend, sadness weighing on his face.

"That is supposed to be my question for you," he replied.

Paul chuckled, "Well, I beat you to it."

Reverend Ole looked up and down the rows of hospital beds. "Things have slowed down, thank the good Lord," he said. "There for a while, I didn't think we'd ever get out from under the number of men dying - every time I turned around, there was another one."

The two men were quiet, each lost in thought.

Paul cleared his throat. "But you didn't answer my question, Reverend."

"Ah," the Reverend waved him off. "It's my job, Paul. I knew what I was getting into over here. It's never easy. But that's what I'm here for. If I can't help you and every other man muddling their way through this war, then what am I here for?"

"Reverend Ole. I know that. But you're human, too. A better man than all of us, but still human."

Reverend Olsen looked thoughtful. Paul waited, hoping he'd actually open up and talk.

Finally, he shifted, stepping closer to Paul's bedside. "From what I understand, you're set to be discharged today."

Disappointed, Paul nodded. Reverend Olsen wouldn't be persuaded to lean on him.

"Well, I just wanted to wish you well before you go and hoped you'd say a prayer with me."

"Sure thing, Rev." He bowed his head and let the Reverend's words for safekeeping wash over him.

"Amen." He opened his eyes at the sound of Anna's voice.

"Anna," Reverend Ole said. "It's good to see you again, dear. Were you able to get some sleep, I hope?"

"Oh, enough to keep going, you know. Thank you for all of your help." She grasped his hand and gave it a squeeze.

"No thanks necessary," he said. "I was just telling Paul, that's what I'm here for." He turned to Paul, sitting up in his hospital bed, and placed his hand on his leg. "I'll leave you two. May God be with you."

Paul responded in the old familiar way he'd done since he was a child. "And also with you, Reverend."

He could have sworn he saw Reverend Olsen wink at Anna on his way out, but if he had, she didn't let on.

She looked at Paul, coming closer to his bedside. "So," she started, "I hear you're ready to bust out of here."

"I wouldn't exactly say I'll be busting out of anywhere," he said, wiggling his toes. "Not with these numb feet. But yeah, I suppose it's time for me to get back out there."

She looked down at the floor, avoiding his gaze.

"Listen, Anna," he began. Her eyes snapped to his. He lost his train of thought when she looked at him and his mouth went dry. Still, this might be the last time he saw her, and he didn't want to blow it again.

"Paul," she tried to interject. He held a hand up to stop her.

"Please, Anna, let me get it out, okay?" She nodded, and he took a deep breath.

"First, I need to tell you how sorry I am."

Shock crossed her face and Paul blew out a breath of relief. If she didn't know what he was apologizing for, she must not have been too upset with him. He held onto that hope.

"For what?"

"Well, I was a total jerk the other day and I've been afraid you've been avoiding me ever since. I was in bad shape, and I lashed out at the first person to try and help. Unfortunately, it was you. I just hope you can forgive me."

Anna stared at him for what felt like forever until it was Paul's turn to be confused when she started to laugh. It started slowly, so that he didn't know whether she was truly laughing or maybe crying, and then bubbled out of her in big gasps. He sat in bed completely befuddled as to what could have struck her so funny. He scratched his head and smiled. Her laughter was contagious and even though he hadn't a clue what she was laughing at, he found himself chuckling along with her.

She wiped at the tears rolling down her cheeks, composing herself, and looked at Paul with a glow in her eyes. He looked at her as if he'd only just seen how beautiful she was. Her hair stuck out in all directions beneath her nurse's cap, the pins no longer doing their job of containing the frizzy ringlets. Any makeup she'd applied earlier that morning had long since worn away. He saw the black smudged under her eyes and the tired way her eyelids remained half-lidded as if she hadn't slept in months. *She probably hasn't*, he thought.

She touched his arm, and he wished he could wipe away the darkness beneath her eyes instead of covering her hand with his own. She looked down at their joined hands, then back up at him.

"I don't know what came over me, but it struck me funny that you think *that* was lashing out." She smiled. "The guy who threw his pills at me or the one who jumped out of his bed and chased me down the rows of beds accusing me of being a spy… they were lashing out," she said. "But you, Paul…you came in here just a few hours after your ship sank. If anyone has a right to be angry, it's you. All of you. And even still, I wouldn't call that lashing out. But," she continued, "I appreciate your apology. And now it's my turn to be sorry. I feel terrible you've been thinking I'm so mad that I wouldn't come see you." She sighed. "It's been crazy here. I haven't had a chance to catch my breath. Believe me, if I could've gotten away, I would've been here with you." Her cheeks flushed, and she stammered on. "I mean, checking in on you, making sure you're recovering well."

Paul smiled. "For what it's worth, I'd have liked to be with you, too."

"And here we are again, catching each other right before one of us leaves."

She unfurled her fingers from his and stepped back. Paul could feel her closing herself off. He couldn't say he blamed her, but he'd be lying if he said he wasn't disappointed. The woman he could picture everything with stood right there in front of him, yet she was slipping away before he'd even gone back to the front.

"Anna," It came out more desperate than he'd intended, but what use was it in hiding how he felt? If he was going to lose her anyway, he might as well give himself a fighting chance of changing her mind.

She turned away. "I can't, Paul."

"You can't what?" He sat up further in his bed, swinging his legs over the side. She kept her back to him, but he could tell she'd covered her face with her hand, her back hunched over to hide her face.

"I can't do whatever this is," she said.

So many questions raced through his head as he hopped down out of the bed. "What do you think this is?" A sob escaped her lips, and he gently pulled on her elbow, spinning her to face him.

"Because I know what I think this is. And even if you walked out on me right now, it wouldn't change a thing about how I feel." He kept his hand on her elbow, afraid she'd call his bluff and walk away. He knew she wanted to stay, but the fear in her eyes told him she might not let herself.

"This war has already taken so much. From both of us. I can't fall for you and lose you too." Her voice shook, and she took a deep breath. "After everything you've just gone through, how can you possibly want to risk any more?"

He looked past her and blew out a breath. "That's exactly the reason why. Sure, you're right. This war has stolen so much from all of us. I don't want to let it steal this, too."

They stood in silence, and Paul moved his hand from her elbow to her waist. "So, you're falling for me, huh?" A smile played on his lips, and she swatted at his arm.

"That's not the point of what I was trying to say."

"I know, I know. But you kind of lost me when you said you 'couldn't fall for me.' It sounded an awful lot like maybe you were falling...or had already fallen...or might fall sometime in the near future," he teased.

He pulled her in and wrapped his arms around her. She stiffened, and Paul loosened his grip. He wouldn't force her to stay. He felt her relax, and she curled her arms around his back, settling her cheek against his chest.

"Everything else is just background noise," he murmured. "Don't let all that out there cloud what your heart is telling you."

"I wish we'd met somewhere else, some other time," she whispered.

"It doesn't matter where we met, Anna. You'd still be it. Don't you get it?" He pulled her back to look at her. "Even if we say goodbye, it'll still hurt. If you tell me you don't want to see where this goes and I die tomorrow, won't it hurt just as much?"

"Don't talk like that, Paul."

"It's the truth, Anna. Wouldn't you rather give your heart what it wants than deny it and be broken anyway?"

She sighed. "It's not fair," she said.

"Don't I know it," he said. "I've asked myself every day since Christmas why the heck am I still alive. It just doesn't make sense."

"It makes perfect sense to me," she looked up at him and smiled. "You're meant to be here, Paul. Even if you don't think you should have survived, too many people need you here."

He snorted. "You could say that about any of the guys who died out there."

She nodded. "Of course you could. I wonder the same about me. You know we were on the same ship over here, don't you? Just one week before you. So why on your trip and not mine?" She pulled back out of his embrace and searched his face. "Don't do it to yourself. You'll drive yourself over the edge wondering why. No one knows why. Why does anyone die? There's only one person I know of that has those answers, and I love Reverend Olsen as much as the next person, but it's not him, either."

~

The bumpy ride in the back of the ambulance gave way to a fresh set of nerves as Paul waited to be reunited with what was left of his unit. He was in the dark about who had survived. He wondered how many of the bodies piled up on the pier belonged to men he knew. The image was fresh in his mind every time he thought about it. *When am I not thinking about it?*

The sickening sour acid rose up in his throat when he pictured those men stacked ten, twenty, sometimes thirty high like sacks of potatoes discarded off to the side of the docks. He couldn't help but feel like it was a disgrace to each and every one of those soldiers who had died for their country. He understood time was of the essence and didn't know what else they could have done with that many dead bodies at once, but it still made him sick. How many actually died that night? It was a question he'd been too afraid to ask - he didn't know if he could handle the answer. *Too many,* he thought.

The ambulance came to a stop just outside a giant tent city on the edge of Cherbourg. Paul looked out the small back window and took a deep breath, steeling himself for what might come next. He'd either find his buddies or find out they were gone.

It was hard to believe Christmas had come and gone, and here he was, on the first of January of the new year, being re-outfitted to live in a tent until new orders came down to move again.

Paul looked down the rows of tents, counting. Forty tents lined the center of the old race track.

The driver opened the back of the ambulance. "Time to go," he said, smacking the door with his enormous hand.

Paul gave him a nod and stepped carefully from the back. Several of his toes were still numb, but the prescribed spirits a few times a day had helped him regain enough feeling that he wasn't bothered by it so much anymore.

He stood on the track and looked around at the men grouped around the campsite. The freezing temperatures and relentless rain had replaced any remaining grass with a slick layer of mud. He wondered where he should go and started in the direction of the nearest tent.

Men watched him, some staring intently, others coming closer, all wanting to see who it was returning from the hospital. From this distance, he couldn't see any familiar faces, and doubt began to creep over him. He'd been so sure he'd reunite with

Harry, at least. Hell, he'd seen him get on the rescue boat. But reality hit him. Even that was no guarantee that his friend had survived. And what about Jack or Glenn? Joe? He smiled when he thought of his city-slicker friend. Surely, he had made it out alive.

He searched the faces of the crowd forming in front of him, curious men walking toward him, hoping for a happy reunion with a long-lost friend. He hoped for the same, but his hopes dwindled when recognition never came. Several men turned around, disappearing inside their tents when they saw that Paul wasn't who they'd wanted to see. The crowd thinned, and Paul trudged forward, discouraged with every step. The shape of a man emerged from the farthest tent, his bright red hair unmistakable, even at a distance.

"No way," Paul said under his breath. He picked up his pace slightly, trying not to get his hopes up. Harry wasn't the only red-headed soldier, he reminded himself. He was still too far away to know for sure, and he didn't want to make a fool of himself by shouting out for his friend, but when the figure looked up and made eye contact with Paul, he didn't have to wonder anymore.

"Paul!" Harry shouted out, and two more men ran out of the tent. The three of them ran toward Paul, and he broke out into a run, closing the distance between them. Relief spread through him at the sight of his friends.

Harry reached him first, clambering into him, embracing him in a messy bear hug, with Jack and Glenn piling on behind him. Paul kept his chin down, buried beneath the arms of his friends, choking back tears he'd rather not shed. Not knowing if they were alive all week - wondering what he'd be walking back into - he'd been holding more in than he realized now that he finally saw them.

Jack was the first to let go, stepping back to look at Paul. They stood there in the middle of the racetrack, awkward embarrassment passing between them at their rare display of emotion.

Paul cleared his throat. "So, these are the new digs, huh?"

Harry clapped him on the back and led the way toward their tent.

"Yeah, it's the finest French luxury out here," Glenn joked.

Jack snorted. "Yeah, just wait until the rain picks up again."

"That bad?"

"What do you think the wood boards are for?" Jack kicked at the wood beneath their feet.

Paul looked down at the makeshift sidewalk that spread from one end of the tents to the other. With every step he took, mud oozed out the sides and through the cracks, sinking deeper into the muck.

"Before we put that down, we'd wake up to a tent full of mud," Harry said.

"Not exactly an enjoyable mud bath in January," Glenn added.

Paul chuckled. He threw his new duffel bag to one side of the tent. He hated that new bag. It was another reminder of everything he'd lost. The scarf Evie had made him, all the letters from home…all of it gone with the ship. He reached under his shirt and felt around for his father's scapular. Somehow, it had made it through the wreckage. *At least I didn't lose this,* he thought.

Jack headed back out of the tent. "You want to warm up around a fire?"

"Yeah, sure, sounds good," Paul said. He walked back out, beyond the wooden sidewalk, joining the other men in the soggy field, and watched Jack and Glenn start a small fire. His thoughts wandered back to the last time he sat before a makeshift fire to warm up, just a week ago on the docks.

"We were starting to lose hope," Jack remarked when he'd gotten the fire roaring.

Paul took a step back from the flames. "What do you mean?"

"You have no idea how many ambulances have come and gone, dropping guys off fresh out of the hospital," he said.

Harry nodded. "Every day we've been running out at the sound of the ambulance rumbling in. And every day it's someone else. We thought for sure you were a goner after a whole week went by."

Paul laughed. "Nah, you can't get rid of me that easily." He looked at each of his friends and realized there was still one missing. "Hey, where's Joe?"

He watched as, one by one, their faces fell and he nodded his understanding. They didn't need to say it.

Glenn cleared his throat. "He didn't make it. He was too scared to jump. Said he'd take his chances staying on board."

"Are you sure he didn't make it though? He could be laid up in some hospital somewhere like I was," Paul said, holding onto hope.

Glenn shook his head, his voice gravelly with unshed tears. "No, he's gone, Paul. His body got picked up."

"He's gone," Jack repeated, shaking his head.

They stood staring into the flames until Glenn broke the silence. "You haven't seen Eleanor at all have you?"

Paul smiled and reached into his pocket. "I haven't seen her, but I do have something to give you."

"I saw Gretchen," he hesitated, "and Anna, too. She gave me that letter to give to you. Eleanor was hoping I might see you again. Anna said she's been worried sick not hearing from you."

Glenn smiled and slapped Paul's arm with the envelope. "Thanks, Paul," he said and ducked inside the tent.

"So, you saw Anna again," Harry remarked.

Paul nodded but didn't say anything.

"Care to share?" Harry pried.

Paul chuckled. "I don't know, Harry. What's there to say, really? I want to give her everything, but I'm too messed up to do it." He kicked at the ground, trying to keep his tone neutral.

"You'll figure it out. Don't let her go just because of all this bullshit," Harry said.

Paul shrugged. It didn't feel so much like bullshit to him anymore. He'd been so confident before their ship sank, hell, he'd even been confident in the hospital with Anna standing in front of him. He'd been ready to take the leap for her. But out here, in the freezing rain that had started misting over them, just enough to make him shiver, he wasn't so sure. Maybe she'd been right to want to cut their losses while they had the chance, even if it wasn't what he really wanted. How could anyone know what they want out here?

He tried to keep his mind focused on what his life would look like after the war's end, even as the Army drilled into them to focus only on the day at hand. *Kill or be killed,* he thought. But

he wasn't some machine that could fight and kill with no re-
morse, no thought for the next day or the day after that, though
surely the high brass would have loved that. His will to come out
alive warred with the despair he felt over the men they'd already
lost, and his confidence waned. If so many good ones had per-
ished, who was to say he wouldn't be next? With no word from
his brother, their ship torpedoed, living in a mud city, it looked
like his luck was running out. A future beyond tents and terrible
food felt too far away to look forward to.

"Any word on what's next?" Paul wondered what their assignment would be now that so much of their regiment had been
decimated.

Harry nodded. "St. Nazaire or L'Orient in a few days is what
we've been hearing."

"Further south, then?" Paul shivered again.

"Yep," said Jack, lighting a cigarette. "So we can guard the
sub pens."

"No kidding," Paul said. The irony of being torpedoed by a
German submarine and now having to guard their pens was not
lost on him. "Aint that some shit."

Chapter 26

ANNA
JANUARY 1945
CHERBOURG, FRANCE

My Dear Granddaughter,
I thought you might need this.
All my love and prayers for your safe homecoming.
Gramps

Anna smiled at the familiar handwriting before pulling out the folded paper behind it. She'd finally had a chance to open the mystery box left for her on Christmas. She immediately recognized her mother's floral stationary. *What does she have to say?* Anna wondered, suddenly overwhelmed with nerves. She wished she could walk outside to read in the cold, snowy air. January had brought more freezing temperatures mixed with rain - oh, how she'd grown tired of the endless rain. But still worse were their orders to stay inside unless they were traveling to and from the hospital. Even now, as she stood in the cold, empty tent, she could hear the drone of the planes and the occasional blast in the distance. It had become more regular, a constant nagging in the back of her mind that they could be next.

She sat down at a table in the mess tent and took a deep breath, focusing on her mother's perfect cursive.

Dear Anna,

You are everything I am not.

Anna rolled her eyes. *We're off to a great start here, Mother,* she thought.

Spare me the eye roll and just hear what I have to say.

She pursed her lips to keep from smiling. She supposed her mother knew her better than she thought.

I have not done the greatest job as your mother, and for that, I am deeply sorry. The relationship we are left with because of my poor communication is not something I am proud of. But I'd like for you to know the truth, anyway. Because it's my truth, and you deserve to hear it. Not because I want your forgiveness- I don't know that I can ever earn that – but because you asked for me to understand your decisions, and it's time I ask the same from you.

My dear daughter, from the moment you were born, you had a fire in your eyes that terrified me. It wasn't something I could relate to – as you know, I enjoy being home, keeping to myself – but you – you wanted to go. You wanted to explore everything you could. I'm afraid I did my best to stamp that light out of you because it scared me. It scared me to think, if I didn't hold on tightly, what might happen? You'd get hurt or sick, and I'd grow even more scared.

It turns out, I grew more scared anyway, despite my best efforts to keep you sheltered from the world. But boy, you proved me wrong at every turn. Perhaps that should have been enough for me to set you free, to watch you soar. You were undeterred by me. Instead, it only fueled my fear and I'm embarrassed to say, made me angry and bitter. They say absence makes the heart grow fonder, and I don't know if I'd agree, but it does put things into perspective. I've been cruel and lashed out because I've been so damn scared. Living in fear your whole life makes it difficult to change. But you're in a war zone now, and I don't think it could get much scarier than that.

I'm trying, Anna. It might not make much sense to you right now, but maybe one day you'll have a daughter that challenges you every day, and your heart will be walking around on the outside of your body, too. Only you'll have learned from my mistakes and do better than me. Don't live your life in fear. If nothing else comes of this letter, I hope it is that.

xx

Anna sniffed. She didn't know what she'd expected from her mother after all this time, but an apology was not it.

She leaned her elbows on her knees and pressed her palms into her eyes. Her mother wasn't asking for forgiveness. Anna could have laughed if she wasn't so damn sad. *We're not so different after all*, she thought.

"I'm scared, too," she whispered.

The only difference between them was that Anna did things scared. She'd railed against her mother for so long it had become second nature to do what her mother didn't want her to do. So she'd do it scared. She supposed she needed to thank her mother, after all. If she hadn't been so overbearing, if she hadn't said no to everything, Anna wouldn't have had to fight so hard to get away. She'd probably not be sitting here in France, bundled up in her woolen overcoat in a cold mess tent, contemplating her life's choices. She'd seen through her mother's facade to the unhappiness below the surface, covered by beautiful blooms and bountiful crops, and she knew she needed more.

"Thank you, Mom," she whispered, words she never thought she'd hear herself say. She wiped her tears away and got to her feet, tucking the letter in the front pocket of her trousers and taking another peek inside the box. She pulled out a small photograph, an image of her mother as a young woman, a broad smile on her face, sitting on the same swing Anna loved so much on her grandfather's front porch. On her lap was Anna, only a year old, reaching up to touch her mother's face.

"Hey, lady," Gretchen's voice rang out in the empty tent.

"Hey yourself," Anna replied, tucking the photo back inside the box.

"I feel like I haven't seen you in days." She swooped in, placing two cups on the table and embracing Anna in a tight hug.

Anna nodded. "Sure seems that way, doesn't it?"

"I thought things would slow down after the new year," Gretchen said. "All that talk about the war's end…I'm not seeing any proof of it." She sighed, offering a mug to Anna.

"What's in there?" Anna eyed the cup. They hadn't had real coffee or tea in weeks, but knowing Gretchen, she probably sweet-talked her way into it somehow.

"Coffee," she said, batting her eyelashes.

Anna arched a brow. "Really," she said, still skeptical. "How on Earth did you find coffee?"

"I have my ways," she said. "Just try it."

Anna looked at the liquid in the mug and sniffed. It smelled like coffee. It looked like coffee. Curiosity got the best of her, and she took a small sip.

"Wow," she said. "It's not bad."

"Of course it's not," Gretchen laughed. "You think I'd drink bad coffee?"

Anna laughed. "But really, where'd you get it from?" She took another sip.

"It's mushrooms," Gretchen said.

Anna spit her mouthful back into her mug. "Excuse me?"

"I found a guy who makes it out of mushrooms. It's actually very healthy."

"I'm sure it is," Anna said. "But really, Gretchen, you could've warned me."

Gretchen rolled her eyes. "You wouldn't have tried it if I'd told you first. And please, you can hardly taste the difference. You said yourself, it's not bad."

"You're right," Anna conceded. "Desperate times," she said, looking into her cup again. She shrugged and took another sip.

"So, what's got you down here in the dark all alone?"

Anna blew out a breath. "I was just reading a letter from my mother."

Gretchen let out a low whistle. "The queen hath finally written?"

Anna giggled. "An apology, if you can believe it."

Gretchen drew back, bringing her hand to her mouth in shock. "Not possible."

Anna nodded, pulling the letter from her pocket. "I don't even know how to answer her."

Gretchen read through her mother's handwriting. "Hmm," she said. "I hate to say it…"

"I know. She sounds almost human."

Gretchen put her hand on Anna's arm. "I say just hold on to it for a few days. No sense rushing a letter after it took her this long to send one to you. Wait until you're really clear on what you want to say."

They stood in the tent, sipping their coffee, watching through the opening at the gradual transition from darkness to light as the sun crept over the horizon, ushering in another snowy day.

"Have you seen Louise or Eleanor lately? I've been so crazy in the field hospital I haven't seen them, either."

Gretchen nodded. "We walked back here together last night. This is the first time we've all been done with our shifts at the same time in ages. They're probably still sleeping," she said.

"What's got you up so early?" Gretchen was usually the first to complain about needing her beauty rest.

"It's getting harder and harder to sleep anymore," she said, shrugging. "Plus, I needed water for my mushroom coffee," she joked.

Anna smiled, but when she looked at her friend's face, she could see the lines of worry and fatigue that mirrored her own.

"How much longer do you think we'll be staying here?" Since they'd left England, there'd been a restlessness about her, like she'd left any ties behind, untethered and unattached to any place they stayed. With Paul having gone back to his unit, she felt the stirring to move even more. She'd remained busy so far, but she hesitated to entertain any idle time for fear of where her mind might wander.

"Actually, Captain Campbell grabbed me yesterday before shift change. She said four more nurses were needed on board a hospital train traveling south of here," she tapped her lip, trying to recall the name of the town. "Something with an R..Re..well anyway, I can't recall the town, but we're leaving soon."

"All of us, together?"

Gretchen nodded. "Maybe we'll get a chance to catch our breath on the train ride."

"That would be nice," Anna replied.

After two more weeks trudging through the snow to and from the tent hospital, Anna had lost hope that they'd be leaving. She walked into her tent, weary and cold after another long shift, ready to strip her uniform and fall onto her cot.

"You look like hell," Eleanor said when she walked through the doorway.

Louise swatted her arm. "Hush," she said. "We all do."

Anna gave a curtsy. "Why, thank you," she said.

Eleanor offered an apologetic smile. "Sorry, I didn't mean it like that."

"What are you doing, anyway?" Anna yawned and dropped her pack to the ground, walking over to where they sat on Eleanor's cot.

"Just cleaning our kits up and getting ready to leave."

"Where are you going?"

The two women stopped scrubbing at their helmets and looked up.

"You didn't hear? We're boarding the train to Rennes tomorrow."

Anna's eyes widened. "No, I haven't seen anyone today. I was so busy getting patients out of surgery. We were so short-staffed today that the doctor pinned his post-op instructions right to the bed sheet before they wheeled them out of surgery. I hadn't even seen him until I was packing up to leave."

"Geez, I guess you'll get some sleep on the train," Eleanor said.

She sat down beside them and pulled her helmet from her bag. "I never would have thought of all the useful things a helmet could be used for aside from sitting on your head," she mused.

Louise chuckled. "I know one thing I'll be glad to never do with it again," she said.

"What's that?" Eleanor stood to empty her helmet of the water she'd been using to rinse her undergarments.

"Eat beans," Louise replied, gagging.

Anna laughed. "I don't think I'll ever want to look at beans again either, in a steel helmet or otherwise."

"I could probably make do if it were wine," Louise joked.

Anna agreed. "Mmm. I haven't tasted wine in ages."

The sound of boots outside interrupted their banter. Anna stood to look, watching an officer try to stamp snow from his boots before entering their tent.

"Mail's here," she said. She hardly expected any of it to be for her, especially not after her mother's letter, which she had yet to respond to. Guilt gnawed at her. *I'm too busy,* she thought, trying to defend herself against her inability to give her mother some kind of acknowledgment. But in truth, she just didn't know what to say. Every time she pulled out a sheet of paper to start, it sat blank before her until she dragged herself to bed, putting it out of her mind for another few days.

The officer opened their tent, shaking snow off his shoulders. "Afternoon, ladies. How are we on this fine winter day?" He smiled, reaching into the mail bag slung over one shoulder.

"Just peachy," Eleanor replied, making him laugh.

"Aren't we all," he said, handing her several letters. "That's all for today," he said, adjusting his hat before turning to leave.

"Well, we'll miss seeing you after today," Louise said, walking with him.

"Is that so?"

She nodded. "We're headed up to Rennes tomorrow morning."

"Ah, well, have a safe trip," he said. "God Bless," he added with a wave and plodded back into the snow-covered field. Louise and Eleanor shuffled through the envelopes.

"Here's one for you, Anna," she said, handing it over.

Anna reached for it. "Strange," she said. "I wasn't expecting anything." She looked it over, not recognizing the handwriting, before tearing it open. She opened up a paper that was heavier than she'd expected.

"What in the world," she said.

Dear Anna,

I do hope this letter finds you and your friends well. My family and I pray daily for your strength and safety. We were sad you had to leave before enjoying Christmas Day with us. However, I thought you might like to have this. Maybe it'll bring you a bit of luck. Give my regards to Louise, Gretchen, and Eleanor.

Love to you all,

Marjorie

At the bottom of the letter was taped a silver coin. Anna stuck her finger beneath the tape, popping the coin free and turning it over in her hand. She gasped, covering her mouth, tears springing to her eyes.

Louise peeked over her shoulder. "What is it?"

"Paul's Peace Dollar," she said. "The one he put in the Christmas pudding at Marjorie's house."

"Hey, no kidding," Eleanor said, sliding over to take a look.

"I can't believe she sent it. And it actually made it through the mail."

She thought about Paul. *Too bad I have no idea where he is now*, she thought. They'd promised to keep in touch and see what happened, but with her work schedule and him not knowing where his unit had even ended up, she hadn't yet heard from him. She convinced herself that it was okay. *It's what I wanted in the first place*, she thought. *No attachments.* But now, turning his coin over, the feel of the heavy silver in her hand, she felt foolish for thinking she could push him away and carry on as if nothing plagued her heart.

"What are you going to do with it?" Eleanor asked.

"I don't know," she said. "I guess I'll hold onto it until I have a good address for Paul. Then I'll send it back to him."

Louise shook her head. "Terrible idea," she said.

"What? Why?"

"You said yourself it's incredible it even made it through the mail. I wouldn't try it a second time," Eleanor said, agreeing with Louise.

"Besides, he'd want you to have it. Especially over getting lost or confiscated," Louise said.

Anna sighed, feeling torn. Finally, she nodded and reached for her pack. She undid the drawstring and shuffled through her belongings, pulling out a small leather pouch. She opened it and dropped the coin inside, joining the few keepsakes she carried with her everywhere. A small photograph of her grandfather, a locket he'd given her that had once belonged to her grandmother, and most recently, the neatly folded letter and photograph from her mother.

～

Chapter 27

PAUL
JANUARY 1945
CHERBOURG, FRANCE

The icy rain pounded the tent above him and he wondered if it would spring a leak soon. After weeks of living in the tent city, eating the vile slop they claimed was food, and shoveling mud out of the tents, morale was at an all time low.

The steady tapping rhythm of sleet on canvas lulled him in and out of sleep. Images of the Leopoldville flashed before him, the way it always did when he closed his eyes. This time though, it was Joe's face he saw up on deck, singing Christmas carols in between draws on a cigarette and complaining about how cold it was out there. Paul could hear his New York accent clear as day, the two of them bantering back and forth. By now, he'd replayed the scene so many times, he knew they were oblivious to the torpedo only for another few seconds, and he wanted to scream. *Stop singing, you damn fools. Your ship is going to sink.* And then, the explosion, followed by a thick black smoke no one could see through and when it finally cleared, he was all alone on the top deck of the Leopoldville. He dropped to his knees, coughing out the smoke that had filled his lungs until he woke from the nightmare, coughing and wheezing in the black of the tent.

He sat up, drenched in sweat despite the damp, cold air, and pulled off his shirt. He scrounged around in his pack for a replacement, using the soaked one to wipe his face, then tossing it to the side. He lay back down and felt his heart pounding in his chest. He closed his eyes, trying not to remember - wishing he could forget and go back to the man he was before Christmas Eve. The man too naive to think he might actually die out here.

"You know what I don't understand?" Paul whittled at a stick with his pocket knife the next morning.

"What's that?"

"We were so damn close to shore. Why in the hell couldn't anyone tow us in? Five miles! Five damn miles. And the damn ship sank anyway."

They were quiet for a while, not because they didn't agree with him or because they didn't share his anger, but because they were stunned by his outburst. Paul O'Reilly was always level-headed - the epitome of calm under pressure. He surprised them with his raw emotion.

"They dropped the anchor," Jack said, his words cutting through the silence.

Paul looked over at him. "Why?" It came out like a plea, begging for the answers to the questions he couldn't shake.

"We were drifting. Captain Limbor was more afraid of hitting a mine than of actually sinking, I guess."

"Well, he went down with the ship because of his shit decision. We could've saved hundreds of men if we'd gotten towed in." He blew out a breath, dropping the stick he'd shaped into a sharp point and lowering his head to his hands, his elbows resting on his knees. "Five miles," he repeated.

Glenn poked at the fire and tossed his cigarette butt in. "That's not even the worst of what I heard," he said.

The other three men turned to look at him. He looked down, clearing his throat. "I overheard some brass talking after I got to the hotel that night," he paused, pain written on his face. "Apparently, our radios were transmitting to the wrong port. All the distress messages were sent to England instead of Cherbourg. Nobody even knew we'd been hit."

Paul shook his head. He thought he might be sick. Anger and sadness pervaded him, mind and body, and he didn't think it could get worse until Glenn kept talking.

"Half the rescue crews were in the bag with it being Christmas Eve and all. So there was no one even available right away. GIs were too afraid to interrupt the bosses at their parties. Not to mention, the ship's engines weren't warm. They couldn't go anywhere for twenty minutes." He swiped a hand down his face.

"That's the difference between life and death right there," Harry said.

"A damn disaster made worse by the absolute mismanagement and idiocy of the ones in command."

"And the sad part is, are we really that surprised?" Jack lit up another cigarette, passing the pack to Glenn.

"They don't really give a damn about any of us," Glenn said.

Harry stood. "Anyone up for a trip into the city?"

"What for?" Paul wasn't ready to let go of his foul mood.

Harry shrugged. "There's still a few mom and pop's open. I like to give them my business when I can."

Paul nodded. "Alright, that sounds fine. Can't be any worse than wallowing in my misery around here."

They'd been confined to the abandoned racetrack, sleeping ten to a tent, and the stench was getting worse by the day.

"Maybe we can find some food that actually resembles... food," Paul said. He was tired of the slop they tried to pass off on them, which sent most men racing to the head all night long, keeping Paul awake with their stomping boots on the wooden walkway in front of their tents.

The truck dropped them in the city's center, at rue Dom Pedro and le boulevard Felix-Amiot.

"Hey, that's where we stayed on Christmas," Harry said, pointing to an elaborate stone building.

"Hotel L'Atlantique," Paul said. "Looks fancy."

"I hope I can find a little something for Eleanor," Glenn said.

Jack threw his arm around Glenn's neck, making kissing noises in his ear.

"Oh, shut up, you're just jealous," Glenn said, shoving Jack off of him.

Jack laughed. "Well, you can just follow Harry's lead. He's sure to find something to send home to Edith."

"How is she, anyway? Have you heard from her lately?" Paul asked.

Harry grinned. "Yeah, I just got a letter from her the other day. She sent it a month or so ago, but it took that long to finally find me." A goofy grin plastered across his face.

"Man, I hope I find a woman who makes me look as dopey as this guy," Jack joked.

Paul laughed, thinking of Anna. He was pretty sure she'd do the same for him if she'd just let him.

"Well, actually, I'm not just happy to have gotten her letter. I'm happy because of what was *in* her letter," Harry said, leading them down the street.

"Oh, yeah, what's that, pal?" Paul raised an eyebrow, wondering what could've had Harry in such a good mood.

Harry stopped short in the middle of the sidewalk. "She's pregnant," he said.

If Paul thought Harry couldn't have looked any happier, he was wrong. Harry radiated pure joy as his friends gathered around him, lifting him up off the sidewalk in congratulations.

"How 'bout that?" Paul said. "You're going to be a dad."

Harry nodded. "Now all I have to do is make it home alive," he said, elation fading from his face.

"Aw, come on, Harry. Don't go all negative on us now," said Glenn.

"Yeah, we survived a sinking ship, for God's sake. Easy sailing from here on out," Jack added.

"How'd you hold such big news in for so long without telling us?" Paul wondered.

Harry shrugged. "I just wanted to soak it in first, I guess. It didn't feel real at first. And then, I don't know. I guess I was afraid to say it out loud like it would somehow tarnish it or make it even less real or something."

Paul clapped him on the back. "I get it. You didn't have to share it with us," he said. "But I'm glad you did. It's the best thing I've heard in a while." He smiled at Harry, squeezing his shoulder, and his friend beamed back at him.

"Thanks, Paul."

They rounded the corner at Rue du Val-de-Saire, and Harry slowed in front of a ladies clothing boutique.

"This place looks too expensive for my wallet," Jack said.

Paul eyed the display in the window. He didn't know much about ladies' fashion, but judging from the silk and linen dresses, fascinator hats, and leather gloves, he had to agree with Jack.

Harry pulled open the door anyway, ignoring his friends. The shopkeeper looked up from behind a long counter covered in fabrics of all different colors and materials. She greeted them with a smile.

"Bonjour," she said, folding a pair of linen trousers and placing them on a wooden table. "How can I help you?" She spoke in stilted English, smoothing another pair of trousers on the counter.

"I'd like to find something to send home to my wife," Harry said in French.

Glenn elbowed Paul. "Did you know this guy could speak French like that?"

Paul shook his head. He knew enough to muddle his way through a basic conversation, but he hadn't known Harry could speak it so well.

The woman smiled, relieved that she didn't have to keep trying her English with the American soldiers.

"You have something specific in mind?"

"Well," Harry hesitated. He motioned to his stomach then turned to his friends. "I can't remember the French word for pregnant."

Paul made a motion like he was cradling a baby while Harry rounded his hands over his belly, hoping she'd understand. "She's pregnant," he said in English. "Something for her and the new baby."

The woman beamed bright with understanding. She held up a finger for them to wait and disappeared through a door behind the counter.

Paul wandered around through the store, not expecting to find anything of interest. A low display case featuring women's accessories caught his eye, and he looked through the glass at the rings, necklaces, leather gloves, and jeweled hair clips. An idea formed in his head, and he looked around for a price tag.

The woman reappeared, carrying a small white box. This time, she spoke in slow, choppy English.

"I have been saving this box for just the right person. It's not often I have a customer looking for baby items." She opened the lid and pushed aside several layers of tissue paper, pulling out one of the hidden items from inside. She offered it to Harry, who reached out, gently touching the pair of delicately crocheted white baby booties. He eyed them in wonder.

"How can anything have such tiny feet?"

The woman chuckled. "Your first child, I assume?"

He nodded, mesmerized by the tiny shoes. She reached into the box again, this time pulling out a silk robe that cascaded to the floor when she held it up.

"Your wife will appreciate a luxurious robe when she's up all night feeding the baby." She gave a small shimmy of her shoulders and smiled. "It will make her feel beautiful."

She sure knows how to lay it on thick, Paul thought. *No wonder her shop is still open.* He watched as she convinced Harry that he needed the booties and the robe.

Paul cleared his throat as she lowered the robe back inside the box. "Excuse me, madam, could you give me a price on an item in this case?"

"Oh boy," Jack muttered. "We've got another goner on our hands."

The woman glided towards Paul, a sweet smile on her face. She was more than happy to have their business today.

"These gloves here," he said, pointing to a pair of camel-brown leather gloves.

"Ah, yes, beautiful, aren't they? Soft as butter, too," she said. She unlocked the case and laid the gloves on top of the glass, gesturing for Paul to pick them up. He ran a finger over the leather and nodded. She was right. They were soft and lined with silk.

"Alright," he said. "You've got me, too."

She laughed. "I haven't even given you the price yet. She must be one special mademoiselle."

Paul shifted uncomfortably under her gaze. "Well, yes, she is. But actually, it's not what you think. I'm sending them home to my sister." He had no clue when she'd ever actually need a pair of gloves like these in Texas, but he didn't care. He had a plan.

The two men paid for their goods while Jack and Glenn waited outside, smoking a cigarette.

The shopkeeper wrapped their gifts for them, thanking them for their business.

"Anywhere left nearby we can find a good bite to eat?" Paul's stomach had been grumbling since they'd gotten off the truck, and he wasn't about to board a train without getting something good to eat.

She clapped her hands together. "There's very few still able to stay open," she said with a sad smile. "But, I think I know of one." She gave them directions, and Paul hoped Harry understood while he smiled and nodded politely.

Paul leaned back in his chair, stretching his arms overhead. He couldn't remember the last time his stomach felt this full. "Good thing we spent all that money on gifts, otherwise, we'd have never found this place on our own," he joked.

Jack laughed. "Hey, at least it didn't come out of my allowance."

"Ah, it's okay. Edith deserves something nice. I hate to think of the time she's had, alone and now alone and pregnant. Without her husband to take care of her like he should," said Harry.

"Harry, don't beat yourself up too bad. There's lotsa GIs in the same exact boat. It's not ideal, but there's nothing you can do about it. I'm sure she's doing just fine," Paul said.

They paid their tab and pushed back their chairs. They walked down rue Dom Pedro, where the shops became more and more scarce. A park stretched out beyond them to the right, where benches dotted the edges of a stone path that wound its way through the grass. Paul imagined it would have been beautiful in spring and summer, but in the throes of winter, the only splash of color came from the green coat of an elderly man seated on the bench nearest to them. Paul watched as he whittled away at a block of wood.

"Hey, check that out," Paul said, walking closer. The old man looked up at Paul with wrinkled eyes and offered him a kind smile with the nod of his head.

"May I?" Paul reached for one of the man's carvings. It was a little dinosaur, complete with sharp teeth and pointed claws. Paul admired the details while Harry picked up another, shaped like a teddy bear.

"Incredible," Harry said.

"The detail is amazing," Paul agreed. The dinosaur fit in the palm of his hand, and he immediately thought of little Danny. "How much?"

The old man stopped his carving and held up his hands.

"I don't think he understands English. Harry, you ask him."

"How much for each of these?" Harry tried in French.

The old man still held up his hands as though he wouldn't take their money.

"I can't take it without paying," Paul said, pulling out his wallet. He and Harry paid the man, tucking the bills underneath one of his wooden creations. When he looked over at the amount they'd left him, he looked up in disbelief. He reached for them, and they each offered him a hand, helping him to his feet. The old man wept as he hugged the two men tightly.

"They made the old man cry," Glenn whispered behind them.

The man sat back down, picking up his carvings once more. Paul watched him for a moment, admiring the skill with which he carved before giving him a wave and backing away toward the street.

"Man, that kills me," he said. "That poor old man could be somebody's grandfather, and he's out there on the street."

"You don't know, maybe he's a rich old man," said Jack.

Glenn snorted. "Yeah, sure, he really exudes wealth."

Jack shrugged. "You never know."

"I doubt he'd have stuck around here this long if he had enough money to get out," Harry said.

Paul looked around at what was left of the city. The streets they'd walked up and down had largely been spared, but everywhere he looked, the depressing sights of a country at war couldn't be ignored.

They neared the station, and Paul stopped in front of the Post. "I think I'll stop in here before we board," he said. "I'd like to get this stuff mailed out." He held up the bag of gifts he'd purchased for Evie and Danny.

Harry pulled out the box he'd gotten for Edith. "I think I'll do the same. No sense lugging around any extra weight."

Glenn and Jack gave them a wave. "We'll see you at the station," Jack said.

Paul sat down at a table outside the Post, digging around in his bag for paper and something to write with. "You go on ahead inside," he said to Harry. I have to scratch out a quick note for Evie."

Harry nodded and went inside. Paul pulled one of the gloves carefully out of its wrapping. He reached into his bag once more, feeling the worn leather of his wallet. He opened it up and pulled out a newspaper clipping that he'd folded into a tiny square. It was the one he'd saved from the Red Cross girls in the hospital.

He rolled it over in his fingers, tempted to unfold it and read what had been written about the Leopoldville once more. He shook his head and tucked it deep inside the pointer finger of the glove until it could go no further. Tucked away safely with no chance of falling out, he slid the glove back inside its paper-lined box.

At least that will give them some idea about how I spent my Christmas Eve, he thought. He was still angry over the gag orders they'd been given. Anyone in Europe could read about what had happened but the men who'd lived through it couldn't write home to their loved ones. Even worse, the men who'd lived through it couldn't write to the families of the ones that hadn't. He thought he'd been pretty clever for thinking of a way to get the article to his family.

He scribbled a quick note to Evie before closing the box.

Dear Sis,

Sorry, I missed getting you and Danny Boy your Christmas gifts. Better late than never right? Hope the gloves fit – I had to guess on the sizing. Try 'em on right away and let me know! Tell little Danny I can't wait to hear his dinosaur roar. Hugs to mom and dad. xox

There, he thought, laying the note on top of the gloves and the little wooden dinosaur. He might not have been able to give his family any hope for where his brother had ended up, but he could at least let them know what he'd gone through. Now, thinking about the absolute disaster the Leopoldville had been, he wondered how much of what his parents had been told about Jamie had been a lie. His hope for finding out his brother was still alive dwindled with every day that passed.

He stood, gathered his things, and walked inside the post. He felt a weight lift when he handed over the package. He'd felt that one little piece of paper weighing him down for weeks, the reminder of what had happened and all the things he couldn't say.

～

Paul followed Harry down the aisle of the train packed with GIs. He looked around for Jack and Glenn. "Maybe they're in the next car down," he said. They squeezed past the rows of soldiers to the back of the car, opening the door to the next one. It was just as crowded as the first, but Paul spotted an empty bench seat toward the back.

Harry pointed. "There they are."

Glenn stood up, waving them over. "Hey, we saved you a spot," he said, pointing to the empty bench.

Harry slid into a seat, and Paul piled in after him, swinging his duffle bag around to his lap.

"Man, they've really got us packed in here," Paul said.

"Yep. Hospital transport is in the front few cars," Glenn said. "I hoped maybe I'd see Eleanor."

Jack laughed. "Poor fool tried to climb up into the hospital car."

Glenn shrugged. "It was worth a shot, anyway."

Paul chuckled. He hadn't even thought about the possibility of Anna being on the same transport train. Though they seemed to be following similar paths across Europe, he found it unlikely they'd end up on the same train. *Still,* he thought, *if she's on this train, it'd have to be some kind of a sign. Then I'd really know God's slapping me over the head.*

"Hey, hey," Jack said, elbowing Glenn in the ribs. "Maybe your girls are here after all." He nodded toward the front of the train car. Paul looked up at the woman who'd just entered, her back turned to him. Her striking red hair was recognizable anywhere.

"Is that Gretchen?"

Glenn stood up from his seat. "Sure looks like it."

The woman threw her head back and laughed at something whispered into her ear. Paul didn't like the way the sleazy GI looked at her, though she appeared to be handling herself just fine.

"Gretchen!" Glenn called out. He cupped his hands around his mouth and called again.

She turned around then, removing the soldier's hand that was traveling too far south on her waist. He shot Glenn a dirty look at the same time Gretchen walked down the aisle. She mouthed a silent *thank you.*

"Well, well, well," she said. "If it isn't the Company I boys."

"Hey, Gretchen, how've you been?" Paul stood to give her a brief hug.

"Never better," she smiled. Her lips were painted that bright red Paul remembered seeing when he woke up in the hospital.

"Fraternizing with the soldiers, again, I see," Jack said.

She shot him a dirty look. "Normally, I wouldn't deny that accusation," she said, "but that guy gives me the creeps." She shuddered and risked a glance over her shoulder. Paul was watching the man too, and he'd finally taken his seat, though he looked at Gretchen every few minutes.

"I'll walk you back up when you're ready so he doesn't bother you again," Paul said.

"My hero," she said, placing the back of her hand on her forehead, pretending to swoon.

Paul snickered. "It's just the protective big brother in me."

"Anna's going to be disappointed she didn't come with me," she said.

His heart sank. "So, she's not here, then?"

Gretchen laughed. "Look at you, from pitbull to puppy in mere seconds."

"Hey, um, what about Eleanor," Glenn interrupted, "did she come with you?"

"They're both here," she said. "They're on penicillin duty, though. Filling up those syringes and prepping doses for the seven o'clock rounds."

Paul felt his heart rate kick up. It didn't matter if he couldn't see her for the entire train ride. Just the fact that she was here, that their paths were crossing again, was enough for him. It squashed any doubts and solidified what he'd felt from that first night. Somehow, someway, it would work itself out. And he didn't feel rushed or desperate. *All in God's time,* he thought, saying a silent prayer of thanks for the message he'd received loud and clear.

"Earth to lover boy," Gretchen said, waving a hand in front of his face. "I'm ready for that escort now."

He offered her his arm and guided her awkwardly up the narrow aisle to the door at the other end, making sure to give the leering soldier a big grin as they passed. When they got to the door, he spun her around so she landed against his chest, enveloping her in a hug.

"Smooth," she murmured.

He lowered his head to her ear, making it look like he was whispering sweet nothings to her.

"Tell Anna I said hello," he said and released his grip on her to open the door.

She slipped through, turning back to give him a half wave and a wink. He could hardly keep the laughter in when he walked back down the aisle to his seat, satisfied that the man had kept his head down, not wanting to look at Paul as he passed.

Chapter 28

After a final look around the cold, bare tent, they loaded into the truck in the dark. Anna watched as the old chateau on the hill disappeared out the back window and wondered what would become of the hauntingly beautiful building before the war's end.

Just before dawn, the four women hopped down out of the truck, steel helmets fastened and full packs on their backs to wend their way through the train station, following the surgeon accompanying them on their way to southern France. He'd prepped them on the cases and ailments they'd be charged with during the train ride, and Anna had admired his precision, eyeing the charts and notes he'd lain across his lap. He was a kind man with a gentle demeanor and Anna watched his steady hands flip through paper after paper, hoping she'd get to continue working with him. His slower, methodical pace would be a welcome change from the surgeons in the tent hospital, slapping poorly written instructions on soldier's chests for her to decipher.

They walked down the sidewalk next to a long line of ambulances waiting to load their patients onto the ward cars. Captain Campbell was there, directing the procession of litter bearers, one after the other, in a smooth line the length of the train.

"Ladies," she said, "it's just the five of us today." She motioned to the next group of soldiers to board the train with their patients.

"We'll make do," Anna said.

Captain Campbell nodded. "We'll have to," she said. "We're only one nurse short, so between the five of us, we should be able to pick up any slack." She slammed the back door shut on an empty ambulance, shouting at the driver to clear out and make room for the next one.

"Ma'am," Eleanor began. "How many patients will we have on board?"

"Two hundred fifty-six," she answered.

Louise blew out a breath, slightly bug-eyed at the number of wounded men being boarded onto the train. "So much for an easy trip to Rennes," she said.

Captain Campbell laughed. "You must've learned better than that by now," she said, ushering forward the next ambulance. "Just remember, your situation is what you make of it. Rest when you need to rest. Don't burn yourselves out. You'll end up not being able to help at all. Now," she turned to face them, "board onto ward car two. They should be full and will need your help calming everyone down after being banged about on the way here."

"Yes, ma'am," Anna nodded. They climbed the steps into the poorly ventilated hospital car. Their patients had only just arrived, so rather than a mix of sweat and infection, the train car smelled of dirt and must, like a house closed up for too many years.

The beds lined each side of the aisle in three tiered berths, with wounded soldiers filling every single one. Anna looked from the bottom bunk to the top, thinking how tricky it would be to crouch down beside the men lying on the bottom. Her eyes slid to the top bunk, and she realized she'd need a step stool to even see the men in the top bunks, so close to the roof of the train they were. She counted down the rows. *Thirty-six men,* she thought. And Captain Campbell said they'd have over two hundred patients. She did the math quickly. *At least seven ward cars,* she thought. *Good Lord. With only the five of us.* They'd have help from the privates and sergeants assigned to the medical detachment, but that still left two cars without a nurse throughout the trip.

"This is…," Gretchen started.

"Not what you expected?" Louise finished her sentence.

"You could say that," she replied.

"How are we supposed to monitor seven cars filled to the ceiling with soldiers?" Anna asked.

"We don't," Eleanor said with a shrug.

"I don't think that's one of our choices, Elle," Gretchen said.

"I just mean it's not actually possible. We just do what we can. Like Captain Campbell said. No sense running ourselves ragged for an eight-hour ride. We just do the best we can."

"When did you become such a fountain of calm wisdom?" Gretchen teased.

The surgeon came bustling toward them. "These guys are all set for now," he said. "I need you to go into the pharmacy car and prep the penicillin before we start moving."

"Yes, sir," Gretchen said.

He stood to the side, making room for them to pass. "Just count till you've gone through ten cars, and then you'll be there," he said.

Anna groaned. "Looks like we'll be getting our calisthenics in today," she said.

By the time the train lurched forward, making its slow departure from the station, Anna was soaked in sweat. Never mind that there were eight ward cars, but the pharmacy was at one end of all eight. Which meant she'd been running through the long line of cars and back again each time she needed something for a patient in pain. The windows had fogged over, the stagnant air inside the train creating a Petri dish compared to the bitter cold outside. She snagged a glance out the window, wiping away the cool perspiration, only to see nothing but dirty snow and hazy skies. She gave up trying to wipe the windows for a glimpse of scenery when everything out there was just as depressing as the sights inside.

She pulled at her blouse, fanning it off of her stomach, sticky with sweat, and leaned against the pharmacy counter. She closed her eyes and took a deep breath. Gretchen came up beside her, and she opened one eye, stifling a laugh at the sight of her friend.

"It's a good thing we don't have mirrors in here," she said.

Gretchen smoothed her hair behind her ears. "Mine's that

bad too, huh?" She pointed at the frizz poking out beneath Anna's cap.

She nodded. "It's so darn hot in here," she said.

"It's all that hot air coming out of those soldiers," she joked. "I think only about half of 'em are even seriously injured enough to need transport like this. Some of those boys are milking it."

"Maybe," Anna said. "It doesn't really matter, though, does it? We have to treat them all just the same."

"How many hours did they say it takes till we get there?"

"Six, I think. Or maybe it was eight. I can't remember."

"I don't know either, but I'm starving," Gretchen said, patting her stomach.

"Gretch, we've only been moving for an hour."

Gretchen shrugged. "I'm getting a workout out there up and down all those cars. Thank goodness they put the stable ones on top. I can't even reach up there."

Anna laughed. "Me neither."

"I guess we better get back to it," Gretchen said, taking the medication she'd come in for. Anna followed her out.

"Don't you need anything in here?" Gretchen asked.

"No," Anna said, "I just needed a minute. I'm drenched." She pointed to her shirt.

Gretchen stopped short. "You are a little flushed. Do you feel okay?" She held her wrist to Anna's forehead.

Anna brushed her off. "I'm fine. It's just sweltering in here. I'm not used to the heat."

Gretchen eyed her.

"Seriously, Gretch, I'm fine." She went around her friend and opened the door, stepping through to the next car. She walked into screams of agony. "Nurse! Nurse! Please! Nurse!"

Anna knelt down beside the soldier lying in the bottom cot. "Hey there, what's going on?"

She checked his pulse while Gretchen pulled back his bed linens. "What hurts so bad?"

Anna looked him over for any indication of swelling while she counted his heart rate.

"It's pretty rapid," she whispered to Gretchen.

"Please," the man moaned again, his temples beaded with sweat.

"Where's your pain?" Gretchen asked again.

He groaned and writhed on the bed but still didn't answer the question.

"Alright, my friend," Anna said, "we'll get you fixed up soon; don't worry about a thing." She widened her eyes at Gretchen, silently telling her they needed the doctor. Gretchen nodded and dashed off. Normally, Anna would have used her best judgment and given him something for the pain, but being on the train with a doctor she hadn't worked with before, she didn't feel comfortable taking matters into her own hands.

"The doctor will be here before you know it," she said. She felt his forehead for any sign of a fever but felt only cool, clammy skin. She looked toward the door, willing the doctor to walk through it. The soldier was incoherent, sweating and groaning with his eyes drifting closed. When he opened them, Anna noticed they were glassy, and even when he appeared to be looking at her, she felt like he was looking through her, like he couldn't see her at all.

The door opened, and Dr. DeBusk burst into the car, steadying himself with the metal bed frames as he walked down the aisle.

"What's going on?"

"His heart rate is elevated, sir. He's in and out of consciousness, screaming in pain that he cannot locate."

"Fever? Any sign of infection?"

"No, sir, I don't believe so, but he's covered in sweat, so I can't be entirely sure."

The doctor lifted the soldier's shirt, palpating his abdomen. "His skin is on fire. How could you have missed that?"

Anna stood up from where she'd been crouched at the man's bedside. She'd never made a mistake on something as simple as a body temperature before. "I'm sorry, Doctor. It's just very warm in here. I suppose I'm not used to it yet," she stammered.

He waved a hand in the air. "It's no matter," he said, continuing to feel around with his other hand. The soldier jerked up, screaming out again.

"Mm. I thought so. He has appendicitis. We need to move him to the surgical car."

"You can't possibly perform that kind of surgery on a moving train," Anna said.

"And what else would you propose? We wait, he dies," the doctor said.

She gripped the metal railing as a sudden dizziness overcame her. She pressed her cheek to the cool metal, relishing the feel of it.

"Are you okay?" The doctor pushed up his glasses, looking Anna up and down.

She pulled herself upright. "Yes, sir," she said, smiling a little too brightly. "Just getting used to the bumpy ride."

"I'm not buying it," he said. He felt her forehead. "You're

warm, too. You need to go lay down."

Anna laughed. "I can't do that, sir."

"The hell you can't. I'm ordering it."

"Sir," she pleaded, "we're short staffed as it is. He needs to go into surgery," she said, gesturing to the moaning soldier. "I'm fine, really. Please. I have to help."

He cleared his throat, raising his eyebrows and considering what to do. He sighed. "If you get any worse, you're lying down," he warned. "I'm not kidding."

Gretchen came up behind them. "Not kidding about what, doc?"

"Anna is not feeling well," he said.

"I knew it!" She exclaimed.

Anna gave Gretchen a look, willing her to shut up.

"I'm fine, Gretchen."

"You're not," she countered.

"I'll rest when we get to Rennes," Anna promised.

"You need to rest now," Gretchen said.

"It's only another few hours, I'll be fine until then."

The doctor looked back and forth between the two women while two privates loaded the soldier onto a litter. He followed the men to the door. "Find me a surgical nurse," he said, "preferably one without a fever," and closed the door behind him.

"Anna, we can handle this. Go rest so you don't get worse," Gretchen begged.

"Gretch, I can't do that to you. It wouldn't be right."

"What wouldn't be right is getting everyone else sick because you're too damn stubborn to admit any bit of weakness."

Ouch, Anna thought. "Just kick me when I'm down, why don't you?"

Gretchen wrapped an arm around her, leading her out of the ward car in the direction of the officer's car. "Sometimes the truth hurts. And sometimes," she added, "it's the only way you'll listen."

They crossed through the pharmacy car and into the officer's quarters. Anna leaned on her friend more than she wanted to admit until they reached the cots.

"Sit," Gretchen ordered, pointing to a bunk, not unlike the ones in the ward cars.

"Yes, mother," Anna said, obeying. She was suddenly too tired to stand on her own.

"That's right, my dear. Now be a good girl and get some rest," Gretchen countered.

Anna rolled her eyes and regretted it instantly. Her head pounded with the movement, and made her dizzy all at once. She flopped backward into the cot, and Gretchen pulled the linen sheet over her.

"We'll keep checking in," she said, feeling her head again. "Geez, Anna, you're burning up. I'll get a cool cloth and be back in a minute."

"Don't worry about me," she said, already hazy with sleep, her eyelids heavy. "Take care of the patients."

Gretchen snorted. "You're one of them, now."

～～～

"Poor thing. She's probably going to miss seeing Paul before we get off at Rennes."

"How close do you think we are now?"

"Maybe an hour, two at most."

Anna pulled her legs into her chest, listening to the familiar voices with her eyes closed. She wondered how long she'd slept and tried to think back to what had happened before she'd been forced into bed. She remembered the soldier writhing in pain and wondered how his surgery went. She rolled to her side and the whispered conversation stopped. She opened her eyes, one and then the other, adjusting to the dim light in the officer's car. She was afraid to attempt sitting up too soon.

"How long did I sleep for?" Her voice came out gravelly, and her throat felt like sandpaper. *Darn,* she thought. She'd hoped a long nap would be enough to get her back on her feet.

Gretchen looked at her watch. "About five hours. Minus the ten minutes when I woke you up to take a shot of whiskey."

"Gosh, I don't even remember that." She sat up slowly, inch by inch, hoping the room wouldn't start spinning again. Eleanor held out a paper cup, and Anna looked inside.

"Just water," she said. "You need to rehydrate. You lost a lot with all that sweat." She nodded at the bed, and Anna looked behind her. An imprint of where she'd been lying showed her just how sweaty she'd been.

Gretchen felt her forehead. "Cool as a cucumber, now. Thank God," she said.

Anna nodded. "I don't feel feverish now. I just have a wicked sore throat," she croaked.

"I'll go see if there's anything left in the dining car that might help," Eleanor said.

"I am starving, actually," Anna said. She leaned her head against the side of the bed frame. "Thanks for taking such good care of me."

"What's one more patient?" Eleanor teased before she left to search for food.

Anna sighed. "This is not how I thought today would go," she said.

Gretchen shrugged. "I'm glad to see some color back in your face. You had me worried."

"I told you I was fine," Anna replied, getting an eye roll in return. "How'd you sneak out of ward car duty, anyway?"

"Most of the GIs are sleeping. Lulled by the train ride like babies," she said. "We've been taking turns walking car to car, but you haven't missed much."

"What happened to the one they took into surgery?"

"He's staying in the surgical car for post-op till we get to Rennes, but I think he's stable now."

"That's a relief," Anna said.

Eleanor came to the door with her hands full and tapped the glass. Gretchen jumped up and slid the door open.

"Your dinner awaits," Eleanor said, placing a tray on Anna's lap with a dramatic bow.

Anna smiled. "Thanks, Elle."

"The stew is hot. I thought that might help. And it wasn't half bad when we had it."

Anna dug in, suddenly ravenous. "I know this is probably not as good as I think it is, but right now, it tastes delicious. I must really be sick." She shoveled another bite into her mouth just as the door slid open. She turned, expecting to see Louise ready to swap with one of the girls, and nearly choked. Paul walked toward her, a lopsided grin on his face.

"You don't need me to slap your back, do you?"

She shook her head and held up a hand, covering her mouth with the other and coughing like mad. Her face was red, both with embarrassment and from coughing so hard. She finally recovered and cleared her throat a few more times.

"Ugh," she said. "If my throat didn't hurt bad enough before, it certainly does now."

"I'm sorry," Paul said. "That's my fault. I didn't mean to startle you."

Anna fanned at her face. "How'd you get permission to be back here?"

"Well, hello to you, too," he teased.

Anna looked down at the tray on her lap. "I'm not exactly in the best shape right now," she said. She felt around on the top of her head and groaned. Her nurse's cap had come unpinned and must have fallen off while she slept, and her hair felt like a thousand knots had been tied through it.

He sat down on her cot. "I beg to differ," he said.

She edged away from him. "You really shouldn't get too close right now," she said.

"I'm not too worried about it," he said. "That is, unless you'd prefer I leave you alone."

She looked at Gretchen and Eleanor, who hadn't made a sound since he'd walked in.

"You two," she said, pointing from Gretchen to Eleanor. "You put him up to this, didn't you?"

Gretchen put a hand over her heart. "What on Earth are you talking about?" She looked up at the door. "Oh, look, there's

Louise. Come on, Eleanor, she needs our help." She grabbed Eleanor by the arm, yanking her up and out the door.

Anna closed her eyes. "I'm sorry they made you come in here. You really didn't have to. It's just a cold, I'll be fine by tomorrow, but I hate to infect anyone else."

"Nobody forced me, Anna. I was hoping I'd get to see you. And if you're worried, I cleared it with your boss, so I promise I won't get you in any trouble."

"Captain Campbell?"

Paul nodded. "How are you feeling?"

"Better than before," she admitted. "I think I slept most of it off. Just a sore throat now."

"Eleanor said you were pretty sick. Your friends were worried about you."

Anna rolled her eyes. "They're being ridiculous," she said, moving her empty tray off her lap.

"Nah, they're just good friends."

She nodded, shifting to lean her back against the bed frame and face him.

"How have you been?" She was a mess and felt self-conscious about seeing him if she looked as raggedy as she felt. But she was also glad to see him. It couldn't have been easy to convince Captain Campbell, and she appreciated that he'd gone and done that for her.

He shrugged. "I'm ready to go home, if I'm being honest."

She nodded. "I don't know that I'm ready to go home," she said, "but I'm ready for the war to end."

"Oh, come on, AB, don't you want to go home to see your grandfather?"

She smiled. "You and that nickname," she laughed. "You'll never give it up, will you?"

"It's cute," he said with a grin. "My old man still calls me Paulie Boy. I've never been able to get him to give it up. All over town, the old-timers call me Paulie Boy. No matter how old I get." He chuckled.

"Wait…" she said, "You mean to tell me your nickname would be…PB?"

"Ha, I guess so, but don't go around calling me peanut butter. I don't think that's much better than Paulie Boy."

Anna laughed, holding onto her throat. It felt like a million little razor blades every time she swallowed.

"Don't make me laugh," she wheezed, then made an 'x' over her chest. "I swear, I won't call you PB," she said.

They sat for a few minutes, enjoying each other's company. Anna broke the silence first. "You know, some people say peanut butter and banana go pretty good together." She looked up at Paul and groaned, her cheeks flushed again. *Oh my Lord*, she thought, *what is wrong with me?*

She felt her forehead with the back of her hand. "That must be the fever talking," she said, trying to backpedal.

Paul chuckled. "Is that so? You know, come to think of it, my sister said that's one of my nephew's favorite snacks."

She watched his face light up at the mention of his nephew. She was pretty sure he'd just made that up, but she was glad to keep him talking about his family.

"How old is your nephew?"

"Well, let's see. He turned one when I was still in ASTP. So, by the time I get back…I'll have missed another birthday."

"I bet he can't wait to see you."

Paul nodded. "So, AB and PB, huh?" He said, changing the subject. "Peanut butter and banana. It's got a good ring to it, doesn't it?"

She laughed. "If you say so." She smiled at him, thankful for his company when she felt so lousy. Her earlier embarrassment over how she must look was all but gone. The way he looked at her made her feel like nothing else mattered.

"I still don't know how you got Captain Campbell to agree to this."

Paul laughed. "Gretchen's not the only one who can turn on the charm," he said, waggling his eyebrows.

Anna shoved at his arm, making him laugh harder.

"No, but seriously, I think she just felt bad for you. Plus, I gave her my best puppy dog eyes," he said. He reached for her hand and she tried to pull away, but he held on tight.

"Paul, I really don't want to get you sick," she said, "Trust me, you don't want whatever this is."

"Sure I do," Paul teased, "I know a really great nurse I can go to." She gave his arm another weak shove.

He looked at her like he was trying to memorize every last line and freckle on her face. She tried to keep her eyes on him, but she felt her ears turn red under his scrutiny and had to look away.

"I should let you get some rest," he said.

She nodded, even though the last thing she really wanted to do was let him leave. He leaned over, kissed her forehead, and she closed her eyes at the contact of his warm lips against her cool skin. He stood to leave. She stood, too, realizing just how badly her body ached with the effort to get out of bed.

"Stay in bed," he said, wrapping an arm around her waist and guiding her back to the cot.

"Wait," she said. "I have something to give back to you." She opened one of the storage lockers and pulled out her duffle bag, glad to have remembered his coin before he left.

She dropped it into her palm and turned around, offering it to him.

"What's this?" He reached out, and she placed the coin in his hand.

"Well, how about that," he said, holding it up. She watched him turn it over in his hand, emotion sweeping over his face that he choked down when he finally met her gaze.

"How'd you get it back?"

"Marjorie sent it to me. She said she hoped it would bring us good luck out here. I was going to mail it to you, but I wasn't sure where you were, and I didn't want to risk putting it in the mail again and having it get lost…" she trailed off, realizing she was rambling.

"See that, I told you it would end up with someone who needed it more than me," he said, handing it back to her.

"What? No, it's yours, Paul. You're the rightful owner of the lucky coin," she said. She held her hands up so he couldn't give her the coin.

"Marjorie sent it to you, AB. And I want you to keep it."

"I couldn't do that to you, Paul. It means too much to you."

"It didn't mean too much that I wouldn't put it in the pudding. And it would mean even more to me if you'd keep it. Let it bring you some luck. Or maybe some peanut butter," he joked. He ran his hand over his hair. "Great, now I'm the one with the bad jokes," he muttered.

She smiled, accepting the coin from him. "If you're really sure," she said, looking up at him.

"I'm really sure," he said. He kissed her forehead again, and her stomach swirled with what she hoped were butterflies and not the stew she'd just eaten.

"Are you getting off at Rennes, too?"

He shook his head. "We're going down a bit further."

"Oh, darn," she said, and she felt the vibration of his laughter against her cheek resting on his chest.

"As nice as it's been having you follow me around Europe," he teased, "I guess this is where we part ways... for now."

She pulled back. "Excuse me, but you've been the one following me around," she said.

He smiled down at her, unwinding his arms from around her waist. "You need to rest," he said, "and I need to get back."

She nodded. "See you soon?"

"I hope so," he answered. She sat down on the bed, too tired to stand. He pulled the sheet up around her, and she squeezed his hand one more time. She watched him back away toward the door until he waved and was gone. She felt colder and more alone than she had since she'd gotten here.

She held his coin in her hand until she started to doze, then tucked it into her pocket before falling asleep.

$\sim$

Chapter 29

PAUL
JANUARY 1945
ST. NAZAIRE, FRANCE

*I*n the commotion of unloading the patients from the train at Rennes, Paul never did get to see Anna on the train again. He watched out the window, hoping to at least catch a glimpse of her, but between the dozens of litters being carried and the line of ambulances at the curb, he couldn't see anything but a swarm of uniforms.

He slumped down into the seat when the train started its slow departure out of the station, counting the ambulances from the window, needing the distraction to quiet his mind. From the little details he knew about their assignment in St. Nazaire, he didn't have too much to worry about. They'd be keeping guard in a largely uneventful area of France. The submarine pens had been boxed in, and, from what they'd been told, the Germans hadn't risked anything yet. Paul hoped it stayed that way until the end of the war. It felt like it was so close he could almost reach out and grab it - freedom from all this. Or maybe his renewed excitement over a future with Anna had put that dangerous hope in his mind. The hope for war's end, when, who was he kidding, he had no idea when or if this war would end. The only thing he had to go on was the growing restlessness and discontent from the guys in his squadron.

He leaned his head against the cool glass after they passed the last ambulance. He thought about Anna and how she'd wanted to mail his coin to him but didn't know where he'd ended up, and an idea formed in his head. He pulled his duffle bag to his lap from where he'd shoved it between his legs on the floor. He took out paper and pen and used his bag to lean on.

Dear Anna,

You've gotten off the train at Rennes, and although I didn't actually see you climb down, I know it's true because I can feel the emptiness you not being here has left behind. It's much more difficult to write a letter on a moving train than I thought it would be, but I had a brilliant idea. At least, I think it's brilliant. Remember how you said you couldn't send the coin because you didn't know where I was? No, I'm not asking for the coin back. It just got me thinking – I can't always tell you where I'll be, but I know you're stationed at the 199th. So, prepare to be bombarded with letters every day that you are there until things are over and I'm on a train heading nearer to you instead of further away.

Paul

The truck drove until the road turned to dirt, and the trees became more dense. They unloaded their gear to set up camp, put up their tents, and stashed their belongings before lining up in front of Captain Gangwere.

"We're short a few men, as you already know," he began. "And we're outnumbered by the Germans."

Shit, thought Paul. *I thought this was supposed to be an easy assignment.*

"Your job is to block off any German trying to enter the pens. It doesn't happen often - they have no idea how few men we have here right now. If we can keep them from getting supplies, they'll have to abandon their posts eventually. Any man you come across needs to be captured, and you don't ever let on how many of you there are."

Paul blew out a breath, looking out past the captain. They were low in a valley, thick woods on one side and tall grasses on the other. The grassy expanse went on and on, providing additional cover for their camp. In the distance, Paul could see some kind of stone building at the top of a hill. He wondered if anyone was still living there. *Not likely*, he thought. Not when this area had already been bombed to the ground. He doubted if any civilians would have risked staying.

Captain Gangwere followed Paul's gaze to the top of the hill. "The chateau is empty," he said, reading Paul's mind. "And I do mean completely empty. Don't go poking around in there thinking you'll find booze or money or anything else left behind. It's too high and open on all sides. You'd be a sitting duck left vulnerable to an easy attack."

Paul nodded his understanding. He had no interest in exploring the old chateau anyway. As far as he was concerned, he planned on getting the job done and keeping his head down. His only goal was getting the hell out in one piece.

"Settle in, boys; you'll be here for a while. But keep your guard up. We should have replacements coming in soon to round out the unit. Until then, it's just us eight. We've got two other squadrons scattered throughout these woods if we need them." He nodded at the trees to Paul's right. "One more thing. You hear that?"

The men stood still, listening for whatever noise their commander wanted them to hear. A high-pitched whistle sounded far off in the distance.

"What is it, sir?"

"German 88's."

"Those are practically mini rockets," Jack said.

"Damn right, they are." He walked over to the pile of supplies they'd unloaded from the truck and grabbed a shovel, handing it to Jack. "Better start digging."

Harry groaned. "Just great," he grumbled. "Digging damn foxholes."

"You can piss and moan all you want. You won't be complaining when an 88 whizzes past your head, and you're safe five feet into the Earth." The commander took another shovel from the pile and got to work alongside his men. Paul respected him for that. Any boss that got his hands dirty, too, was welcome to call them out as far as he was concerned. He could've given the orders and watched them work. But that wasn't the kind of man he was. Paul thought about Colonel Rumberg then. He'd have been right there with them, too. His thoughts wandered while he moved dirt shovel by shovel. They were short four men. Four men gone from their squadron alone. Joe was one of them.

"Feels like I'm digging my own grave," Harry complained.

Paul chuckled, "You better cut that out."

Harry shoved his shovel beneath the grass, stepping on it for leverage. "Just speaking the truth," he said.

"Well, find a different one then," Paul said. "How 'bout instead, I'm digging this damn hole so I can get home to see my newborn baby when this is all over with." He kept going, angry shovelful after shovelful. Harry stopped and stared at him.

"You better do something about that, you know," Harry said.

"About what?"

"All that anger you got pent up inside of you. It'll destroy you if you let it." He looked at Paul and went back to shoveling. It was Paul's turn to stand and stare at his friend.

"You're right, I am angry. I don't know how the hell you aren't. Maybe it was something in the water that did it. Seeing so many good men doing the dead man's float. But yeah, Harry, I'm angry."

"You've gotta let it go, Paul."

"Let it go? Is that what you did?" He tossed his shovel on the ground. "Just pretend it never happened, is that it? Carry on like we didn't lose a damn thing?"

The men around them were quiet, some still shoveling, a few too afraid to make a move, watching the scene unfold before them.

Paul stalked off through the woods. He knew the other two squadrons were setting up camp here, too, so he wasn't worried about being in the woods alone. Plus, he was too pissed off to care or make a rational judgment call. He walked to the edge of a river - he had no clue what river it was - and watched the water meander by. He closed his eyes and counted. He didn't know how many minutes he stood like that before he heard rustling behind him. Any other place, he wouldn't have bothered to turn around, but he had sense enough about him to look in the direction of the noise. Harry's red hair gave him away, and Paul turned back toward the water.

"You know, I should push your ass in," Harry said from behind him.

Paul chuckled.

"I didn't mean to piss you off back there."

Paul shrugged. "It doesn't matter, Harry. You're not wrong. I am angry."

"We all are. Don't get it twisted and think we've just gotten over it."

"It sure seems like it. More so than me, at least. I still see it, Harry." He turned to face his friend. "Every time I close my eyes, I relive it. Over and over and over. Only it gets worse every time. Not only do I watch Rumberg die, now when I fall asleep it's Anna, or you, or my sister." He looked at the ground, "My brother." He put his hands on his head in frustration while Harry stood and watched him, listening.

"And I'm angry over what happened, yeah, but I'm even angrier that it's eating me apart, and I can't stop it. I can't escape it. What is wrong with me that I can't get to the place you're all at? To just keep going, put it all behind me."

"We're all struggling, Paul. You're kidding yourself if you think you're the only one still trying to sort it all out. You're not any different than any one of us, so just put that idea to rest right now. You know what I think it really is, Paul? You're so used to being cool under pressure. You're not easily rattled. You're the guy we all go to for help. Hell, you've helped me keep my head on straight more than a couple times. And now you're in a place where you're the one needing help, and you think we'll look at you differently, like you're not equipped to be the go-to guy anymore. But guess what?"

Paul arched a brow.

"That's not how this works. You're not any less of the man you were before that ship sank. If anything, you're an even better one."

Paul scoffed. "I wouldn't go that far, pal."

"I would. We all would. You did a damn good job rescuing guys off that ship. Guys that would've otherwise died. And I'm sorry that Colonel Rumberg died, but it's not your fault. I'm sorry you're left with these demons to wrestle, but we all have 'em. You think I don't feel guilty, too?"

Paul looked up from where he'd been kicking at the dirt. "What the hell for?"

"Paul. I made it off that ship without even getting my pants wet. You don't think that plays in my mind? That I should've been man enough to stay and help? That I was too much of a coward to stay? So I jumped. And I stayed safe. And yeah, I was damn relieved at the time. But now? Now I feel like a jerk. Like I took the easy way out. The selfish way out."

"Stop, Harry," Paul said.

"No. I'm telling you the truth. You're not alone in this. So don't shut us out and pretend like you are. Pretend like the rest of us are all okay and you're the only one who's not. Let us in. It's the only way. No one else can help you. No one else went through it. We know, too."

Paul took a deep breath. "Thanks, Harry. I'm not going to lie to you and say I don't still feel the way I feel. But I'll try not to isolate myself."

Harry nodded. They stood on the riverbank, watching the current go by.

"Wonder if we'll have time to cast a line. Some fresh fish would taste pretty good compared to the slop we've had."

Harry stepped closer to the water, looking for fish beneath the surface.

"How much shit am I in for taking off?"

Harry turned back around. "Ha. Captain Gangwere said it's your ass if you get taken by the Germans."

Paul laughed. "Figures."

Chapter 30

ANNA
JANUARY 1945
RENNES, FRANCE

*A*nna woke to the sound of an explosion so loud it shook the cot she was lying on. She sat up in bed and looked around, gaining her bearings. She was so congested she couldn't breathe through her nose, but she swore she could taste gunpowder in the air.

She stood on shaky legs, thankful her friends had thought to leave her a fresh uniform at the foot of the bed. She'd been so sick getting off the train at Rennes she hadn't been good for anything except crawling from one cot to the next. She changed out of her nightgown as fast as her body would let her, just as another explosion shook through the building. She could have cried. Here she was, sick as a dog in a new city without any real idea where she was. She knew she was in the 199th General Hospital. But other than that, she was blind to her surroundings. Rather than cry, though, she buttoned her blouse, stepped into her shoes, and ran from the room. In the dark hallway, she held onto the wall, listening for anything that might tell her which direction to go. She held a handkerchief over her runny nose and walked down the hall to the stairwell. She heard voices echoing upward from the floor below.

"Oh, thank God," she said when she reached the bottom of the stairs. It opened up into a lounge where her friends sat around one of the low round tables scattered about.

"Anna," Gretchen jumped up and ran to her. "What are you doing up?" She led her to the table, pulling up a seat.

"As if I could sleep through those explosions! Shouldn't we be evacuating?"

She looked around at groups of nurses at the other tables in the room and wondered why no one else was panicking. *Am I crazy? Did I dream all that?* But no, here comes another one. There was no mistaking the whistle that preceded the sound of a bomb making contact with its target. Anna's eyes were wide with fear while everyone else acted like it was nothing.

"The girls that have been here a while said it's normal," Eleanor said with a shrug.

"That noise is not normal," Anna replied.

"There's nothing we can do about it, anyway," Gretchen said.

Anna looked at Louise. At least she looked slightly more concerned.

"I don't like it either," Louise said. "But they're right. There's nowhere else to go."

She'd been in Rennes only a day, most of which she'd slept through, and she was ready to leave. She blew her nose and sat down at the table.

"How do they work through that awful noise?" She shook her head. "Their nerves must be shot."

"You'll get used to it," a nurse from the table next to them said. "Took me a few weeks, but now I hardly even notice."

"Hardly notice? The first one tonight shook my whole cot!"

"Oh, you were up in Room 37, weren't you?"

Anna nodded.

"Yeah, that's the south side. It gets the brunt of it. When you're down in the ward with patients, you'll forget all about it."

Anna doubted it, but she smiled at the nurse. "Maybe so, but I'm not going back to bed up there."

~~~

After a week of chills and body aches, Anna had finally turned a corner. On her last day of bed rest, she sat down at the little wooden desk in the corner of the room. She'd moved out of the terrifying south side room where she'd stayed the first night, joining Gretchen, Louise, and Eleanor in a tiny dorm room. Her mother's letter still hung over her head, and she figured she'd better write now before her shift started in the morning.

She opened her leather pouch, glancing at Paul's Peace Dollar before taking out her mother's letter and unfolding it on the desk. She read it again and again, trying to decide what to say.

My Dear Mother,

I apologize for the delay in my response. I've been in Rennes for one week now, though I've not been able to see patients. Rather, I've been one myself. Nothing to worry about – I'm much better now. I came down with the flu on the train ride here. Thankfully, today is my last day of bedrest, and I can resume my duties tomorrow morning.

She sat back in the chair, drumming her fingers on the desk, unsure of how to address what her mother had written. She had so much she wanted to say until she sat down to write it. *Oh well,* she thought, *just do it.*

Mother, I hope you know that an apology is not necessary, though I am glad to have received your letter, and I appreciate very much your willingness to bridge the gap that divides us. I am not angry with you. I'd like nothing more than to move forward into a good place, no matter our differences. I think you'll find, as I have in my time here, that we aren't so different as we once thought.

Sending my love to you and Dad,

Anna

"Ready?" Eleanor stood at the door, waiting for Anna the next morning. Anna nodded, straightening her cap.

"I think so." Her stomach swirled with butterflies, nervous for her first day of work in a new hospital.

"I'm sure they'll take it easy on you, at least for today," Eleanor joked, opening the door to the ward and circling behind the nurse's station.

Dr. DeBusk came barreling around the corner, skidding to a stop when he saw Anna. His eyes lit up. "Anna, you're just the person I hoped to see."

"Good morning, Dr. DeBusk."

"Feeling much better, I hope?" He didn't wait for her to answer. "My surgical nurse is out today. Another one down with the flu."

"Oh, dear, I'm sorry to hear that."

"Yes, yes, poor thing," he said distractedly. "I need you today."

"Oh, sure," she said, nodding. "I can take your post-op patients."

He smiled. "Actually, I don't need you for post-op. I need you in surgery."

Anna's eyes went wide. She'd never assisted in the operating room before. "Sir, are you sure there's no one else with more surgical experience?"

He shook his head. "I've seen your work, Anna. You have plenty of experience."

"Thank you, sir. I do appreciate that, but…"

"Great, it's settled then. First patient is scheduled for 9am," he said, backing away down the hallway. "Eleanor, you'll handle post-op today."

"Sure thing, Doc."

Anna looked at Eleanor in shock. "What am I going to do?"

Eleanor gave her a blank stare. "You're going into surgery in…" she looked at the clock. "Ten minutes."

Anna closed her eyes. "But I've never gone into surgery before," she whispered.

Eleanor looked indifferent. "Anna, you'll be fine. You're a good nurse."

Anna walked down the hall toward the operating room in a daze. Her first day working at the 199th General Hospital was also her first day assisting in surgery. She didn't even know what kind of surgery she'd be assisting with. For once, she was thankful for Captain Campbell and her strict orders to stay in bed an extra day. That extra day meant she was well-rested and clear-headed for today.

She entered the operating room, the first patient of the day already lying on the table in the middle of the enormous room, an overhead light shining down on him. *No time to be scared,* she thought. She plastered a smile on her face and faked a confidence she did not feel.

"Ready?" Dr. DeBusk smiled kindly. "We've got a simple debridement this morning," he said.

Anna nodded. "From where, sir?" She'd done plenty of debridements on soldier's wounds. *I've worked myself up for nothing,* she thought.

Dr. DeBusk looked up from his notes. "The liver," he said.

She steeled her face. *Liver,* she thought, breathing slow, steady breaths. *Ok, it's ok, Anna. You're just here to assist. Nothing to worry about. It's just a bit further inside the body than you've done before. No big deal.* She finished her pep talk and got to work, gathering the doctor's instruments and organizing them on a tray beside the table.

Anesthetic was administered, and the soldier drifted into sleep. Anna watched in wonder as the doctor cut in just the precise location to access the soldier's wounded liver. She handed him each instrument as he requested it and watched him skillfully remove the slug that had lodged itself inside. He placed it onto the metal tray with a soft plink that echoed through the cold room.

"Alright, I think he's all set," the doctor said, inspecting his work one more time. He began to stitch the soldier, then handed it off to Anna. "You can take it from here," he said.

She hesitated, then took over for the doctor, expertly sewing up the rest of the incision. When she'd knotted the last stitch, she breathed a deep sigh of relief, letting out a shaky laugh.

"I hadn't realized I was holding my breath," she said, bringing her hand up to cover her wildly thumping heart.

Dr. DeBusk chuckled. "By the day's end, you won't give it a second thought."

She smiled, grateful for the doctor's confidence in her ability since she wasn't feeling it herself.

She wheeled the patient out of the operating room with the help of an orderly, passing off the doctor's notes to Eleanor. She gave him his first dose of penicillin and returned to the operating room.

"We have an emergency coming in," Dr. DeBusk said, and the butterflies in Anna's stomach kicked up again. "Another debridement, though this one might be a bit trickier."

~

Anna filled a basin with soapy water and submerged her dirty uniform inside, scrubbing the stains from the white fabric. Today had challenged her more than anything else had. She had thought the Leopoldville had been the hardest night of her career, and it still was, but today's difficulties had challenged her in a different way. Today had been rewarding rather than heartbreaking.

She wrung out her uniform and drained the basin, carrying it all back to her room to dry in front of the radiator.

"How'd it go today?" Gretchen greeted her before she made it halfway through the door. Anna laughed, closing the door behind her.

"It was…" She searched for the right word. "I don't know

how to describe it. Incredible. Exhausting. It wasn't like anything I've ever experienced before. I was terrified this morning. I still don't know why Dr. DeBusk wanted me in there with him. If he'd have given me a choice, I'd have said no."

"That's why he didn't give you one," Louise said.

"You're probably right."

"She's definitely right. You don't give yourself enough credit," Eleanor said.

"Thanks, guys," Anna said, hanging her wet uniform. "Dr. DeBusk opened up a man's heart today. I assisted him during heart surgery. Never in my life," Anna said, sitting on the edge of her bed.

"And? How did it go?" Gretchen looked just as excited as Anna felt.

"He took out shell fragments and pieces of fabric that had lodged in the pericardium. By the time he finished, the soldier had a regular heart rate and his blood pressure was back to normal. I swear, it felt like just a few minutes rather than a few hours."

She was physically drained, her feet and back sore from standing in the operating room all day, but her mind was alive with a renewed sense of wonder and exhilaration, something she'd been afraid the war would steal away from her.

~

Chapter 31

PAUL
MAY 1945
ST. NAZAIRE, FRANCE

*P*aul sat in his lawn chair, looking up at the sky. The rumblings of a war nearing its end had begun to circulate, and they'd started to relax a little more with every day that passed. Each one was the same as the last - patrol the roads in, check for any signs of movement nearing the pens, and march back. Every couple of weeks, they'd organize with their entire platoon, taking longer walks with the tank leading the way through the areas where Germans were known to have their bunkers.

Rain and cold kept them in their tents or trucks or gathered around a fire. The first few days of sun, Paul had taken full advantage, afraid it might be a cruel trick that would disappear altogether. He sat in his folding chair, thinking about what his dad would be doing on the farm, halfway around the world, in this weather. He couldn't wait to be back on a tractor instead of a troop truck. He smiled at the thought of little Danny sitting on his lap for a ride on the big tractor.

He wrote out a letter to Evie, his mom and dad, then started one more.

Dear Anna,

Well, we've made it to May 1ˢᵗ. Seems to me it was a lifetime ago that we were on a train bound for the south of France. Not much new to report since yesterday…ha..ha..I guess that's a good thing. I hope you're still getting my letters. Anyway, we're about to head out on a patrol with the rest of the platoon. I'll let you know how it went tomorrow.

- Paul

"Ready to go?" Harry rapped his hand on the top of Paul's steel helmet.

"Yep," he said, standing to fold up his lawn chair.

They marched over to the rest of their unit behind the tank they'd be following for cover. He'd be the point person today, taking the lead behind the giant machine. They gathered their weapons and fell into formation, waiting for the word to proceed. They performed these raids every few weeks, checking German bunkers for any activity. Some weeks, they'd bring in a few prisoners; most weeks, though, they found no one.

"Hey, maybe this will be our last patrol," Harry said, optimistic.

"I sure hope so," said Jack.

The tank crawled along ahead, knocking down the high grass, making a path for them. They kept their weapons raised, checking left and right, until the tank came to a sudden stop.

"On the ground!" Paul went down to the ground just before bullets flew over their heads. A bunker that had been empty on the last patrol was now raining bullets down on their platoon. The Sherman tank was their only cover, and he waited, crouching behind the tank while the man inside it fired into the German bunker, shaking the ground beneath him. Paul aimed his rifle, taking a shot at the hole between the sandbags that had been piled up. He fired endlessly, praying he'd make contact and end the ambush they'd found themselves in the middle of.

Movement to his left made him take his eye off his target. "Stay in position!" He screamed so loud and for so long that his voice went hoarse, and he still screamed through the pain. "Stay back! Get back into position!" The soldier to his left continued to advance ahead of him, moving out of safety. Paul tried to grab hold of the soldier's foot to drag him backward when he saw the flash of red hair at the back of his neck beneath his steel helmet.

"Harry! What the hell! Get back!" Paul grabbed at him again, crawling forward. He kept his rifle up, firing a shot into the bunker and refocusing on Harry. His friend had his gun up, firing his own shot at the Germans, when Paul heard a horrific sound. He took his cheek off his gun just in time to watch Harry hit the ground, his steel helmet blown backwards from the impact.

"No!" Paul lunged forward. "Medic! Medic! Medic!" He heard himself shouting over and over, panic and desperation coursing through him. He crouched over Harry, shielding him from more enemy fire, not caring if he got hit himself. Harry's helmet hung off his head at an odd angle, and Paul carefully pulled it off the rest of the way, blood pooling on the ground beneath him, soaking through the knees of his pants.

"Medic!" He screamed again, staring into the lifeless eyes of his best friend. The medics approached, forcing Paul to step back away from Harry. He felt like he was standing outside of his body. This couldn't possibly be happening. He was dreaming. Jack ran up from the rear, screaming like he was crazed, with his semiautomatic in his hands. Paul should have told him to stay in his position. He should have chased after him, forcing him back behind the tank. Instead, he stood there, his rifle held loosely in his hand, while smoke and dirt filled his eyes and nose, and the air swirled around him. Visibility was poor, and even if he could've seen anything, his brain wouldn't tell his body to move. He watched the medics carry Harry away, beyond the front lines. He wanted to follow them, wanted to breathe life back into his friend. *This can't be happening,* he thought again. *This isn't real.* He felt his knees begin to buckle when Glenn came up beside him, pulling him out of the trance he was in.

"Paul, we gotta keep moving."

Paul nodded, moving his feet one in front of the other with Glenn's prodding. The smoke started to clear, and everything stopped all at once except for the drone of the tank engine. The ringing in his ears was so loud it took him a minute to realize the gunfire had stopped. The tank made a slow forward approach, and Jack came into view, nudging three Germans out of their bunker with their hands up in surrender.

As soon as he saw them, Paul broke out in a run, anger, and grief colliding inside of him at the loss of Harry. He tackled one German soldier, pummeling him to the ground, his face raw and bloody, until Glenn pulled him away. He was blind with rage, wanting to finish what they'd started.

"Easy, Paul. It won't bring him back," Glenn said, holding onto his arm. Only then did his knees finally give out on him. He fell to the ground. The thought of Harry going ahead of him, taking a bullet to his head made him sick to his stomach. His helmet should have protected him. He bent over the ground and vomited, wiping his mouth with the back of his hand.

"Why, Harry? Why?" He cried out, his face muddy from sweat and tears mixing with dirt. He looked down at his uniform, splattered with the blood of the German soldier and soaked with Harry's blood, too. It was too much for him. Too much, but also, not enough. It would never be enough to bring his friend back. Anna had been right. This war stole everything precious and good from their lives.

Glenn and Jack got on each side of him, pulling him to his feet, carrying the entirety of his weight while he hung limp, wrought with the pain of watching his best friend die.

"He wasn't supposed to move in front," Paul sobbed. "Why the hell didn't he follow protocol?"

Glenn hung his head. "I don't know, Paul. I really don't know. I don't think we'll ever know."

Jack cleared his throat, swallowing down the lump of emotion. "I know why. He took that bullet for you, Paul," he said, and Paul looked at him, Jack's eyes swimming with unshed tears. "It would've been you."

"It should've been me. Dammit! The man has a baby on the way. God, why?"

The tears wouldn't stop then, thinking about a pregnant Edith, anxious for her husband's return, hopeful he'd be there to witness the birth of their first child. He thought about Harry's baby growing up without his father. And it was Paul's fault. He should have been the one to take that bullet, not Harry.

"I promised him he'd make it back to Edith," Paul whispered.

"Harry knew you couldn't keep that promise. You were his best friend. He knew that. Don't doubt that for a second," Glenn said, pulling Paul so close that their foreheads touched. He held Paul there by the back of his neck until the rest of the platoon caught up to them and they were forced to keep trudging through the freshly mown path of the tank.

Two weeks after Harry died, Paul was on another train, sitting alone with his thoughts. He'd withdrawn from everyone. Jack and Glenn, though they tried, couldn't penetrate the deep sadness that ran through him now. It had been bad enough losing Colonel Rumberg, Joe, and countless other soldiers the night the Leopoldville sank, but this... he didn't think he'd ever recover from a loss this big.

One week, Paul thought. *He couldn't have held on for one more week.* It had taken that long for them to get word of the German surrender. The war had essentially been over, and yet, Harry was still taken from this Earth.

He looked over at the seat beside him, where Harry should have been. Instead, just his pack lay there. Paul had put up a fight when the commander came to take Harry's belongings. He was determined to deliver Harry's things to Edith himself. Even if it took him a year to get there, he had made a promise to his friend and he intended to keep it.

He thought about that day by the river when Harry had called him out. *Let all that anger go*, he had said. *Don't let it poison you, Paul. Well, Harry*, he thought, *what am I supposed to do now?* He didn't think he could ever let go of all the anger he felt - or rather, he didn't *want* to. If he was angry, he still remembered.

But what happened when he let go of the anger and the memory started to fade?

Paul's mind wandered to Anna and the last time he'd seen her - on a train just like this one. He'd made a promise to her, too. He hadn't kept that one, either. *Yet another way you've failed*, he thought. Once Harry died, he couldn't bear to pick up a pen. What could he possibly say? He couldn't write the words he wanted to say and anything else felt too trivial. He couldn't fake it with Anna, but the guilt ate at him, especially when he read her latest letter.

Dear Paul,

I don't expect a response, but I will keep writing every day until maybe, eventually, you want to talk to me again. I can't say I don't miss the surprise of getting your letters - I suppose I'd started taking them for granted - I won't lie. But, I think I can understand why they stopped coming. I hope I'm not too presumptuous to say that it wasn't because of me - I'm holding out hope that you'll still want something to do with me. Because I treasure our friendship, Paul. Even if that's all this turns out to be, I won't deny how I feel anymore because you were right. It hurts either way.

xx Anna

He leaned his head against the hard seat and reached beneath his shirt for the scapular he'd worn every day since his father had given it to him. It was worn and frayed, little brown strings hanging loose from all four sides. He could hardly believe it was still intact after the past year. Maybe his dad had been right. Maybe it had given him extra protection. But he didn't really think so - a piece of fabric didn't make him any more worthy of being saved than any of the other guys. But maybe it had strengthened his faith, a reminder every day that God is nearer to him than he thought. *I could use that reminder again right about now, God,* he thought. *I'm questioning everything I know about you, Lord. Just like Dad said I would.* He thought about his father and what he'd do given the hand Paul had been dealt. He'd probably be thankful to be alive. But it wasn't that easy. How could he be thankful to be alive and carry all this guilt around at the same time? He knew everyone would tell him the same thing - he had nothing to feel guilty for. But what did they know? They hadn't witnessed their best friend take a damn bullet for them. He still couldn't wrap his head around it. Harry had wanted nothing more than to get out of this hellhole and back home to his wife. Harry, who'd been so anxious to be a brand new dad. Yet he sacrificed his own life so Paul wouldn't die. He wanted to scream. *Why?* The fact that he'd never get an answer to that question killed him. He hung his head, another wave of grief washing over him.

He felt like he was in a constant tug of war between two parts of him. The old Paul, with fresh eyes, optimistic about what lay ahead, and the Paul he'd become - torn apart by grief and despair and too sad to even think about his future. He'd joked with Harry about not wanting to become some crotchety old man, dwelling on his wartime experience. But right now, he didn't see any other way for him. Because right now, he didn't feel like he was dwelling on anything - he felt like holding onto his pain was the only way to honor the guys who weren't riding on the train with him.

Chapter 32

ANNA
MAY 1945
RENNES, FRANCE

*S*pringtime came cautiously - bulbs peeking through the barely thawed ground only to shrivel up after another late frost - and then, all at once, the incessant rain rewarded them with the greenest grass and the most vibrant red tulips stretching toward the warmth of the sun.

At first, Anna hardly noticed the change. She'd gotten used to staying in the hospital for so many months that she'd forgotten to pick her head up once in a while to look out the window toward the prospect of spring. When she finally walked outside, she was greeted with new life, a warm breeze, and all the signs of change in the air. Her first instinct was to strip her feet of their shoes and socks and soak up the feeling of the Earth and all its goodness. She resisted the urge, settling instead for a walk in front of the hospital, where she could bend down to run the blades of grass across her fingertips. She sat down on the edge of a low stone wall, breathing in the sweet smells around her. In sharp contrast to the bleakness of war she'd grown accustomed to, now, when she looked around, the glory of spring had blossomed. With it, of course, came thoughts of home - where will that be? She sat and wondered, for the first time without worry, what her future outside of Europe would look like. She reveled in the feel of the sun shining on her face, tempting her to shed her cape to feel the warmth on her arms. She kept it fastened tightly around her neck, not risking a chill after the flu she'd had just a few months ago. The long winter had made her eager for the warmer months and the prospect of summer. The chill in the air reminded her that the chance of winter rearing its head again wasn't over yet, even while the birds chirped from the trees that lined the road in front of the hospital.

It had been an uneventful few months since she'd joined the 199th General Hospital. She was thankful for that, especially as the rockets picked up, keeping her awake each night. She hadn't gotten used to the noise - rather, she'd gotten used to operating on less sleep, lying awake in bed, praying each night wouldn't be the night they were hit. It had felt like an inevitability hearing the whir and roar of rockets being launched. But, as the other nurses had predicted, they'd made it all these months and were still in one piece.

Most nights, Anna would reach beneath her cot, feeling for the shoebox she'd kept there. Inside, she'd carefully organized each one of the letters she'd received from Paul. She smiled, thinking about the first one he'd sent. She'd scoffed at the idea of him sending her a letter every single day that they were apart.

Who knew when they'd finally see each other again? She wasn't very romantic, she realized, thinking it was silly, an idea made in the spur of the moment after seeing her on the train. When reality set in, she was sure he'd be unable to keep up with the letters every day. She'd tucked the first one away in the little pouch where she kept his coin and put it out of her mind until several days later when the mail arrived and just as many letters arrived from Paul. So many, in fact, that she could no longer fit them in the little leather pouch.

He'd stuck to his word. She had accumulated a letter for every day they'd been apart so far. Some days, he wrote only one line, and others were two or three pages. They didn't show up every day - sometimes she received four or five at a time, and she'd savor them, reading only one a day until more came in. She was beginning to recognize the kind of day he'd had when he wrote - some days, he poured his heart out on the paper, telling her everything that ran through his head while he was holed up somewhere in the woods. Other times, he was more lighthearted, telling her about the pranks they played on one another when they got bored and making her laugh. Those were the ones she shared with the girls, wanting to spread the joy she felt when she read them.

She wrote him back, too. She tried as often as she could, though she usually came up short, unable to match his letter a day. She knew what was happening, but she kept her heart guarded, unwilling to admit she could lose it to a man through the words he'd written on the page.

Crowded around the little radio in the hospital lounge, nurses and doctors held hands, awaiting the news they'd been hoping to hear. Gretchen squeezed Anna's hand, and she smiled at her friend, though her mind wasn't on the broadcaster's voice at all. She couldn't think about anything other than the growing pit in her stomach. She hadn't received a letter from Paul in several days. She knew not to expect a letter every day. The delivery was unpredictable at best, but this was the longest she'd gone without hearing from him. It was all she could do to keep her mind from wandering to all the reasons why he'd stopped writing, the worst of which filled her with dread and worry that ran so deep she could hardly eat.

She tried to focus on Winston Churchill's voice, crackling through the radio.

'Finally, almost the whole world was combined against the evil-doers who are now prostrate before us. Gratitude to our splendid Allies goes forth from our hearts. We may allow ourselves a brief period of rejoicing, but let us not forget for a moment the toils and efforts that lie ahead.'

Gretchen lifted Anna's hand in the air, cheering with the entirety of the room. Anna let herself be carried away by the celebration, hugging her dear friends. The program turned over, featuring the most popular songs from the last four years. She danced around the room, linking arms and singing along to the words of *'Praise the Lord and Pass the Ammunition.'*

She'd enjoyed the moment of celebration, a reprieve from worry, until the start of her shift. She walked down the hall with Eleanor, still smiling with the buzz of excitement and relief they all felt. They walked past the front desk, heading into the ward when they passed Captain Campbell.

"Oh, Eleanor, just the person I was looking for. This letter was left for you. It must have gotten mixed up with my own mail."

"Thank you, ma'am," Eleanor said, taking the envelope. Anna smiled, hiding the disappointment she felt over another day without a letter from Paul.

"It's quite a day, isn't it?" Captain Campbell beamed at the two women. Anna kept her smile plastered to her face.

"Yes, ma'am, it sure is."

"Well, I'll leave you to it," she said, waving as she walked away.

Eleanor tore into her letter. Anna tried not to watch her friend, tears pricking her eyes. What was it that had made Paul stop writing? She sniffed, scolding herself. *Don't be a silly fool. Eleanor's letter could be from anyone. It's none of your business.* She straightened her shoulders and smoothed her uniform before pulling open the door to the ward. She held it open for Eleanor, but when her friend didn't follow right behind her, she turned around. Eleanor was stopped in the middle of the hallway with one hand covering her mouth. She looked up at Anna and held the letter out to her.

"I know why Paul hasn't written," she said. Anna let the door bang shut, walking back toward Eleanor and taking the paper from her.

"What are you talking about?" Anna scanned the handwriting, reading as fast as she could. "No...no, no, no." It was all she could get out.

Eleanor looked over her shoulder as she read. "Paul isn't handling it well at all, from what Glenn says," she said, flipping the letter over and pointing to the last paragraph.

"Oh, God," Anna said. "Harry's wife is expecting." She closed her eyes, willing the tears not to fall. Guilt washed over her. *God, how selfish I've been. Worrying about not getting a letter when the man has written every damn day. His best friend is dead.* She thought about the grief Paul must be feeling after losing a lifeline like Harry had been for him.

She wiped her eyes, handing the letter back to Eleanor. "He was so proud of Harry," she said. "They were so close to coming home." She looked up at the clock above the ward door and blew out a breath. "We have to get in there. We'll be late."

Eleanor pulled her into a hug. "I can cover for you if you want to go back to the room."

Anna shook her head, pulling away. "What good would it do? I can't do anything to help him from here. He's shutting me out," she said. She opened the door again, and Eleanor squeezed her hand as she walked by.

"Don't let him."

Anna snorted. "And how do you suppose I do that?"

"Just keep writing. Even if he never responds, write to him every day. It's your turn now. Convince him not to walk away. That is, if you think it's worth fighting for."

Anna nodded. She'd never felt more sure. "He is."

All week, Anna watched Eleanor spend every minute of her free time with Glenn. She'd been caught by surprise when he'd stood in front of the hospital, waiting for a chance to see her friend the day he'd gotten to Rennes. And all week, Anna had held out hope for a visit from Paul that never came. She never stopped writing, and he never wrote back. She'd stopped sending them through the post and gave them to Eleanor instead, knowing that Glenn went back to their barracks every night. She'd started to wonder if she should stop. Did he want her to give up? She had no way of knowing. She sat outside the hospital, thinking she should probably stop once their company moved on from Rennes again. *That would be the best time to end things*, she thought, when Glenn wasn't around to deliver her letters anymore.

Eleanor and Glenn walked up the sidewalk hand in hand, waving to Anna when they got closer.

"Hey, Anna, good to see you," Glenn said.

"You too, Glenn." She smiled and tipped her head up to the sun. "Beautiful day out, isn't it?"

Springtime and the war's end had brought with it a renewed hope. Even the patients she saw every day felt it from their hospital beds. The anticipation of going home was palpable.

"Actually, it's the best day yet," he said, grinning. "Though I think tomorrow will be just a bit better." He winked at Eleanor, who smiled up at him, then sat down next to Anna. She looked like she might explode with excitement.

"We're getting married."

Anna's mouth dropped open. "Wow," she said. "Congratulations! That's wonderful news." She reached out for Eleanor, enveloping her in a hug, then hopped down off the wall to hug Glenn, too.

"The thing is," Eleanor began, biting her lip and looking at Glenn.

"What is it?"

"It's just that...well...we're doing it tomorrow."

"Tomorrow? As in...less than..." she looked at her watch, "twelve hours away?"

Eleanor nodded.

"Reverend Ole said he'd marry us," Glenn said, grinning like mad and reaching for Eleanor's hand.

"But..." Eleanor grabbed Anna's hand with her free one. "I need you to be there. Please? As my witness?" She searched Anna's face with pleading eyes.

"Oh, Elle, I don't know if I can get anyone to cover my shift," Anna said, knowing full well she could and that the real reason she didn't want to go was because she didn't want to come face to face with Paul.

Eleanor shook her head. "I knew you'd say that. So, I already cleared it with Captain Campbell. Gretchen and Louise will be there too. It'll just be a small thing."

Anna looked at her friend. She didn't just want her there as a witness if Gretchen and Louise were already going to be there. She just wanted her friend by her side on her special day. She smiled at Eleanor, "I wouldn't miss it." She could get through one awkward day with Paul and crawl under the covers when it was over. *I've gotten through worse,* she told herself.

"What will you do about a dress?" Anna focused her attention on her friend's big day.

Eleanor waved her off. "You know I don't care much about all that stuff," she said.

"She could wear her pajamas and fuzzy slippers for all I care, and I'll still be waiting at the altar," Glenn added.

Anna grinned. They really were perfect for one another.

He turned to look at Anna and his face became serious.

"Listen, don't beat yourself up over Paul. He's not talking to any-one. It's not just you."

Anna nodded and looked past Glenn to the hydrangeas planted in a row against the hospital building. They were heavy with white, puffy blooms. *Annabelle hydrangeas,* she thought, thinking of her mother. *One of her favorites.* She'd watched her mother year after year, taking great care to support the blooms that would otherwise flop to the ground, their stems not strong enough to hold them up on their own. These had just begun to flower, the stems not yet bowed from the weight.

"Thanks, Glenn," she said, finally. "Do you know where you're off to after your stay here?"

"I think they've got to calculate our time or something like that. See who's eligible to go home. Otherwise, we'll probably be sent to the Pacific."

Anna raised her eyebrows. "And here I thought the war was just over for everyone. I guess it's never that easy."

Glenn laughed. "Definitely not. Especially not in the Army."

Eleanor jumped down off the stone wall. "Well, it's almost time for our shift," she said. Anna smiled. Her friend didn't want to talk about her soon-to-be husband leaving town again. They walked toward the hospital entrance, and Glenn gave Eleanor a quick peck on the cheek.

"See you tomorrow," he said, smiling. Anna waved to him, linking arms with Eleanor and walking into the hospital.

"You're getting married tomorrow and you're still going to work your shift tonight?"

"Of course," Eleanor said.

Anna shook her head. "I should have known."

"I've been telling you all along," she said, "you can do both." She arched a brow at Anna.

"I think that ship has sailed," Anna said.

"Why do you say that?"

Anna shrugged. "I think once they leave and Glenn's not here to keep giving Paul my letters...I might as well stop writing them."

Eleanor stopped walking. "Are you sure? I thought you didn't want to give up on him."

"I don't. But I can't force him to love me either. If he doesn't want to try...we're barely in the same town longer than a week, and now...I don't know. I don't know if I can even help him. I'm not naive enough to think my love is some kind of magic cure for the pain he's feeling."

Eleanor squeezed her hand. "You know I support you no matter what you decide."

Anna nodded.

"I just hate to see you two throw a good thing away," she said.

"I know. I do, too, but I don't think it's going to work out."

"Well, then, he's an idiot," Eleanor said.

~

They got off their shift at eleven o'clock, and Anna forced Eleanor into bed. "You need as much rest as you can get before your big day."

Gretchen sat on her bed, organizing her makeup. "Ooh, I've got the perfect colors for you, Elle," she said.

"No," Eleanor protested. "No clown makeup."

"Oh, come on. I did your makeup the night you two met. It's

only right you let me recreate the look," Gretchen pleaded.

"Fine," Eleanor conceded, "but no red lipstick."

Gretchen pouted. "Fine," she agreed.

The door to their room opened, and Louise walked in, struggling to get a giant garment bag through the doorway. Eleanor sat up in her bed. "What did you do?"

"It's not what I did," Louise answered. "It's what Captain Campbell did. I haven't even looked inside yet, but I'm dying to see what's in here." She laid the bag on Eleanor's bed, covering her legs. "It's for you," she said, gesturing for Eleanor to open it. She unzipped the bag down the middle, revealing a cream-colored suit jacket with a matching skirt, adorned with tiny pearl buttons down the front.

Eleanor gasped. "Where could she have gotten this from?"

"Beats me," Louise said. "I'm just the delivery girl."

"I figured I'd just wear my nicest uniform," Eleanor said, "but this…I can't believe it."

They admired the silken material until Louise zipped the bag back up, hanging it over the door.

"I can't wait for tomorrow," Gretchen exclaimed, bouncing on her toes.

"You and me both," Eleanor said, settling back down into bed. She yawned, pulling the covers up to her neck. "Night, girls."

Anna waited until her friends were asleep to tiptoe out of the room. She walked down to the nurse's lounge with a pen and paper, and her robe wrapped tightly around her. It was nearing midnight, and the room was empty except for the occasional nurse on break.

She sat down at a table in the corner and tucked her legs underneath her. She looked down at her blank paper and blew out a breath. *I should just go back to bed,* she thought, but she put her pen to the paper anyway, letting the words flow out of her.

Dear Evie,

I hope I am not overstepping my bounds by writing this letter to you. Paul may be unhappy with me for doing so, but he is a dear friend, and after all he has told me about you, I felt it was only right that you heard from someone. His friends in his unit may have already written, so forgive me if I'm repeating what you already know.

Paul's best friend Harry was killed in action a few weeks ago. I don't have details, and it's not my story to tell, but from what I understand, Paul has stopped writing to everyone, not just me. He only speaks to his friends as it pertains to work. Normally, I wouldn't meddle in someone else's business, but I care a great deal for Paul, and, well, I can't seem to just turn those feelings off. He confided in me about your brother, and I send my apologies that you have not heard from him yet, either. Knowing your parents already have one child missing, I suppose I hoped to save them the worry of wondering why Paul's letters have stopped. Though he is struggling, he is alive. I thought you deserved to at least know that.

Fondly,

Anna

She sat back and reread her letter. *Do I send it?* She was torn between wanting to help and not wanting to be meddlesome. She contemplated what to do while her nerves kicked into high gear, worrying about what she'd say to him tomorrow. She looked at the clock. *Make that today,* she thought, watching the hands on the clock click over to twelve-thirty.

She folded the letter and decided *not* to decide tonight. She needed sleep, a clear head, and then maybe she'd know better what to do.

~~~

Anna woke to chaos in the little dorm room. Gretchen was flinging clothes out of her trunk and all over her bed.

"What is going on?" Anna sat up and stretched, blinking away the sleep from her eyes.

"I've got to dress all of you for a wedding, that's what," Gretchen snapped.

Anna snorted. "I think you need some coffee and maybe a bite to eat first."

Gretchen closed her trunk and glared at Anna.

"What?" Anna put her hands up. "What did I do? I just woke up."

"Am I the only one concerned with the significance of a wedding happening today?"

Eleanor rolled over to her side, watching Gretchen try to pick out matching outfits. "What wedding?"

"Ha..ha..Eleanor, you should be just as nervous as I am," Gretchen exclaimed.

Eleanor sat up and shrugged a shoulder. "What for?"

Gretchen stopped throwing clothes. "You're getting married!"

"Gretch, why would I be nervous about that? Like I said yesterday, I'd have been fine wearing my uniform. I'm not really worried about what I wear."

Gretchen threw her hands up. "I'll never understand you, Eleanor Reeves."

Anna laughed. "I'm going to get coffee," she said, grabbing last night's letter off of her trunk. *And mail this out before I'm too chicken to do it.* There was no sense worrying about it when the man wouldn't speak to her anyway.

By noon, the girls had gathered downstairs in the hospital's chapel. Reverend Olsen greeted them with warm hugs, congratulating Eleanor. They sat in the front pew, waiting for Glenn to arrive.

"Imagine that, the bride is ready before the groom," joked Louise.

"Well, we had a bit of an advantage," Eleanor said.

Glenn came bursting through the chapel door, running up the aisle toward Eleanor. She stood up, facing him in the cream suit, fitted perfectly with its pearl buttons gleaming down the front. Gretchen had done her hair and makeup for what Eleanor swore would be the last time, and from the look on Glenn's face, it had been worth it.

"Eleanor," he said, "you're beautiful."

She looked down at her feet - shoved into the pumps Gretchen had insisted she wear. She'd tried to argue that she didn't want to end up with a sprained ankle like Anna had, but it had been a losing battle.

"Reverend Olsen," Eleanor said, turning to the minister. "Is there any way we could do this outside in the garden?"

"I don't see why not," he said, picking up his bible.

"It's a beautiful day outside, and it's a bit dark in here," she said, looking around at the poorly lit chapel. It looked like it hadn't seen much traffic or been used much at all in the last several years.

They walked back down the aisle, and Anna noticed Jack standing in the doorway. Her stomach did a flip when she neared him, and she couldn't help but look around for Paul. But when she walked past Jack out into the hallway, he wasn't there, either. She looked back over her shoulder, but she knew she hadn't missed him. Jack caught her eye and offered her his elbow on their way outside.

She hesitated and he laughed. "I promise I won't bite," he said. She smiled and looped her arm through his, letting him escort her into the little garden on the side of the hospital.

"I'm sorry Paul's not here," he said.

"He's not coming?"

Jack shook his head.

"Well, I'm sorry too. For Glenn," she said. She couldn't believe Paul wouldn't even try to pull it together for his friend's special day. "He must really be a mess, huh?"

"That he is," Jack said. "He tries to hide it behind work, but we all know that's not really him." He stopped walking. "I don't really know how to get him back, Anna. Harry's death…" He shook his head.

"I'm so sorry, Jack. It's been hard for all of you. I wish I knew what I could do. I've written to him every day. I keep hoping something might spark a response, but I think it might be time for me to leave him alone."

Jack kicked at the dirt. "Anna…It's really none of my business, and you have every right to move on…"

Anna sighed. "That's the thing, Jack. I don't want to move on. I just can't keep up a one-sided relationship. It's like no matter what I do, whether I keep writing or not…" she trailed off, looking for the right words.

"Keep writing," a voice said from behind her. She looked up at Jack, who offered her a small, hopeful smile. She hesitated before turning around. Paul stood just a few feet away, his hands shoved deep in his pockets. He had a look on his face she couldn't quite read.

"Please," he said. The flash of pain she saw in his eyes ripped through her, and she wanted to run to him and wrap her arms around him, tell him that everything would be okay, that they'd figure it out together. But he was beyond silly placations, and this wasn't her day. She wouldn't steal the thunder from Eleanor. She gathered up all of her courage and nodded at Paul, then turned and walked away, wending her way between the rows of flowers to join Eleanor and her friends.

She watched Paul take out his pocket knife and cut several small peach rosebuds from a bush nearby, then walk further into the garden and cut a hydrangea bloom. He held them all together and walked up to Eleanor, placing a kiss on her cheek. "Congratulations," he whispered and handed her the makeshift bouquet.

"Thanks, Paul," she said. "I'm really glad you're here."

Glenn reached out and squeezed his shoulder. "Thank you," he said, his voice thick with emotion.

~~~

Anna carried her heels in her hand and walked over to the low wall at the far end of the garden where she'd watched Paul try to quietly disappear.

She leaned against the stone wall beside him, keeping her bare feet planted in the grass. "Penny for your thoughts, PB?"

She thought she saw the whisper of a smile cross his face.

"Pretty wild, huh?"

"What's that?"

"Eleanor and Glenn tying the knot."

"I think it's pretty great. They're a perfect couple."

He nodded, the expression on his face sad. She stood beside him and waited.

"I just kind of always thought we'd be first," he finally said.

"First?"

"Yeah, you know," he pointed to where Eleanor and Glenn stood with their arms wrapped around one another. "The first to get married."

He glanced over at her. She felt like she'd been punched in the stomach. The air left her lungs in a rush. She hadn't expected him to say anything like that to her today. She'd braced herself for the awkward encounter, unsure of what she'd actually say when she faced him after all these months apart. Of course, she'd had those same thoughts. She'd pictured their future, hell, she'd even pictured their children and scared herself half to death. But she hadn't expected him to say he'd felt the same way.

"And what do you think now?" She stood up, away from the wall, and pinned him with her stare.

He looked down, avoiding her gaze. "I don't think I know much of anything anymore."

"That's not true, Paul. You know how you feel, but you're hiding behind your grief instead." She touched his arm. "I know you're hurting, but Harry would be so disappointed if you gave up on your life when he wanted you to live it."

Chapter 33

*P*aul sat on the riverbank with Reverend Olsen. The good old reverend had made it a point to visit him weekly since he'd gotten back to Rennes. At first, he just sat and listened, sulking miserably while Reverend Olsen tried to get through to him. Today was different. Paul was ready to talk.

Reverend Ole smiled at Paul as he listened. Paul told him how he'd been fooling himself before Glenn's wedding. At first, he hadn't thought he could even go. How could he when he felt like a shell of the person he was before? But when Jack pulled him out of the tent and proceeded to ream him up and down, telling him what a shitty friend he was - telling him that bullet had been wasted on Harry - Paul had staggered backward and walked away without a fight. For the most part, he agreed with Jack. And that's what he hated the most. There was a small part of him, a whisper of a voice that said he could change it if he wanted to. He could be that person Harry was proud to call a friend.

By the time he ran back to the tent, Glenn and Jack had left. He'd changed into a clean uniform and followed them to the hospital, resolved to at least be man enough to show up for his friend. He knew he owed Anna an explanation, and she deserved that much. The problem was, she deserved more than he could give, and he planned to tell her that, too.

Except that, when he finally saw her, the wires in his brain must have crossed because he'd blurted out all that nonsense about marrying her.

"God, I'm an idiot," he said when he'd finished regaling the events of the last week.

Reverend Ole chuckled. "No, you're not. You're hurting, Paul. Give yourself some grace. It's not easy to move forward without someone you love."

"So you think I need to let her go, then?" Paul picked at a blade of grass, disappointed that Reverend Ole hadn't told him what he wanted to hear.

"I was talking about Harry."

Paul looked over at the Reverend. "Don't look at me like you didn't have love for that man. You two were inseparable. Brotherly love can be just as painful, you know. It's going to take time to get used to."

"What if I never get used to it?"

Reverend Ole shrugged. "You might not. But eventually, you'll get tired of being miserable day after day, and your regrets will pile up until you can't climb out of the pit you've dug yourself into. Unless you learn that two things can coexist. Joy and sadness. It's never one or the other. I won't tell you to go off and marry the girl, hoping it'll bring you happiness capable of swallowing up the grief. It doesn't work like that either. It takes work. The question is, are you willing to put in the work? For Anna, but most importantly, for you. Are you worth it? Harry thought so. Why don't you?"

They sat for a moment before Reverend Olsen picked up the Bible that lay beside him on the bench and opened it. Paul closed his eyes as the words washed over him.

"Those who live in the shelter of the Most High will find rest in the shadow of the Almighty. This I declare about the Lord: He alone is my refuge, my place of safety; he is my God, and I will trust Him. For he will rescue you from every trap and protect you from deadly disease. He will cover you with his feathers. He will shelter you with his wings. His faithful promises are your armor and protection. Do not be afraid of the terrors of the night nor the arrow that flies in the day. Do not dread the disease that stalks in darkness nor the disaster that strikes at midday. Though a thousand fall at your side, though ten thousand are dying around you, these evils will not touch you. Just open your eyes and see how the wicked are punished. If you make the Lord your refuge, if you make the Most High your shelter, no evil will conquer you; no plague will come near your home. For he will order his angels to protect you wherever you go. They will hold you up with their hands so you won't even hurt your foot on a stone. You will trample lions and cobras; you will crush fierce lions and serpents under your feet. The Lord says, 'I will rescue those who love me. I will protect those who trust in my name.

When they call on me, I will answer; I will be with them in trouble. I will rescue and honor them. I will reward them with a long life and give them my salvation.'

Paul hung his head, letting the Reverend's words sink in. He still didn't understand why he'd been spared.

"Paul," Captain Gangwere approached, waving a paper. "Paul, I got word on your brother."

Paul shot up, closing the distance between him and the Captain. "How? What does it say?"

"He's alive, Paul. He's alive, but he's emaciated. He's being transported to a hospital with the rest of the POWs that escaped, but they think he'll survive."

Paul took the letter, reading as fast as he could. Jamie was alive. After all this time, after all the doubt and dwindling hope, his brother was alive.

"He was captured in Italy. He escaped from Camp 59."

Paul closed his eyes. "My God," he said. They'd all heard the rumors about Camp 59. It was a miracle he'd escaped. His eyes welled with fresh tears, and he turned away. "Thank you, sir. I, uh, I just need a minute." He took the paper and sat down at the river's edge, breathing deeply. When he'd asked his superior officer to look into what happened to his brother, he'd expected to find out he'd been killed in action.

"Hey, Reverend Ole," Paul said. "You're right. I'm so damn happy Jamie is alive. But I'm sad as hell that Harry's not here to share the news with."

Chapter 34

PAUL
MAY 1945
FRANCE

"Anna, you know I don't want to do this." Paul tugged at her hand, but she held on, her grip tightening as he tried to pull free.

She led him closer to the edge, the water lapping at their toes. She smiled up at him, holding onto his arm as he grimaced, his eyes trained on the water in front of them. He'd do anything for the woman standing next to him, even if his palms were sweaty with fear. He knew it was irrational. Just because the Leopoldville sank didn't mean he'd lost his ability to swim. He knew the water here was calm and clear, perfect conditions for a swim in the warm July sun. Couples all around them dove in, peals of laughter and delight ringing out across the beach when they surfaced. He tuned them all out, focusing on the feel of the cool water on his feet. On all the ways this day differed from the last time he'd been in water. *I'm not trapped. It's not freezing. It's not going to pull me under.*

Anna squeezed his arm, waiting patiently while he wrestled with his thoughts. He looked back at the group of their friends, spread out on a blanket they'd brought just for today's celebration on the beach. Gretchen passed a bottle of wine to Louise while Eleanor sat on Glenn's lap, her arms hooked around his neck. Paul pictured Harry sitting on the empty spot of the blanket, celebrating with them. *Where he should be,* Paul thought.

What a strange place to be, he thought, somewhere between overwhelming grief and the precipice of joy. Feeling like you couldn't go on - or perhaps you could, dragged kicking and screaming, not wanting to let go of the memories even if they killed you - but also ready to go. Ready to put the pain and sadness and overwhelm behind you. He shook his head. *It'll never be behind me,* he thought. But maybe he could put it in God's hands instead.

He missed his best friend. But holding back from the rest of his life wouldn't bring Harry back. It would only take him through the rest of his life as an angry young man to a crotchety old one and that wasn't the future he wanted. He looked down at Anna. The future he saw in her eyes was the one he wanted.

"I'm scared, Anna," he said, honestly.

She held fast to his arm. "Aren't we all? Do it anyway, Paul. With me. Do it scared."

He gave a nearly imperceptible nod. "Ready?"

She grinned. "On the count of three."

She moved her hand to intertwine it with his.

"One, two…," Paul jumped, dragging her with him into the

cool, blue sea, lifting her up out of the water as he came up from beneath the surface. The laughter that bubbled out of her while she splashed at his face filled his soul with something he'd slowly lost over the last year. She wrapped a hand around his neck, wiping water droplets off of his forehead with the other.

He moved onto his back, and the two of them floated easily in the calm water, their breath in steady rhythm with one another, his hand still firmly grasped on hers.

"Doesn't it scare you that I'm not that same man you met at that company party last year?"

His question took her by surprise and she arched a brow that he couldn't see, floating beside him. "Does it scare you that I'm not the same either?"

The gentle tide brought them closer to the shore until they could stand waist deep, and he felt the sand washing out from beneath his toes.

"You know what I mean, Anna. I'm not as..." He hesitated, searching for the right word to describe the way he felt about himself now.

"I'll tell you what I see. And you tell me if I should still be scared. I see a man who has defined himself as a soldier - a damn good one, mind you."

Paul chuckled and rolled his eyes. "That describes about ninety percent of us, but ok, go on."

She narrowed her eyes at him before she continued. "A damn good soldier who is always there for anyone who needs him. Who has seen things and felt things and is forever marked by war."

He nodded. "And that's what I'm worried about. That's not necessarily a good thing."

"That's where you're wrong. Because I'm marked by it too. We all are. I might not have lost my best friend out there, but Paul, I treated too many boys who should've been at home studying for a math test instead of carrying a rifle on their back and now they're buried somewhere across Europe. I'm not the same woman I was, either. If we were, we'd be monsters. We were naive less than a year ago. Hell, I thought if I shut you out, my feelings would just disappear, and I wouldn't care about what happened to you."

"Ouch," he said, splashing water at her.

"What I'm trying to say is, now we know better."

"So you're saying you couldn't get rid of your feelings for me?" Paul grinned, teasing her.

"Not even if I tried," she said, "and believe me, I tried." She laughed then, splashing him back.

"Real nice," he laughed, picking her up and launching her back into the water.

"How dare you," she exclaimed when she came up for air. He swam out farther, laughing as she chased him. He let her catch up, pulling her to him before she could try to dunk him under the water.

"Should we join the crew?"

She shrugged a shoulder. "I suppose," she said, taking off ahead of him.

They raced each other up the sand to the blanket, tripping and falling over one another. Paul stretched out, his hands propped up behind him. Anna took a cup of wine from Gretchen and rested her head on his shoulder. It was the lightest he'd felt since Christmas Eve. They watched the people swimming and listened to bits of conversation from their friends while they soaked up the celebratory afternoon. The sun was hot on their skin late in the day, casting a glow across the water, making Paul squint.

He looked down at Anna, a contented smile playing on her face.

"Penny for your thoughts, AB?"

She smiled even wider, the way she always did when he used her nickname.

She met his eyes, her head still resting on his shoulder, a look on her face he couldn't decipher. "I think I want the garden, Paul." She closed her eyes as if she were hiding from her own words, and he threw his head back. His laughter made them tumble backward, and he looked up at the brilliant sky.

He squeezed her tight against his side. "I think I can make that happen."

～〰～

Epilogue

tanding in his parents' living room, Paul scanned the new frames his mother had added to the mantle above the fireplace. Photographs of him and Jamie in their uniforms adorned each side, and in between were news articles, one he hadn't read before, detailing the escape of American prisoners, his brother being one of them. And the other, an article all too familiar to him.

"I don't know why Ma insists on framing these things."

Paul turned and smiled. He saw his blue eyes reflecting back at him. They were often mistaken for twins, he and Jamie. His mother called them her Irish twins, and he supposed he could see why. Though his brother was nearly two years his senior, there was no mistaking their resemblance to one another.

He shook his head. "Beats me. I'd be happy to never see that again," he said, pointing to the article about the Leopoldville's sinking on Christmas Eve.

Jamie chuckled. "I must say, little brother, that was pretty slick."

"What's that?"

"Evie told me about the gloves you sent. Where'd you get an idea like that?"

Paul shrugged. "I don't know. I just…" he trailed off. They hadn't talked much about what they'd been through. Any time Paul tried to bring it up, Jamie shut him down. It was like they'd gotten home and just jumped back into life, ignoring any reminders of the past. "I didn't want them to worry about me, that's all. But I thought if anyone got a telegram…I don't know, Jamie. They deserved to know." He tried to choose his words carefully. He had been angry with Jamie for not writing. But that was before he'd experienced war for himself.

"As soon as I opened up that box and saw a pair of gloves, I knew something was up," Evie said. The two men turned to find Evie leaning against the doorframe, a smile playing on her face. "I said to myself, 'I'll use these just about as much as we use this fireplace.'"

Paul and Jamie laughed, making their way over to their sister, who wrapped her arms around them both. She led them toward the front door, stepping over the old Labrador, basking in the stream of sunlight coming in through the screen door.

Jamie shook his head. "Look at this old dog," he chuckled.

Paul opened the door. The dog lifted his head like he was deciding whether or not to follow, and promptly flopped it back down again.

Evie laughed. "Spoiled rotten," she said.

Paul sauntered down the steps, his eyes tracing the path of the new driveway they'd installed just to the right of his parents.

Winding down behind the barn, he could hear the hammering of nails on the little white cottage being built.

His dad came out of the barn, a smile overtaking his face when he spotted all of his children together. "It'll never get old seeing the three of you back here," he said.

Evie snorted. "Don't get used to it. I've had about enough of sharing a bathroom with these two." She gave Jamie a shove, and he wrapped his arm around her in an easy headlock, messing up her hair while she squealed.

The cottage came into view, and the four of them stopped. "Just about finished, now," Paul said.

A little red-headed boy came toddling along from behind the house, with Anna not far behind. The boy's eyes lit up, and he picked up his pace, making a beeline for where Paul stood.

"Hey there, little guy," he said, squatting down and opening his arms wide as the toddler neared. He avoided the embrace, wrapping his chubby hands around Paul's father's leg instead. His father let out a deep laugh, picking up the little boy and swinging him around as Paul got to his feet.

"Well, how about that," Paul said, looking incredulously at Anna.

She smiled. "He sure loves his Papa," she said.

~⌒~

ANNA

She took her time, meandering down the path at a slow pace. It was smooth enough that she could push the wheelchair with ease. Paul had gone above and beyond anything she could have imagined, as usual. She hadn't been able to stop smiling since he'd brought her home to Texas.

She thought about that first visit two years ago, coming home from Europe and arriving at her parent's house in New Jersey. Before they had any idea what they were doing. Her mother had given him a grand tour, smiling widely and hugging them both - hugging them! The change in her mother had nearly knocked her off her feet. It had been a beautiful ending to the summer, walking back to the gazebo for lemonade.

Anna remembered it like yesterday, walking up the steps first, turning around, watching her mother fall to the ground, Paul catching her just before she could hit her head on the gazebo railing. Anna had knelt beside her, cradling her mother's head in her lap, holding her hand, tears streaming down her face until the ambulance arrived.

She looked down at her mother in the wheelchair and put her hand on her shoulder. Her mother looked up, placing her own hand over Anna's. She couldn't help but get emotional when she thought about nearly losing her. That ride to the hospital, Anna had prayed through her sobs, angry at the unfairness of it all. *How could she be taken away just when we're finally mending the scars of our rocky relationship?* When the doctors had finally come out to the waiting room, Anna fell to her knees, flooded with relief. A stroke, they had said. She'd had a massive stroke and would likely never walk again. *But she's here,* Anna thought.

Anna wheeled her mother through the garden Paul had built. He wasn't one to skimp on a project. He always told her to go big or go home, to which she'd laugh, roll her eyes, and go along for the crazy ride. In no way did she need a garden of this magnitude, but he wouldn't be deterred. He must have memorized all of her favorite parts from her mother's garden, and she had to wonder if he'd had a little help from her mother herself.

She watched her husband walking down the path ahead, Danny on one side and their little red-haired boy on the other. He'd told her mother he had a surprise for her today, a secret project between him and his two best boys. She looked behind her, smiling at her dad who was walking slowly beside her grandfather as he hobbled along. She could hardly believe all the people she loved were here in one place. If someone had told her she'd be living in Texas, and her whole family would move halfway across the country to be nearer to her, she'd have scoffed at the idea. *But*, she thought, *that's what happens when grand babies arrive.* She smiled, smoothing a hand over her stomach.

Danny, now a feisty almost five-year-old, ran ahead, the little toddler chasing behind in his bare feet, just like his mother. Paul turned around, grinning at Anna.

"You going to let him run that far ahead?" Anna shielded her eyes, watching the little boy trying to keep up with his big cousin.

Paul stopped, letting her catch up. "He knows where he's going," he said, kissing the top of her head.

"And where exactly is that?" Anna laughed at the impatience in her mother's voice. It was true that she'd turned over a new leaf. But some things a person just couldn't change, and for Anna's mother, being trapped in a chair made her grumpy.

"You'll see," Paul said with a wink, gaining a frustrated sigh.

"You better check on those little rascals," Anna said when the boys rounded a corner and disappeared from sight.

"You go on," he said, taking over behind the wheelchair. "We'll be right behind you."

She jogged ahead in her bare feet, following the two boys. When she rounded the corner, she gasped. She stood still, taking in the scene before her. She covered her mouth as tears sprung to her eyes. Paul came up beside her, wheeling her mother up to the garden bed he'd built just for her.

"This is what you've been working on every night?"

He nodded and bent down toward Anna's mother. "What do you think, Mrs. Mitchell?"

The planting box was tall enough that she could be wheeled right to it, the perfect height for her to dig her hands into. On the other side, he'd built a bench with a high back, perfect for accommodating two rambunctious little boys to dig their trucks into the soft soil.

Her mother pointed to the toys already being filled with dirt. "I think," she began, "they'll need to take those diggers somewhere else once I plant my seeds in here."

Paul and Anna laughed. "I think that means she likes it," Anna's father said, walking up to the group gathered around the new garden box.

Anna wrapped her arms around Paul's waist. "Thank you," she whispered.

She wandered over to the grass and sat down, watching her husband and son dig in the dirt with her mother and marveled at how incredible this life was. *How completely unpredictable*, she thought.

"Hey, I forgot to tell you," she called to Paul, "Edith said she'd be in town by tomorrow afternoon. I told her to come any time, and the boys can play together."

"Have you told her about his name yet?" Paul ruffled the little boy's hair, dirt sprinkling out of it as he filled his dump truck again and again.

She shook her head. "I thought you should be the one to tell her."

"Rowan!" Her mother scolded and Anna stifled a laugh. "Don't throw the dirt, sweetie," then looked over at Anna, "he's just like you."

She smiled. She couldn't disagree with her mother. Rowan James, she thought. Her son may have inherited the color of her hair, but she hoped he'd always be proud to carry a bit of his Uncle Harry with him and his Uncle Jamie, too.

"What's that you say - you haven't told Harry's wife Rowan's name yet?" Her father sat down beside her, making her chuckle when he pulled off his shoes and socks, digging his toes into the grass. *So that's where I get it from*, she thought.

"She knows his name...we just haven't told her what it means yet," Anna said.

"What's that?"

Anna looked at her father, then smiled up at Paul. Little Rowan was perched on his lap, dirt flying all around them. "It means little redhead," she said.

～⌒～

Author's Note

I was a naive twenty-year-old when I walked through the doors at the National Purple Heart Hall of Honor, nervous for my first day of work. I never expected what was supposed to be a part-time job to make ends meet while I figured out what I wanted to do with my life would leave its mark on my heart, even after all these years.

Watching veterans tell their stories - many of which had never been told before - was both incredible and heartbreaking. What has been built at the Hall of Honor is a beautiful experience I hope everyone has the chance to see.

The Leopoldville tragedy was just one of many incidents I learned about during my time at the Hall of Honor. I suppose I have Pete Bedrossian, one of my bosses, to thank for handing me a folder full of the names of soldiers who had earned a Purple Heart that fateful Christmas Eve of 1944. Had I not been given that assignment, had I not entered the date 12/24/1944 over and over, hundreds of times over several days, my curiosity wouldn't have been piqued, and I wouldn't be writing this today.

Wondering what exactly happened to the 66th Division led me down a rabbit hole I've not yet come out of. I became fascinated and appalled. My heart ached for the young men on board that night. The seed had been planted in the back of my mind for a story that I just couldn't let go of.

About fifteen years have passed since I first learned of the Leopoldville, but I often came back to that idea, a pipedream that I thought might eventually be fulfilled by someone else. Someone more qualified than me.

But, somehow, by the grace of God, after all this time, it was still my story to tell. With the encouragement of my husband, I began to take it seriously. Maybe I could do it. Why not me?

I dove deeper into the research and interviews of soldiers and their families, where images came alive, and details revealed not only what happened that night but also what happened before and after the sinking of the ship.

This novel, while fictional, has been kept as true to the actual events as I could possibly keep it, with a bit of creative license taken where necessary to fill any gaps and keep the story moving in an enjoyable journey for the reader.

Anna and Paul, though fictional characters, are based on real people from the past. In Anna's case, she came to life from a small portion of Allan Andrade's Leopoldville: A Tragedy Too Long Secret, in which he was able to interview a World War II nurse, Helen Livesey. Helen had traveled across the English Channel on board the Leopoldville just one week prior to the men of the 66th Division. Because of this, "she always felt tied to the men of the 66th Division and their fate (Andrade, p. 39). While she wasn't on the docks that night, and she did not marry a soldier in the 66th, it wouldn't have been unbelievable if she had. She did, in fact, travel through England and France, make rank as a First Lieutenant, and marry a soldier. Much of her character, along with those of Gretchen, Louise, and Eleanor, were pieced together from interviews with Army nurses as well as their letters home, as referenced in Judy Barrett Litoff and David C. Smith's We're in This War, Too.

For instance, the watermelon party, the accidental Vicks and ink bottle switch, the ten- mile hikes, and many other scenes portrayed throughout Beyond the Surface, though seemingly outrageous, are based on actual events.

Similarly, when I thought about who I wanted the main character of Paul to be, my goal was always to honor as many of the real men on board the Leopoldville as I possibly could. Paul is the compilation of many different soldiers whose stories have been told in the nonfiction works of Allan Andrade, Joaquin Sanders, Ray Roberts, and Larry Simotes. Paul is the culmination of so many soldiers - ones who survived and ones who did not.

Some names have been changed in addition to Anna and Paul, but several were kept the same as those I learned about in my research. Men like Colonel Ira Rumberg, General Kramer, Reverend Olsen, and Captain Gangwere are all men who influenced and helped to shape each soldier on board the Leopoldville on Christmas Eve.

I can only hope that I have done justice in my retelling of the story of the brave soldiers lost in the depths of the English Channel that tragic Christmas Eve night. After all, it is their story.

---------------- ⤳⤳ ----------------

ACKNOWLEDGEMENTS

---------------- ⤳⤳ ----------------

I couldn't have seen this book through to its finish had it not been for so many wonderful people supporting me.

To my husband, who has always believed in me even when - especially when - I didn't believe in myself. For being my biggest fan, loving me, and always keeping me in good supply of freshly baked chocolate chip cookies, words cannot express how grateful I am to have you by my side. If it weren't for you, your steadfast strength, and your constant encouragement, I wouldn't be writing these words today.

To my children, who have no idea just yet how much their little lives have breathed life into me every single day. Everything I do is for you both. I hope when you pick up this book, you know that you can fulfill any of your dreams. If mom can do it - mostly while waiting in the school pickup line - you can, too.

To Mom and Dad - you've cheered me on since I was picking buttercups on the soccer field and quitting nearly everything

I started - I finished! I'm so thankful to call you my parents and to have always felt your love.

To my mother-in-law, Pam, whose enthusiasm and encouragement has never wavered - thank you.

Sleep-deprived and with my daughter hanging onto my legs, I submitted an idea I wholeheartedly believed in. Hope*Books said, "Yes! We believe in it, too!" I am forever grateful that you agreed this story was worth investing in and allowed me to tell it.

~

Resources

Andrade, Allan. *Leopoldville: A Tragedy Too Long Secret*. 2009.

Sanders, Jacquin. *A Night Before Christmas: The Sinking of the Troopship Leopoldville*. 1964.

Barrett, Judy, and David C. Smith. *Liftoff: We're In This War, Too*. 1994.

Simotes, Larry. *Two Strikes and Not Out: The Story of George Bigelow and the Sinking of the SS Leopoldville*. 2017.

Roberts, Ray. *The Leopoldville Trilogy: Survivors of the Leopoldville Disaster, Sequel to Survivors of the Leopoldville Disaster, and More Tales of the Leopoldville Disaster*. 1997.

"The Leopoldville Disaster." (2009). In P. Producer (Executive Producer), *Deep Wreck Mysteries*. Production Company.

Camp Blanding. (1944). *IRTC Handbook*. Retrieved from https://www.floridamemory.com/items/show/343599

WW2 Online. *Oral History Project*. http://www.ww2online.org.

James, Liam. "Winston Churchill's VE Day speech that marked the end of the war in Europe." The Independent, 8 May 2020, https://www.independent.co.uk/news/uk/home-news/winston-churchill-ve-day-speech-end-war-ww2-read-full-a9503661.html

Printed in the USA
CPSIA information can be obtained
at www.ICGtesting.com
CBHW031254060824
12781CB00007B/12

9 798891 850705